This book should be returned to any Lancashire County Council Library on or before the date shown

Lancashire County Council Library Service,
County Hall Complex,
2nd floor Christ Church Precinct,
Preston, PR1 0LD

www.lancashire.gov.uk/libraries

D0774591

Also by Andrea Bolter

Her New York Billionaire
Her Las Vegas Wedding
The Italian's Runaway Princess
The Prince's Cinderella
His Convenient New York Bride

Also by Nancy Robards Thompson

A Down-Home Savannah Christmas
Southern Charm & Second Chances
Maddie Fortune's Perfect Man
Fortune's Surprise Engagement
Betting on a Fortune

Discover more at millsandboon.co.uk

CAPTIVATED BY HER PARISIAN BILLIONAIRE

ANDREA BOLTER

HER SAVANNAH SURPRISE

NANCY ROBARDS THOMPSON

MILLS & BOON

All rights reserved including the right of reproduction in whole or in part in any form. This edition is published by arrangement with Harlequin Books S.A. This is a work of fiction. Names, characters, places and incidents are either the product of the author's imagination or are used fictitiously and any resemblance to actual persons, living or dead, business establishments, events or locales is entirely coincidental.

This book is sold subject to the condition that it shall not, by way of trade or otherwise, be lent, resold, hired out or otherwise circulated without the prior consent of the publisher in any form of binding or cover other than that in which it is published and without a similar condition including this condition being imposed on the subsequent purchaser.

® and TM are trademarks owned and used by the trademark owner and/or its licensee. Trademarks marked with ® are registered with the United Kingdom Patent Office and/or the Office for Harmonisation in the Internal Market and in other countries.

First Published in Great Britain 2020
by Mills & Boon, an imprint of HarperCollinsPublishers,
1 London Bridge Street, London, SE1 9GF

Captivated By Her Parisian Billionaire © 2020 Andrea Bolter
Her Savannah Surprise © 2020 Nancy Robards Thompson

ISBN: 978-0-263-27885-9

0620

MIX
Paper from
responsible sources
FSC™ C007454

This book is produced from independently certified FSC™
paper to ensure responsible forest management.

For more information visit: www.harpercollins.co.uk/green

Printed and bound in Spain
by CPI, Barcelona

CAPTIVATED BY HER PARISIAN BILLIONAIRE

ANDREA BOLTER

LANCASHIRE COUNTY LIBRARY	
3011814048627 9	
Askews & Holts	06-Oct-2020
AF AFR	£6.99
NKI	

For Megan

CHAPTER ONE

THE EIFFEL TOWER. It had been a long time since Jules had woken up to the sight of one of the world's most famous landmarks. When his eyes clicked open after the heavy slumber he hoped would cancel out his jet lag, he'd used the remote control on the nightstand to raise the blackout blinds and let in the light of the Paris morning. There the tower stood in view through his window, in all its wrought iron lattice glory.

Jules's apartment was an example of the many Durand Properties, his billion-euro real-estate empire, he owned in the city with their mixture of historic architecture and every modern convenience. High ceilings, crown moldings and original chevron wood floors reminded him that this apartment in the Seventh Arrondissement, as Paris's districts were referred to, was over a hundred years old.

His eyes fell shut again. While there was no question that his hometown was one of the most magnificent cities in the world, he was uneasy returning to Paris. Traveling across the globe, buying more and more properties everywhere he went had become his way of life. The last sleep he'd had on land was on the fifty-seventh floor of an ultra-luxury hotel in Singapore. Always on the move, Jules liked living in hotels, anonymous and temporary.

After rubbing his eyelids with the heels of his hands, he reopened them. There was the window again with its spectacular view. The tower, watching over the city as it always did. Yep, he really was back in Paris.

Mindlessly scratching his bare chest, he knew he should get out of bed. Tomorrow, he'd resume his habit of starting the day with an outdoor run. Today, he'd acclimate. A busy morning lay ahead with reestablishing himself at the Durand Properties headquarters and completing the job he'd returned to France to do. It was time to take the reins from his irresponsible mother and father, who had been on their own globe-trot for far too long. Although parenting his parents was hardly how he'd envisioned this chapter of his life, blood was blood and he'd do anything he had to.

As if reading his mind, the buzz of Jules's phone beckoned and one glance at the screen's caller identification let him know it was his mother. He swiped to answer.

"Where in the world is my tall handsome son?" Agathe Durand's singsong led him to believe she was calling from a different time zone, as she was never chipper in the mornings. Her voice was high with that continental-traveler tone she used to fool people, to disguise the fact that she was perpetually discontent with her life.

"My apartment, Mother. You're not in Paris?"

"Tel Aviv."

"Tel Aviv. Dandy." Spending Jules's money, of course. "Dare I ask, is Father okay?"

"Yes, your exasperating pater is fine, although keeping me from properly enjoying Tel Aviv. The man wants to sit in cafés eating falafel all day instead of being out and taking in the sights."

There she goes again, Jules thought. Blaming his father for her own unhappiness. As she did the entirety of Jules's childhood. At their age, Jules hoped their domestic dramas were behind them, especially now that Hugo was confined to a wheelchair after a fall had broken his back. Yet, with his parents, there was no telling. The unpredictability of which drove ordered-and-organized Jules crazy.

"Never mind touring Tel Aviv. You're supposed to be in Paris. That's why I'm here." Arranging to meet them in the same place was often a challenge and Jules had sat waiting in many a foreign train station or airport, eventually receiving the call that they'd missed their departure.

While his parents continued their decade-long knack of finding an antique piece of jewelry to buy and then sell at a high markup, or one of them getting work in some corner of the world at a tavern or on a farm, Jules had been largely footing their bills. Hugo's physical condition now prohibited him from any hard labor. Agathe's bon vivant facade was not what it used to be and she was no longer able to charm her way into dinner or a night's lodgings.

As their only child, Jules felt a responsibility to them despite the dysfunction he'd grown up in. Money was something he had plenty of to give. So while peace and satisfaction were apparently out of the question for his parents, at least he could make sure they didn't disappear somewhere into the abyss. Now their wanderings had become impractical and dangerous. He needed to ground them.

In short, the gig was up for these nomads Jules called parents. It was time they stayed in one place. Paris, where they'd raised Jules in a shoddy apartment on the outskirts of town, long lost to creditors, was where they were born and where they would die.

"Oh, Jules, we'll be there eventually."

A wince reminded him of similar phone calls from years gone by. Only it wasn't both of his parents calling during any hour of the day or night far from home. It was his mother who, at least a dozen times during Jules's childhood, would become bored or angry with her housewifely doldrums. So she'd pack a suitcase and disappear, abandoning Jules and his father. With theatrical vows that she needed to *see* the world and would never return, she'd only get as far as visiting relatives in other parts of France for a few days. Inevitably, she'd regain her senses or outstay her welcome, not having the wherewithal to get any farther. She'd return to her husband and son with promises that she'd never leave them again. Until she did.

In later years, she began dragging Hugo along with her, which gave her the courage to venture greater distances. A bitter and cold man who was never able to maintain steady employment, it made no difference to him where he laid his head at night.

But this move would be final. Once Jules got his parents back to Paris and into one of his apartments where they'd have a safe roof over their heads, he'd base himself here again and look after what their aging health would demand. As laughable as it was to use the term for people his parents' age, it was time for Agathe and Hugo to *grow up*. In the process, Jules would call Paris home again as well, which he had been resisting but knew was overdue.

"If you had seen the way your mother behaved with our taxi driver last night, you'd be as horrified as I was," the voice of Jules's father came through the speaker. Obviously, Hugo had gained custody of the phone in Tel Aviv and was reporting to Jules lest his wife consider herself blameless for their latest row. "She absolutely threw herself at him. The young man was gracious, of course, but even he was embarrassed."

"You're just jealous," Agathe called into the speaker. Why Jules's parents had to fight during a call to him was anyone's guess. There was plenty of other time left in the day for them to badger at each other and then let things subside like they always did, neither of them having the gumption to actually end their marriage. They were becoming more childish every time he spoke with them.

"While I can't think of anything I'd rather do than listen to the two of you argue over the phone, I need to finish the apartment I have for you and run my business. You were supposed to meet me in Paris to make some decisions about the renovation. I'll put you in one of my hotels while we finish the work. Get here." He ended the call, annoyed. Hopefully, he was making the right decision in forcing them back. He couldn't think of another solution.

After showering and donning his uniform of a Savile Row business suit, he found his daily breakfast of a green vegetable smoothie in the refrigerator, which he had instructed the housekeeper to prepare. He readied himself for his workday in what was to become his new routine. Durand Properties occupied an enormous building in Montparnasse. It had been months since he'd set foot in his actual office, the staff spending more time with him on telescreens than in person.

Jules maintained a crack management team to collaborate with him on operations, leaving him free to do what he did best. Seek out real estate to purchase and rehabilitate, resell or lease. He was good at his job, he reasoned, as he'd amassed over two hundred properties on four continents.

He stood at his bedroom window and peered down at the street traffic while he sipped his green drink. People hurried this way and that, many headed to the metro stations where they'd travel underground to their daily destinations.

His eyes fixed on a young couple. The woman had a short haircut and wore a striped dress, gesturing wildly with her hands as they walked. Jules couldn't hear her from his second-floor apartment, but from her facial expressions she seemed to be shouting at her companion. The man, bearded and in jeans, listened silently. At one point, he deftly kissed her on the cheek without causing either of them to lose their stride. From arguing to kissing, their familiarity with each other made Jules guess they were a couple that had been together for a long time. Did interactions with women always have to include commotion?

"Yes, Karim." He turned from the window and paced the wooden floor as he took a call from his personal assistant at the office, who Jules spoke with several times a day regardless of his own whereabouts.

"Jules, I've checked with Lanon in Project Development about acquiring an interior designer to do the apartment for your parents. She tells me that all of our designers are swamped and if we pull anyone away from their current project, we won't make our completion dates."

"I see." Jules contemplated his assistant's report. A few years ago, he had bought a large building in the Second Arrondissement with apartments that would be a good fit for his parents because he was able do the structural changes needed for wheelchair access. Which was not always possible in the stately old buildings of Paris. Plus, it was in a lively neighborhood with plenty of shops and public spaces nearby. His tenant there had moved out, although later than he had expected. So the unit still needed paint, furnishings and decor, and some further accommodations given his father's mobility restrictions.

"I'll be in the office shortly. Please check with Giang in Resources as to how we should go about finding a designer immediately."

Of course, it couldn't be just anyone. Since the designer was to work with Jules as a son of the inhabitants as well as an employer, it wasn't a typical project. He'd want to select this hire himself.

"I already have. He suggested we contact some of our high-end furniture suppliers, as a lot of designers come through their doors."

"Good, then. Kindly get that done."

After the call, Jules knotted his tie in the mirror. He squared himself in the eye. The two little permanent creases between his eyebrows always gave his face a serious demeanor.

This morning, there was also worry in his big brown orbs. Converting abandoned factories into housing for an entire village in India was one thing. But taking charge of his parents' affairs, staying in Paris to be with them in their elder years was going to be his biggest project yet. He was fundamentally as unsettled as they were.

For some reason, he thought of that pretty girl in the striped dress on the street yelling at her man.

Returning to the window, Jules saw the couple far down the block now, as tiny as dolls from his viewpoint. He shifted his gaze to the Eiffel Tower one more time.

Paris.

The City of Light.

Home.

Jules had never felt lonelier.

"I might have good news," Yasmine Jaziri told her roommate, Zoe Gaiman, as she sat down at the outside table of the café on Boulevard Saint-Michel, the long-time haven for young people and students in the city's Latin Quarter.

Zoe nursed her lemon soda as she allowed Yasmine to get settled in. When the waiter approached, Yasmine ordered a glass of red wine.

"Let's hear it." Zoe couldn't wait. She could use some good news no matter who or what it pertained to.

"My boss, Si, told us that Jules Durand is desperately looking for an interior designer."

"Jules Durand? As in Durand Properties?" Zoe bubbled. The real-estate development corporation, which owned dozens of buildings in Paris and many more throughout the world, was founded and led by a certain Jules Durand whom Zoe had read about in a magazine article. The fact that he was much younger than would be expected for someone so accomplished had made an impression on Zoe, and she'd remembered the name. Also, judging from the couple of photos accompanying the magazine story, Jules Durand was twenty-five kinds of good-looking.

"Apparently, he has an apartment he needs work on, and quickly," Yasmine continued.

"What, he asked Si if he knew anyone?"

"Yeah. Si mentioned it at the staff meeting this morning." Yasmine appriticed for Si Wu, a renowned furniture designer. Trendy and finely crafted side tables that cost more than Zoe earned in a year kind of thing. It made sense that Jules Durand would buy from a studio like that. "I can get you the contact information."

"I doubt he'd consider me qualified." While Zoe was a burgeoning interior designer, Durand Properties was not going to be interested in someone with her level of experience. She'd been in Paris for a year and had only managed to secure a few small jobs. A tiny restaurant that needed a new look on a budget. A nursery school that was updating their two classrooms. The couple that needed to utilize their parking garage for storage. Not much more than what she had been doing in Maupont, the small town near Lyon where she grew up. She had fled to make a name for herself in Paris, not to mention leave painful memories behind.

"What can I get for you two mademoiselles?" the older mustached waiter asked when he returned with Yasmine's wine.

"Thank you, we're just having drinks," Zoe quickly answered. There was no money in her budget for an expensive dinner. She and Yasmine had agreed they'd meet to savor a slow drink and watch the parade of Paris go by. At this point, even that was a treat.

The waiter snarled, no doubt hoping they were going to order food. Zoe shrugged her shoulders at him with a cute smile. It failed to crack his gruff exterior.

"It doesn't hurt to try," Yasmine continued on about Durand Properties. "You have nothing to lose."

"You've got that right."

Zoe had come to Paris on a hope and a dream, and feared that neither were coming to pass. Even sharing a one-bedroom apartment with Yasmine, whom she'd met through a mutual acquaintance, she couldn't afford this expensive city. Something had to give or she'd soon be letting her brothers in Maupont know that she was coming home, defeated.

"Just send an email," Yasmine encouraged. "You have some nice photos from the jobs you've done. Include those. You know what you're doing."

Sweet Yasmine. Always a word of encouragement. She assessed her roommate sipping from her wineglass Her thick dark hair was stick straight, as opposed to Zoe's corkscrew red curls that grew every which way out of her head. Yasmine hailed from Tunisia and had moved to Paris to study, eventually landing under Si Wu's tutelage. Even though Zoe's fantasy of success and a life in Paris seemed to be crumbling, she'd always wish the best for Yasmine.

"I suppose it wouldn't hurt to try and see if I can get a meeting." Not with Jules Durand himself, she hoped. That would be too nerve-racking. He'd probably have an underling interview prospective designers, wouldn't he? The CEO would have much more supervisory tasks in front of him.

What was she even thinking? Jules Durand's company, with some of the most notable buildings in Paris, was not going to hire someone who knew how to make a room look larger by placing mirrors in the correct locations! They would employ designers with CVs as grand as the rooms they'd be filling.

The waiter returned with a tray full of delicious-smelling food for another table. Zoe's nose followed the aroma as far as it could.

"Yasmine, you know what? You're right. I do know what I'm doing. I don't doubt my abilities." She liked saying those words out loud. "Durand Properties might be just the break I need."

"That's the spirit."

The possibility that if she did pursue the opportunity she might encounter Jules Durand himself niggled at her. Staring back at her from those magazine photos with his eyes as dark a brown as hers were as light a blue, he was one intense man. His were the kind of eyes that could take over a girl's thoughts. Make her wonder if the impossible might be possible. Not Zoe, of course. None of that was for her. But it might set someone else to speculation.

"Okay, get me the contact information."

Two days later, Zoe and her portfolio strode toward the Durand Properties headquarters. In her one good black suit with the coordinating silky blouse underneath, she felt professional and terrified at the same time.

Just as Yasmine had promised, the contact person at Durand Properties was easily reachable by email. He, in turn, sent her an e-log from which to choose an appointment time. Several of the slots were already filled, leading Zoe to deduce that other people were being interviewed, as well. Which didn't bode well in her favor as her competition might have more experience than she did.

Nonetheless, she was excited. This was why she came to Paris, to work within the walls of the incredible architectural marvels, both old and new, that graced this remarkable city. She loved it here, where the boulevards teemed with energy. She didn't want to return to sleepy Maupont, where the most she could hope for was the odd job revamping a guest bedroom or small office. Where, walking down every street, she'd see someone she knew who would give her that look of sympathy and pity for what would define her family's name there for the rest of eternity. No, Paris wiped the slate. Gave her a fresh start. And it was where she wanted to live for the rest of her life.

As Zoe neared Durand Properties, a modern glass building that occupied an entire square block, she ducked into an alleyway. Removing the comfortable shoes she'd been walking in, she opened her bag and extracted the business heels that pulled her outfit together. After the switch, she approached the entrance door, *Durand Properties* etched into the glass with a distinct script. An intercom system allowed her to announce her arrival, then the latch clicked and she was able to open the door.

She remembered that Karim Harbi, the man she spoke with on the phone, had told her to check in at the welcome desk before taking the elevator to the fourth floor. The woman who sat behind the counter verified the appointment and pointed her in the right direction.

When the elevator door opened to the fourth floor, Zoe stepped into a central reception area, the likes of which she had never seen before. People bustled to and fro. All the walls were made of glass, affording panoramic views of the city from every direction. The fourth being the top floor allowed Zoe to see that the slanted roof was made of a reflective type of glass and solar panels that could harness the sun's heat.

In the center of the space was a wide staircase with open steps and gray steel railing. Two women descended while engaged in conversation. Off to one side, a long concrete reception desk was staffed by three employees, two women and one man, all stylishly dressed in neutral colors, speaking into headsets. Several seating areas were grouped throughout with blond wood furniture, some with red upholstery, others bare. A cluster of men in suits sat at one talking amongst themselves. Low coffee tables held massive arrangements of red flowers. Abstract stone fountains placed here and there compensated for the lack of artwork given that there were no actual walls other than the glass perimeter. It was, quite simply, the most stunning workspace Zoe had ever encountered.

"Mademoiselle Gaiman?" a young man greeted her as she was taking in the surroundings. His voice served as a good reminder to make sure her jaw wasn't hanging open at the impressiveness of it all. "I am Karim."

His accent and dark skin suggested he was another young person who had come from somewhere else to Paris with a dream in his pocket.

"Nice to meet you."

"If you'll follow me, Monsieur Durand is ready for you."

What did he just say? As it was Karim she had been interacting with so far, Zoe had convinced herself that she'd be having her interview with him. Or with someone in their human resources department. Or someone other than Jules Durand himself.

"Karim," she coughed out, "is it typical that Jules Durand is the first to meet with perspective employees?"

"No, of course, a company of our size has a department devoted to personnel. But this is a special project of a personal nature. Jules will better explain when you meet with him."

Heart suddenly thumping against her chest, Zoe cleared her throat. Karim led her to a massive corner office, private by being delineated with its own glass walls. It was as carefully furnished as the reception area. As they approached, Zoe could see a meeting section with a wood table and chairs. There was also an area with two drafting tables, computer banks and shelves that held architectural blueprints. To the side of that, two white leather sofas faced each other with armchairs beside them creating a conversation space. There was a vase of more red flowers on a countertop beside a sink and refrigerator. A treadmill faced outward to the view. The single office in its entirety was large enough to house a family of four. At the stone desk in the center of it all, a man who Zoe recognized to be Jules Durand sat in a high-backed black office chair speaking to someone through an earpiece.

As she got closer, which for some reason felt like marching toward a firing squad, she could make out the furrows between his eyebrows that she'd taken notice of in those magazine photos of him. They gave him a sort of stern look that was somehow wildly sexy at the same time. In a dark gray suit, white dress shirt and forest green tie, he was as stunning as his office building. His aura, his buzz permeated the air and reached her all the way out in the corridor. This man was over six feet of pure power. Adrenaline pounded through her.

On impulse, Zoe began forking her fingers through her corkscrew curls in hopes that her hair didn't look too unkempt. She threw her shoulders back and stood as tall as she could which, given that she was a shorty, wasn't much.

Cheering herself on, she had this. She was a hard worker, had done nice designs in the past and deserved a chance to move onto bigger projects. Not to mention that the only way she was going to be able to stay in Paris was if she rose up to the next rung on the career ladder.

She was going to dazzle this man, regardless of how imposing he was.

He was going to hire her. No doubt about it.

Karim pulled open the heavy glass door to the private office and, after Zoe stepped in, took his leave.

"It's an honor to meet you, monsieur," Zoe began as she took an uneven step forward, which made one of her shoe heels wobble. Then she heard a cracking sound. But before she could do anything about it, the heel snapped and buckled under, jerking Zoe Gaiman forward and causing her to fall flat on her face into Jules Durand's office.

"Are you all right?" Jules dashed from behind his desk to attend to the interviewee who had just, literally, burst into his office. Presenting his arm for the young woman to use for balance as she stood up, he felt a surprising tingle when she wrapped her small fingers around his bicep.

"Yes, I'm fine," she quipped dismissively, although

nonetheless leveraging all of her weight onto his arm. The portfolio of photos and sketches she had brought along to impress him with was now scattered around her. A quick cheat of a glance told Jules that they were good.

Once she hoisted herself to a standing position, he took notice that she stood not much more than five feet tall. And she had a wild tangle of hair. Had her fall dislodged a more conservative hairdo? Because, at the moment, it looked like a crazed tree straight out of a Van Gogh painting. A wine-induced hallucination of reddish, no, almost orange spirals pointing toward every angle. It took all of his gentlemanly decorum not to reach out and touch one of her curls, so curious was he to know what they would feel like.

She retrieved the culprit that was responsible for her dramatic entrance. Indeed, the pointy heel had almost fully separated from the body of her shoe and dangled limply from its infrastructure.

"Darn it. These are my only..." She decided, flustered, not to finish the sentence. Instead, she slipped the broken shoe back onto her foot and used two hands to smooth down her skirt and jacket before extending her palm for a handshake. "I'm Zoe Gaiman. I hope you can forget what just happened and we can begin the interview over again." She blew a breath upward, possibly in an attempt to send some errant hairs back to their designated place.

As he returned her handshake, Jules couldn't consent to her terms because he had an inkling that he would never forget anything about Zoe Gaiman.

Her fingers were as soft as he'd imagined they'd be.

Together, the two of them bent down to gather up

the sheets of her portfolio. He gestured for her to take a seat opposite his at the desk. Hobbling on the broken shoe, Zoe made her way to the chair and slid in.

With a tap on his computer, a photo appeared on his screen, the secondary screen that faced Zoe's seat and on the large monitor that serviced the seating cluster to his right. In the past few years, Jules had conducted most of his work from his laptop while ensconced in suites of the world's finest hotels and in Durand Properties satellite offices. Naturally, he'd frequently returned to Paris for meetings and functions. But his highly efficient office here was underutilized. That was about to change, as he'd be basing himself here permanently.

"The apartment in need of design is in this building," he explained about the first photo to Zoe. Five years ago, he'd purchased the building, which had been divided into eight apartments, not knowing at the time that he'd be dedicating one to his parents. "Here are some photos."

To her credit, Zoe seemed to have recovered after her visit with his office floor and she studied the slideshow he presented. "There's an elevator, I take it?" she inquired.

"Yes. Which is critical. You see, this apartment is for my own parents to inhabit. My father is wheelchair-bound."

"Oh, so that's why Karim said this was a personal project. It looks as if the front entrance to the building has the width to accommodate a wheelchair, but the interior doorways have been widened? That must have been a tight squeeze."

"My architects supervised those modifications." Jules was impressed. Zoe was the third designer he'd interviewed today and neither of the other two had noted that obvious need for wheelchair clearance in the apartment's doorways.

He glanced away from the screen to make contact with her sky blue eyes, which had a crystalline shimmer he found very intriguing. She also had an adorable swath of freckles that ran from one cheekbone across her nose to the other. And that hair!

Women and their attractiveness or lack thereof was of no interest to Jules, so he surprised himself in even taking the time to observe Zoe's unique beauty.

"I see from your portfolio pages—" he pointed to what was now a haphazard stack that she'd lain on the spare chair beside her "—that you share my appreciation for blending the old with the new."

"Yes, I like to bring in every functional convenience but make the living space warm and stylish at the same time. And I did a course in special-needs accessibility. Let me show you some photos."

He peered over while she riffled through her pile. One looked like a guest room converted into an office, the other a classroom. Did she have the proper experience for an entire Paris apartment, especially one for his parents where he knew he'd demand perfection? Zoe showed him an unimpressive access ramp leading to a converted garage with a few grab bars installed here and there. Jules's contractors had already done the structural modifications on the apartment. Still, at least she said she'd studied accessibility.

He opened another program on his computer. "Here we have some suggested color combinations for the paint and furnishings in the main living spaces. We can look at the bathroom and kitchen afterward. I assume you're familiar with this software that automatically generates a primary color scheme with complementary shades for accents."

"I don't use auto-generated color combining."

"Excuse me?"

"I wouldn't want a computer to decide a paint shade to match a sofa color for me. That's not how I work."

With two fingers, she twisted a ringlet that fell over one of her ears. Jules had no way to determine if it was actually out of place. It was nothing short of ludicrous how curious he was about her hair. Although, now it was what was coming out of her mouth that alarmed him.

"Mademoiselle Gaiman, as you might imagine, Durand Properties employs every bit of technology available that can assist us in our work."

"With due respect, Monsieur Durand, computer-aided design is, of course, a marvelous advancement. And the furniture placement programs and whatnot on the market these days are timesaving tools. But I also have to feel a project. In my heart—" she paused to bring her fist to her chest for emphasis "—and in my soul."

"I see," he tittered, surprised at this young woman's pluck. People usually yessed Jules Durand, too intimidated to disagree. He wasn't sure whether or not he liked Zoe's assertiveness. Ever so briefly, his mind flashed on a very private way he might show her with his lips who was the boss.

He quickly refocused with, "I'm afraid I don't employ souls. I employ professionals who, in turn, follow industry standards and new developments."

"Does the way yellow spring flowers play against the five o'clock sky rely on a digital approval system?"

"I beg your pardon?"

"When the waves of the ocean ebb and flow, creating a natural rhythm that syncs with a shoreline wind. Can your computer software replicate that?"

Jules was becoming a bit irritated. While there was something mesmerizing about this young woman, he had a job to offer and expected it done his way, and certainly wasn't going to work with someone who questioned his methods.

Especially in dealing with this apartment for his parents, Jules wanted the project done quickly, as he expected Agathe and Hugo back in Paris soon and he couldn't accommodate time-consuming mistakes. He had no leeway for prima donna designers who constantly changed their minds and, for example, repainted several times before being satisfied with their choices.

He needed his parents securely ensconced, not traipsing all over the earth like vagabonds with his father in a wheelchair. It was ironic that Jules himself had called no place home for years, either, although his time away was well spent amassing a fortune.

Everyone was going to stay put in Paris. For all the turbulence of his upbringing, with his mother's abandonments and then returns, and his father's unstable employment history, Jules would ground them now. He'd become the de facto patriarch.

"I thank you for coming in, Mademoiselle Gaiman." He pushed his chair back from the desk, ready to show her to the door. "Obviously, we have an incompatible approach, but I do wish you well." Oddly, the idea of never seeing Zoe again gave him pause and he hesitated.

"Wait…" Zoe threw her palms up, trying to halt him before he stood. "If this apartment is for your own parents, don't you want it to breathe with life? Shouldn't it be a blanket of comfort? That sings in peaceful harmony. Why don't you show me the apartment in person? So I can feel it."

That was the second time she had mentioned *feeling* the apartment.

Jules didn't do feelings. He didn't choose properties based on spring flowers. He relied on engineers and architects and inspectors and financial advisors for whom the tools of the trade brought a scientific precision. Jules liked that. There was no room for gamble in his orbit.

Yet, chance was exactly what was in front of him. He'd get no data collection on how long his parents would live. There was no spreadsheet that could forecast if his mother would finally find serenity within the boundaries of a permanent residence. No analysis would report how good a job Jules would do as their caretaker.

So the last thing he needed was any further unpredictability. While he respected that Zoe was probably a very creative person, and thought he might contemplate for the rest of his life how hair grew out of someone's head like that, he had other prospects to meet with. This interview was over.

"Thank you for your time, Mademoiselle Gaiman."

He stood, hoping she'd follow suit. Which she did, but not before shooting a penetrating look at him that made his ribs rattle. Were there tears pooling in those bright blue eyes? "Good luck with the project," she muttered.

Jules saw Zoe Gaiman to the door with her tottering on her broken shoe heel all the way.

CHAPTER TWO

OBVIOUSLY WE HAVE an incompatible approach.

Jules Durand's words from the day before played over and over again in Zoe's head as she brought two cups of coffee to the teeny tiny balcony of her and Yasmine's apartment.

The window space with its wrought iron railing was barely big enough for two folding chairs and a stool they used as a table, but they loved to drink their morning coffee out there. It was special little things like that which made Zoe hopeful she could always call Paris home.

No matter that their balcony faced out to the rear of their building and overlooked the back of the building on the next street, which didn't afford a view of much of anything. They could still breath in the Paris air and see the way the sunrays cast this way or that, inspiring artists for centuries to capture that special light through their paintbrushes.

"You see the way the sun almost glistens off of the strawberry jam on your toast?" Zoe said to Yasmine as she handed her one of the mugs. "That's what I was trying to explain to Jules Durand. Everything is integrated in the world around us."

"Do you think that Jules Durand, of Durand Gazillion-Euro Properties, needed you to explain *anything* to him?" Yasmine asked before taking a sip of her coffee.

"Apparently not," Zoe snickered, as she maneuvered one of the chairs to the precise angle so that she could sit in it without falling over the railing.

"You haven't told me all of the details of your grand entrance."

"Yeah, I made quite a first impression. The only silver lining is that at least when I fell into his life, my suit skirt didn't hike up to show him my unmentionables."

"Glad you can see the bright side."

"Have I mentioned how much I hate high heels?"

"You say you like them because they make you look taller."

"It might not be worth it."

"So, did Durand give you a hard *no* or was it a *we'll let you know* kind of thing?"

"Oh, it was most definitely a *no*."

Thank you for your time, Mademoiselle Gaiman.

That was a hard *no* if Zoe had ever heard one. Especially with the kingly tone of voice he used and the way he stood up from his desk. Like he couldn't get her out of his office fast enough. She'd been so frustrated she almost ended up leaving in tears. Her shoe, his domineering demeanor, the rejection.

Although one thing not lost on her during their too short meeting was that if she'd thought Jules Durand was nice-looking in the photos she'd seen in a magazine, it was nothing compared to him in person. His thick black hair was cut short but left a little bit longer in front, accentuating the dense eyebrows with those crinkle lines between them. His eyes were deep and very dark, leading to a long narrow nose. With his closely shaven face and knife-blade jawline, Zoe had especially noticed his full lips, which were a pale pink. All united, it was one gorgeous face.

"Why are you smiling?" Yasmine interrupted Zoe's mental recap of the most handsome human she'd ever seen in her life.

"Am I?" She hadn't realized her musings were visible. "No reason."

"Tell." Yasmine chomped on her toast.

"Only that he was, you know, not too hard on the eyes."

"No kidding. I've seen pictures of him. He's tall and has a great build, too."

"He's the long and lean type. Not bulky."

Zoe thought of the impeccably cut suit he'd worn. And how regal he'd looked in it.

"He's always showing up on those eligible bachelor lists. And says he'll never marry, that the institution is not for him."

"He definitely has a way of letting you know he's in charge. Not very equitable."

Zoe looked to the sky. Maybe his arrogance was self-confidence, and that's what had brought him success. Or the other way around, that achievement had made him so sure of himself. In any case, there was more to him than that. A man who had given such detailed thought into setting up a workable home for his parents spoke to her. Maybe because she missed her own parents so much, his care and concern touched her heart regardless of his personal manner.

No matter, though. Zoe had no interest in the man other than professionally. In any man. Men could be distracting and lead to love. Love could lead to loss. She'd had enough of that already.

After she'd fallen into Jules's office, and her portfolio with examples of her work had scattered all over his expensive carpet, she hadn't had a chance to show him one job she had done for a wheelchair-accessible guesthouse in her hometown of Maupont. Maybe it wasn't on the same scale as the apartment he was redesigning in Paris, but if she'd have been able to show him photos of that project, might she have fared better in the interview?

What's done was done. Unless…? Could she call him and try to get another interview? No, that would seem like begging. She'd asked to see the apartment and he'd refused her. He was clearly uninterested in her style. As he said, they were incompatible.

"Do you have any other upcoming interviews?" Yasmine inquired.

"Not a one."

Zoe stretched her spine against the chair back. Still tired, her nights had been fitful lately as she tossed and turned, trying to figure out what to do next. She didn't want to retreat to Maupont, which was not the world's gleaming center of art and architecture where she'd dreamed of vital and fulfilling days and evenings.

Back home, her three older brothers ran the furniture shop that her parents had owned. Returning wouldn't be what she wanted, but they'd put a roof over her head and she'd help at the shop. Where sofas and headboards and lamps had ignited in her a fascination with indoor spaces that she longed to make a career of. And studied to do so.

Unfortunately, there was limited opportunity in

Maupont and its surrounding towns. Rarely was there new construction. Small business owners and residents lived modestly and seldom had money for large remodeling jobs. Or even needed interior design. Nothing there would ever give Zoe the chance to really spread her wings, to exercise her potential. She wanted big clients with big projects and big budgets. Paris budgets.

Plus, every road in her hamlet led to a sad memory. The town square where her parents took her and her brothers to play as children and afterward bought them an ice-cream cone. A small bistro where her parents would occasionally go out to dinner on a date night. How her mother would make that extra effort to put on a nice blouse and lipstick.

Or the train station. Zoe especially didn't want to have to regularly see the train station. When they were kids, her father would take them to watch the trains go by. They'd wave through the windows to the passengers, with Zoe always imagining the faraway places they might be going.

Sadly, the train station would instead come to represent the chilling reality that defined the Gaiman family. When Zoe and her brothers were young adults, their mother and father boarded their train to take the trip to Milan that they had been saving for. Little did the four siblings know that they'd never see their parents again. The train derailment that was the top story in all the local news killed their mother and father instantly.

Because almost no one ever moved to or from Maupont, all the townspeople there still looked at Zoe and her brothers with pity. It didn't seem to bother her brothers, or they didn't notice it as much as she did. The bent neck and mashed lips on people's faces that said

I feel sorry for you even if they were talking about the weather.

When her parents were still alive, Zoe had been reluctant to move away from them, even to chase her ambition. They were a close-knit family. Zoe got her university degree and worked on those small local jobs she acquired through shop customers that only served to make her thirst for the more complex ones. After her parents died, she and her brothers got on with things, selling their childhood home and taking over the shop. But eventually, Zoe knew that she either had to try to make her dreams come true or stop having them. There was nothing keeping her in Maupont. Her brothers supported her decision. And so to Paris she came. Now she feared her hopes had come to an end.

Snatching the last piece of toast from Yasmine's plate, Zoe nibbled on it.

Her phone rang. She glanced at its screen. The caller identification was blocked.

"Hello," she answered with curiosity.

"Zoe Gaiman?" The low voice was familiar. "This is Jules Durand. Would you be available to come see the apartment at one o'clock? I thought we might talk over the project again."

"Hello again, Mademoiselle Gaiman," Jules called out as he saw Zoe walking toward him. He'd arranged to meet her in front of the building where he'd soon house his parents.

"Monsieur Durand." She held out her hand for a shake. It was the second time he'd shaken her hand and couldn't avoid noting, as he had last time, its remarkable suppleness.

"Thank you for meeting with me."

"I have to say I was surprised that you called. I assumed you thought our interview fell flat," she said with a chuckle. "You know, *fell* flat?"

A tiny twitch raised the corners of Jules's mouth. "Yes, I know what you were referring to." He'd almost felt her embarrassment by osmosis when she tripped on that broken shoe and became intimately acquainted with his finely woven carpeting. No one would want to meet a prospective employer in that fashion.

"So, may I ask, monsieur, are you still considering me for the job?"

"I'll be honest with you. I was not impressed with anyone I interviewed."

"I see. I was the best of the worst in your estimation?"

"I didn't mean it that way."

"How did you mean it?"

"I…um…" Why was he befuddled around this young woman whose qualifications were less than he'd expect for this project that was of such personal importance? Something about her threw him off-kilter. Seeing her again made him realize just how much. It would probably be a very bad idea to work with someone as distracting as she seemed to be.

Nonetheless, she really was the best of the bunch that he'd interviewed. When he thought about the six applicants he'd met yesterday, Zoe did stand out. Plus, at least she had a bit of experience with accessibility needs. He thought he should meet with her again.

He watched as she turned her attention to the two wood doors painted navy with their bronze doorknockers adorned with depictions of a lion's head. The handles were original to the 1860 construction of the building. Of course, nowadays, a state-of-the-art coding system facilitated entry.

"I think it'd be a challenge for your father to get his wheelchair across this threshold." She pointed to the bottom of the door where there was a sliver of open space before it met raised concrete. "That wasn't visible in the photos yesterday."

"Yes." Jules liked that she was jumping right into the task at hand and had remembered that his father's needs were of primary concern. "My architectural team is working on some options. Let's go inside."

Jules punched an entrance code into the keypad and the door unlocked with a click. He pulled it open to allow Zoe in. As she breezed past him, sunshine caught that untamed jungle of curls atop her head. It was amazing the way the sun decided which spirals to highlight and which to let serve as contrast.

What was he talking about again? He had projects all over the globe, this apartment to finish while his parents were at present drifting the streets of Tel Aviv. He didn't have time to care about the sun's reflection on Zoe's hair.

If he were honest, it wasn't just his parents' whereabouts he had the most trepidation about. It was the prospect of spending so much time with them, of being face-to-face again with the tumult he'd been embroiled in his entire life. Despite Jules's demand that they return to Paris and *grow up*, as he sarcastically phrased it, he was going to have to keep an emotional distance. The commotion and neglect he'd experienced as a child had been kept at bay by his career and his world travels. Put to the test, those scars had only a very thin skin covering them.

Yet, this was something he had to do. The desperation in their voices during phone calls, the phony suave sophisticated pitch in his mother's tone signaled to him that their roving had to come to an end.

Once in the building's foyer with its marble floor, Jules tapped the button to call for the elevator, an old-fashioned cage style that had been added to the building in the early 1900s.

"Your parents will be able to maneuver this?" Zoe asked in reference to the accordion iron door that needed to be slid back in order to enter the not-so-large cabin of the elevator itself.

"The wheelchair will easily fit and there's room for another person or two to stand."

With no wheelchair inside at the moment, Jules was able to keep to one side of the cage with Zoe at the other as the elevator rose. Which was good, because he'd prefer not to stand beside her if he had the option—she might smell good. His eyes had already betrayed him with their inability to resist inspecting her hair in the sun. Now they were locked in battle with his brain that was instructing him not to look at her legs under that pink knee-length dress she was wearing. His mind lost the fight and his eyes pronounced the legs lovely and shapely. To which Jules almost frowned. Why did she have to be so attractive?

Once they reached their stop, Jules opened the cage and showed Zoe to one of the two apartments on the fourth floor. With another private code, he opened the front door.

"This doorway has enough width, and no threshold," she observed.

"Thank you. I'll let my architects know you concur," he said snidely, though she didn't react. He supposed she was trying to impress him.

The small entry area into the apartment led in one direction to the kitchen and the other to the dining and living room, which they stepped into. The floor-to-ceiling windows with double-glass doors that faced the street, as was typical in so many Paris apartments, would let in lots of fresh air. "Nice light," Zoe commented.

She looked behind her and then retraced her steps. Jules could tell she was imagining the entrance from the point of view of someone in a wheelchair.

"There are no hard turns from the front door to here," Jules confirmed.

"True. I'm thinking about a small shelf beside the front door at wheelchair height—" she gestured to the short wall in the entry area "—with some attractive bowls or baskets where your father could lay down his personal belongings or purchases when he came in. Maybe a painting or a mirror above it."

"Perhaps you'd like to make some notes," he suggested. "Did you bring a tablet or laptop?"

"I don't need to just yet. I'll remember."

"I expect every conversation we have to be documented."

"Yes, Monsieur Durand. I was just tossing out a thought."

"I'd like any ideas to be presented to me in writing or through images and cataloged with a filing scheme so that we might refer to it later."

"Every idea." Zoe gave him a side-eye as if she was

surprised by his request. Was she or was she not a professional? Her licensing and education seemed to be in order when Karim had researched her background.

Jules supposed she hadn't worked for a big corporation before and had a more casual relationship with clients who only needed a room redecorated and so on. It was frustrating that he couldn't find an applicant better suited to how he did business. He assumed that if he hired Zoe, she would want to do a good job and he could train her to use his methods. Although, as soon as he had that thought, it occurred to him that Zoe Gaiman didn't seem like someone who did things other people's way.

"I'm feeling Chopin in here," she said, making swirls with both wrists and outstretched fingers to animate. He noticed how tiny and fine-boned her hands were. "Soothing piano chords for soft hours after your parents have been out and about all day."

Case in point about methods. "May I ask, what does *feeling* Chopin mean with regard to the task? Neither of my parents play the piano."

"No, not literally. It's a mood."

"Is it?"

"Would you like me to write it down?"

He almost laughed. Was this young woman so opinionated with everyone she met, or just him?

The last thing Jules needed in his life was someone to argue with. He'd grown up in one long yelling match. He could remember crying in his bedroom as a little boy because his parents were so combative with each other. It was traumatic.

No, Jules worked conventionally and systematically and he expected all of his employees to do the same. If there was a dispute or disagreement, it was to be handled by one of his project managers. Although, in this case, he was to be the project manager as he would be directing the job given his personal interest in it.

Zoe must have sensed that he wasn't pleased with her little snip because she got that same glassy-eyed look as she'd had in his office when he dismissed her from the interview. Like she was about to cry.

Oh, women! Jules shook his head a little. One minute Zoe was bossy, the next emotional. After growing up in the mayhem of his parents, which was largely triggered by his mother's malcontent, he knew that he had a skewed view of women. He had wanted to believe that most women were not like his mother, full of acrimony and temper. Yet, he hadn't been able to prove his theory.

There'd been no one in his life he'd seen model a healthy relationship. When his parents weren't tearing each other down, they had a dull resignation toward one another. As if they both felt they were stuck in a trap, that there was no other choice. Neither had the guts to leave for good or put any effort into making things better. Agathe did her disappearing act but always returned. She donned a mask to the outside world and could masquerade as an extrovert, one who was apparently at present throwing herself at young taxi drivers in Tel Aviv. Hugo now had his wheelchair to hide in and blame.

Jules had no other relatives or people around him to set a positive example. And the women he'd subconsciously chosen during his university years and in his early twenties were dramatic and needy. It was what he knew. Once he gained success in his career, the opportunists began to descend on him, all sorts of women who would slowly reveal themselves to be only after what Jules could give them.

It seemed absolutely clear that women and Jules weren't a match.

He certainly had normal human desires. So, he developed a three-date rule. Which was serving him well. He could date a woman, but no more than three times lest he or she start to think any kind of connection was developing.

Jules was free to have the company of a female for dinner or drinks or recreation, even followed by physical intimacy should they both want it. He was allowed to repeat up to two additional dates with that same woman. After that, he cut things off, blaming his busy schedule if he liked her enough to explain why he wouldn't be calling again. His system worked like clockwork. He couldn't think of a single time he'd been tempted to break his rule. Zoe Gaiman's sassy and sexy mouth was of no concern to him in that regard. Coupling was not on Jules Durand's schedule.

"Do you think your parents will be doing a lot of entertaining?" Zoe asked Jules as they continued to survey the apartment.

Impress him with something, her brain screamed.

She'd already irritated him by commenting on something his architects were taking care of. Then she let out a little jibe about his rigid approach to work. That led to an awkward silence, which had been blowing like a breeze through the room for an uncomfortable number of minutes.

"I doubt it," Jules stated matter-of-factly. "Why do you ask?"

Hmm. Whenever Jules mentioned his parents, Zoe noticed a change of timbre in his voice. Like he was talking about people he didn't really know, other than that they were aging and his father was wheelchair-bound. Zoe wasn't sure what to make of that.

Don't voice your every thought like you always do, she counseled herself.

While Jules Durand was obviously a difficult man to deal with, Zoe needed to get this job. A reference from him could open doors for her. Her career could really take off if she got this right. The apartment was glorious—it had all the classic Parisian touches with the double-door windows and brass doorknobs. She would adore working on it, and others like it. Maybe she could *yes* him into thinking she agreed with everything he said and then do things her way after all. She'd do such a good job for him, he'd never notice. Although, clearly, Jules was not a man who missed anything.

"I was just wondering about what size the dining table should be, whether it would be frequently used for seating more than your parents. When *we* choose it—" she emphasized the word *we* as if she'd already gotten the job "—we could go with an oval or round shape for safety, no pointy corners. And we could order a couple of the chairs on casters so they'd be easy to roll out of the way if your father wanted to pull his wheelchair up to the table."

"That's worth a consideration."

"I'll make a note of it," she chipped, which earned her a funny double take from Jules, those creases between his eyebrows becoming very pronounced.

Standing next to Jules Durand, coupled with the afternoon sun creating a pleasant temperature, Zoe had a freeze-frame moment. If she got this project, her vision for herself could be coming to pass. By contrast, if she didn't, she'd have no choice but to return to Maupont, at least for a while. Maybe she could save up money and try Paris again in a couple of years. The mere thought of that brought a slump to her shoulders. She didn't want to return to her hometown with her tail between her legs, a failure, and nothing but harrowing memories to look forward to when she got back.

"Is something wrong?"

Zoe subtly dabbed the outer corner of each eye to wipe away the drops that those very thoughts had produced. "No, not at all, Monsieur Durand. This apartment just really speaks to me about the beauty of Paris."

A wistful smile crossed Jules's lips, the first one Zoe had seen. She almost keeled over, and this time it would have been *his* fault.

If Jules Durand was handsome with his serious professional face on, the way he looked while smiling was something from another dimension. Laugh lines defined his mouth, which opened enough to display perfectly straight white teeth. Yasmine had told her she'd seen his photo on those silly Paris's-Most-Eligible-Bachelors lists the gossip magazines did. It was not hard to see why, although she did wonder why this gorgeous and powerful man was still a bachelor.

Zoe didn't exactly know what caused him to grin, but she'd walk ten miles in the snow to be able to do it again. *Make Jules smile.* She'd add that to the list he wanted her to keep.

"I appreciate your enthusiasm," he said by way of explanation. "It is a marvelous property, without question."

They smiled at each other for a minute that Zoe

would swear had nothing to do with architecture. Thinking quickly to prolong the positive interaction she asked, "Can we have a look at the kitchen?"

"Please." He gestured for her to enter ahead of him.

He pulled his phone from his pocket.

Standing side by side, surveying the kitchen, Zoe became immediately aware of being in such close proximity to him. He produced an inner heat that she instantly liked and felt drawn to. With him being so much taller, she could have nestled her face against his shoulder and, strangely, thought about doing just that.

Instead, she had to not only discreetly turn her head, but also crane it upward to get a glance of his face in profile while he tapped into his phone. As he concentrated on what he was doing, his strength and potency was tangible. It made the skin prickle all over her body. She'd never been in the presence of someone who controlled the oxygen in a room.

Once she was able to pull her eyes away from him, she saw that the built-in kitchen cabinetry was complete, but doors were not affixed and there was no backsplash as yet.

"I'm thinking of this for the cabinet." He showed her what he'd cued up on his phone. French country wood with intricate arch carvings. She didn't like them. The apartment had enough ornate touches. She'd choose something simpler for the kitchen. But she didn't say anything. Yet.

The client was always right, so the saying went. That was until she could sneak in her own ideas and make clients think they had thought of them on their own.

Just get the job, she advised herself again.

A cream-colored granite countertop was in, which

delineated the kitchen from the front entry area. An idea came to mind that she couldn't resist pitching, even though it would mean redoing work that was finished. "Why don't we lower that granite counter and take the cabinets out from underneath?" Again using *we*. "There is plenty of other storage elsewhere and that would leave open space so that your father could just wheel right up under it. We'll make it a breakfast bar with a chair of the same height for your mother."

"Go on."

"I know it would require a change order and add some cost. But you don't have the cabinet doors yet so at least those won't be wasted."

Jules's heavy eyebrows hitched up.

So, Monsieur Durand was going to be surprised every time she had a good idea? That was fine with Zoe. She had lots of them.

"I can picture that. I'd like to see the specifications. In writing."

"Also, if we go with a style that's less fuss…" Zoe stopped herself again. She wasn't going to tell him that she didn't like the cabinet-door style he'd chosen. There was time for that later. He seemed to be responding favorably to the suggestions she was making for his father's special needs. She should stick with that for the time being. "I'd also like to shorten the length of the counter so that your parents have more room to pass through. And if the stone is cut properly, that extra piece of countertop can be salvaged to create the entry shelf I was talking about."

Jules looked at his watch that Zoe assessed clearly cost more than the salary she made last year. Was she losing his attention?

"I've got an appointment in ninety minutes. Followed by two more. I need to get some lunch."

"Oh," she stuttered after his abrupt change of topic. "I'd love to talk more about the project sometime."

"Yes. We'll have lunch and discuss it further. Was there something unclear about that?"

"Only that when you said you needed to get lunch, I thought you meant... Never mind, Monsieur Durand."

"Why don't you call me Jules?"

"And I'm Zoe."

"Yes. I know."

"I mean, call me Zoe."

"Your name."

Why were they back having so many miscommunications after they had just jived a few seconds ago about the countertop? She didn't understand the way he thought. Although she had the sense that she'd like to.

During the elevator ride down, Zoe observed everything she could about the building's structure. On the street, she followed Jules a few doors down to a bistro he knew. She was thrilled at the moment. Like something from a movie, she was in Paris with a dashing billionaire. It almost wasn't real. They took seats at one of the small tables outside in the fresh air. Everyone who walked by seemed so chic as they went about their business. French women really did knot their scarves a certain way and beard stubble on men never looked better.

When the waiter presented them with menus, Zoe had a moment's panic. She didn't want to assume that because Jules was wealthy he was going to buy her lunch, as he hadn't expressly said so. With her dwindling bank account, she'd need to mind what she ordered.

"Two glasses of the Domaine du Candulon Sauvignon Blanc," Jules ordered before the waiter left. Then asked her, "Is that all right?"

She didn't want to tell him that she'd had so little work she needed to conserve her money. A glass of wine couldn't cost that much, could it? Except that when she found on the menu which vintage he'd ordered, she was wrong.

"I'll take a garden salad with grilled chicken. Would you like the same?" he asked Zoe when the waiter returned. "I'll buy lunch, of course."

Zoe wondered if she was blushing. At how utterly mesmerizing that famous real-estate tycoon Jules Durand was telling her that he'd buy her lunch!

But she wasn't going to bat her eyelashes and let him choose what she'd eat. "No, thank you. I'll have the forest ham and creamed butter on a baguette."

"Really?"

"What do you mean?"

"I prefer a lunch of lean protein and vegetables. That nourishes me for the afternoon."

Another difference between them. Zoe ate anything that was put in front of her and had a special love for the baked goods of Paris.

It shouldn't surprise her that Jules was rigid about his lunch, just as he seemed to be with everything else. Zoe wondered what, if anything, made this man cut loose. Did he have a wild side? Something about the possibility of that rumbled low down in her belly.

She gobbled the first half of her sandwich when it arrived, causing Jules to smirk a bit.

"Were you starving?" he commented on her dedication to her lunch.

"It's just so delish. Do you want a bite?"

"I don't eat bread early in the day. The carbs slow me down."

She shrugged and took another humongous bite of her sandwich. There was no bread o'clock in her regime. "So I'm guessing you won't want to order dessert?"

Jules ate his salad with vigor while fielding messages on his phone. He shook his head. "I've got to take care of this right now. If you'll pardon me."

"Go ahead," she said, still chomping enthusiastically at her sandwich's salty richness. Should she be pretending she had urgent business to attend to on *her* phone, as well?

"Karim," he spoke into the phone, "set up a meeting for me with Kowalczyk. Today."

After issuing five different sets of instructions to Karim, Jules finally put down the phone and sipped his wine. He made an assessment of Zoe, as if he were sizing her up. "I have a full schedule, and a number of projects that have presented challenges in addition to moving my parents into the apartment. Therefore, I can't spend any more time interviewing for an interior designer. Zoe Gaiman, you have just gotten the job. Effective immediately."

CHAPTER THREE

JULES SIPPED HIS green breakfast drink while gazing out his office window at the morning sky. He and Karim had just finished their morning meeting, the newly in-person chat as opposed to the daily teleconferences they'd been having with Jules checking in from the four corners of the world. There was a lot on Jules's mind, with properties in various states of flux from Kyoto to Morocco to Perth that all needed his review. Yet, he found himself staring out into the distance, longing for something, not knowing what.

"Mother," Jules answered with a tap to his earpiece when his phone's buzz identified the caller. He girded himself before asking the inevitable. "Where are you?"

"Still in Tel Aviv, darling. We met a fabulous French couple last night. Two gentlemen who own inns up and down the Loire Valley. I spent the evening dancing with Gaspard and Louis, while your father sat and drank."

Jules pursed his lips. How like his mother to be critical of his father who, obviously, wasn't the type to be out on the dance floor in his wheelchair.

He could hear over the phone that Agathe was wearing her disguise again, like she was genuinely attacking every day with gusto. He could hear the reedy thinness in her voice, as if she were trying to convince herself as much as she was him.

"At your ages..."

"Oh, heavens, Jules," she cut him off, "you sound like an old fuddy-duddy. When was the last time *you* were out dancing all night?" Ah, so Agathe also had managed a dig at her son.

But with a shrug that no one saw, Jules tried to think of a time he'd stayed out dancing. Never. That was the answer. He did not spend his evenings carousing. Early to bed and early to rise was more his routine. He couldn't say it was fun, but it made sense for his life.

"To what purpose do I owe this delightful update?"

"We're a bit short on funds."

Jules scowled. Not really about the money, which he had plenty of. But his mother's frivolous attitude irked him. "This is the last time. There are plane tickets to Paris already purchased in your names. I've hired a designer for the apartment and unless you want to leave all the decisions to us, you'd better get here." That wasn't much of a threat to her and Jules knew it. She wouldn't care, might not even notice, what style of cabinet door was in the kitchen or the fabric of an armchair.

Agathe was no domestic maven. She always thought she married beneath her and said so at every opportunity, even though her family was of the same working class as Hugo's. They met while he was tending a bar at a local brasserie in the Paris suburb where they both lived. Agathe and some other girls from the neighborhood happened to wander in one night. When Agathe told the story in retrospect, she'd say she was attracted to what she called Hugo's *sad* eyes. The same eyes Jules inherited, according to his mother. Hugo and Agathe began to date and before long she found herself pregnant. Their wedding was held three months before Jules was born.

He remembered as a young boy that his mother spent her days on time-wasting activities like watching television and pouring her first glass of wine before lunchtime, never embracing motherhood or embarking on a career. And Hugo drifted from one job to another, ornery and short-tempered perhaps due to unresolved issues about his own relentlessly critical father.

Jules grew up in a household filled with mood swings that felt like arduous climbs up a steep mountain followed by sharp drops down, wherein the trek began again. And again and again. His parents' fighting might have begun over something as trivial as Hugo leaving his coat on a chair instead of hanging it up. Then the bickering would escalate over several days' time, culminating in his mother packing her olive green luggage and leaving, claiming she'd never return. Jules lost track of how many times it happened, but at least a dozen.

By his teenage years, he was no longer rattled by the abandonment he'd endured as a younger boy, when he'd stick his head out his bedroom window to watch his mother storm down the street away from their dingy apartment, yanking on the handle of the suitcase tottering behind her on its worn-out wheels.

Hugo barely looked up from his newspaper when she left or when she returned. Jules never found an ally in his father. The most Hugo would manage during his wife's absences was to bring home a few groceries at night and sign his son's school forms. There'd never been any commiseration with his father over his mother's behavior.

Jules had his first job by thirteen years old, sweeping the sidewalk for any shopkeeper who would pay him for the task. When he was twenty years old, during his university years, Jules had saved enough money to buy a ramshackle apartment in a downtrodden area. He cleaned it up, leased it and began to learn the ins and outs of being a property owner.

"*Toda raba.*"

Agathe must have thought she was being cute by thanking Jules in Hebrew for agreeing to send money.

He ended the call and returned to scrutinizing the sky. It was a cloudy morning in Paris but the weather forecast predicted it clearing later in the day when he'd be meeting Zoe. The thought of seeing her again brought a smile to his face, which was welcome after he'd just been irritated by his mother. Zoe's orange curls. The petite willowy body that had zigzagged through the crowded boulevard yesterday with snakelike flexibility. The ideas for the apartment that she was so sure and confident about. She'd had some worthy suggestions. That she was full of enthusiasm peaked Jules's interest.

As unlikely and unexpected as it was, something about Zoe had gotten under his skin. He'd thought about her before he'd fallen asleep last night and again first thing when he woke up. He'd even checked his watch a couple of times already, eager for their afternoon appointment. Which was absurd. He kept people at a tidy distance aided by the fact that they were often intimidated by his wealth and position. He served nicely as his own barrier.

Daydreaming about seeing a woman again was not how Jules played the game.

By the time he'd finished having lunch with Zoe

yesterday, he had too much else on his mind to continue looking for a designer and decided to give her the project. Lest his new hire think she'd be given free rein on the apartment, Jules planned to show Zoe some of his other properties in Paris. To make clear what he liked. While he appreciated that she spoke up about her thoughts, he'd make sure that by the end of the day Zoe understood that all final decisions were to be his.

Despite his affirmations about who was in charge, when he saw Zoe coming up from the metro station later that afternoon, Jules felt a lurch in his gut. She was so pretty with her bare legs under a full floral skirt worn with a low-cut midnight blue top. As she got closer, he noticed the freckles that dotted her face were not the only ones on her body. Her collarbone and exposed décolleté were adorned with more of the pigmentation marks that he found oddly charming. For a minute, he found himself almost angry with her for being so lovely. Women didn't sidetrack him, and he was determined to keep it that way. What sorcery was this one carrying up her bright blue sleeve?

"Zoe."

"Jules."

He gestured to the building a few steps away. "Built in 1901. I want you to see an interior design we did in one of the apartments. The tenants are at work and have allowed us to let ourselves in."

She commented once they had entered, "No elevator?"

"No, in this particular building one hadn't been put in over the years, and we couldn't do the structural changes it would have required."

"So it's not suitable for elderly people."

"No, but we've never had any problems leasing it. The stairs are good exercise."

Zoe followed Jules up the steps and by the third floor she was huffing for breath.

"Would you mind slowing down a minute?"

Jules sneered to himself, his face not visible to Zoe behind him. He had indeed been bounding up the stairs. Was he trying to impress her with his physical prowess? So unlike him.

They entered the apartment. It was another well-preserved example of historic Paris interiors.

"Oh, so you went very traditional here?" Zoe commented at first glance.

"Yes, we chose the Tiffany lamps and the rug has details woven in Chinese silk."

"Do you lease all of your properties already furnished?"

"No, just as often they're empty. But here in Paris, our clients tend to be of a standing that utilize the full services we can offer. Expense is rarely a consideration."

"And they choose the design themes?"

"What are you implying?"

"Nothing." Her voice rose an octave. "You've got red walls, gold draperies, the large wood-framed sofas with embroidered cushions."

"I take it you don't like it?"

"Only that I gravitate to more comfortable styles. It's just my personal preference. Again, my opinion, but I think there's opportunity to highlight the period pieces without dominating the whole room in this sort of bordello style."

"Bordello! I'll have you know these fine antiques took a year to locate and cost ten times what it would have to simply recreate the pieces. We used university documentation for authenticity."

For as many times as he'd thought about Zoe in the past twenty-four hours, he seemed to have forgotten that while there was something extremely appealing about her, she was exasperating, as well. Jules did not surround himself with uninhibited people who voiced every thought they had. Squabbling was the last thing he wanted to do with employees, and saw to it that he never did.

Oh, no. His parents were evidence that life was too short to be spent arguing, even for the Zoes of the world who found discourse to be some type of sport. So, it was with a jaw tensed shut that he continued to glare at her, trying to remind himself that her personality didn't matter. As soon as the apartment for his parents was done, she'd be out of his world forever.

"No disrespect intended. I'm sure your tenants love their surroundings. I was just thinking out loud. Isn't an exchange of brainstorming exciting?" she asked in earnest. "You wouldn't have hired me if you wanted someone who would agree with you all of the time."

"And I expect you not to make me regret my decision."

Jules massaged the divots between his eyebrows and began the diaphragmatic breathing a podcaster had been explaining through his earbuds on his morning run earlier.

"Do you have brothers and sisters?" Zoe asked. Was she trying to change the subject?

"No. Why?"

"Only that I grew up battling with three older brothers. Let's just say that confrontation is something I'm quite used to."

So was Jules, but for all the wrong reasons.

Therein lay the difference. Zoe understood arguing as something organic and useful. Jules's parents fought in a way that belittled the other and had no end goal.

Zoe was right, though. Arguing over a bordello—*ha*—lamp did not mean anyone was leaving or being hurt. It was just heated conversation. Jules didn't know why Zoe pushed those buttons in him. Or perhaps it was the apprehension of spending more time with his parents, who hadn't evolved in their thirty-four years together but hadn't parted, either. In their own weird way, they were still very much a couple. Agathe no longer had it in her to leave Hugo's side. But fighting was simply their way, their cycle. Jules had long ago decided it wasn't going to be his. Hence, his three-date rule to be sure he didn't accidentally hope for a different outcome.

As they left the apartment, Zoe swept passed him and he got a whiff of what smelled like coconut shampoo. Without realizing it, his head bent toward the scent as if to follow it through the doorway. He quickly righted himself, shocked by his own actions. Zoe was making him *feel* things. Which was frustrating and baffling because Jules Durand had gotten as far as he had in life by shutting down feelings. At all cost. How high would the price get?

"I don't understand him at all," Zoe exclaimed to Yasmine as they sat cross-legged on their small sofa while watching a cooking show on television. "In one moment he's nice to talk to and then in the next he gets holier than thou."

She reached over for one of the strawberries in the

bowl on the coffee table in front of them. After several hours spent with Jules looking at a few of his luxury properties around town, they'd parted company. He offered to have his driver give her a ride home but she opted for the metro, knowing that she also wanted to pick up some food on the way. She and Yasmine nibbled on the berries, the chicken and loaf of bread she'd brought home. They'd eat the leftovers tomorrow.

The TV chef was shelling a lobster with her impressive knife skills.

"Well, he gave you the job, didn't he?"

"Theoretically. Although he makes me nervous that I could blow it just as easily with one wrong turn."

"Don't make one, then."

Yasmine was right. Zoe needed to keep tabs on her freewheeling style. There was no money left to keep hope churning if she lost this job.

The meeting had gotten off to a rocky start when she likened that first apartment to a house of ill repute. But it was so over the top she'd just blurted out her opinion. Censoring herself didn't come naturally.

"That's probably why he's at the top of his field," Yasmine continued. "By doing things his way."

"How he talks about design choices is driving me crazy. This color matches with that building material, which mathematically coordinates with a certain number of chairs. It all makes perfect sense but there's something so flat about all of his computer software and texture charts."

"At work, we have designers who come into the shop with specifications like that. They want a sofa in blue velvet shade number such and such, and bigger than x but smaller than y. Then just as many come in not certain what they're after but they know it when they see it."

"Right, so I'm the latter, he's the former."

"Just because you're not a high-tech planner like he is doesn't mean he won't be happy with the outcome."

Zoe broke off a piece of the country bread and stuffed it in her mouth. The center was chewy and moist with an airy crumb that made her mouth do a happy dance in response. The chef on TV tossed a large knob of butter into a sizzling skillet.

Zoe thought back to the lunch she'd had with Jules when he told her he didn't eat bread at certain times of the day. While she certainly didn't begrudge anyone healthy eating habits that worked for them, this was Paris! Where even the simplest bread was elevated to an art form. How could he resist the smells and tastes that beckoned to passersby from the storefronts at every turn?

Once again, it was systems and discipline that defined this man's life.

"He can be so annoying."

"Oh, so you're attracted to him! That explains everything."

"What?"

"He wouldn't peeve you if you weren't into him."

"I'm not *into* him." What a silly term that was! "I'm *into* keeping the job and staying in Paris."

"Okay, I'm just saying there's a twinkle in your eyes when you talk about him."

"There is not!"

"Suit yourself," Yasmine said and then wedged a too-big strawberry into her mouth. They both laughed.

On TV, the chef swirled the butter until it was brown and then gently eased the lobster pieces into the pan.

Even if she did find Jules alluring, an elegant billionaire like him wasn't going to be interested in the frizzy-haired little designer he half regretted hiring. For starters.

The second reason for any contemplation of Jules's appeal being ludicrous was that Zoe was never going to get involved with a man. She was never going to love. Nope. That was already decided. The edict signed and certified. Because if there was one thing Zoe had learned the hard way, it was that to love meant to accept the possibility of loss. And Zoe couldn't afford to lose anymore. As it was, the bits and pieces of her heart were barely being held together. She might be willing to take a risk on a paint color, but not with her love.

The phone call she would never forget replayed in her mind.

It hadn't been but an hour earlier when Zoe and her brothers had accompanied their parents to the train station to see them off for their long-planned trip to Milan. Zoe's mother had dressed nicely for travel, an expression of her excitement about the journey to a fashionable city.

Zoe would forever remember the burgundy-colored pantsuit with a patterned blouse underneath that her mother wore. Her long hair was held back with a pretty barrette. She had even convinced their father to sport his black leather jacket and dress jeans so that they looked like a smart couple on the go. Zoe and her brothers had presented their mother with a nosegay as a bon voyage.

At twenty-three, Zoe had long finished growing and

was clearly the short one of the family, taking after her maternal grandmother who had been barely five feet tall and had the same unique red hair. Her three brothers towered above her as they all gave hugs to their departing parents.

After getting on the train, her mother had made sure to blow kisses to her children as they pulled out of the station. They were to be gone for ten days. No one could have guessed that these four siblings waving on the platform would never see their parents again.

Afterward, back at the furniture store, Zoe retreated to the office to do some bookkeeping while her brothers manned the sales floor. When the phone next to her rang, she casually picked it up, assuming it was a potential customer inquiring about an item. Instead, the caller identified himself as a police officer, and from his subdued tone Zoe knew instantly that something was wrong.

Her ears listened but they could barely hear. With each word uttered, the voice on the other end of the line sounded farther and farther away.

Train derailment… Fifty-seven dead… No survivors… Sincerest condolences… Counselor to come by…

What followed was a blur of days upon days of neighbors bringing over soups and casseroles and cakes that had no taste. Coffee was no different than water, midnight was not distinguished from dawn. Relatives Zoe hardly knew descended from both within and outside of France, sharing their sets of remembrances. Psychologists and social workers spoke in the hushed and modulated pitches they no doubt received training for, designed to calm the listener but which struck Zoe as forced and artificial. The questions never ceased about what was going to happen next, to Zoe and her brothers, to the store, to the house they'd grown up in.

There were the tears that wouldn't stop. Like a re-circulating fountain, for as many as erupted from Zoe's eyes, there were still more behind those waiting to spray forward. She'd hardly believed she could cry that much without dehydrating all the liquid in her body.

As the weeks went by, the visitors and stringy meat stews stopped arriving. The spring of tears eventually lost some of its force. It erupted every day, but the flow wasn't as strong and didn't last as long.

What replaced it was something small but heavy that sat on top of Zoe's rib cage and never moved from its spot. It reminded her that her small body couldn't house a second souvenir of bereavement like the one she carried. She'd never ask it to. Yet, the potential for loss was all around. When Zoe caught herself caring too much about anything, that little spot pinged and sent a subtle vibration through her body. A warning sign she relied on.

So whether or not she was fascinated, and pinged, by Jules Durand was a moot point. Obviously, a fling with her boss, and yes his attractiveness was indisput-able, would be a very bad move. And anything more serious was out of the question for her. Not to mention that she had no cause whatsoever to think that he was interested in her.

There was absolutely no reason to keep replaying the moment at that second property they'd visited today, the attic apartment with the steel-framed skylights. It was an innocent gesture of chivalry, the way he placed his hand on her lower back to usher her through a doorway. That it sent a wicked shiver up her spine, snapping her shoulders to arch sharply, didn't mean anything at all. Nothing at all.

It simply wasn't important that she still had the sensation of his large hand on that exact spot, imprinted like a tattoo. When he'd whispered, *Come this way*, he'd meant nothing by it other than to guide her into the room. But his low voice had been so close to her ear it reverberated for the rest of their time together.

Why was she still thinking about that interlude?

Come this way.

Dish completed, the TV chef placed the pieces of lobster onto a serving plate and drizzled the brown butter on top. She then sprinkled on toasted breadcrumbs and chopped parsley, declaring that the most important ingredient in any recipe was quality.

"*What* is that smile about?" Yasmine probed. Were Zoe's thoughts visible on her face?

She stuffed another strawberry into her mouth.

"It doesn't have to be modern, but it should be sleek!" Zoe's voice was becoming a bit sharp as she and Jules disagreed in front of the cabinet door options at the kitchen furnishings shop. "I still say that looks too village cozy. From what it sounds like with your parents' constant travel, I'm sure your mother likes things simple."

"You've never even met my mother."

Jules remembered the kitchen in the dark apartment he grew up in as being plain, with no particular decorative choices. Just as Agathe had no specialties as a cook. Much of what Jules grew up eating was premade food or picnic items.

Nonetheless, he liked what he liked and thought

the more traditional French country style might add a homey feel. Even if his mother didn't care, at least it could look inviting.

Whereas Zoe favored lacquered lightwood doors without any beveling and brushed nickel hardware. "The tone of the wood is warm," she pressed. "I think that will give you what you're after."

"The client is always right," he quipped with what he knew was a cheeky grin. Zoe rolled her eyes in exasperation. That made Jules chuckle. He nudged it further, "Am I correct?"

Zoe narrowed her eyes like she was regarding him with suspicion.

Which goaded him on. He repeated, "Yes?"

She pointed to a space-age turquoise cabinet door made of plastic. "How about these?" She held her smile for a second to pretend she was serious.

Her determination was admirable, if somewhat exhausting. In spite of himself, he'd become tolerant of their friendly dissimilarities about design. They were on their third disagreement of the day, Jules noted as he looked at his watch. At this rate, the apartment should be completed in five years.

"I'm getting hungry. You don't want me to cross over into *hangry*, do you?" He used the made-up word that signified the shift to anger that lack of nourishment could bring.

"That's because all you drink in the morning is that green goopy concoction. You need something that will stick to your ribs."

"What do you suggest, a pastry?"

"Yes, covered in chocolate," she said with an emphatic nod of her head that made a couple of her curls bounce in the process. Jules still marveled that Zoe's hair had a life of its own, falling this way or that as she moved. "I'm kidding but, you know, an egg, a bowl of warm grains, a yogurt. In short, breakfast."

Words were coming forth from her but he couldn't get his attention off Zoe's mouth as it moved. As a matter of fact, studying her lips was a far more intriguing notion than thinking about the dinner party he had to attend tonight. A large development group from Kenya was visiting the Durand Properties headquarters and meeting with a number of Jules's key people in preparation for a large project in Nairobi.

All the negotiations had been already hammered out, and the evening was just to fete the developers by inviting some of Paris's high society for a dinner cruise on the Seine. Jules loathed that part of his job, the socializing and small talk. He should have invited a date to help chitchat and swat away the gold diggers in glittery dresses who always found their way to him at these things.

Jules had a few female acquaintances in Paris, professionals in the industry who were married to their careers. They knew that Jules wasn't open to anything but occasional companionship. In truth, though, while they were polished and accomplished women, nothing about any of them had sparked his fancy. It felt like too much of a chore to reach out.

After Zoe had checked out the shelving in the back of the store, she walked toward him, biting her bottom lip. Out of nowhere, the desire came over him to nibble on that supple lip himself rather than let her continue do it. How might that plumpness feel between his teeth?

As she moved toward him in what he experienced as

slow motion, he imagined himself sitting at his work desk. And Zoe entering his office, this time not flat on her face from the oopsie she'd taken at their first interview.

Instead, she'd be wearing the close-fitting stretchy black dress she had on today that showcased her compact curves and played nicely against the pale skin of her legs. A devil's deliciousness overtook him when he thought of her striding toward his desk. Toward him. To him. For him. He envisioned himself with a press of a button activating the mechanism that would close all the blinds in his office, giving him total privacy.

The hairs on his arms stood up at the possibility. While Zoe sauntered her way across the office, he'd push his chair back from the desk and beckon her close. His hands would take hold of her hips and pull her to him. With a firm grasp, he'd lift one of her legs around him and then the other, raising her until she sat facing him on his lap, straddling him in his office chair. He'd enjoy exploring the soft flesh in his hands, his pelvis thrusting up to meet her.

As a matter of fact, he fought to prevent his hips from making any motion now, in the middle of the kitchen furnishings shop. Covering his mouth with one hand, he continued to watch Zoe browse in the store, his eyelids at half-mast in his arousal.

In his fantasy, once he'd spent a long leisurely time with the parts of her that were, literally, in reach, his palms would move up her spine. One vertebrae at a time up to the back of her neck where his fingers could finally tangle into that glorious head of hair that he was sure would be as silky and springy as it looked.

Grabbing a fistful of those locks, he'd tilt her head so

that her face was close to his and he'd start feathering light kisses down onto that pretty mouth. That wouldn't hold him for long before he'd begin nibbling little pieces of those lips between his teeth, until he heard a moan of pleasure escape from her throat. At which point he'd kiss her with his full mouth.

Over and over. And over.

Until her lips were red and swollen.

Until…

"Are we getting lunch, or what?" Zoe bounced over, startling Jules with her zest. He felt a strain against the zipper of his pants and casually buttoned his suit jacket to conceal any evidence. She said, "You look hungry."

"I am." She didn't know how right she was.

He instantly refocused, shocked at where his mind had been. He couldn't remember the last time craving had come over him like that. Musing about women wasn't on his agenda. Or never had been, anyway.

It wasn't that Zoe affected him in a way that no other woman had, he told himself. He simply wasn't used to spending so much time with anyone. This was temporary. The apartment would be finished soon enough, his parents would move in and bewitching Zoe would be out of his life. That would be in everyone's best interest.

"I've got a business function to go to tonight," Jules said after he guided them out of the shop and to a market café where they could grab a light bite to hold him until evening. Again, he began to dread being *on* for a boat full of people he barely knew. With no stop for reconsideration, the words fell out. "It's a dinner cruise on the Seine. Are you busy this evening? Would you come with me?"

CHAPTER FOUR

"You're asking me to come with you for a cruise on the Seine?"

Zoe seemed surprised after Jules invited her to the evening with the Kenyan developers so that he wouldn't have to go alone.

"If you'd like. Some notable people in the Parisian property world will be there, too. You might even make some contacts that could be useful."

There. Jules reframed the invitation in his mind so that it made sense to him. Zoe might benefit from the networking. And he'd be more at ease socializing if he had an ally on his arm. He most definitely did not invite Zoe because he'd just spent a solid fifteen minutes at the kitchen furnishings shop fantasizing about kissing her.

"Oh, well, thank you."

"Are you free?"

"Yep. Nothing on my calendar."

Then why was she hesitating?

"So…is that a yes?"

"I'd be happy to. Only, um…"

"What is it?"

"It's only that…what's the dress code for something like that?"

Ah, so that's what was bothering her.

"I suppose the women will be in cocktail dresses. Do you have something suitable?" Jules could tell that while Zoe had a stylish sort of look, her clothes were clearly inexpensive.

"Maybe you'd rather ask someone else," Zoe said as she busied herself collecting the empty containers on the table from their quick lunch. Gathering everything into her hands, she deposited them in a nearby bin. "You know, more from *your* world."

"*My* world?" Jules knew what she meant but couldn't help mulling it over. Yes, he was acquainted with some of the wealthiest and most prominent residents in Paris. But he enjoyed their company no more or less than he did a construction worker he might talk with in Finland or a waiter in Bangkok.

Jules didn't get close to people. Any people. It didn't matter whether they were rich or poor, buyer or seller, old or young, male or female. Although he knew what Zoe meant about his world, it wasn't one he felt any particular place in. After a boy spends his childhood watching his mother pull a suitcase down the street and finds no ally in his father, he learns to go it alone. Jules only trusted Jules.

Strangely, Zoe, tidying up in her budget but body-hugging black dress, was the first woman he'd ever met that caused him to think twice about all the self-protective decisions he'd made. Not that it mattered, though. She was an employee, not a romantic interest. He didn't have those. She was going to accompany him to a business event. That didn't even count in his three-date policy. Plus, there would never be a second or third to make him question his rules.

"Is the issue that you don't have anything to wear?"

"I don't really go to many dressy occasions."

Jules didn't know a thing about Zoe's background. Whether she'd grown up with money, a childhood that was happy or sad. He knew that she was eager to get the apartment job with him. She'd mentioned that she had a roommate, which made him guess that she leased wherever she lived rather than owned.

"If it's all right with you, I'll buy you a dress. We can pop over to a shop on the Champs-élysées right now."

She whipped her head toward his. "*Pop over* to the Champs-élysées?"

"Yes." He texted Karim to find him a recommendation for a boutique.

"Oh, ho-hum, my boss suggested we *pop* over to buy me a cocktail dress."

A belly laugh erupted in him at her intonation. Jules couldn't remember the last time he'd laughed so heartily. He took her hand and said with a tug, "You're quite something, Zoe Gaiman. Come on, I have other things to finish today besides outfitting you for the evening."

On one of the hallowed side streets off the Champs-élysées, in the area where some of the world's most famous fashion designers had their headquarters, Jules's driver pulled to the curb so that he and Zoe could exit the car. People wearing the latest looks walked this way and that, some chic and on trend, others swallowed up by outrageous clothes that seemed fit only for a runway or featured in a glossy magazine. Tourists intermingled with people whose careers were made or broken on these streets. Fashion was in the air.

In the front windows of their destination, a few dresses hung on bald white mannequins. While they were evening gowns, and more formal than was called for the dinner cruise, Jules approved of their under-stated style. He wanted Zoe to join him for the evening as one of his tasteful young designers, not some flashy arm candy who was going to steal the limelight from his visiting developers.

Karim had phoned the shop ahead of their arrival so they were greeted by the owner as soon as they entered. A tall thin woman with white hair, probably in her sixties, and dressed in a flowing beige outfit introduced herself as Fia.

"Monsieur Durand, it's an honor. How may I assist you today?"

"This is my colleague Zoe. We have a corporate affair tonight, a dinner cruise on the Seine. Cocktail attire. It may get cold so let's include a wrap. Also shoes and accessories."

"Of course." Fia studied Zoe, no doubt estimating her dress size but also her coloring, height and whatever else she could gleam about her. "May I present some options?"

"Please."

Jules noted the airy boutique. Racks of clothes lined the walls with quite a bit of open space in the center save for a couple of tables where small handbags and sunglasses were displayed. It was a well-curated collection, which Jules appreciated, as there was no time to sort through dozens of possibilities.

"Can I offer either of you a glass of champagne?"

"Sure," Zoe wasted no time in answering.

"If you have a mineral water, that would be nice," Jules added.

Fia gestured for them to sit on the sloping black

leather and chrome armchairs that were clustered around a white round coffee table. A previously unseen assistant brought the drinks and then disappeared.

Zoe let out a whistle, then mashed her lips when Fia returned with three dresses. She said, "Let's give these a try. If you'll follow me."

While the ladies departed to, presumably, a fitting room, Jules handled the messages that had come in. There was a voice mail from his father's doctor confirming upcoming appointments. Jules hoped his parents would return to Paris in time to keep them. After a fall down a flight of stairs three years ago broke his back and claimed his mobility, Jules insisted that Hugo be proactive about other facets of his health.

He tagged the message for the file he'd already created called Parents Medical. Others were designated for Residential, Financial and Governmental. If he ran his parents' lives like he ran his business, perhaps he could circumvent the unruly atmosphere he'd grown up in. It was a tall order, but organization was the only thing that kept Jules secure.

Which is why sitting in this dress shop in the middle of the workday suddenly seemed crazy. But not nearly as crazy as that prolonged fantasy he'd had about kissing Zoe and, worse still, the fact that it kept replaying it in his mind. He needed to divert his brain to more productive matters should any future thoughts of that nature arrive.

That affirmation was ticking across his frontal lobe when Fia and Zoe returned to the showroom. Fia had put her in a sleeveless dark orange structural-type dress that had cutouts in the fabric where some sort of mesh was sewn in to cover the flesh that was bared. One slash was across the shoulder while another revealed part of her rib cage, and another still opened across the thighs. It was a creative, fashionable design.

The dark orange color mimicked Zoe's magical hair in a complementary way. But those mesh patches were too sexy. Jules didn't need the extra battle he'd have all evening, trying to avert his eyes from the glimpses of her body under the open weave. Couldn't they just choose something simple and basic?

Fia kept a respectable distance so they could discuss the dress privately.

"I love it," Zoe exclaimed as she approached him, holding her arms outstretched to show off for him.

Her enthusiasm made him want to laugh, like she was the proverbial kid in a candy store.

"Not right for the evening," he stuttered. Deciding not to reveal anything else, he tossed out, "Besides, your exposed bits would get cold. Next."

"Oh, so I don't even get a say," she exclaimed with a cute mock indignation.

"That's right," Jules replied with a wink. A wink! When was the last time he had winked at someone? Never? What was Zoe doing to him?

She returned to the dressing area and then reappeared in the simplest of black dresses with long sleeves and an embroidered band around the high neckline. Boring. Perfect.

"Distinguished," Jules ventured.

"For someone's grandmother." Zoe wrinkled her nose, pivoted and marched back to the fitting room.

While he waited, Jules approved the project schedule for the Miami development. He had several appointments before the cruise and needed to prepare. Hoping the third dress would be the charm, he watched Zoe saunter toward him.

This one was a draped number in a silver metallic fabric. She looked like she was wearing a superhero cape.

"Hate," they both said in unison.

"So, where does that leave us?" He rubbed his palms together. They could continue this all day, actually not an unpleasant proposition, but it really wasn't that important. "Let's get the black…"

"The orange one," Zoe interrupted.

"Fine." Jules could surely control his response to a dress, couldn't he? He waved Fia over and told her of the decision. "Can we outfit her with a coat, shoes, bag… What else do we need?"

"Might I suggest a hair and makeup stylist? Zoe, perhaps you'd like to wear your hair ironed straight for the evening," Fia proposed.

"No, she wouldn't." Both women snapped their heads to glare at him. He must have sounded like an overbearing brute. But he was so enamored of Zoe's nature-defying curly locks that he couldn't stand the idea of them being tamed. Knowing there was nothing he could say to downplay his overreaction, he went for a simple, "I've got to get going. Are we finished here?"

Afterward, he had his driver drop Zoe off at the home decor showroom she wanted to visit for work on the apartment. Jules watched from the car window as she walked away. Shopping had been far more enjoyable than it should have been. Why was doing the most mundane things with Zoe so charged with enthusiasm and vitality? Arguing over a lamp, admiring a purse, seeing her eat a sandwich. As she strode farther away, he inexplicably wished she would turn around and come right back, reclaiming her place beside him in the car. Only when she was finally completely out of view through the window did Jules instruct his driver to pull away.

After the makeup and hair stylist left her apartment, Zoe slipped into the orange cocktail dress and brown stilettos. As long as she lived, she'd never forget the cracked heel that sent her, literally, falling into Jules Durand's office. Navigating a metro station, with all its stairs, in tonight's shoes, would be a recipe for disaster. Fortunately, Jules had sent a car.

Her roommate, Yasmine, wasn't at home so Zoe texted her a quick selfie for feedback on her ensemble. But it was just Zoe and her bedroom mirror to decide if everything was in place. Jules had said a number of influential VIPs in the Paris real-estate scene were going to be in attendance. Making a good impression could lead to jobs that would allow her to stay in Paris. Plus, Zoe had to admit, she wanted to look good for Jules. After all, he'd financed her look from top to bottom.

She couldn't stop thinking about how brusque he'd been when the shop owner, Fia, suggested Zoe straighten her hair for the evening. She had no idea why that had mattered to him but his response had been vehement. And territorial in a way that was shocking at first but very, very, very sexy upon reflection. That take-charge dominance. She'd never met anyone who had such authority over every situation he encountered. Jules's way of doing things was what had brought him success and fortune. He was right to have utter confidence in it.

As to her hair, the stylist had applied several products that accentuated her curls and groomed them into a more tidy pile. A long narrow clip that echoed the slash designs in her dress brought everything together. Reaching for the off-white swing coat that went with the outfit, she reflected on how Jules had made a point to tell Fia that Zoe needed a wrap for the cruise. Yes, it was more evidence of Jules Durand being on top of every little detail, but there was also something so caring about the thought. He didn't want her to get cold. He'd make a fine caregiver to his parents when they returned to Paris.

She had a moment's wonder about his personal life. How many women had Jules made sure didn't suffer an evening chill? She knew from the eligible bachelor lists that he wasn't married and assumed that if there was a woman currently in his life she'd be the one teetering on stilettos to accompany him.

After the driver helped Zoe into the car, she watched out the window as she was whisked through the Paris dusk. It was impossible to say at what hour the city was more beautiful. To her eyes, it was stunning every minute of the day or night. The early evening skies cast a ruddiness on the boulevards as the sun receded. The car crossed over a bridge and Zoe could see the boats of various size and type that were already on the river, most of them with open-air decks and glass-enclosed cabins. Jules's cruise would be joining them shortly.

"You look marvelous," Jules said, as he appeared curbside to usher Zoe out of the car, he and his driver having obviously communicated about her arrival.

"You do, too," she blurted, and then regretted it. But looking good he was, in another exceptional suit. This one was slim-cut and navy, with a navy shirt and a brown tie to match the brown oxford shoes. Everything cut from the finest cloth, constructed with impeccable workmanship and fit to perfection, of course. Zoe couldn't help but take in his personal panache. As she'd thought during every encounter with him, Jules was the most striking man she'd ever seen. It took effort not to swoon.

"Shall we?" They walked a short distance to the dock. He crooked his arm for her to take as he helped her onto the boat's gangway at the riverbank, with the Eiffel Tower as their background. Zoe could hardly believe she was participating in a moment this glamorous. It was like something out of a magazine, dressed-up people on the Seine for an evening ride.

"A pleasure to meet you," Zoe found herself saying over and over again as Jules introduced her to his developers and their significant others who mulled around on the top deck of the luxury boat. The men wore suits and tuxedos while women, both old and young, were dazzling in their fashions and jewels. Bartenders serviced two stations, pouring drinks on order, while waiters passed pretty Kir Royales, champagne tinged with blackcurrant crème de cassis that gave it a red tint. Jules reached for two of the flutes from the silver tray and handed one to Zoe. Hors d'oeuvres were passed on trays lined with flowers and votive candles.

Seating clusters of wooden chairs covered in white sailcloth invited relaxation, but most of the guests stood congregating to keep watch on the Eiffel Tower as the boat pulled away. The captain spoke through a loudspeaker system, pointing out landmarks without sounding too touristy. Audio devices were handed to those who requested translation into other languages.

A thrill overtook Zoe as they passed by the sights, from Les Invalides to the Musée d'Orsay and the Louvre. It was as if she were seeing the Paris attractions for the first time, which she was from the river's view.

She'd be lying if she didn't admit that the moment was profoundly romantic. Paris really was the city for lovers. It wasn't hard to imagine that Jules was her real-life man. That between boat cruises and Michelin-star restaurants and fabulous parties, there was something real and genuine between them. That at the end of every evening out, one more glitzy and exciting than the next, they'd return home to the plush bed they shared where they'd lie down on fine linens to make love and sleep in each other's arms.

Carried away with her musing about Jules really being hers, she barely noticed that she had moved closer to him as he chatted with a guest. Until she distinctly felt her shoulder against his solid arm. She quickly snapped out of it, collected her wits and checked herself and everything around her.

"Do I look like I don't fit in?" Zoe asked Jules once the gentleman he was speaking with stepped away.

"Why do you ask?"

She gestured discreetly with her head at three women across the deck, two blondes and one a brunette, dressed flawlessly from head to toe, all three of their heads craned toward Zoe and Jules. "They keep staring at me."

Jules tipped his flute of Kir Royale in their direction as recognition. "It's not you they're staring at. It's me."

"Why?"

"Haven't you heard? I'm one of Paris's most eligible bachelors," he snickered.

"Oh, my gosh," Zoe quipped. "They're looking at you like you're prey."

"And it feels that way. Nothing but power plays and drama with the likes of them. They're real-estate agents who make plenty of money. But nothing is ever enough. Vultures, indeed."

Zoe decided to inquire on what she'd been curious about. "I take it you're not in a relationship, or else why would you have asked me to accompany you tonight?"

"Most definitely not. Not now and not ever. Three dates is my limit."

He went on to explain about his three-date policy, which was quite sensible, yet the words stung Zoe's face. It wasn't as if she had thought Jules invited her tonight because he was interested in her personally. She knew better than that. He was Jules bloody Durand! He would never date the spunky little designer from Nowhereville.

Not to mention the fact that she was not open to dating, either. There was no way she was ever going to take a chance on adding to the pain that she toted like a piece of luggage. No, thank you. She'd go it alone.

So, she fully understood Jules's three-date rule because it was similar to her body's ping alert system. The little siren that reliably told her she needed to pull back from something that was making her feel.

Yet, somehow, the finality of Jules's declaration about dating was harsh.

The cruise passed by people who sat along the riverbanks eating from picnic baskets, and the sweethearts kissing and waving to the passengers in the boats. Jules shook his head as if in disbelief. "I forget how extraordinary Paris can be."

"I've wanted to live here for as long as I can remember."

"Where were you born?"

Zoe described her hometown of Maupont. "The air is clean. People look out for each other. But it's a relic. A couple of historic churches that draw some tourists. Otherwise, nothing ever happens there."

"Did you visit Paris when you were growing up?"

"Just once as a child. And then I came with friends as a teenager. My parents had the furniture shop to run and weren't much for the city. Until they planned their dream trip to Milan when my brothers and I were older and could manage the store for them."

"Did they enjoy Milan?"

"They never got there."

"Why?"

"Look at that." Zoe pointed to a building with an especially elaborate facade. Now was not the time to have brought up her parents. She'd tell Jules about them sometime. But she couldn't take a chance of getting emotional tonight in front of his guests.

"So you decided you wanted to move here…" Jules sensed that she was withholding something and was savvy enough to allow her a segue.

"This probably sounds crazy but it all started with a sofa." Zoe was grateful to move on to another conversation. "A metal-framed sofa covered in a bluish-gray textural tweed modeled after a style from the 1950s."

"You came to Paris on a sofa?" Had he picked up that she was on the verge of tears and was trying to lighten the mood? "Most people use a car. An airplane. Or a magic carpet."

Zoe smiled and peered up to meet his dark eyes that

glistened in the night sky, as reflective as the moon's illumination on the river. What stunning eyes they were. Observant and thoughtful, yet that spark of playfulness that was dying to pry free was evident in their center. His eyes might be one of her favorite sights in Paris, although she'd keep that vote to herself.

"I loved that one sofa we had at the shop so much. My dad put it in the window display with a complementary side table and lamp. It was what got me interested in interior design. I used to imagine creating a whole room, a whole mood around that one piece. To me, it was elegance and flair. I conjured up a lifestyle that went with that sofa. I was devastated when someone bought it."

"And that led you to Paris?"

"In a way, yes. Once I knew I was going to be a designer, I wanted to be in the capital of style. Where else?"

"So wishes do come true."

Zoe let that dangle. She didn't want to tell Jules that it was only because he'd given her the apartment job that she had any hope of staying at all. That she hadn't been able to break in to the industry in a sustainable way. And that she was one paycheck away from having to go back to the furniture shop where, when last she visited, her brothers had put an ugly dining table and chairs in the shop window instead of another beautiful sofa like the one that had inspired her so.

"Now, of course, I want to visit all of the great sights in the world. Where's your favorite place?"

He contemplated the question for a long time. Zoe wondered why his answer was delayed. "Here," he finally stated. "I've been away for so long I'd forgotten how there's something breathtaking around every corner."

The captain announced that dinner was being served. As the guests chose one of the four staircases leading down to the glass-enclosed dining cabin, Zoe was stunned at the lavish appointments. Gleaming polished wood and shiny brass met her at every turn. The dining tables were dressed in iridescent tan-colored tablecloths and white flower centerpieces twinkled with taper candles arranged at different heights. Charger plates at each diner's place were made of copper and the several forks and spoons at every setting promised a multi-course meal. Likewise, four different-shaped stem glasses per guest meant that the wine had been carefully chosen.

Jules sat Zoe beside him and, after the waiters poured the first wine, stood to offer a welcoming toast that earned him polite applause. The starter course was served, smoked salmon atop a cucumber and artichoke confit, drizzled with herbed cream. It was delicious. Over the dulcet improvisations of the jazz trio that entertained from a small stage, Zoe did a respectable job of hobnobbing with the spouse of one of the developers seated on her other side. She wanted advice on where to shop for purses in Paris. Certain that the stately older woman was not interested in the bargain stores she and Yasmine combed through, Zoe mentioned some high-end shops she'd heard of.

The captain told guests that they were passing under the Pont Neuf—the new bridge. Which was a misnomer, he explained, as it was actually the oldest standing bridge in Paris. He pointed out that the structure had twelve arches and, in addition to the equestrian sculpture of Henry IV, almost four hundred stone mascarons adorning the cornices, their grotesque faces originally thought to keep away evil spirits.

During the entrée, which was a choice of spice-rubbed lamb and Greek quinoa or tart Provençal with wild mushrooms, the captain gave a history of Notre Dame. The cheese course followed, a lovely composition on the plate of three varieties and thick triangles of dense grainy bread dotted with dried fruits. After the boat reached its designated turnaround, the captain continued, relaying information about the Place de la Concorde, the Grand Palais and other sights along the route. As stunning as all those locations had been to Zoe when she'd stood in front of them on the street, under the night sky in the boat's glass cabin she felt like she was in a magical place that only existed in dreams. Not to mention the handsome vision sitting beside her.

Dessert and liqueurs were served buffet-style on the upper deck to better enjoy the final landmarks of their cruise. When Jules left Zoe's side to pay special attention to important clients, she had a pleasant conversation with a couple of Paris developers about utilizing small urban spaces. She hoped she'd made some sort of positive impression so that if she were ever to contact them via a reference from Jules, they would remember her.

After the individual almond cakes with apricot buttercream filling topped with warm dark chocolate sauce, the captain began his return to the riverbank. Just as the clock struck eleven o'clock, the boat faced the Eiffel Tower, obviously perfectly timed for the passengers to best see the hourly light display. With the drama that only Paris could incite, the entire tower began to flicker with golden sparkles, shimmering, glittering and as brilliant as a multi-faceted diamond. It was a spectacle to astonish even the most cynical. Like a woman who throws her shoulders back and owns her beauty, the proud monument twinkled. Everyone on the boat, on the banks and, indeed, from views all over the city halted in time to gape.

Jules stood beside her. Zoe almost thought she could see the reflection of the tower in his eyes. With some sort of knowing smile, they acknowledged that they were sharing a moment. Together.

"So we've found something we agree on," Jules said as he led Zoe off the cruise boat toward his waiting car.

"Paris," she answered with a sweeping arm gesture.

His driver opened the passenger door and they both slid into the back seat.

"Are you tired?" Jules asked her.

"Not too tired. Why?"

"Shall I show you some buildings I love?"

"Do you own them?"

"You may be surprised to know that I don't actually own all of Paris."

"Well, there are always career goals."

Jules shook his head at his cheeky companion.

He rattled off a few landmarks to his driver who dutifully nodded.

First was the Musée d'Orsay, which they'd caught a look at from the boat. Jules lowered the car window and pointed to it. "This is my absolute favorite building in Paris."

"Yes, it's amazing."

"It was originally a railway station done in the beaux arts style."

"Talk about renovating and repurposing."

"Apparently, in the 1970s it was scheduled to be torn down before someone came up with the plan to turn it into a museum."

"Thank goodness." Zoe pointed at the building. "How the structural metalwork integrates with all of the ornate details. Incredible."

"When the barrel-vaulted main space and the train platforms were sectioned off with walls inside to hang the art, museum critics hated it at first. They said the building competed with the art."

Jules was enjoying this, chatting with Zoe. Even though he moved fast and accomplished more in a day than others did in a week, a part of him was numb. There was a switch that had never been flipped to the On position. Zoe was in sharp contrast. Her enthusiasm for everything in front of her was such a breath of fresh air, so alive and unfamiliar.

He wondered why Zoe's parents never boarded that train to Milan. She'd changed the subject when he'd asked about it on the cruise. Did they split up? As a child, he often wished his own parents would, although he was never sure which one of them would be worse to live with. Navigating around both of them had taken up so much of his focus from as far back as he could remember.

When his mother was away on her pointless desertions, young Jules would look out the sooty window of their dank apartment on its ugly and nondescript block as if he were searching for her. Or stare, mystified, at the dirty laundry and unmade beds. He worried it was his fault that she'd left, clearly she wasn't a nurturer like most mothers were. He resented his father's inability to put a halt to the situation, or to comfort his son, and considered him weak. Jules never felt loved and never learned to love in return.

He became an angry young man and channeled his rage into becoming hyper-structured, planning out everything from what he was going to wear the next day to how he was going to acquire his next property. He found an ironic comfort in controlling what he could in his life.

After amassing extreme wealth, he started to send money to his parents. He knew it was wrong, that the child should not have to support the mother and father, but he did it anyway as his fortunes grew to the point that the expense had no impact. Blood was blood and he considered it his duty.

When he thought of it all right now, sitting next to vivacious Zoe while they drove through the storied boulevards of the city center, Jules felt a hole in his gut. He was becoming painfully aware that with his chosen lifestyle, he was missing out. That he wasn't leading a full existence, one that deserved some happiness and heart song.

There had to be more than being a parent to parents who were never even good to him, with whom he shared no pleasant memories to coast along on. And more than making billions of euros, most of which sat compounding into more money in never-used investment accounts. The word *enjoyment* had never been on Jules's radar. He was starting to see that if he didn't lighten up inside, darkness was going to cloud over him.

"Now, this works. But how?" Zoe marveled as they approached Centre Pompidou in the Fourth Arrondissement, which snatched his attention back to the present. The high-tech architecture, with its inside-out style where the mechanical systems such as plumbing and electrical were exposed and color-coded on the outside of the building, was one of a kind.

"Some people think it's a monstrosity," he said of the structure that was part art museum, part library and part event space.

"It's a fine line between what works and what doesn't when you do modern on a big scale like this."

"Good point."

Jules was so glad he'd brought Zoe along on the cruise tonight. It was meeting her that had set his mind to wondering about pleasure and about dark shadows. About sharing sunsets. He'd never met a woman he could imagine having a longstanding companionship with, and would never take the chance of ending up in a rancorous union like his parents. Yet, he had to admit the idea of attachment to someone had been crossing his mind, especially in the past few days.

With his face still close to Zoe's as she peered out the window at the Pompidou, he chose instead to study those orange ringlets of her hair up close. They really were a miracle from another realm. Her brain must be filled with some magical powers.

Entranced by a woman's curl?

Yes, Jules definitely needed to bring some diversion into his life. Maybe he should take up tennis.

And what about that dress? He cut his eyes to steal a glimpse of the slash across the shoulder. The design was clever in how it revealed the shapeliness of her décolleté. The hair, the sexy dress, Zoe's peppy companionship at dinner, it had all worn him down. The hour was late and Zoe's seductiveness overtook him. Craving became need before he could restrain it.

As the driver pulled away from the Centre, Zoe turned her head toward Jules, presumably to say something.

Which he didn't allow because before she could speak he leaned over, brought his lips to hers and delivered a long melting kiss. It was better than anything he could think of that had happened in the recent or distant past.

CHAPTER FIVE

IN AN INSTANT, Zoe was pulled under into a warm and pleasant universe where all she could feel or taste was Jules. While she was able to discern that only their lips were actually touching, it felt like he was all over her, like together they'd merged into one being and she didn't know where she began and he ended. Then, abruptly, he blurted, "My apologies," and jerked backward to his proper place in the car's back seat.

He'd previously instructed his driver to take them to Montmartre, where Jules was intending to show her some notable buildings. With a hand flat against his chest, he emphasized, "How utterly inappropriate. I don't know what I was thinking. I'm so very sorry."

Zoe stilled. Not a cell of her was able to move. She was stuck in an unnatural position, half turned toward the man who had just laid his lips on hers, yet her hips were twisted the opposite direction from looking out the window. Although her brain told her to straighten out, her body wouldn't cooperate.

She'd been hoping to make another clever comment about the architecture Jules was showing her but the words weren't able to make it out because he had covered her mouth with his. His lips had obviously delivered some type of paralyzing potion because all she could do was look into his eyes, perhaps waiting for an explanation. And listening to that constant ping inside her chest confirmed that her emotions were exposed for the plucking. Like plump, ripe fruit from a tree.

"That's okay-ay," she stuttered, adding an extra syllable to her simple words. Zoe most definitely wasn't *okay-ay* but she felt she should say something. Jules looked so pained, the furrows between his eyebrows digging in.

Jules Durand, *the* Jules Durand, had just kissed her, and making billion-euro real-estate transactions was not all he was good at. His kiss was masterful. He slid effortlessly from paper soft to insistent to erotic. From sweet to spicy, nice to naughty. It went on for hours. Okay, it was minutes but it felt like a week. As he finally, abruptly, stopped, Zoe wanted more, internally screaming with a tormenting deficit when he yanked himself away. It was a kiss she would remember forever. And despite his apologies, the kiss hadn't been forced upon her, if that was something he was worried about. No, as soon as the sensation of his firm lips against hers registered, she'd sunk into it, and gave as much as she'd received.

"I promise you that will never happen again," Jules rasped, clearing his throat. "You know I don't generally act in the spur of the moment."

"Of course," she replied in a monotone. "Neither do I." Obviously, it had been a mistake. They were colleagues and nothing more.

So why did his promise that kissing her would never happen again smart like a rejection? Maybe because Zoe hadn't been on a date in a long time and Jules's touch ignited dormant embers of desire that had been smoldering deep within her. She'd had a few dates in Maupont, but no one had ever activated the ping. Not like he just had.

She had to remind herself that even if Jules had any interest in her, which he didn't beyond as an employee, no serious liaisons were in her future. Funny that around him she kept forgetting that decision.

Uneasiness permeated the car like a strange scent as the driver continued whisking them down one street and then another, traffic eased in the late hour. Jules sat up very straight and kept his eyes forward. Zoe finally summoned the ability to adjust her body to face the front, as well.

After a few minutes of traveling in silence, Jules used his matter-of-fact voice. "Zoe, I've noticed that you are a very…what's the word…enthusiastic person."

"Is that a polite criticism of some sort?" She resisted the urge to swivel her head toward him so they spoke with all four eyes focused out the car's front window, privacy glass still separating them from the driver.

"Not at all. I admire it. I've been calculating that the amount I work coupled with what will be my new responsibilities with my parents won't leave a lot of time for…recreation?"

"You mean work and life balance?"

"Work and life balance, yes. Work has been my life. There is no balance."

"So, what do you do for fun?"

"Fun?" He scratched his chin as he contemplated the question.

"To relax, to decompress."

"That was fun."

"What was fun?"

"Kissing you just now. That was fun."

Yeah, she'd have to agree. It was birthday-party-with-triple-layer-cake-and-candles fun locking her lips with his.

"Maybe you should try it more often," she suggested tentatively, not sure if she was being flirted with.

"No. Most definitely not. Kissing, romance, all of that is not an option. What do you think of golf?"

After Jules had his driver take Zoe home, she slipped the key through the lock to her apartment door.

"Yowza!" Yasmine exclaimed as she came in. Zoe's roommate wore red pajamas covered with a graphic design of puppies and she ate ice cream with a spoon straight from a large container. "You look ah-may-zing."

Zoe kicked off the stilettoes that had been killing her but were worth it for the stature they'd given her. After falling into Jules's office, she'd vowed never to wear heels again but the dress Jules had bought her for the cruise seemed to beg for the extra zhoosh. She'd sent a selfie earlier but apparently the ensemble was even better in person. Yasmine leered at her from top to bottom.

"The dress worked, that's for sure," Zoe reported. "I felt good in it and you should have seen me hobnobbing with Parisian VIPs! I can really talk the talk. Maybe something will come of it."

"What about you and the billionaire?"

She wasn't sure that she should tell anyone, even her roommate, about Jules's accidental kiss that would have no meaning tomorrow. Zoe did not want to be quizzed on every move made by Jules Durand.

"There's nothing going on there. He's my boss. I didn't embarrass him so I'd call the evening a success."

"Were there other attractive men there?" Yasmine snooped before spooning a big bite of ice cream into her mouth.

There might have been handsome men in attendance, after all this was Paris and there was the Kenyan contingent as well, but Zoe had failed to notice. She'd barely taken her eyes off Jules other than to exchange pleasantries with the guests he'd introduced her to. They'd been side by side most of the evening. In fact, when he stepped away to greet someone or get a drink, she'd felt the empty space beside her whoosh like a chill.

Zoe took a spoon from the drawer and dug into Yasmine's ice cream for a scoop. She asked wistfully before tasting it, "Have you noticed that this city is a really romantic place?"

"Are you kidding me?" Yasmine scrunched up her face.

"Sometimes I wish I was in love with more than just sofas and paint colors."

"Aha, so maybe a certain someone is making you rethink your no-serious-relationship rule."

"Hardly," Zoe answered too quickly. "In fact, he himself has a *three-date* rule, which I think is very sensible." She explained Jules's rubric.

"Uh-huh," Yasmine replied unconvincingly and licked her spoon.

Zoe had a full day's work on the apartment ahead of her in the morning, so she changed out of the dinner outfit, washed up and went straight to bed. Except that sleep didn't come. Lying on her back and staring up at a shadow across the ceiling, both her body and her brain still vibrated.

Darn Jules for planting that delicious kiss on her! Because even though he retracted it with his words, Zoe's lips were still reacting. How, in a blink, his kiss had sent sensations up and down her like hot blood that coursed through veins parched from drought.

His kiss kindled mental portraits of lovers in Paris. Walking arm in arm, appreciating every bridge over the shimmering river. Strolling down a boulevard, gesturing and animated in their conversations, so much to tell each other. Those same lovers admiring a painting, sharing a pastry, kissing in a dusty bookshop, unable to contain their need for one another. And once they got home, exploring the depths of their desire until the raw sunlight of dawn opened the skies.

Why did Jules have to kiss her? Now Zoe couldn't stop whirling about possibilities she'd forbidden herself to dwell on. She knew herself enough to be sure that she was a person who loved wholly and fully, so casual encounters were never going to do for her. It was all or nothing, and she'd chosen the latter. It wasn't helpful to have her resolve put to the test.

In that way, she was a little like Jules. Having a plan. To protect her heart. And in a strange fashion, tonight he had behaved like her. His kiss was on impulse. Had he thought about it, he certainly wouldn't have done it. Instinct propelled him to her. Instinct was what Zoe usually relied on. What was happening?

That. That was fun.

Jules's earlier statement resonated between her ears.

She scolded his words inside her head to be quiet and to let her fall asleep. Instead, the voice got louder.

Kissing you was fun.

Fun. What a stupid word Jules had used, he reflected during his morning run. He was a thirty-four-year-old billionaire. Obviously, he didn't get this far this quickly in life by having fun. Children in a playground had fun. Frivolous party girls in tiny dresses at nightclubs had fun. Carefree heirs to fortunes lolled about on yachts having fun. Jules worked. Thought. Worked some more.

As was his usual routine for his run, he briskly walked for two blocks in order to loosen up and get his circulation flowing. For the next two, he brought himself to a light jog. Then he stopped for his sequence of muscle stretches to prevent injury. Once he was fully warmed up, he increased his speed to a run and, before long, his breathing rose to meet the exertion.

Images flickered through his mind. Morning runs in the sweltering humidity of Manila. Through the bite of a Chicago winter's dawn. Along beaches in Maui. Yes, he had business in every corner of the earth. He'd toured historic sights. Tasted unique foods. Participated in extreme sports. Been awed by natural wonders. Had interludes with beautiful women. But had he found any *fun*?

This was where he'd take his morning run now. Under the unmistakably Paris skies. These streets were to be his permanent neighborhood, his home turf. Was there *fun* around any of these city corners? What exactly was *fun*, anyway?

Kissing Zoe was *fun*. There was no way he could deny that, even though his brain struggled for a more academic understanding of the word. It was an unfortunate accident that he'd now have to correct by never letting it happen again. He'd told her as much when he apologized for acting on a whim. What was it about her that had propelled him to make that move without self-intervention?

Jules rounded another corner. His breath had reached heaving and he welcomed the perspiration. He checked the fitness settings on his watch to make sure his speed and heart rate were in target range.

Zoe was an underling who'd escorted him to a business function. There wasn't anything personal between them. They hadn't even known each other long enough to be called friends. Absolutely nothing could have predicted that he would claim her mouth like that, fixing his lips to hers until they both had to come up for air.

In all honesty, it wasn't entirely unprecedented. There was that steaming hot fantasy about Zoe striding across his office in her black dress and straddling him in his office chair. When he envisioned his hands grabbing onto everything they could reach as their lips collided in a forbidden middle-of-the-work-day merge that would have shocked his employees on the other side of the glass if they knew what was happening behind closed blinds. Were that little daydream to have come to life, he and Zoe would have spent time on his expensive carpeting, and it wouldn't have been because of a broken shoe.

He hadn't given those images a second consideration. Well, maybe, he hadn't given them a fifth. Or was it a fifteenth? In any case, when she asked him in the back seat of the car what he did for pleasure, apparently he'd shown her. A smile crossed his lips at the recollection, and he lifted the bottom of his T-shirt to wipe the sweat from his face as he finished his run.

After showering, he sipped the green drink the housekeeper had left. Reading over some reports for the condo development in Krakow that was frustrating him with budget overages, his mind kept drifting back to Zoe's sweet lips.

Fun.

Kissing her in the car, he'd acted without premeditation. There was another word he'd been contemplating. *Spontaneity.* Something unplanned. Occurrences that had no place in his world and could, by their very nature, only lead to mistakes. Like kissing Zoe, in case he needed any proof. Worse still, he feared that what he was feeling was more than a sexual charge from his encounter with her lovely mouth and his musings on what her body might feel like in his hands. There was a knocking inside of his gut, like some sort of wake-up call.

He was fighting to ignore it.

Jules didn't need anything more to deal with. For so long without a place he had called home, he'd been able to board intercontinental flights and jet away from any longing that might have made its way under his skin. From uncertainties that had started popping up more and more frequently, about connection and priorities. Contemplations he couldn't shut down.

It was harder here. Jules had never been a lover in this city that celebrated them. He'd spent the occasional carnal night or weekend with one of the exotic women he'd met in faraway locales. Superficial encounters that happened between people who would never meet each other again. After which it was easy to say goodbye.

As he knotted his tie and collected his things for work, that increasingly persistent nagging came at him again, telling him that it was no longer enough.

Grabbing his attaché case and other belongings, he stepped out his door, vowing to stop thinking about saying good morning to Zoe—every morning—for the rest of his life.

"I've been invited to Prague with a lovely family I met who are in need of childcare," Agathe's shrill voice pierced through Jules's phone when he and Zoe were at the apartment a few days later. He stepped into the kitchen out of earshot and left Zoe in the living room.

"Oh, good heavens, Mother." He could only imagine what lies she'd told this family to get them to believe she was capable of looking after children.

"It's not as if your father would care if I…" The strength in Agathe's voice faded, as if she herself were tired of her own script. Jules certainly was.

His loud exhale contained particles of disgust. It was as if a recording that they'd both heard a thousand times was playing. "You are not going to Prague."

"I hate him," she squawked feebly.

"Yes, Mother, I know. You always hate him until you don't." Love was ridiculous. The universe was giving him another reminder to steer clear of it. "Stop this nonsense and get on the plane to Paris."

Jules ended the call and returned his attention to Zoe. She had brought some paint samples and brushed one swath of each color onto the wall. While he really didn't know her well, he could tell that she wasn't like his mother with inconsistent mood swings and a general bitterness, as if life owed her something that it wasn't delivering.

What kind of mother would a woman like Zoe be? Yes, the type who takes her kids to the park and then buys them an impromptu ice-cream cone, eliciting more delight than a planned snack would. But would she also know how to put boundaries on that impetuosity, to raise children who learned how to focus on school exams and work diligently toward goals?

Jules had long ago decided that he'd help the population by not bringing more children with unfit parents into the world. After the instability he grew up in, he was convinced he'd go too far in the other direction and be a controlling and regimented father.

Letting the paint dry, next Zoe analyzed the lighting that had been installed in the hallway that led to the bedrooms and bathroom.

"I wonder if we could better mimic natural morning light with some additional overheads here. Since we haven't painted yet, it wouldn't be too big a job to add on. Let me think on that." She sat down cross-legged on the bare floor in the middle of the hallway. She slowly looked around her, panning side to side, then up and down, as if there was some new information to be gleamed. *Feeling it.* Like she was summoning the dead to vote in.

"Are you conducting a séance?"

"No. But that's a great suggestion. Let me consult my tarot cards. And what are your parents' zodiac signs?"

Jules knew she was joking but his call with his mom had stripped him of any sense of humor he might have been able to muster.

"I have lighting analysis software and you can try your ideas with that," he declared.

He knew his tone was harsh. Still sitting on the floor, Zoe glared up at him. One of her corkscrew curls bounced forward on its own volition and covered one eye. She swept it away with the back of her hand defiantly.

Something in Jules wanted to sit down on the hardwood floor next to her. Maybe take off his shoes. Maybe hold Zoe close. Maybe be in the moment and see what happened.

But he didn't do that sort of thing.

Instead, he offered an olive branch. "Can I take you to dinner?"

The cruise on the Seine was date number one. Except it hadn't been a date because it was a business function. The kiss afterward was a freak accident and he'd already apologized for his mistake. The quick lunches they'd grabbed definitely didn't get logged. Tonight would be date number two, only it wouldn't count, either, as they would be discussing the apartment. It was all figured out. There would not be any more physical contact. Although, dinner would bring him dangerously close to date number three, should they need to spend another evening together in the future. If one was counting these things.

"What do you think of the medium-blue paint?" She stood and led him back into the living room.

"It's bold but the room can take it."

"Jules, did you just make a decision based on preference?" This time she got him to crack a smile. "You'll find it shocking to know that I consulted a color-scheme program. Warm colors advancing and cool colors receding and all those *rules* you like so much."

"Aha! What did that lead you to?"

"Well, at first I was thinking that everything needed to be soothing. Perhaps it's a day that your parents are out and about in the intensity of the city. That they need a gentle cocoon to come home to."

"And then?"

"Then I thought that maybe a home with verve and energy was better for globe-trotters. One that was stimulating in its own right. So I came to this." She pointed to the paint swatch on the wall. "A much darker blue than I would have expected to try. With the main decor colors being forest green, rust and khaki. Something about that feels like the colors of travel."

"Colors of travel? There you go *feeling* again."

"Since they've done so much of it."

"Hmm."

From what Zoe knew, his parents' endless journey was enviable, not a rootless search for belonging and contentment that the Durand family apparently knew nothing about.

"You can't deny that you still have to respond to the suggestions a software program lays out. There are still subjective..."

Jules grabbed Zoe's hand and pulled her toward the front door. "Let's go eat and we can see how the paint colors *feel* to me in tomorrow's light."

Jules led them around one corner and then another and then another, which put them on pedestrian-only Rue Montorgueil in the First Arrondissement. Known as an international foodie paradise, the cheese shops, fishmongers, patisseries and restaurants serving food from every corner of the world beckoned.

After much discussion, they chose a bustling Thai restaurant and took two seats side by side at the counter facing the open kitchen. Zoe opened her laptop and called up a lighting placement program to show him the changes she wanted to do.

"Comes in handy, doesn't it?" he teased again about her use of the computer-aided design, raising an eyebrow in a mock-gloating manner that was adorable. She begged herself to stop reminiscing about that kiss the other night, the one he'd promised never to repeat. Yet, she found herself wishing he would.

If only he wasn't sitting so close to her. Shoulder to shoulder, they both occasionally looked up to watch the chefs in front of them flipping noodles over scorching high heat, the finished products lush with jewels of diced meats and colorful vegetables.

Jules's long muscular arm pressed against hers as they huddled over the laptop screen. Her whole being buzzed when she was close to him. And as they dug into their delicious pad Thai, the rich peanut flavor somehow added to the sensuality. It was a combination of sensations that made her almost light-headed, and had the power to make the loud and crowded restaurant fade into the distance of her consciousness. Zoe wanted to lick the sweet sauce from Jules's lips. Wanted to drop into his arms and press herself against his solid chest. Wanted them to hold onto each other like there was no tomorrow. No one on earth had ever made her feel that way. She hoped nobody ever would. It was really too much.

"I'm not a fool," Jules said as they took a stroll after

dinner. "I know that there's an artistic element to what you do. If I didn't appreciate that, I wouldn't need a designer. I'd simply let the computer make all of the decisions."

They approached the nearby Musée du Louvre. Closed for the evening, crowds still mulled about photographing the world's most famous museum under the moon's glow. Originally a castle, with construction that began in the twelfth century, it became a museum in the 1700s. The campus, its enormous main courtyard and the glass-and-steel pyramid that stood at its center, was instantly recognizable.

"You told me you fell in love with design via a sofa. Did you take art history in school?" Jules asked.

"Of course."

"What kind of child were you?"

Zoe gulped. It was still hard for her to discuss anything about her past without missing her parents so much that the anguish threatened to knock her to the ground. "I suppose I was a happy enough kid. As much as you can be with three older brothers."

"Was your parents' furniture shop successful?"

"Define *success*."

"Touché."

"They made a living in a small town where there wasn't much opportunity. They were in love, so I'd define that as succ…" Her lower lip quivered uncontrollably, leaving her unable to complete the sentence.

"What is it?"

Zoe dabbed away the tears that clouded her vision as they got closer to the pyramid. "One of the last things my mother ever said to me before my parents died was that she hoped I'd someday meet someone as wonderful as my father."

"Your parents died? At the same time? Was there an accident?"

She'd forgotten that she hadn't told Jules about her parents' fate and did so now. "One day they were unlocking the shop door in the morning, turning the old-fashioned sign from Closed to Open and then back to Closed at the end of the day. You go through the motions, thinking you've eked out an existence, that you can count on, that you're content." The ping in her chest hurt so much it could have been a knife blade. "And in the next moment they were gone."

"Oh, my gosh," he responded. "That's an unimaginable tragedy."

"Maybe it's what turned me into the adult I am. I've become one of those *seize life* kind of people, but really it's that I have to be because I'm terrified it can all be taken away in a flash."

"So that's why you're not a planner."

"Touché back to you." She looked out to the courtyard. "There's one thing I'm very organized about. My mom was wrong about wanting me to meet the right person. I'm never going to be with a partner."

"Because they might die?"

Zoe was surprised at Jules's bluntness. Although that was something she liked about him, his way of cutting through to the quick of something.

"Yeah. What are the odds of dying at the same time as the love of your life? Pretty low. So that means there's a fifty percent chance of them dying before you."

"This from a person who says she doesn't bring mathematic systems into her life."

At the base of the Louvre Pyramid, they cranked their necks back to take it in from bottom to top, in unabashed awe.

"What about you, with your three-date rule? Talk about structured."

"I witnessed something very different growing up. Chaos. I can't have that in my life."

"So women equal disorder?"

"Something like that. In any case, it's much easier not to take chances."

"We're on the same page about that. You don't go on fourth dates and I don't get close to anyone."

"Bravo for us. We've figured out our own safety nets."

They both laughed into the night, pretending to be so pleased with themselves.

CHAPTER SIX

"AGATHE AND HUGO, this is my associate, Zoe Gaiman," Jules introduced his parents in the lobby of the Juin Hotel, a boutique inn he owned on the Left Bank. The black-painted exterior outside with its silver awning displaying the hotel name led to the smart interior.

The black-and-white-tiled floor complemented the wallpaper with its design of black pineapples, the fruit a historic symbol of hospitality. Jules had been very pleased when this hotel had gone up for sale a couple of years ago and he'd been able to purchase it. It had been in operation for seven decades.

Zoe shook Agathe's limp hand and bent gracefully down to shake Hugo's from his seat in the wheelchair.

"Jules, you didn't tell us you were seeing someone," Agathe exclaimed in her overly dramatic manner. He hadn't seen her theatrics in person for a while and thought she grew sillier and sillier with age.

"I'm not dating anyone, Mother. As I just mentioned, Zoe is my colleague. She's a talented designer who's assisting me in readying the apartment for you."

"Colleague," Agathe repeated with hiked eyebrows. She retrieved a lace handkerchief, as if something from another century, from her small handbag and used it to blow her nose. Hugo's pallor was gray.

Jules was surprisingly relieved to have Zoe come along for the reunion with his parents, especially after he'd told her more about his childhood, more than he'd ever told anyone. He tallied up just how much time he'd been spending with her. Oddly, the realization didn't displease him. He'd felt comfortable asking her to come along for moral support, although he didn't voice that in as many words.

When he refused to send more money to his parents in Tel Aviv and Agathe's scheme to become a Prague nanny had fallen through, he'd finally squeezed them enough financially to the point where they had no choice but to use the plane tickets he'd provided.

It had been six months since he'd last seen them. On a trip west from Dubai, Jules had stopped in Hungary where they were working as models for a painter who was doing a study on older bodies.

Just the sort of thing his mother had spun into a grandiose tale of adventure, the reality was that the artist in question lived in poverty on a barely operational farm and wasn't paying them a salary. They slept on a haystack in a barn and fetched their eggs every morning from underneath a chicken. When Jules arrived, he found them with dirty bare feet and his father exhausted by a persistent dry cough. Not exactly how seniors, one with health issues no less, should be spending their time.

It was then he'd decided that enough was enough, that he'd need to take charge and prevent any more bad decisions. He needed to look out not only for their well-being but also for their safety.

Had he found them happy and taking good care of themselves, he might have been willing to let them continue their endless drifting. After all, they didn't need employment. He could certainly afford to finance their wanderings. But his father was drinking too much and his mother was, as always, belittling and threatening to desert him, even though it had been years since she actually had. She no longer had the adeptness to run away on her own like she had in years past.

"You're coming home where we'll see proper doctors and you'll live as respectable Parisians," Jules had proclaimed at the painter's farmhouse. "I'm not going to receive a phone call from some remote corner of the world to find out you've been eaten by wild animals or have starved to death."

After that endless row in Tel Aviv, the time had finally come. He'd house them at this hotel until the apartment was ready.

"Monsieur Durand, may I show your parents to their suite?" The hotel manager, who wore a suit and tie with a name tag adorning his jacket's lapel, joined the group.

"Thank you, Huy."

Two bellmen appeared to handle the luggage.

"Zoe." Jules placed his hand on the center of her back to escort her toward the elevator. He wasn't expecting his palm to be greeted with the plushness of the baby pink sweater she wore that seemed to promise something even softer underneath. He supposed it was only natural that his mother would have immediately assumed that Zoe was a romantic interest. That the thought wasn't repugnant was a first for him.

"Shall I push the chair for you?" Jules offered to his father.

"Obviously, I can do it myself." A bark of an answer—not unexpected. Resentment that Jules was controlling their fates. Had his father planned for his elder years, perhaps he wouldn't have been reduced to that. Jules noticed how brawny Hugo's biceps had gotten from their labors. His father speedily pushed the wheels of his chair until he had gotten halfway across the lobby ahead of the rest of the party.

Jules had a moment of terror over what he was embarking on. Bringing these people back into his life who were, for all intents and purposes, dreadful parents. Was he trying to stage a do-over? Did he think that if he cared for them now it would somehow right all the wrongs, salve all of the hurts? How much control did he *really* have?

Once they arrived at the suite, Jules asked Huy to send up some sandwiches, fruit and juice. "We'll see the orthopedic doctor next week to have you fully evaluated, Father. When was the last time the two of you had a complete physical examination?"

"While you're at it, get your mother a psychological exam," Hugo snapped.

Agathe pretended not to hear him as she inspected the suite. "So this is what my prison cell will look like," she stated without looking at any of them. Jules had overestimated his mother's interest in not embarrassing him. Obviously, civility in front of Zoe, who she'd never met, was of no matter to her. Had Jules known his parents were going to be *this* badly behaved, he wouldn't have brought her to witness it.

Jules's forehead became very tight. A headache was developing and he considered taking some aspirin. He hissed in Agathe's ear, "It's only temporary, Mother. I suppose my elite hotel that's fully booked year-round doesn't have the charm of a Hungarian haystack, but you might actually enjoy indoor plumbing."

"Agathe, have you seen the view?" Zoe called from the window. Jules's mother joined her. They looked out to a pretty street with apartments across the way, all the windows adorned with flower boxes. "Isn't Paris lovely?"

"I lived here for too long, dear," Agathe exhaled. "I'm underwhelmed by a few peonies in some store-bought dirt."

"Mother, stop being so rude."

"Soon enough, we'll have the apartment ready and then you can truly settle into your new home," Zoe persisted. "I hope you'll like all the choices we made."

She was clearly trying to help, and Jules wanted to kiss her for it.

His headache was turning into a throb.

"My electricians are installing your hallway redesign this morning," Jules informed Zoe during a FaceTime session. He'd been busy with his parents and they hadn't seen each other at the apartment for a few days. But each morning, she'd met with him on a video chat. Zoe had to admit she looked forward to the early call and was always dressed and ready for him at the designated time.

She'd be lying if she said he wasn't on her mind, but the distance was an important reminder that after this job was finished she didn't know how frequently they'd be in contact. "I'd like to show you some sketches I had for the bedroom furniture placement."

"Sketches?"

"Yes, Jules." She took on a jokey tone as, by now, their different working methods were no surprise to each other. "I had some ideas after I met your parents last week."

"What sort of ideas? That we'll need armed guards to keep the troops in line at their residence?"

Zoe watched Jules through the screen. He was sitting tall at his office desk, the view expansive behind him even through the screen on her tablet. Although Zoe couldn't say for sure which was a better vista to gaze upon, Paris's rooftops or Jules Durand in his brown suit, white shirt and red tie.

It was shocking to think that Zoe had become a part of this man's high-flying lifestyle. Seeing him on the screen like she was watching a television show, he sipped his thick green breakfast concoction, sorted through papers on his desk and fired off messages from his computer. He was a master class in multitasking. She couldn't help but admire how much Jules got done in a day.

She'd also come to know another side of him. Although he made a joke about his parents needing military peacekeepers, she could recognize in his face, in his posture, in his voice, that he was under a lot of stress. She even saw vulnerability in those dark brown eyes.

Zoe could hardly blame him after what she'd witnessed when meeting Jules's parents at his hotel. His mother was ungrateful and unpleasant and spoke without any kind of self-filter. Hugo wasn't much better. Jules was short with them, already exhausted by his caretaking mission.

The more she thought about it, the more it bothered

her that neither of them said thank-you to Jules. For their plane fare from Tel Aviv. For the hotel suite and upcoming apartment. For any of it. She didn't know all of what had transpired between them but it was enough to make her want to protect him. It was ironic that she wanted to don a suit of armor to defend the big tall billionaire.

Studying him on the video call, Zoe noticed how the clench in his shoulder blades made him look stiff sitting in his chair. Analyzing his striking face, the divots between his eyebrows were the most sunken she'd ever seen them. She figured he hadn't fully fathomed what he was getting himself into by bringing his parents back until they'd actually arrived.

She went ahead and voiced her concern. "Jules, you look tense. Did you go for your run this morning?"

He'd told her that morning exercise was vital to his routine.

"Yes." He took another sip of his drink.

"And you have a busy day full of conferences and acquisitions?"

For the first time during the conversation, he looked directly into her eyes on the screen in response to her semi-sarcastic comment.

"Yes, Zoe. I run an empire, you know. And tense doesn't even begin to describe it."

He was having a hard morning, and she was starting to get the feeling that he had come to consider her someone he could talk to, someone who had something to offer him. That he could be real around her, which was rare for him. There was definitely something inside of him that he needed to release. More than strain. It was like there was another man inside the accomplished one she watched through the screen, one who fit in Paris.

A man with a big romantic passion he kept under the surface. Maybe the city itself could eventually set that free for him. Or maybe she could.

What was the good in that, though? Helping Jules unlock his inner spirit was no concern of hers one way or another. She was never going to be the person he'd share that emancipation with. No one was. He'd made that clear. Although, if she were being honest, the notion had popped up in her mind more than a few times. Especially after that delicious mistake of a kiss, the one she was still replaying. What would it be like to be his lover, his best friend, his wife?

It was hard to picture the man who swore by his three-date rule and had spent most of his adult life living in the world's sleekest hotels, participating in domestic pleasures. Would he look forward to coming home to her at night? A designated hour that work ended for the evening? When they would prepare a home-cooked meal, eaten cozily at their little round table for two? Would he stop at the store on the way home to buy medicine when she called suffering from a runny nose? Might there be a beloved pup curled up at his feet while they watched a movie on a lazy Sunday?

No, he had people who went to the store for him. His life was too busy for a pet. A cute little table for two? Absurd!

"What do you have over there?" he commented on what he was viewing from his end of the FaceTime chat. "Is that a toolbox on your table?"

She explained that the hammer, nails and whatnot had been left out as she and Yasmine were attempting to repair a bedroom dresser they'd found broken and abandoned on the street. "We always need extra storage," she explained. "We're going to sand it down to the original wood and then stain it."

"That's what you do in your spare time? Restore other people's garbage?"

"We've never tried it before."

Zoe absentmindedly touched his cheek on her tablet's screen, as if she could penetrate through all the way to his skin.

"What happened?" He reacted to her movement. "Why did you just touch your screen?"

Oops! "Oops," she covered quickly, having forgotten how that move would appear at his end of the connection. "I was just wiping a smudge." While she'd been staring at his face as he spoke to her, it was as if his likeness on the screen rather than in person gave her license to let out some of her own bubbling emotions.

She'd become deeply attracted to him. No doubt about it. What she had initially found irritating about him, she'd come to respect. He'd been able to channel his organizational and decision-making skills into a billion-euro corporation, in spite of an upbringing that offered no encouragement. What he was willing to do for his parents, out of duty and not because they deserved it, was noble. He was a force for good in a world that needed it.

And she wanted to peel away more of his outer layers, to set free the fiery man that she kept getting glimmers of. Glimmers that were keeping her awake at night, so compelling were the *what-ifs* her brain was now constantly ticking with. What if she herself was open to romance, to love? One thing she knew for sure was that if she were, she'd want to be with Jules.

Zoe had been convincing herself for so long now that

she would never enter into a serious relationship. In fact, terror gripped her at the mere thought of something happening to Jules, and they weren't even together.

After her parents' instant deaths, Zoe was despondent for months. The pain of having both parents taken at the same time was a hurt so savage it had the strength to tear her apart limb by limb. She thought she'd never rise up from the sorrow, from the grief.

It was like walking in a daze for a couple of years. To lose her parents was bad enough, but in such a shocking way was too much to overcome.

When she finally did emerge, the lack of opportunity in Maupont was unbearable. She needed change. One day, she visited the cemetery where her parents and grandparents were buried. She had a heart-to-heart chat with them at their gravesites and asked them what to do. It was then she realized she had to come to Paris. She had to pursue her ambition. And at the same time, she decided firmly she could never accept the unknown that getting close to someone would bring. Therefore, she'd avoid it completely.

So it made no sense at all that she was pretending the apartment they were renovating was for themselves, creating a beautiful home that they designed together where they would live in bliss.

Mademoiselle Gaiman pull yourself together, she mentally admonished herself. *Tuck that attraction into the top drawer of the dresser you're repairing and never open it again.*

Nothing useful could come from these musings. Jules had given her a professional boost for which she'd forever be grateful. That was it.

"In addition to the electrician, the painters will be

at work today," he said, while looking down at some paperwork from a different project. "I'll stop by at the end of the day."

Here she'd been having such lofty thoughts about unchaining Jules's more carefree side and about tables for two, while he had his mind on his business. Still, man did not live by green drinks alone, and the recipe wasn't going to keep him healthy if he didn't have some downtime and recreation.

"Why don't we meet there at five o'clock?"

"Yes, five is good," he answered without raising his head.

"After that, what would you think about spending the rest of the afternoon doing something relaxing?" She hadn't meant to ask him that, or maybe she had?

"I don't relax." He was, once again, barely listening as he concentrated on other matters.

"Do you think maybe you should?"

"I'll put *Find Ways to Relax* on my to-do list."

"There you go! I'm sure you'll find something really rewarding if you make it a *should* not a *want to*."

"Are you being sarcastic again?"

He lifted his eyes and his stare shot point-blank right through the screen. Her heartbeat fluttered. She relived yet again that intense kiss they'd shared. What had really happened there? For all his rules and regulations, something overtook him in that moment. She couldn't stop wondering what.

Although she had no reason to, no obligation to, she felt compelled to help him unwind a little. He needed it so. She could safely do that much without too much risk to herself, couldn't she?

"What do you think? Could you shrug off your many responsibilities for a couple of hours?"

"What did you have in mind?"

"I'll show you."

When Jules met Zoe in front of the apartment, he grinned at what he saw. There she stood straddling a bicycle while holding the handlebar of a second, both with white wicker baskets in front that were decorated with artificial flowers. "I borrowed Yasmine's bike for you."

"I can see."

Zoe looked so adorable it took Jules a couple of breaths to settle into the moment. She wore a short and flowing dress made from a fabric with pink, blue and yellow flowers on it. Her hair was tied back with a pink ribbon and she wore retro-style sunglasses and a pair of flat leather sandals. She was a vision of happy, carefree Paris, even though Jules knew by now there was depth and pain beneath her cheery exterior.

He reached for one of the bike's handles and in the process their hands touched each other's. How thrilling the sensation was. After entering the building, they propped the bikes against a wall and did a quick check of the progress on the apartment.

"I haven't ridden in years," Jules confessed when they were back on the street. He held the borrowed bike, amused that he'd be riding with the girly white basket in front. While hotel concierges throughout the world had tried to encourage him to see their fair cities from a bicycle seat, Jules had always refused. He preferred his efficient morning run for his exercise. And a driver to whisk him anywhere he wanted to go.

"Bicycling through Paris, isn't that just a classic thing to do?"

"I used to bike when I was a kid." Indeed, Jules could clearly recall the exhilaration he'd had riding through the streets, pedaling as fast as he could through the outskirts of town where he lived. That was one of the few good memories he had. The wind blowing his hair back, his body leaning into turns or curves he had to maneuver. Whatever challenges the road brought were easy compared to what awaited him at home.

He adjusted the seat to accommodate his height, his fingers remembering the mechanisms of the bike as if it had been yesterday. In fact, Yasmine's bike was so basic it reminded him of a child's. None of the precision advances of sportsman bikes available today. "Where to?" he asked Zoe, aware of how rarely he'd asked that question of someone else, as it was always him making the decisions.

"Follow me."

The long list of things Jules needed to take care of flickered across his mind like news captions ticking across the bottom of the screen on television. But another part of him, one he hadn't seen in a long while, told him it was okay to let everything sit for a couple of hours. His parents were at the hotel and Karim had rescheduled a couple of meetings. The world really wouldn't come crashing down without his constant supervision.

Zoe gestured for them to turn at the intersection and again at a side street, where traffic was light and they could pick up speed.

Deciding to surrender the ride to Zoe's control, he let her stay a little bit ahead of him. Which afforded him a lovely view of her on the bike. Her petite frame was shapely. The thin fabric of the sundress billowed as she pedaled, allowing glimpses of the creamy skin of her thighs. The back of her pale neck was exposed by the ribbon that bound her hair.

Before long he was imagining his lips grazing the back of that neck underneath her hairline. He flashed back to how impossibly silky her pillowy lips were when he kissed her. How scorching and potent his tongue was with his mouth on hers. He wouldn't mind doing it again.

What if he pulled his bike up right next to hers and then at a moment when they stopped at a traffic light, he'd just lean over and touch his lips to hers? He was glad that she was a bit ahead of him so he didn't have to hide the silly grin that swept across his face at the idea.

As he was beginning to suspect, Zoe was leading him to the Luxembourg Gardens, one of the most storied and visited locales in Paris. Not only was it a must-stop for many tourists, Parisians considered it a prime spot to relax and take a break from the active and densely populated streets of the inner city.

"Let's sit by the Medici Fountain," she said as she dismounted her bike once they entered the garden gates.

"My favorite part of the gardens," he said as he gazed at Zoe. The curls that had emancipated themselves from her pink ribbon framed her face. The trail of freckles that traveled from one cheekbone across her nose to the other were fresh and natural in the late afternoon light.

"Mine, too."

They walked their bikes to the fountain with its long rectangular water basin surrounded by shady trees. A place that had been immortalized in countless paintings and photographs. Metal chairs lined each side of the basin, where people had been coming to bask for centuries. The expanse of still water gave way to the fountain with its statues and columns.

"What a nice idea to bring me here," Jules mused, swept into the beauty and peace surrounding him. Were the plane trees fragrant or was that his imagination?

"Let's sit."

They scoped out the available seating. A group of older men occupied part of the space, their chairs turned toward each other in an impromptu circle as they talked using many hand gestures. A woman read a paperback while holding her teeny dog. Schoolchildren, under the watch of a nanny, squealed and played a hopping game. It was almost a step back in time, the tableau set long ago. Jules had to admit he welcomed not being able to spot a cell phone.

He pointed to a couple of empty chairs and pulled them to the basin's edge, the scrape of the metal legs audible as he did so.

Once they sat, Zoe produced bottles of cold water from her bicycle's basket and handed him one, which was most appreciated. Popping the cap, Jules took a sip.

"Look at how much shade these trees provide," she said, noting the way the sunlight broke into shards as it danced on the basin's water.

"Perfect lighting design, right?"

"If you listen for it, you can hear the leaves rustle."

They sat in silence for a few minutes, indeed hearing the leaves' song. Jules could actually sense his heart rate slow, his breath become easy and unrestricted with deep inhales and even longer exhales. It was as if oxygen was reaching cells that had been starved of it for years. A pleasant tingle meandered through his blood vessels. His palms opened and tilted upward. "You were right. A person does need to do a little bit of nothing on occasion."

"This is some darn good nothing, isn't it?"

"Yes," he whispered and fell into a meditative state for a few minutes. His eyes closed. Everything fell away except a gentle wind on his face and the presence of Zoe beside him.

Eventually she said, "Our next destination will be a bit of something, though."

"Intriguing. I'm in your hands." Jules bit his lip. He hadn't meant to say something so flirty—it just slipped out. Zoe was turning him into someone he'd never met. A man he might like to know, to become. Who embraced existence on mental, physical and spiritual levels. Someone open and emancipated. A man who said yes.

After they'd thoroughly enjoyed the fountain and its surroundings, they ambled through more of the garden. Zoe led them to a café within the grounds where people sat savoring an early evening drink or snack outdoors. She chose a shady table and when the waiter approached, Zoe took the lead.

"We'll have a *tartelette des fruits*, a *fondant citron* with Chantilly *crème* and a crepe with cocoa noisette spread. Two hot chocolates and two glasses of champagne. And give the bill to him." She pointed to Jules, eliciting a belly laugh from him and a chuckle from the waiter.

"You're trying to corrupt me?" Another flirt. Not only couldn't he stop himself, he didn't want to. "You know I don't indulge in sweets."

"Exactly. On your relaxation day, you're not going to eat leaves. You're only going to look at them. Although maybe we'll have them with dinner later."

"We're having dinner?"

"If you play your cards right." She shot him a sly smile.

Zoe, he wanted to scream! *Stop saying sexy things!* Bad enough that he was thinking them. She'd already gotten him to ditch all the items on his agenda to go bike riding. And here they sat surrounded by the flora, dirt under their feet. Now she'd ordered desserts! If he didn't watch himself, Zoe might tear down the carefully guarded kingdom walls he'd created. Which, it seemed, a part of him was desperate to let her demolish.

The waiter delivered everything on a large silver tray. Zoe and Jules each put a napkin on their laps and their forks went to work.

He thought surely his eyes were going to roll back in his head at the taste of the warm crepe. He savored the thick hazelnut and chocolate flavor as it swirled around in his mouth. "Oh, my goodness."

"You've heard that expression," she said with a satisfied smile. "Life is uncertain so we should eat dessert first."

As she took a bite of the fondant Chantilly, a bit of whipped cream lingered on the side of her mouth. Jules leaned over and with a swipe of his thumb, removed the swirl from her face. And immediately, without thinking about it, licked it off. Afterward, he was a bit embarrassed at the informality.

She didn't seem bothered by it, though, and they continued peering at the gardens laid out in front of them. Vivid flowers in every shade of the rainbow surrounded the circular lawn with its statuary in front of the Luxembourg Palace.

Time passed at a leisurely pace Jules was so unaccustomed to. Every last speck on each plate was consumed and not a drop of the drinks remained. He and Zoe conversed about books and music and movies. About politics and history. The more they talked, the more he wanted to continue, speaking on any topic that came into their minds.

The moon began to rise when they decided it was time to go.

"Really, we should pick up some salads for dinner after all those sweet indulgences," she decided.

"We could bring them back to my apartment."

Jules hadn't had a guest in his Paris apartment in years, as he had used it so infrequently. He welcomed the idea. Like it was an actual home where he might have friends over. A weak voice in the back of his head tried to caution him that if he was counting, this was his third date with Zoe. And perhaps bringing her to his apartment was a bit too intimate. But his rationalizations and equations were no longer making sense to him.

Zoe gasped comically when she saw the size of Jules's apartment.

"Make yourself at home," he said casually. And then was surprised when she took him literally, unclasping her sandals and tossing them in a corner as she gave herself a self-guided tour. She took note of his upscale furniture and well-appointed office, every cord and cable to his high-tech setup discreetly out of view.

"Can I have a look at the rest?"

He'd have laughed at her lack of pretension if he weren't so charmed by it.

"Have at it, *cherie.*"

She moved to the kitchen, opening cabinets and drawers. Naturally, everything was done with top-notch building materials and craftsmanship.

"Premium quartz," she mentioned as she touched his countertop.

In the master bedroom, she bounced her small hand across the foot of his oversized bed, testing the firmness of his mattress. "Is that a Leon Villar?" she asked about the abstract landscape painting above the headboard.

"It is."

"Did you see his show at Galerie Pauline Caron?"

"I saw the show in New York."

He was glad for the painting discussion as having Zoe in his bedroom was unnerving. Namely, because he couldn't stop picturing laying her down on his bed, and letting his hands, mouth and more explore all of her body that he'd not yet seen. That flimsy little dress she wore would slip over her head in one pull, and whatever was underneath he'd remove with a quick slide.

Jules's feet moved toward her. He called for that warning voice in his head but it had become so faint he really couldn't hear it. It had morphed into a distant buzz that he was easily able to shush.

Her look in response to him moving closer was affirming. Lips slightly parted, the sparkle in her eyes welcomed him.

There was only one thing to do, and so he did it. He wrapped his hand around the back of Zoe's neck and brought her face toward him as he bent down to bring the first of many kisses to her inviting mouth.

It was better than any dream he'd ever had. As Jules

delivered yet another shower of light kisses to Zoe's lovely face, each brush of his lips against her skin presented a dilemma. On one hand, he wanted to slow himself down and register each kiss before he went on to the next. But a conflicting need was ready to devour her with urgency. It was a delicious agony, choosing between the two and settling somewhere in the middle.

Just a few minutes ago, they were picking up salads from a nearby market, after their pastry-fueled sunset at the Luxembourg Gardens. Dinner in tow, they'd brought the bikes to the entrance foyer of Jules's flat. He'd have his driver return them to her apartment later. Better still, he'd also send Zoe and her roommate new bikes with all the latest innovations.

Now he was kissing her at the foot of his bed. He held his lips above hers, just close enough for her to feel his breath and want more. The hiss of her inhale emboldened him.

Both palms cupped her face. He dragged his mouth away from hers, with a tormenting pull, so that he could feather his way down to her jawline. She lifted her chin toward him, a blessing that allowed him to apply his kisses in a continuous line. The journey took him from the plump bottom of one earlobe and down one side of her face. He wasn't done until he traveled her jaw to the other side. The thrum of pleasure that elicited from somewhere low within her prompted him to discover more.

When he brought his face against the cool of her throat, his teeth bared themselves and began tiny nibbles. He reveled in her aura, breathing in her powdery sweetness. With an easy tug, he undid the ribbon that by then had been containing only half of Zoe's physics-defying orange curls. Her hair cascaded down over her shoulders, as shiny and alive as Zoe herself was.

His fingers wove through her locks—something he'd been wanting to do since he'd met her, so mesmerizing were they to him. In fact, he took pleasure from just pressing an individual curl tightly and then releasing it to watch it spring open.

"My hair is fascinating to you?" she asked after he'd performed the operation several times.

"I can't stop myself from touching it."

"Don't, then. Don't stop anything."

Their eyes met, his wearing a dark veil of arousal and hers crystalline with alertness. Jules paused with a moment of clarity. Nothing about this made sense. Why would he want to disrupt his carefully laid-out plans?

Don't stop anything.

She'd just cooed those words straight into his soul, although she might not know the extent of her effect on him. Before he could second-guess himself anymore, his hands glided down to her two shoulders. He caressed them, his fingers taking note of each of her bones and their alignment. His hands were so big they covered her shoulders completely.

He bent to kiss from the bottom of her throat down to the low neckline of her sundress. When his tongue reached the fabric, it flicked under the thin cotton. Just knowing that his mouth had met skin that the dress had been concealing stirred his very core. Her head fell back as she welcomed his exploration, which he continued with focus. His mouth took the temperature of which spots on her throat and her décolleté felt the warmest. Between her breasts was a honeyed heaven where his lips had to linger.

Eventually straightening up, he locked her in an embrace, as he suddenly needed to feel her tightly against him. Although she was petite, he found her not fragile but resilient, her body arching to meet his every move. When he molded her to him, she became pliant. Yet, she was anything but passive. Tender sighs mingled with erotic moans.

"Zoe, you're doing something to me I hadn't planned on."

"You've lit me, as well."

Filled with emotion and sensation and a primal hunger in his belly that wouldn't be contained, he pulled her down onto the bed with him. Climbing on top of her, he acknowledged how lucky his hands and lips were to be roaming over Zoe's velvety beauty. In his eagerness, he kissed her every way his body told him to. A peck on her nose. An assertive bite to the crook of her neck. The taste of the inside of her wrist.

"I haven't felt this much desire in…" Jules stopped himself before revealing what might be his best-kept secret. That he hadn't wanted someone like he wanted her. Not *in years*, which was what he had been going to say. But ever. Ever!

And it wasn't just sexual attraction he was experiencing. She'd opened his eyes to the possibility of a true connection with someone. Something that was honest and fulfilling and sustaining.

After what he witnessed as a child, he'd never trust anyone with his heart, but it was nice to know he could even have those feelings. That he was still human. Zoe showed him an alternate universe where love and beauty were everywhere. She'd changed him. He'd always be grateful for, or maybe tormented by, the gift she had given him.

"What, Jules? What are you trying to say?" Her voice sang out from the avalanche of kisses he was bestowing on her.

"Only that… I'm glad you're here." With that, his mouth found hers again where their tongues met for an extended swirl that pulled Jules into an ocean's tide. His hand began a journey along her thigh, slipping under her dress.

When he leaned his neck back, the passion he saw in her eyes must have been a mirror. He swept Zoe's flowery little dress up over her head and tossed it on the chair beside his bed.

CHAPTER SEVEN

ZOE COULD HARDLY believe she was being seduced by, and for that matter seducing, Jules. She told herself she'd better enjoy this unbelievable moment in time because it would be gone in a flash and was unlikely to ever happen again.

You're doing something to me I hadn't planned on.

His words were spoken in the heat of desire. She had the good sense to not take them seriously. Still, she was a sophisticated denizen of Paris who was free to indulge in a night of impassioned intimacy with an extraordinary man.

So, with the ever-present eye of the Eiffel Tower visible through the window of Jules's bedroom, Zoe pulled him tight, her warning ping screaming from within. She'd never been with a man like him. The few boyfriends she'd had back in Maupont were of adult age but they were still boys, fumbling and tentative, unsure of themselves. Jules was 100 percent man. His power and command as an executive was matched by the strength and confidence emanating from him as a lover.

After he'd taken off every stitch of clothing she wore, he quickly undid the buttons of his shirt and cast it off to the side, as well. Then he was on top of her again, his weight melding her into his bed. She wrapped her arms around his shoulders, his lean muscles defined underneath warm smooth skin.

His hands moved down her outline and then underneath her to bring her body up even closer to him as he pressed his still-clad maleness against her bare and now pulsating center. There they kissed and swayed, embarking toward a destination they didn't yet see.

When craving demanded more, Zoe reached between them to unbuckle Jules's belt and unzip the fly of his pants. Excited by the fullness that she stroked with her palm, her other hand yanked at his remaining clothes. With a devilish grin, he backed away from her to peel off his trousers. He reached for a condom in his nightstand and unrolled it before returning to her arms where their bodies finally truly joined and became one.

Zoe gripped him, wrapped her legs around his waist, as they flew up to the heavens, now knowing where they were going. They ascended higher and higher and higher still until, together, they soared freely as one.

When they landed back down, he collapsed on top of her. Her fingers combed through his hair with a sense of possessiveness, like he belonged to her. It was a heady sensation. Her every breath oozed an earthy, womanly sensuality she'd never known in herself.

After a serene interval of recuperation, Jules announced, "I want to eat."

"We still have our salads."

He separated himself from her, which, at first, was a torturous desertion. It had only been to gather up a few items of clothing. He stepped back into his boxers and black slacks, though he left the top button open, pulled his belt from the pant loops and cast that aside. Zoe slipped on her dress and undies, leaving her bra where it sat on Jules's side chair. He reached for her hand and led her, barefoot, into the kitchen.

As he sat her down at his chrome bar table with its two stools facing each other, Zoe wondered how many women had occupied the second seat at his table, literally or figuratively throughout his world travels.

"Have you ever lived with anyone?" she asked as Jules opened the fridge.

He lashed his head toward her in a way that made Zoe apprehensive that she'd angered him with her inquisitiveness. Instead, the look in his eyes was glassy and sad, especially shadowed by the bluish light coming from inside the refrigerator. "No. I told you. That life is not for me."

Something in his face and the way his response sounded like a question melted Zoe's heart. This man was as precious as the monuments of Paris he so revered. He deserved to be happy, to be able to count on someone. He was worthy of love. How tragic it was that his past was robbing him of a future. Although the same could be said of her.

She studied the movement in the taut muscles of his back as he reached for the salads. Her body went liquid again at the sight, a reminder of what had just transpired in his bed. He flicked on some under-cabinet lighting that gave the whole room a gentle glow, nice for the late hour. After placing the food and cold drinks on the table, he perched at the stool opposite her.

They ate in quiet for an interlude. Zoe's body was still lost in his embrace but her mind had gone to thought. When a little too much time passed, it became oppressive. She believed him when he said that he didn't get close to people and would never couple with anyone. Making love with her had not changed that one iota. Why would it? It wasn't as if she was used to a scenario like this, either. She'd come to Paris to make a career for herself, hopefully to have interesting friends and a full life. Since she'd been here, she hadn't been in a man's bed nor shared hers.

After keeping his eyes on his salad, the awkwardness got to Jules as well and he flicked a remote control on the table to turn on the television. They watched the news together, although she wasn't paying attention to the words coming out of the anchorman's mouth—something about roadwork in the Eighteenth Arrondissement.

There was no denying that an overwhelming yearning had been satiated between them in Jules's bedroom. They fit perfectly together in that respect, as if their bodies were meant for each other's. Only for each other's. But something passed between their hearts as well, something poignant, life-altering. She couldn't have been the only one to have felt it. Although, she had the sense that tomorrow she'd need to figure out how to put all of that to the side and move on with their professional interactions. Jules had made his intentions, or lack thereof, clear from the beginning.

Perhaps they were the cliché of those European types who casually mixed business with pleasure? If so, she should be able to laugh this off, just one night of many free-flowing encounters. After the ecstasy Jules brought her, the heights of giving and receiving pleasure that were new to her, to turn to a self-conscious kitchen snack in the dead of night did not come naturally to her. In fact, for reasons she couldn't coalesce into one explanation, she was fighting back tears.

But it was time to pretend that they didn't care about each other. That's how these nonchalant affairs went. Chitchat was in order and luckily Jules provided. "I'm concerned the two wing-backed chairs for the bedroom are too big in scale." He was referring to the furniture delivery for the apartment that had arrived earlier today. Before the bike ride and the Luxembourg Gardens and her tongue tracing down his spine.

"I'll look at it again with fresh eyes tomorrow," she answered in a scratchy late-night voice, determined to keep up. "It's true that they're more decorative than anything else since it wouldn't be worth the trouble for your father to get out of his wheelchair to sit in them. I'd like to fill in that space, though."

"I still like the idea of a bench. The depth would be so much shorter."

That conversation petered out and they went back to watching the news.

"Well, it's late and I'd like to get some sleep," Jules said after they finished eating.

Did he mean that he wanted *them* to get some sleep or that he wanted her to leave? Again, Zoe racked her brain, trying to figure out how worldly adults who have had sex but aren't together handle these situations. No wonder she didn't do blasé encounters. It was too confusing.

"I... I should be going, then," she managed, figuring that was the safest thing to say.

"You're welcome to stay..." His voice was unconvincing and he cast his eyelids downward. He was feeling as uneasy as she was, so different from the master-of-the-universe persona he usually projected to the world.

On one hand, she wanted to hold him all night long, perhaps including more of the divine lovemaking they had created and then nestling herself into him as they fell into one dream. On the other, she couldn't get away fast enough, to provide herself with a shield before any more affection toward him would promise inevitable disappointment. Being wise, or so she thought, she chose the latter.

After returning from collecting her things in the bedroom, she slipped on her shoes. "Are we still going to see your apartment on the Grands Boulevards later this week?"

"Yes." He tapped on his phone. "I've just called a driver to take you home. Let me walk you down."

At the late hour, Paris was subdued outside of Jules's building but still awake. Some young people laughed loudly as they passed by. A few cars and motorbikes tooled down the boulevard. When the driver pulled to the curb, Jules opened the door and helped Zoe into the back seat. He leaned in to give her a kiss good-night that belied their parting. It was a kiss that informed them, in case they hadn't figured it out yet, that they'd entered the danger zone. Their feelings for each other were anything but meaningless.

"I'll need a phone conference with Kowalczyk and his contractor today," Jules instructed Karim as they walked out of a meeting at Durand headquarters that had his head spinning. "If he doesn't get his materials cost under control, I'm pulling out."

"I let his people know."

"Run me a comparison sheet on what he'd budgeted versus what his estimates are now."

"Yes, Jules."

"And call our legal team and find out what my obligations are at this point."

"I will do that." Karim spoke in a calm monotone that Jules appreciated. Jules would be spending more time in person with his assistant now that he'd be based in Paris. The thought didn't displease him.

"Get the architect on the phone," Jules instructed as he rounded the corner to his office while Karim continued forward.

Entering his office, Jules tossed the file he was holding onto his desk, shrugged off his jacket and loosened his tie. Mounting his treadmill, he set it for a slow walk to help him blow off some steam.

With the city laid out in front of him, he realized that he was overreacting to the work setback. He'd dealt with developers who went over budget many times. His agitation didn't have that much to do with Krakow.

What was bothering him was how uncomfortably things had ended with Zoe last night after they'd made love. It had been so authentic and uncomplicated, spending that time with her at the Luxembourg Gardens and then at his apartment. Like a dance that he already knew the steps to, being with her came easily. He hadn't needed to strategically fortress himself with walls to keep out emotions. Although, maybe he subconsciously had in the end. Because after all the surprising naturalness of them getting out of bed together to eat a late supper in the kitchen, Jules stepped out of himself and saw the situation like someone looking in. And in that instant, the realness he felt turned itself fake in his stomach like rotten food. And he had to get away from it as quickly as he could.

Tucking a woman into a waiting car in the middle of the night. Three-date rules. A vow never to marry. Jules Durand had become the man he'd set out to be. Only now it was someone he didn't like.

"Hello," Jules said with a quick kiss to her cheek when he met Zoe in front of one of his buildings a few days later as planned. Most of the decisions on the apartment for his parents had been made but he'd promised to take her to one of his most show-stopping properties.

He seemed cheerier than he had when they'd parted in the wee hours that night after they'd made love, with her peering out the back-seat window at him as the driver pulled the car away, distress washing over Jules's exquisite face.

"You own this?" she asked, even though the answer was obvious. "The entire building?"

"1869. Haussmann."

Georges-Eugène Haussmann, the prefect under Emperor Napoléon III who redesigned a decaying city into the metropolis and crossroads Paris remained to this day. Haussmann demolished the medieval city neighborhoods that were unhealthy, overcrowded and dangerous, and replaced them with a new Paris. Enormous apartment buildings were built, not to be considered as individual structures but as part of an urban landscape with wide avenues and public squares. That signature architectural style became the look of Paris, the front-facing windows and horizontal designs of similar heights, building-front after building-front cut from cream-colored stone.

Zoe's mind boggled that Jules owned one of those buildings, and at what price it might fetch on the modern market. She shook her head. "I know I'm a small-town girl but it's hard to believe I actually know someone who owns a Haussmann on the Grands Boulevards of Paris."

Jules's mouth twitched. She could tell he wasn't actually smiling at her lack of savvy, only that she'd voiced it out loud. "All right, Mademoiselle Small Town, my property manager arranged for us to see one of the apartments in the building. From what I'm told, my tenant uses a wheelchair and we've made some excellent accommodations for her I'd like to show you."

"Wonderful. Lead the way." Zoe pointed to the entrance door.

So far, so good, she noted of the easier rapport they were managing today. Although, entering the building, she moved close to him and it was all she could do not to lean in. To beg those strong shoulders to encircle her, a return to the magical private universe they'd escaped to in his bed.

All business, Jules used his passcode to enter the apartment.

"Wow," Zoe exclaimed. "Did we just walk into the Palais Versailles? I've never seen anything like this." It appeared that every wall that was not part of the building's intrinsic structure had been removed, artistic pillars concealing foundational beams that were necessary to retain. In doing so, a vast expanse had been created, almost beyond what the eye could see. "I can't believe this is a center-city residence."

"By taking out as many walls as we could, we've

made it easier for Madame to maneuver around the apartment."

"Less doorways and corners. Not to mention the majesty of it all."

"I'm very pleased with how this turned out. And when Madame decides to move out, I'm sure many tenants would appreciate this open plan."

"Ya!" Zoe shrieked, getting a giggle out of Jules. "This has to be the best apartment in Paris. The Grands Boulevards are my favorite part of the city, anyway."

"Come here." He took her hand and brought her to the farthest windows where there was a clear view of the opera house, Palais Garnier.

"Did you know that the opera house was once the nexus of Paris's high society?" she asked.

"What operas have you seen at the Palais?"

"None. I've never been."

"You've never gone to the opera in Paris?"

"I've never been to an opera anywhere."

"We'll have to correct that immediately. Do you have plans tonight?" He didn't wait for an answer as he pulled his phone from his jacket pocket. "Karim, get me an opera box for tonight."

Zoe heart rate sped. Jules was calling his assistant to get opera tickets for them? Just like that?

After the strangeness at his apartment, she hadn't known what to expect today. She'd been working on his parents' apartment independently while Jules was dealing with other properties. She'd updated him during FaceTime sessions but the uneasiness between them had still hung in the air. It was a relief that he was less quirky today.

"I thought you didn't make spur-of-the-moment decisions," she chided him, giddy energy propelling her to make a joke.

"I must be spending too much time with you." He grinned back. "Do you have anything to wear?"

"Can I wear the orange dress you bought me for that cruise on the Seine?"

"You could. But let's buy you something new."

She shrugged her shoulders. "Whatever you say, boss." The quip earned her another chortle from Jules. Their jokey manner was keeping them from dealing with the reality of their night together, both the incendiary lovemaking and the prickly aftermath. But if he wanted to play it that way, so would she. Maybe they could find an equilibrium. In any case, she was going to the opera.

"We may as well go to Galeries Lafayette." Paris's most famous and sophisticated department stores were conveniently located nearby. Jules tapped into his phone again. "Karim, I also need a personal shopper at Galeries Lafayette right away."

After touring the rest of the apartment, they walked the few blocks to the store and entered into its massive sales floor. Each of the store's upper levels, which were flanked with archways, were visible from the center of the ground floor. That drew the eye upward to the styling of the art nouveau multi-colored steel and glass dome. It was another architectural masterpiece. Zoe marveled, "This store is a museum piece in and of itself."

An elevator took them to their floor and they were shown into a sequestered salon. The overstuffed furniture was upholstered in a baby pink and the carpet a pretty caramel. A dais surrounded by mirrors anchored the space.

A young saleswoman introduced herself as Safa. She wore a navy sheath dress with a multi-colored scarf tied around her neck just so, the knot at one side where it magically stayed in place. "I understand you'd like something special for the opera?"

"We would." Jules nodded.

"Did you have something in mind?"

Jules turned to Zoe. "What would be your fantasy opera outfit? I'll wear a tuxedo."

"Old-fashioned romance, I guess. Is black velvet okay?" she questioned. After all, Jules was paying for another dress. She expected he'd want to approve it as he had last time.

"If that's what you'd like."

"I'll be back with some suggestions," Safa said and then exited the salon.

When Jules arrived at Zoe's apartment that night to pick her up for the opera, Yasmine was home, as well. "Ni... ice to meet you," she stammered. Zoe couldn't blame her, as Jules's mere presence seemed to overtake their tiny apartment. It was as if all of the furniture moved out of the way to allow his entrance.

With his substantial height and precision haircut, his slim-cut black tux gave him that look of modern royalty. Every inch of him was faultlessly chic, from the jacket's thin lapel to his luxury wristwatch to his shoes on which a scuff would never dare appear. It was almost comical the way Yasmine's eyes all but bugged out like a cartoon character.

But when Zoe stepped into Jules's view in her ensemble, it was she who drew the approving gaze. As a matter of fact, he cleared his throat in response, which Zoe found adorable. "You look spectacular," he said.

No one had ever called her that before and she almost blushed. Memories of making love with him flooded her. The way his body, his fingers, his mouth had appreciated her and made her feel *spectacular*. Her heart sat heavy with the knowledge that she might never share that glory with him again. Even if she had the opportunity, she'd have to turn it down. Her emotions had already grown perilous. Nonetheless, one of Paris's most attractive bachelors was taking her to the opera, and she was going to turn her mind to savoring every moment of the fairy-tale evening.

So, she quite enjoyed the lustful way he looked her over from top to bottom. He, of course, had sent a stylist to the apartment to help her get dressed, and her unruly hair had been corralled but left curly in a half-up, half-down do. Her smoky eye makeup was dramatic and the most perfect shade of pale lipstick complemented her complexion.

Zoe absolutely loved the dress she'd picked out from the choices the saleswoman at Galeries Lafayette had brought them earlier. Crushed velvet, it had a wide and low-cut neckline. So jet-black it was almost blue. The shapewear undergarment she wore enhanced her bosom, displaying as much voluptuousness as was tasteful. The dress fit her like a glove, hugging all her curves until it reached a lower calf hemline that was flattering on her. And the nude heels gave it a freshness that the more customary black shoe wouldn't have.

"I think there's something missing," Jules stated after his long gander. He stepped closer to her as he removed a midnight blue jewelry box from his jacket pocket. Flipping it open, large diamond stud earrings sparkled from their satin berth. "These are for you."

Yasmine gasped so loudly that both Jules and Zoe snapped their heads toward her. He smiled at her roommate's zest. Jules took one of the earrings from the box and removed its backing. "May I?"

"Yes!" Yasmine blurted. The three of them giggled. With, mysteriously, the knowledge of how to fit earrings onto a woman, Jules graced her lobe with the heavy jewel. His thick fingers understood the task, gently sliding the post in and then affixing the back. The whole process was so profoundly erotic Zoe's eyelashes fluttered and beads of sweat began to form between her breasts. Then he repeated his ministrations with her other ear. She tried to calm herself with slow breaths but to no avail. She was no match for this man's charms.

Pleased with his handiwork Jules decreed, "Perfect."

And divine everything was, as his driver delivered them to the Palais Garnier, one of Paris's most famous addresses for centuries. The ornate building's exterior was decorated at every inch with statues, columns, friezes and sculpture done in stones and metals. It wasn't hard to see why ghostly lore and novels such as *The Phantom of the Opera* were set in amongst such splendor.

Jules escorted her inside and when they reached the Grand Staircase, Zoe could hardly believe she was there. The swooping double staircases crafted of fine marble led up to either side of the foyer. They were even more magnificent in their detail than she had seen in photos and paintings.

"You know, part of the reason these staircases were designed to curve as they do was so that people could get a clear view of who was here and what they wore," she said. "This used to be *the* place for gossip and scandal."

"You've read up, I see."

He crooked his arm to begin leading her up those lavish marble stairs. "Careful with those high heels—" he winked "—we don't want you falling into the opera like you fell into my office. Modern-day scandal as Paris mogul takes adorable klutz to *Madame Butterfly*."

"You're never going to let me live that down, are you?"

"Not a chance."

She scrunched her face but he knew that she appreciated his humor. Still, she took hold of one of the elaborate balustrades and kept her other arm in Jules's. Feeling quite splendid, she reached the top of the stairs, secretly grateful to do it without bobbling.

"My gosh," she exclaimed as they took their seats in the box he'd reserved. The sumptuous horseshoe-shaped auditorium was rich with its red and gold decor. A bronze and crystal chandelier led to the ceiling painting done by Marc Chagall. "I'd read about this Chagall ceiling. I've forgotten when was it done?"

"In the 1960s."

"I think what I was reading said they installed it over the ceiling's original artwork."

"Another example of the old and the new merging in Paris."

When the lights were lowered for the opera to begin, Zoe's stomach twisted. The moment, the splendor of the opera house and her enchantment with Jules should have been perfect. Yet, the extreme discomfort the night after they'd made love still twirled within her like a ballerina's pirouette. She hoped her inner pinging would quiet down enough for her to enjoy the performance.

And Puccini's beauty and poignancy did captivate her attention. She sat motionless and spellbound for the entire first act.

At the first intermission, Jules suggested they visit the Grand Foyer, the long gilded hall with crystal, gold leaf and ceiling paintings that seemed to stretch the length of a city block. The social scene in the Paris of years gone by had gathered in this hallowed expanse, apparently sometimes several nights a week. Zoe could see why. It was opulence rarely seen outside of a palace. Zoe imagined women in the elaborate dresses of centuries past, corsets and gold braiding, tiny shoes with buckles and powdery wigs. Or, later, women with red lipstick and their short hair tucked into cloche hats. The foyer was a history lesson come to life.

"I want to show you something," Jules said as he took her hand. She wasn't able to hide the jolt that his firm grasp produced in her. He took her out to the loggia, the large span of balcony where the night air invigorated Zoe's face.

Tears pooled in her eyes at the sight of everything. The loggia overlooked the Place de l'Opéra, the open public square and the wide boulevards of what was called the Haussmann-Opéra neighborhood. Just as rideshares and scooters now moved people to and fro, she could picture the same streets filled with horses and carriages. Times were different but, in a way, Paris had stayed the same. That was why she'd moved here. To be part of the past and the future of this inimitable city.

"Jules, thank you for tonight. For bringing me here."

"I need to tell you something." He turned his face to

her as they stood in front of the view. "I want to apologize for the other night. I shouldn't have let you leave like that. As I've told you, I don't enter into romantic attachments. My attraction to you got carried away and then after our beautiful lovemaking interlude I...panicked I suppose is the right word."

She girded herself. Here would come the words she was expecting, the words that she knew were in both of their interests. He'd say definitively, lest there be any confusion, that what happened between them was impulsive and that he doesn't *do* impulsive. That they should just chock it up to a mistake, which would never occur again. Just as their original kiss had been.

It really would be for the best. She'd shake her head in agreement. Neither of them were open to falling in love. There was no benefit to continuing a personal acquaintance. They were colleagues and nothing more.

Take a mental snapshot, Zoe.

Because this was all she was getting. This night, this loggia, this stunning and affecting man. She'd cherish and replay all of it until her dying day.

"And?" She encouraged him to finish, wanting her pain served up quickly like a bandage being ripped from delicate skin.

"And..." He lingered before leaning down to take hold of her face and give her a profoundly sensual kiss that snaked all the way down into her belly, coiling in her very soul. "And I want a do-over. I want you in my bed again. And this time I want to hold you all night."

After they returned to their box seats, the tragic longing of Cio-Cio San's famous second-act aria paled in comparison to the music in Zoe's heart.

CHAPTER EIGHT

JULES PLACED A wisp of a kiss on the head of a still-sleeping Zoe in his bed. He grabbed some running gear from a drawer and padded quietly out of the room, not wanting to wake her. After he dressed for his early-morning exercise, he opened the fridge to make sure the green smoothies were there. He and Zoe would have those for breakfast when he returned.

On the street, cafés were open to meet the needs of those already out and about. Shop owners pulled back their safety gates, fishmongers stacked the latest catches on ice. Jules ran past a fruit vendor, the proprietor in a white apron inspecting his offerings, pulling off apples that he deemed unsellable and tossing them into a box under his display stand. Neon lights in a supermarket window looked eerie in the still-sleepy morning, but customers entered and exited. The optometry office, the bank and the pet groomers were not yet open.

Traffic chugged along but few horns honked. In the hum of daybreak, Jules could think. Before demands yanked his concentration from one thing to another to another still. That Krakow project still had him worried. He was missing some information and he'd need to schedule a teleconference as soon as he got to the office.

He increased his running pace. And would his parents be able to make a new chapter of their lives here? Could they manage to set aside their differences, at least some of the time, to grow old together with any amount of grace and respect? Nothing in their past suggested that they would but out of sheer will Jules was hoping against hope that he could create some kind of unit between the three of them that had never existed in the first place.

At the moment, though, he didn't want to think about their issues any more than he did those in Krakow. There was only one thing he wanted on his mind.

Zoe. Charming, vivacious, warm-hearted Zoe. With whom he'd spent a night that alternated from sweet affection to savage hunger. That left them sweating and panting to the point that they could hear each other's breath afterward as they lay spent on his bed. And instead of being satisfied, Jules wanted more.

He ran past his local boulangerie and got a whiff of the yeasty baked goods he was able to see through the shop's open street-facing window.

After he had kissed Zoe so passionately on the loggia of the opera house and stated that he wanted her to come home with him, he waited in a haze of awareness for the rest of the performance, his body flinching and flexing, desperate to be free of his tuxedo. It was an exquisite torment. Their night at his apartment afterward was well worth the wait.

Reflecting on all of it as he ran, oxygen surging through him, one fact caught him by surprise. If one was to be counting, taking Zoe to the opera had been date number four. He'd disregarded his longstanding promise to himself never to go past three dates with a woman.

At the beginning, he'd rationalized that Zoe was a colleague so his tallies didn't even count. Now, he no longer cared. Maybe everything in his world could come together as one big messy whole. Once he stabilized his parents, finally stopped the commotion that he'd been running from his entire life, he'd allow in some joy. And romance. Was anything about that plan realistic, or was he being as silly as a teenager with a crush?

The existence he'd been leading had to change. It wasn't normal, wasn't healthy. When he moved aside the clutter in his brain, he knew that. A man could become nothing but a hard shell living alone, communicating only superficially to his parents or regarding business. His hot red blood would drain, his juices would dry up, the vital force of his solar plexus would shrivel.

Suddenly, while he was running and observing the life on the street around him, it was as if he could see with a bright clarity that had long been hidden. What made existence worthwhile was to spend it amongst other people. Having a shared experience. The ups. The downs. The maybes. Caring and being cared for. And it was Zoe who had opened his eyes.

On a whim, he circled back and started running in the direction he came from. With a ridiculous amount of excitement, he entered the boulangerie whose smells had tickled his nose when he'd run past earlier. The green smoothies could wait. Jules ordered two cafés au lait and four croissants, which were still warm in the bag the cashier presented.

When he got home, he went straight to the bathroom and started pouring a bath in his enormous Carrara marble tub. In his bedroom, he found Zoe just waking, stretching her sinewy arms above her head.

"Good morning."

"You've been out?" she cooed, her voice still subdued from sleep.

"My run."

"Mmm…how ambitious."

"Early bird and all that. Would you join me in a bath?"

"A morning bath, how luxurious. Do you do that every day?"

"Never."

A shy smile crossed her lips and Jules's heart twanged.

He fetched her a toothbrush and gave her a few moments of privacy in the vanity portion of his bathroom suite. Meanwhile, he found some bubble bath his housekeeper must have bought for him and yelled through the door, "Gardenia or citrus?"

"Citrus."

Once she emerged, he helped her step into the bathtub made to comfortably fit two.

"Ah…" she whooshed as she immersed herself in the fragrant bubbles.

Jules lowered himself in, as well.

He positioned them just as he had planned in his mind as he carried the coffee and croissants back after his purchase. With him leaning back against the tub's marble, he pulled Zoe between his legs so that her back rested against his chest and he could be a human pillow for her.

"I can't believe you can see the Eiffel Tower even from your bathtub," she remarked on the view through the picture window that was strategically positioned to afford total privacy. "I'd never get anything done if I had a bathroom like this."

Jules couldn't argue. With the oversized glass shower that had several faucets and jet options, plus the extra-large tub with a whirlpool motor, this room was a special oasis. Connected to the bath and shower suite was a separate water closet, double sinks in cabinets with lots of storage and a dressing table with a lighted mirror. He'd owned this apartment for years but hadn't lived in it for more than weeks at a time. Now that he thought about it, this was probably a woman's dream come true of a bathroom. A measure of his isolation was that he'd never noticed before.

"It does promote relaxation."

"Kudos to your designer on this one."

Jules couldn't remember who had done the renovations on this apartment. He'd been out of the country at the time.

"I've never taken a bath here."

"What? Why?"

"It never occurred to me." He kissed the top of Zoe's shoulder, her skin slick with soapy water. "Until this morning." Wrapping her in his long arms, he fully enveloped her and held her as close to him as was humanly possible.

The bubbles danced beautifully across her bent knees. Lucky bubbles. He kissed the top of her head over and over.

This freeze frame in time was very appealing. It was as if all at once during his run, he *got it*. That the benefits of sharing a bath, a life were well worth any sacrifices of control. His intellectual self knew that most partners didn't walk out on the other and then come crawling back, begging for forgiveness over and over again. None of what Jules grew up in was normal. In a flash, he believed for the first time that history did not have to repeat itself.

A kind of delight came over him, like nothing he'd ever felt before. Sure, there was a rush when a project was completed or an attractive property was acquired. Yet, what he experienced this morning was something different. Better. It was pure and simple optimism.

Almost unwilling to let go of Zoe for even a minute, he leaned over to the tub's ledge and handed her one of the coffees he'd bought.

"Mmm," she sighed after a sip. "Delicious."

"Like you." He dried his hands on a nearby towel so he could open the bag of croissants. Breaking off a piece, he reached his hand in front of her so that he could feed her a bite.

"Croissants for breakfast? I thought you started the day with handfuls of lawn grass or some such."

Jules laughed, his bellows echoing throughout the bathroom. "It was a spur-of-the-moment decision."

"I approve." When he fed her more, she held onto his hand so that she could take the second bite more sensually, her tongue flicking the tips of his fingers.

Their soak was about to take an entirely different turn when Jules's phone buzzed from the bedroom. Because early morning had slid, albeit lusciously, into business hours he felt he should take it.

"I'll be right back."

"Sure. But give me the rest of the croissant first."

Another chuckle made him wonder who he was. Had he learned the meaning of the word *fun*, after all?

He hoisted himself out of the bath, wrapped a towel

around his waist and went to his nightstand to retrieve his phone. His mother's voice tampered the elation that Zoe and bubbles had given him.

"I'm at the Gare du Nord." The train station. Dread thudded in the center of Jules's chest. "I am not wasting one more moment of my life on that louse you call a father. I'm leaving and this time I am truly never coming back. I'll need some money and I'll be in touch with where you should wire it."

"Mother. Stop this nonsense. Do not get on that train. I'll send a car for you. We're not doing this anymore."

"All aboard!" Jules could hear the loudspeaker in the distance.

"Mother!"

"I'm boarding now. Goodbye, son."

Lounging in the bath until her skin was pink and shriveled, Zoe followed Jules's instruction to linger as long as she wanted. As to what was so urgent based on the phone call he'd received, he merely said that he had to go and that it couldn't wait. He'd quickly donned full business garb and his serious face. Zoe assumed it had something to do with the projects he'd mentioned were running over budget. The succulent kisses goodbye he gave her didn't need any explanation.

Zoe could get used to bathing in a huge marble tub with a view. The lazy sunlight shining on the Paris rooftops made the tableau look like a painting. She oozed into some steamy daydreams of her and Jules and bubbles, his big hands making sure every spot on her body was properly soaped. Every. Spot. Those same hands that surely knew what they were doing to her on dry land last night. After the opera and the exchange on the loggia, when he begged her to understand that he'd panicked after they'd made love the first time but that he was sure he wanted her in his bed all night long. She slid underneath the water and allowed the warm cocoon to surround her.

Then, only after she'd eaten every flake of the croissants Jules had surprised her with after his run, she finally got out of the tub and used a thick fluffy towel to dry herself off. With just her black velvet dress from the night before to put on, she quickly left Jules's apartment for her own where she could change into daytime clothes.

Her next stop was Si Wu's studio to approve the living room furniture before having it delivered. Si had previously come to the apartment and, along with Jules, they'd worked out the furniture order there. It was a symbol of respect for Jules that the renowned furniture-maker had paid him a house call. Now, at his studio, Zoe appreciated roaming around his showroom, eyeing the sophisticated yet contemporary pieces Si was famous for.

Since her roommate, Yasmine, worked here, she had a chance to say hi. Yasmine came down from the stepladder she was on, having reached for something. "Didn't hear you come home last night, roomie."

All Zoe did was nod back, a smile breaking across her face.

"Zoe, hi, come, let me show you where we're at," Si cut in. He was a high-strung man with black-rimmed eyeglasses who talked and walked very fast, darting across his large studio. Zoe hustled to keep up with him. Si pointed to the rust-colored button-tufted corner piece that had sofa seating on one side and an L-shaped chaise lounge on the other. He rattled off in his rapid-fire manner of speaking. "I can add another module if you decide you want it larger, button-tufted is always so sharp looking, and wears well, what do you think?"

She inspected the creation and thought about it, picturing it in the place she'd chosen. The fine craftsmanship was evident in every facet. It was a gorgeous piece that would anchor the room. But she did have a question. "As you know, one of the occupants uses a wheelchair." Jules hadn't specifically asked her not to mention that the apartment was for his parents when they started working with Si, but she didn't think it was anyone's business. "Does it have to be so low to the ground? I'd like the tenant to be easily able to get in and out."

"I can do some custom legs to give you a little more height. You don't want to end up with a bed sort of look, especially for the chaise section, unless you do?"

Zoe was almost giddy to be having this conversation with the famous furniture designer, even if he did have an odd way of speaking. This is what she'd dreamt of. Customizing fine pieces, which, together, became a home with personality. There were no price tags on Si's furniture, unlike the showroom of her family's store in Maupont where customers needed that information. At a studio like this, a person couldn't afford his designs if they needed to ask the price.

"The dining table and chairs, end tables, side chairs, bench for the bedroom, nightstands, bed frame, daybed for second bedroom, window table, all being delivered today," Si rattled off the inventory from memory. "Is that okay with you, Zoe?"

That she was here was all because of Jules. Despite her less than graceful entry into his life, he took a chance on her. In more ways than one. She bit her lip, recalling the sensuality they'd shared last night, tuning into each other's pleasure, giving and taking, and bringing the other to ecstasy. With Jules, both professionally and personally, she felt confident and mature. Maybe her inner tide had finally turned.

"What happened *this* time?" Jules barreled into the hotel penthouse where, earlier in the week, he thought things had been a bit calmer with his parents.

"Your mother is up to her old tricks," Hugo said as he wheeled himself closer to his son and then made a dismissive wave with his hand. "It was somehow my fault that the toast got cold and then she was off and running on her tirade. I never provided enough for her. We're reduced to taking marching orders from our son who is locking us into an apartment so we can rot. Her life has been meaningless."

"To which you replied?"

"She's right. With no one to blame but herself."

"Lovely."

"This time she swears she's going to stay away until she dies so she never has to look at my sour face again. Direct quote. Reminds me of the old days."

Jules's brow furrowed, annoyed at his mother's harsh words and at having to endure his parents' theatrics yet again. While her behavior hadn't been better, at least Agathe hadn't been running away from her family the past few years. Whatever the mental process was that triggered her need to escape, with the help of Jules's money, she'd been dragging Hugo along with her. But now her old habits had reared up again, skyrocketing Jules's emotions right back to the old days.

It seemed perfectly fitting that because he'd let Durand Properties make it for half the morning without him, something he so seldom did, and he was getting genuine pleasure from a bubble bath and buttery Parisian pastries with Zoe, that his parents would ruin it for him.

"We'll have to get a nurse in to help you for the time being," Jules voiced as his mind began to spin.

"Don't be ridiculous," Hugo protested. "I don't need looking after like an invalid."

But Jules was already firing off a text to Karim to contact an agency that could find someone suitable. Taking swift action to solve a problem without any sort of debate was what had kept him from falling apart as a child, as a teenager and as an adult. It was his salvation.

No amount of order could make things right with Zoe, though. All the realizations he thought he'd come to this morning quickly burned up in smoke as if they were tossed into a bonfire. What on earth had he been thinking? That happy-in-spite-of-everything nonsense he'd begun believing was just an escape. No one, no woman he'd ever met, not even Zoe, could convince him that partnering with someone wouldn't lead to disappointment, betrayal and despair.

It was pure poppycock that humans were made to share their place in the world with someone. Quite the opposite. The safer a distance a man kept from others and their distortions, the more likely he was to fully develop himself, to find his own way and not be swayed by the needs and limitations of someone else.

Jules saw himself in his father's sneering face. They were survivors, by whatever means necessary. That much they shared in common regardless of their opposite paths. Hugo chose to be alone within a marriage. Jules wouldn't even go that far. Neither should waste time and energy dwelling on how things might be better.

Agathe must have panicked. He'd overestimated her ability to appreciate the stability he was offering. Stronger measures were necessary. For their safety. Jules was the responsible party. He couldn't take a chance that his mother would wander off without him knowing her whereabouts. He would bring in a social worker to administrate and supervise physical and mental evaluations. Bring in round-the-clock care if that's what was called for. Their situation was too much for him to manage on his own. Just like with his properties, he needed a professional team. Organization and logic would prevail, as they always had.

For now, it would be simple enough to get his mother to return this time because, without money, she wouldn't last long even if she did impose herself on some distant cousin for a few days like she used to. After that, he'd bring in a squad.

Jules knew what else he needed to do.

After he'd heard through his mother's phone the train conductor calling passengers for boarding, the desperation in Agathe's voice took Jules back to his childhood. Memories marched along his brain like ticker tape. He replayed all his mother's departure walks down the street outside of their apartment building. How young Jules would stick his head out the window to watch her. He'd rest his arms on the rotted wood of the windowsill that always left scratches on his arms. Agathe's dress or coat might be different from one season to the next, but there was always the olive-colored suitcase.

The rattle of its wheels on the sidewalk was a sound he would never forget.

Before Agathe's call, for a fleeting moment in the bathtub with Zoe, he'd supposed that he could let go of all of that. Convinced Zoe's optimism had changed him. But it turns out, that was as temporary as the bath bubbles that had coated her luscious body.

Because Agathe leaving again had emotionally exhausted him. It was the last straw. He needed to put his armor back on. He wasn't capable of such a big shift as what being with Zoe would bring. It was too late for him. He was actually fragile. Feelings had no place in his world. Shutting down was the only way he could exist. That was what he knew, his lifeline, and he couldn't surrender it. That part of him had to be selfish. The wise part, the overseer, couldn't let him pile on any more disappointment. He was done. What if he put his trust in Zoe and she left him? He wouldn't survive the loss.

Or what if he was the one to leave? After all, as much as he could intellectualize about what had happened to him as a child, it was a fact that history sometimes did repeat itself. Despite his best intentions, maybe he wouldn't be able to go the distance in a long-term relationship with her. He couldn't bear the idea of her hearing *his* suitcase teeter away. Of her poking her head out the window to watch him desert her. He couldn't bear the hurt that his leaving her would cause. He'd had no example on how to do relationships right. Certainly, he'd get it wrong. He loved Zoe too much to take a chance on breaking her heart.

He *what*?

Love. How had that word escaped from the far recesses of his psyche? It wasn't even a word he used often. Was he *in love* with Zoe? Presumably, if a person was in love, they'd do everything in their power to shield their beloved from harm. To not only cherish but to protect. Logically, then, Jules himself was the potential harm to Zoe. Therefore, if he was in love with her, he should safeguard her from him. As a matter of fact, love obligated him to. Yes, he loved beautiful, sexy, talented Zoe Gaiman. So the most important thing he could do, the best way he could demonstrate his love, was to get out of her life.

His mission was clear.

When he'd left her earlier, inviting her to stay in the bath as long as she wanted and let herself out, they agreed to meet later at the apartment to supervise the furniture placement. At this point, perhaps it was going to be his father and a caretaker moving in, but nonetheless the renovation was coming to a close.

The front door was ajar when Jules arrived at the apartment, allowing him to see Zoe arranging some decorative items on the teakwood dining table that had arrived. The light streaming in through the windows added a golden halo to her natural radiance. His stomach clenched at the reminiscence of her satiny lips and of the responsive body that had arched for him over and over during their lovemaking. At the closeness that had formed without him being consciously aware of it, the secrets shared, the compassion for each other, the silly differences between them in the beginning so superficial now.

He'd allowed those forbidden daydreams he'd been having to crystalize into sharp focus for a split second. Them as a couple. His home as theirs. A kiss on the nose. Dancing by candlelight. Sharing an apple.

To have and to hold.

One last look at her through those rose-tinted glasses. Then he had to put a stop to his visions or they might kill him. In that respect, he *had* changed since childhood. Now he knew how to slay dragons, how to decimate obstacles that threatened him. Yes, that was it—love was an obstacle to freedom.

Zoe turned around as Jules entered the living room. "Oh. Hi. I didn't hear you come in."

"Did everything get delivered?"

"Si is doing a modification on the sofa sectional for me. Everything else came."

"Good."

"What's wrong?"

When Jules had abruptly raised himself out of the bathtub where they had been sharing a little slice of heaven a few hours ago, he hadn't explained about his mother's call from the Gare du Nord. While he'd shared quite a bit with Zoe about his past, he wasn't certain how much he should include her in any current matters. Now that he'd recognized what he needed to do, he was glad for that defensive decision.

Obviously, she was able to tell that something wasn't right. He moved nearer to her, though not too close, figuring it was better for him to say what needed to be said if he wasn't touching that honeyed skin he'd been caressing for hours last night after the opera.

"You know," he began, "we've never discussed any ongoing professional relationship after this project finished."

Zoe blinked a couple of times, sensing that the coming news was not good. "Ongoing professional relationship," she rasped the words he'd just spoken.

"I think you're a wonderful designer," he said, gesturing across the apartment. "It turns out all of your instincts were spot on after all, no matter how much I teased you about your methods."

"But…" She squinted.

Jules's lungs couldn't inhale a full breath. What he was about to say would alter the course of both of their lives forever. Compelled, but without the certainty he usually relied on for decisions, he carried on.

"What I'd like to do is connect you with some of the property developers I know here in Paris, who will hire you based on my recommendation. Smart and reliable designers are always in demand."

She nodded in comprehension, sweeping away some curls that had fallen forward. "So you're saying you wouldn't want to work with me again?"

Jules took a step forward but then forced his legs to stay put. Throwing his arms around her was the *wrong* thing to do in this moment. Yet, he couldn't stop fighting with himself about it.

"Zoe, I'm so sorry." *I love you.* "But I know myself well enough that I can't work with you again professionally because I can't see you anymore personally."

She jutted out her chin, choking back emotion. The entire set of her face changed, became drawn. "Oh, were we *seeing* each other?"

"Whatever it is we want to call it. To be perfectly honest, these weeks with you, making love, the Luxembourg Gardens, the opera, made me wonder for the first time in my life if I might be able to open up to a committed union with someone."

"And that someone isn't me."

"No." His Adam's apple pulsed. Frustration wasn't

allowing him to even say what he wanted to. "It is you. I've never felt anything for anyone like what I feel for you. That's the problem."

"I don't understand."

"I've never seen a healthy relationship in action. I wouldn't know what that looked like, how to do it. I'd ruin it. I'd never be capable of trusting someone or letting them put their trust in me. I'm better off as a ship that passes in the night."

"That's right, your three nautical voyages rule. I think with the opera we made it to four."

"You're angry. I'm so very sorry." *I love you.* "You've given me a taste of romance and enchantment. It was a divine state of being. But that's not for me, and never will be." He loathed rejecting her, the very person he'd most like to cherish until his dying day. Hated the words coming out of his mouth, even if they were the truth. For her and for him. His mind knew what his heart didn't want to accept.

Zoe composed herself. She was a survivor, too. He'd see to it that opportunities as a designer would come her way. He'd influence her future to the extent that he could from afar.

"We knew at the beginning that neither of us were intending to enter into anything serious," she stated bravely. "That was something we had in common."

After the loss of her parents, the risk of caring about someone and being cared for was great for her. She'd go it alone, too. Although her face said otherwise. Her eyes couldn't disguise the anguish.

With the weight of the world bearing down on him, Jules said, "I'll treasure this time together for the rest of my life."

Half of her mouth managed a hitch of a bittersweet smile. "Right. We'll always have Paris."

While she hadn't seen Jules enter the apartment a few minutes ago, Zoe surely watched him leave. As he walked out the door, the sight of the back of his head with the sharp swath of his dark thick hair and his slim frame in his pinstripe suit was unbearable in its perfection. She felt that her heart was attached to him and being stretched like a cord that would only go so far and then it would fray and disintegrate. Which it did when he disappeared out of view and she could finally let the tears flow.

After telling her that they'd no longer have a personal or professional relationship now that the work was done, he'd done a quick inspection of the completed apartment and then said he had another appointment. Zoe didn't know if that was true or that he just needed to get away from her. Which she could understand. He was clearly upset and conflicted—it wasn't as if he regarded calling things off with her lightly.

Her eyes couldn't turn away from the open front door as she wiped tear after tear from her eyes with the back of her hand. Even though she was in agreement with him that there was no future scenario that saw them together, the piece of her that had allowed visualizations of a different outcome stung and burned. It proved the point exactly, that Zoe didn't need any more pain, which would only have grown worse if the inevitable came after she'd become even more invested in Jules.

Once every fiber in her being was certain that he wasn't coming back to tell her, like he had at the opera, that he'd made another huge mistake, she pivoted in slow motion to take in the totality of the apartment. Without the strict budget that the clients she'd worked for back in Maupont were bound by, this apartment was Zoe's best career achievement so far. The practicality and accessibility, combined with the furnishings and appointments that announced style, had all come together whether Jules's parents would appreciate them or not.

She had the presence of mind to photograph the apartment for her portfolio. Jules had promised to act as liaison for her to get other design work in Paris, and for that she'd be forever grateful.

In the master bedroom, she'd talked Jules out of the rug he wanted because she was concerned that it was hard to maneuver over with the wheelchair. The bed was cool and inviting with baby blue and white linens. Twin nightstands held lamps and charging stations for electronics, with room for books or drinks. Gauzy curtains flanked the windows, and black-and-white seascape photographs adorned the sidewall. She'd had the wing-backed chairs returned to the shop she and Jules had bought them from, deciding instead on an upholstered bench from Si that would be easy for Hugo to use. There was plenty of passage space everywhere in the room.

Tears still streaming down her face, she snapped pictures of the second bedroom, which had been multipurposed nicely with a daybed that functioned as an extra sofa at an easy height for Hugo if he wanted it for afternoon naps or perhaps to enjoy the state-of-the-art television setup. Or if, in reality, the time came that he'd need a caretaker to spend the night. The long table underneath the picture window could be used for projects or as a desk, without the obstruction of drawers underneath.

The compromise about the kitchen that she and Jules had argued about worked perfectly, simple and clean cabinets painted off-white but with the yellow stone backsplash he'd wanted for a homey touch. Stacks of luxurious towels, storage shelves and artwork finished the bathroom. End tables place-marked where the sofa would fit into a corner in the living room, Jules having promised to send Zoe a photo when it came in.

Room by room, Zoe documented her accomplishments, exhaling loudly with no one to hear her, letting the tears continue to flow as they saw fit. When she was finished, she used the key codes to lock up, knowing this would be her last visit here. On the street, she walked toward the metro station, although not exactly sure of her destination. She didn't want to go home to an empty apartment, and Yasmine was at work at Si's studio.

Zoe descended the station stairs and decided where to go, though only halfway admitting it to herself. On the train, all the seats were taken so she grabbed onto one of the poles to anchor herself. From that position, she observed the fellow passengers surrounding her. That marvelous mix that was Paris, with people of every race, color, belief, orientation, size, age, homeland. Tourists, students, workers, families. Everybody headed somewhere. Stories to be told all around her.

Slitting her eyes to make her spying less obvious, she watched a young couple. The skinny man inked with tattoos up and down his arms held his dark-skinned gal from behind, pressing into her in a very sexual way, leaving no space between their bodies. She leaned her head back against his chest, a glazed-eyed bliss on her face. He whispered something into her ear that made her smile.

A city for lovers.

Zoe had been part of that folklore, ever so briefly. At the breathtaking loggia of the opera house. In the fine clothes and the diamond earrings Jules had bought her. Where her temporary lover kissed her without reserve and told her how much he wanted her in his bed again. How she'd floated up to the chandelier and Chagall ceiling after that, in an opaque trance for the rest of the performance while Jules maintained physical contact. At first, he'd held her hand, the pad of his thumb rhythmically caressing her skin. Later, he put his arm around her shoulder and held her there, the backs of his fingers stroking her neck.

In memory, what started on the loggia was one long embrace that lasted all night long, until they reveled in the morning's bubble bath. Zoe didn't know it at the time, but Jules's phone ringing signaled the alarm that would end the dream.

What would be the fate of the sexy couple Zoe eyed on the train? Happy forever or split by the weekend? Circumstances, wounds, fear, jealousy, fate, destiny. There were so many variables.

She exited at the station and trudged toward her destination. She entered the Luxembourg Gardens to wander around the perimeter of the café where she and Jules had been a pair of those Parisian lovers. Where they talked and laughed. Where she stuffed his face with a warm crepe and gooey pastries. She wouldn't have cared if they'd drunk plain water, as long as she was with him. The most amazing man she'd ever met.

A man of great intelligence and even greater character. Who awakened in her a primordial and grounded femininity that hadn't been unearthed before. Jules made her ping, made her second-guess her commitment to self-protection regardless of the cost. No one, nothing, would ever move her like he had. At least she hoped not.

When her phone rang as she wandered the gardens, she had a minute's hope that it was Jules until the screen identified a number she didn't recognize.

"Hello."

"Is this Zoe Gaiman?"

"Yes."

"This is Dr. Tran at Hospital Sainte-Térèse."

"Yes." Zoe's breath quickened. This couldn't be good.

"Yasmine Jaziri named you as her emergency contact."

"What happened?"

"Yasmine has been admitted into the hospital for observation. She collapsed at her workplace."

"I'll be right there."

CHAPTER NINE

Zᴏᴇ ᴄᴏᴜʟᴅ ʜᴇᴀʀ the clack of her own shoes as she rushed down the hospital corridor. She wasn't used to the sounds and the smells. Equipment in every direction blipped, dinged and beeped. There was an aroma of cleaning products that, no doubt, were responsible for the sterile whiteness of the hallways and floors.

"Yasmine Jaziri," she asked when she reached the nurses' station after following the instructions the doctor had given her over the phone. She'd left her session of disheartened reminiscing about Jules at the Luxembourg Gardens. As soon as she'd gotten the word about her roommate, she called for a rideshare, not wanting to spend time getting to the hospital on the metro.

Locating the room number the nurse gave her, Zoe poked her head in first, in case Yasmine was being attended to and needed privacy. Seeing that she was alone and asleep, Zoe tiptoed in so as not to wake her and sat down beside her bed in the visitor chair.

It was shocking to see Yasmine hooked up to tubes and wires. Some led to monitoring equipment. Zoe knew enough to note that her roommate's blood pressure and heart rate were stable, obviously a good sign. An intravenous line led to bags of fluids and medications. Yasmine seemed to be breathing normally while she slept. Although her dark complexion was more ashen than Zoe had ever seen it and her lips looked dry and chapped.

Time idled while she waited for Yasmine to wake up or for a doctor to enter with information. Zoe scanned everything in the room from an interior designer's point of view. It was drab but certainly functional, with a wall of built-in cabinets and drawers to organize supplies. Colorful geometric-patterned curtains tried to add some cheer as they flanked the one window. The view was of another building on the hospital's campus but it did allow in desperately needed natural light, as the overhead fixtures gave off a harsh illumination. Zoe thought she might go crazy from listening to the endless buzzing of equipment. Hospitals were not the most pleasant places.

"Well, hello there," Zoe said softly when Yasmine moved her head and slowly flickered open her eyes.

"Zoe," she scratched out, her throat obviously parched.

The bedside tray held a cup of water with a straw. "Are you allowed to drink anything?

"Yes, the nurse brought that before…before I fell asleep, I guess. My memory is a little fuzzy."

Zoe picked up the water and handed it to Yasmine, making sure the straw was close to her mouth and that she had a firm grasp on the cup.

"What happened?" The doctor on the phone said that Yasmine had collapsed but he hadn't had any further details.

After she took a few sips of the water, Yasmine handed the cup back to Zoe who returned it to the tray.

"One minute I was reaching for something on a high shelf and the next I was on the ground surrounded by the emergency medical responders Si had called for."

"Mademoiselle Jaziri, you lost consciousness," a low baritone joined the conversation as a man in a lab coat entered. "I am the attending physician, Dr. Tran."

He turned to Zoe. "You are a family member?"

"No, I'm Yasmine's roommate. Her family are all in Tunisia."

"Doctor…" Yasmine cleared her throat "…what is wrong with me?"

"It appears to have been severe dehydration. Everything looks okay but we'll need to do some more testing to see if there's an underlying condition and to make sure you didn't sustain any injuries when you fell."

"Oh, my gosh, what kind of injuries?"

"It's unlikely there are any based on the examinations and your present condition, but we'll want to do some brain imaging as a standard precaution."

Yasmine's eyes became wide as saucers. Zoe knew she was terrified and reached over to hold her hand. It was cold to the touch.

"I'll be back shortly and we'll get these assessments started as soon as we can. I really don't expect we'll find anything of concern, although we'll err on the side of caution."

"Thank you, Doctor," Yasmine managed as he left the room.

While the situation was serious, Zoe had long accepted that life was full of surprises. A young woman reaching up for something at work wasn't likely to crumple to the ground and need medical assistance. A hardworking couple going on a short holiday in Milan wasn't likely to be killed when a train ran off its track. Stuff happened.

Case in point, that in spite of the devastation Zoe had gone through after her parents' deaths that left her certain she'd never get close to anyone ever again, Jules Durand had happened. And it had shown her a prospect where two people did believe that they could be there for one another through thick and thin. Or were at least willing to give it a try and get by on hope.

Good fortune had actually graced Zoe. Jules called things off between them sooner rather than later. Any more days or nights she might have spent with him would have compounded the already heavy hurt she was towing like a ball and chain. Instead, at least now it was over and done. She didn't have to wait for the sneaky, inevitable stab to the chest. It had already come.

Alone she had decided to be. Alone she was. Everything was according to plan.

"That was a pretty good report from the doctor overall. How did you get so dehydrated, anyway? You did look a little bit off when I saw you at the studio."

"I got busy. I forgot to drink anything. Now that I think about it, it's been that way all week. I get involved in what I'm doing and I don't stop for breaks or lunch."

"That would never happen to me." Zoe smiled to cheer her up. "I eat all the time."

"With the hot billionaire?"

"Not anymore. That's old news."

"What? After the earrings? And the opera?"

Zoe touched one of the two diamonds that hadn't left her ears since Jules had placed them there. "My Parisian affair. That's all it was."

She'd known Yasmine for a year and while they co-existed peacefully as roommates, they weren't best friends. Zoe didn't have best friends. She was on her own in Paris, just as Yasmine was. Young women in a huge city, trying to forge a life for themselves but with no one watching their backs.

Yasmine's eyelids struggled to stay open.

"You should get some rest."

"Will you call my parents and tell them where I am? They're going to be so worried."

"I will."

Needless to say, Yasmine's mother was terribly distraught when Zoe explained the situation. With family and work obligations, neither of Yasmine's parents could immediately leave Tunisia for Paris to be by her side. Zoe promised to call her every time there was anything to report from the hospital. With audible tears, Yasmine's mother said that her daughter needed to move back to Bizerte, that this was the exact type of incident to prove that Paris was too far from home.

Zoe knew that a mother's love was talking rather than a voice of reason. But there was something to what she said, which directly related to the thoughts Zoe was starting to have. She sat back in the visitor's chair and propped her legs up on a corner of the bed while Yasmine slept. She was feeling rather tired herself.

Her fingers twisted one of the earrings. What Zoe had been mulling over was that maybe she should return home. To Maupont, to her siblings. Even though Jules had promised to act as liaison and find her more work, her brief time with him had only served to shed light on how lonely she really was. As much as she tried to outwardly present the idea that she didn't want or need anyone but herself, the lack of connections stared her in the face in this most social of cities. She no longer believed her own lies about choosing to go it by herself.

Boring Maupont. Designing the odd room renovation or workspace. But at least she'd have her brothers. They hadn't felt the ping in their chests, cautioning them not to get too close, not to feel. No warning alarm held them back. Two were married and she liked their wives. Perhaps they'd have children soon. That was something to look forward to. Fate might take any of them from her, but they'd have each other to rely on. She'd never be quite so solitary as she was now.

And as much as she loved Paris, she feared every building, every flower, every croissant would remind her of what she didn't get to have with Jules.

She leaned her head back and her eyelids grew heavy as, amidst the unfamiliar hospital drone, she allowed herself to drift off to sleep.

"I most certainly will not send you money. I've booked you a train ticket back to Paris yet again," Jules had scolded his mother, "and I expect you to use it."

With no options Agathe had, in fact, returned to the city. Jules had a driver pick her up at the train station and shuttle her to what was to be her new home. He and his father joined her there. Hugo greeted his wife with, "You again? I thought you promised never to return."

"This has got to stop!" Jules yelled. "Since you've been financially irresponsible for your entire lives and have no assets saved for your senior years, you are dependent on me. So you will live by my rules. Resent it or not, you've turned me into the parent. It should hardly be a horrible sacrifice to live in this apartment."

"Don't talk to us like we're children," Agathe tossed back with a snub of her nose.

"Yet, that's exactly how you behave."

"You wouldn't be the success you are if it weren't for us."

"You mean in spite of you."

"Don't talk that way to your mother," a gruff Hugo bellowed.

"Oh, have we found something you two agree on? That's a first." Jules frowned, finding himself unable to employ any self-censorship. This endless cycle with his parents was intolerable, and that wasn't all that was bothering him. "I introduced you to the interior designer who did the apartment. Both of Zoe's parents died in a train derailment."

Agathe blinked. "How awful."

"Yes, it's unimaginable. Life is fleeting. I can't understand why the two of you have chosen to live yours in constant opposition with each other."

"Your mother hates me because…"

"Enough excuses," Jules barked, cutting his father off. He'd had it and needed to fully express himself, to finally give voice to what he'd never said aloud to them. "Have either of you ever stopped to think what effect your constant fighting had on me, your only child? What it was like to have your mother leave with a suitcase over and over again, vowing never to return, even though she always did? And a father who couldn't keep a job because he was too stubborn to follow instructions and obey rules?"

A hush fell around them. His words were sinking in, both to himself and to them. It was liberating. To let out what he'd held inside. The words seemed to shock all three of them. After a lull, he found a calmer but pained voice, "Look at me. Really look at me. Beyond the professional success. Your son. Your child." He wanted to scream. For the boy who endured what he had. For the man who was crippled by the damage. "The atmosphere I grew up in of conflict, abandonment and uncertainty has left me unable to form relationships. I don't even have close friends. I've shut down any thoughts of marrying. Or having children. And I've only recently understood how much that has cost me."

Hugo and Agathe looked at each other, genuinely moved by their son's lament.

"I suppose we were too mired in our own strife to notice its impact on you," Hugo admitted.

Agathe shook her head as if she were just coming to a realization herself. "I was a horrible mother."

She was, and Jules was not going to assuage her with a denial. "What's done is done. But this has got to end. Because the craziest thing of it is that deep down you do care for each other. Why else would you, Mother, have always returned home when you left? And you, Father, always took her back? You could have split up. I'd hardly have been the first child whose parents had divorced. Yet, you didn't. And after I grew up, despite your bickering, you've roamed the world together."

"At your expense."

"That's not what matters. Life expectancies have gotten very long," Jules replied, "and even with father's physical limitations, you two could have several wonderful decades together. *We* could."

"What do you say, you nutty old bag?" Hugo threw a guffaw to his wife. "I suppose I must like you a little."

"All right, you good-for-nothing sod," Agathe answered back. "I might actually love you a little. No more drama."

"Let's not ask for the stars," Hugo snickered.

He wheeled his chair over to her and tugged on her arm until she leaned down for him to plant a kiss on her cheek.

Jules swallowed hard at the sight—he couldn't remember the last time he'd seen anything similar.

"You and Zoe did do a lovely job on this apartment," Agathe admitted.

"I know I've probably never said it, son," Hugo acknowledged, "but we're very proud of you." In fact, those weren't words he'd ever heard from his father. And for all of Jules's self-sufficiency, they meant a lot.

"Zoe and you?" Agathe inquired. "There's something between you that's more than just business, isn't there?"

How could his mother have intuited that during the short time they'd spent together at his hotel, when Agathe had been on particularly bad behavior? Was the bond between Jules and Zoe that obvious? Although it was almost impossible to say out loud words he didn't believe, he spat, "There was. There isn't anymore. How did you guess?"

"I can see it in your eyes. A mother knows." All three of them smirked at Agathe's comment as she was, obviously, anything but a typical mother. "I don't think you want to let her slip away."

After he left his parents to acquaint themselves with their new apartment, he got into the waiting car and picked up his phone. He remembered a school professor who'd said that one of the signs of a good leader was someone who would admit when they'd made a mistake. Jules had made the biggest one of his life. Even his mother could see it.

It was time to right the wrong. Witnessing his parents conceding to a reconciliation had moved him greatly. Gave him a new hope. Made him realize he was forever changed. He had a fresh distinction now. He was, and always would be, a man who had loved someone. Did love someone. And his mother was correct. The last thing he should do is turn his back on that precious gift of love. Yes, life came without guarantees. Yes, somebody with no experience in something was bound to stumble.

And yes, one could never be happy unless one followed his or her heart.

Jules's heart was walking around Paris on two curvaceous legs with a remarkable tangle of orange curls on its head. He needed to go claim that heart before it was gone and never to be found again.

When he tapped in the number to his heart's phone, the call switched directly to voice mail. What he had to say was too important to leave on a message. He did ask her to return his call as soon as possible. That it was urgent. He texted the same words and then instructed his driver where to take him.

Jules repeatedly rang the doorbell to Zoe's apartment. There was no response. He knew she wasn't at his parents' apartment, because he'd just left there. There was nothing else that needed to be purchased so she wasn't shopping for any finishing touches. Could she be out on a date? With a man, one who didn't put up barriers?

No, Jules assured himself. Zoe had been as adamant as he was that she would avoid the potential damage of love. He doubted she'd be out with a romantic interest so soon after he'd wounded her. She still might not be open to reconsidering her own rules. She'd been just like him in that respect. But the situation had changed. He'd have some convincing to do. That was okay. Whatever it took.

Not knowing what to do with himself, he went to a sports shop and bought two top-of-the-line bicycles for Zoe and Yasmine, and had them put in his car. He then had his driver return to Zoe's block. Perhaps she'd come home soon. He finished a sparkling water at a café before surrendering and going home. It wasn't until late that night when Zoe called and explained about Yasmine.

"Can I come to the hospital?"

"It's too late for visitors."

"Tomorrow, then."

"Let's wait and see."

Zoe woke up disoriented. Her phone buzzed in her pocket, but she let it go to voice mail. With eyes still closed, a backache reminded her that she'd been sleeping in a chair all night. She was still at the hospital. Although when her eyelids blinked open, she saw that neither Yasmine nor her bed were in the room with her. Zoe's mind whirled, imagining the worst, just as the hospital attendants wheeled Yasmine back into the room. She was sitting up in the bed and had a healthier color to her face.

"They took me downstairs for the brain imaging," Yasmine told Zoe. "I didn't want to wake you when I was wheeled out."

"Do we know anything?"

"No, but the doctor said he'll put a rush on getting the results. He thinks everything will be fine and that if I'm stable I can go home tomorrow."

Zoe stood to stretch. She felt like a twisted pretzel. And she was exhausted. While she'd managed to sleep here and there, she'd woken up many times during the night to the strangeness of the hospital. Darkness had finally opened into dawn. "If it's okay with you, I'm going to get some breakfast."

"You should. Thanks so much for staying with me."

"I'll be back in a little while."

Zoe forced her body into a fully upright posture and exited the room. Walking down the hospital corridor, she recalled the jumble of thoughts she'd had during the long night.

When her parents died, Zoe thought she'd never get over her grief. A black cloud blocked her from the sunlight for months after the accident. Their absence blinded her from seeing any goodness. The pain held her down, trying to strangle her.

That's when it all became certain. When she came to rely on the pings. In case she started to forget, the internal warning would remind her that she'd never let anyone close ever again. While two of her brothers went on to marry, and the other had a steady boyfriend, Zoe couldn't follow that path. Her heart was too soft. The risk was too high. In making her way to Paris, she'd vowed to throw herself into creativity and not people. She'd immunized herself like a vaccination would, preventing love from seeping into her bloodstream.

Over eggs and juice, Zoe was aware of the beeping in her pocket again. A glance at the phone screen told her not only that it was Jules but that she'd missed three of his calls. Why had he initially called yesterday? Something about the apartment, no doubt. Having briefed him last night about Yasmine, these morning calls were probably out of concern.

When she rang, he sounded relieved to hear the doctor's expected prognosis. "May I stop by?"

She didn't want him to come. Or did she? Jules wasn't part of Yasmine's life. He wasn't even part of hers anymore. He'd made a clean break with Zoe, and Yasmine's hospitalization didn't change that. She'd be better off continuing to practice being on her own, experiencing life's ups and downs such as roommates being in the hospital. "I don't think you should."

On the other hand, why wouldn't she want him to come? She didn't have many friends in Paris. Hospitals were big scary places. Why wouldn't someone want to have an ally, or even just a familiar face? How distorted her view of relationships had become. When she got back to Maupont, she'd put some genuine effort into finding a few girlfriends to pal around with, maybe university mates she'd lost touch with.

Solitude suddenly washed over her like an ocean's wave.

Jules said, "I'd like to see the both of you."

Zoe had a moment to protest. She didn't take it.

Zoe was back in Yasmine's room when Jules stepped into the doorway. A sight for sore eyes to be sure, he held a beautiful arrangement of yellow flowers in a glass vase. "May I come in?"

"Of course," Yasmine answered, shooting a knowing look in Zoe's direction.

"These are for you." He placed the flowers down on the stand beside Yasmine's bed.

"They're so pretty. Thank you."

They conversed a bit until Yasmine's eyelids began to flutter. Jules took the cue. He stood at her bedside. "Assuming you're going home tomorrow, can I give you a ride?" He knew that Zoe and Yasmine were alone in Paris, with no family, and he thought of a way he could be useful. That was one of the many things Zoe lo…

"That would be wonderful. Thank you," Yasmine said as her eyes fell shut.

"Step into the hallway for a minute with me?" he asked Zoe, who was on the other side of the bed. She nodded, although apprehension bounced in her stomach.

"What were you calling about last night?" Zoe wasted no time once they'd left the room. To be with Jules in the antiseptic surroundings of the hospital was unnatural. Wrong. And it almost angered her. This was a place for families, for significant others, for lifelong relationships. Where people died or were healed or brought babies into the world. It wasn't a place for Parisian bosses and the underlings they'd had affairs with to chat.

He made contact with her pupils and followed them when they tried to move away. "Do you remember when we went to the opera and I told you I wanted a do-over?"

"Yes."

"I need an even bigger one this time. I've made another horrible error. And I'm here to correct it." He wrapped his hand around her small shoulder, his warmth instantly radiating through his palm into her. "I want to be with you, Zoe. I don't know what I'm doing and I'm bound to take dozens of wrong turns but I love you. And we're going to be together."

Overwhelm had her feeling dizzy. She'd spent the wee hours of the night making sense of his breakup, re-affirming her aloneness. He'd been crystal clear, know-ing himself, stating his mind. Now he'd changed it and she was just supposed to jump in? Her internal ping sig-naled so loud and fast she was sure the nurses in another ward were going to confuse it with medical equipment.

"I can't, Jules. You helped me realize that. I'm not good for anyone."

"You're good for me! Just when I was sure I'd be alone forever, something I wouldn't have predicted in a million years occurred. You. You fell, literally, into my life," he teased her about her first impression, "and you destroyed my ordered world with its rule books and protocols. You've shown me that our hearts can be free. And limitless."

When he'd told her at the apartment that he didn't want to see her anymore professionally or personally, that was news she hadn't thought she could move past. Instead, it was this, the opposite, that was even harder. To turn away from what half of her admitted she so desperately wanted. Yet, she had to. She was the only one there to protect her. Zoe had to be her own knight in shining armor.

"I'm sorry. I can't."

After they stood in the corridor staring silently at each other for as long as they could take, Zoe granted Jules's request to return to the hospital the next day to take Yasmine home. She couldn't deny him that.

"Tomorrow, then."

Time passed with Yasmine undergoing many exams

and tests, and the two roommates making the best of hospital television programming. The nurses were kind enough to give Zoe soap and towels so that she could shower, as she didn't want to go home and leave Yasmine alone at the hospital.

During the artificially lit hours of the night, Yasmine slept peacefully while Zoe's mind whirled. Even though she might have wished for Jules's return, she hadn't been expecting it. Forcing her to face her demons yet again, to reconsider what was real and what she was hanging onto simply because it had become familiar. After endless cups of tea from the kind nurses, and after running down her phone's battery wasting time on the internet looking at furniture, Zoe decided to take a little walk around the hospital ward.

She was used to the blinking lights and identifying sounds by now. There was very little other noises beside a faint and constant buzz. Visiting hours were long since over. A custodian mopped the floor. Someone else restocked bedding onto a cart. Zoe didn't mean to snoop but she glanced into a couple of patients' rooms as she passed them by. A very elderly man, tiny and frail, breathed with the help of an oxygen mask on his face. In the next, a much younger man had bandages on his head. Had he undergone surgery, she wondered? Or had he fallen? Had he been in an accident? Was he the victim of a crime? Her brow furrowed in concern. He couldn't have been much older than twenty.

How unknowable the universe was! Look what had happened even just in her orbit. Yasmine's spell of dehydration could have made her collapse while crossing a street, where she might have been hit by a car, or could have broken her legs or sustained brain damage that left her unable to walk or talk. Zoe's parents might have traveled safely to Milan and be home in Maupont right now. Every moment of existence was a treasurable gift that needed to be treated as such and never taken for granted.

And Zoe finally couldn't deny that however many days and nights she had left on this earth, she wanted more than anything to spend them with Jules. With him, the world could be complete and full and she could belong. She knew that she'd helped him find a little whimsy and delight from within the seriousness of his life, the fallout of his past. But he probably didn't know how much he'd given her, besides just a job.

Without intending to, he made her feel connected to him and part of something larger than herself, something that mattered and was worth having at any cost. Together, they were an interdependent entity. He taught her that planning for the future wasn't to be feared, that it could be a positive thing. His commitment to his parents in spite of what they put him through moved her. In his arms, she'd learned about a joining of souls and bodies far beyond what she'd ever known was possible. And she wanted to keep experiencing that merge for eternity. They sometimes had opposite ways of looking at things but like yin and yang, Jules and Zoe fit together as a whole.

She would never get over the grief of her parents' untimely deaths. Nor should she. Grief was a measure of her love for them. The grief could be welcomed. It could be cherished. And most importantly, Zoe needed to stop using it as an obstacle.

She was in love with Jules Durand. And she needed

to tell him so as soon as possible. Hopefully, it wasn't too late.

Dawn couldn't come fast enough.

With morning cheer, she phoned to let Jules know that Yasmine was being discharged. "Everything is okay. She can go home."

"That's wonderful. I'll be right there."

After he arrived and while Yasmine was collecting her personal belongings to leave, Zoe took Jules's hand to pull him aside. The smile that lit up his eyes told her that nothing had been jeopardized, nothing would ever be too late. She caressed the back of his hand with her thumb. "This time it's me who needs a do-over."

He began nodding excitedly. "Yes. Yes, my love. I think we've got a lot to work through between us. We're going to make many mistakes. Need many do-overs."

"We'll get through them."

"Does Yasmine take good care of herself as a rule? Does she eat plenty of vegetables and take vitamins?"

"I think so. Nice of you to inquire." Zoe's health-conscious man. Was her future going to include icky green drinks and early morning runs? That was okay if that's what he wanted. As long as there were pajama days and plenty of cheese, too. She'd hope to live a long and balanced life. With Jules.

"I'm asking because I want to make sure she'll be okay on her own."

"What do you mean?"

"I was thinking that perhaps she could move into one of my properties."

"Why? Where will I live?"

"I want you to move in with me. And marry me. And be by my side for the rest of our days. Will you do that?"

"I will." The cautioning ping in her gut almost tore her open. That was another thing she'd have to walk with, to accept. She could do it. As long as she was with him. "I love you, too, and I want to be with you forever." Zoe threw her arms around Jules with a force that knocked even him off-kilter. Something she was very good at.

* * * * *

HER SAVANNAH
SURPRISE

NANCY ROBARDS THOMPSON

This book is dedicated to my husband, Michael, because of you, I am living my dream. I love you.

Also to Susan Gorman for our shared love of corgis. Thank you for helping me name Zelda's corgi, Bear.

Chapter One

The only thing worse than the morning-after walk of shame was waking up married in Las Vegas and not remembering how it happened.

Kate Clark's left thumb found her ring finger. The presence of the cold metal band that Aidan Quindlin, her on-again-off-again sweetheart since high school, had presumably slid into place last night sent her ducking into fetal position as she made herself small under the soft white cotton sheet. Because maybe if she made herself tiny enough, she would disappear before Aidan, who was sleeping soundly next to her, woke up.

Kate's whole family had gathered in Vegas for

a weeklong celebration of her grandmother Gigi's marriage to her longtime love, Charles Weathersby. It had been a fun party, with delicious food and free-flowing drinks.

Kate had not gotten drunk. She couldn't have been. She had only had a couple of sips of Love Potion Number Nine, the signature cocktail of the Weathersby wedding reception. Granted, Kate had never been much of a drinker. The so-called Love Potion had been a sickeningly sweet concoction that tasted like a mix of grape juice, cough medicine and toilet bowl cleaner. Not that she had ever tasted toilet bowl cleaner, but she could imagine.

The drink had tasted so bad that she hadn't been able to stomach more than two sips.

How could anyone end up in a drunken, marriage-minded stupor after only two sips?

So there was no way she could blame her Elvis wedding on the alcohol.

Unless Love Potion Number Nine was *that* potent. Doubtful, but…why were the details of last night so foggy?

Kate rolled over onto her back and opened her eyes, blinking at the ceiling. Her stomach was upset, but she didn't have a headache. She stole a glance to her right. Aidan was still beside her, looking gorgeous even as he slept. She squeezed her eyes shut again, trying to sort out what had been a dream and what really happened. Because she had had some crazy dreams last night, dreams that were merging and blending with the surreal images of what might've happened last night to get this ring on her finger. But she couldn't be sure.

She recalled a gangly Elvis officiant. The way she remembered it, after he had said, "I now pronounce you husband and wife," he had burst into a heartfelt rendition of "Jailhouse Rock."

Kate remembered insisting it wasn't their wedding song, then gangly Elvis had changed keys and started crooning "Don't Be Cruel."

Surely that part was a dream. What kind of a wedding chapel would offer those song choices for the recessional? An Elvis-themed wedding chapel, of course.

It had to have been a dream, because she remembered turning in circles, looking for Aidan, only to find him up on the dais singing "It's Now Or Never" to her.

Obviously, she had already taken the now-or-never sentiment to heart.

It must've been her guilty conscience working overtime, because she didn't want to be cruel. Not to Aidan. Not again, like the times before. But she didn't want to be married, either.

It wasn't him she was rejecting. Good, kind, solid Aidan.

This was definitely all on her.

Panic skittered through her. *Why had they done this?*

Why? Because the joy radiating from Gigi and Charles had been almost palpable. It had been contagious. That much, she remembered. Who would not get a little sentimental when they watched their eighty-five-year-old grandmother finally marry the love of her life?

Kate vaguely remembered the entire family dancing to the song "Come On, Eileen." They had also danced to "Love Potion Number Nine," the song with the same name as the wedding punch. She cringed at the foggy memory.

What did they put in that stuff? Whatever it was, it should come with a disclaimer. Surely a couple of sips wouldn't have made her lose her mind.

And yet she'd woken up married.

Kate also remembered looking at Gigi and Charles, and suddenly fearing that she would end up alone in the world. She had turned to Aidan—and she always turned to Aidan, didn't she? Last night she had turned to him and thought, *I should propose to him right now. Toss it up to fate.* If he said yes, she would stop second-guessing love. She had to stop running. Because she would never find anyone better than Aidan Quindlin.

That part was clear and decidedly real.

So was the moment she and Aidan had exited the banquet hall. Kate had tugged on his hand. He had turned to her, smiling, his eyes saying yes even before she had popped the question.

She groaned inwardly, throwing her arm over her eyes.

Just breathe. And think logically.

Of course, there was always the chance that Aidan would be just as horrified to wake up married to her.

She took a few more deep breaths and let her mind sift through the facts.

Obviously, the "Jailhouse Rock/Don't Be Cruel/It's Now or Never" medley had been her subconscious screaming at her. Gangly Elvis had been real. Or had he?

Someone had married them. She just wasn't clear on who.

Was it legally binding if she couldn't remember the officiant? Couldn't remember saying *I do*, couldn't remember exchanging vows?

How could it be legal if she hadn't remembered what she had to do for the rest of her life?

Covering herself with the top sheet, she slid up into a sitting position, leaning against the quilted headboard, drawing her knees to her chest.

On the nightstand next to the bed was a small white book that looked like a photo album. She picked it up and opened it. The first page contained what looked like wedding vows:

I (name), take you (name), to by my husband/ wife, secure in the understanding that you will be my forever partner in life…

There was more, but her head was swimming and she couldn't get past the fact that their names weren't even filled in. It was so generic.

She flipped the page and found what appeared to be a marriage license. Not only were their names filled in, she recognized her signature, even if she didn't remember signing.

She snapped the book shut. Her stomach roiled and a clammy film of hot panic encased her like a second skin. She lowered her head to her knees, willing the sick feeling to pass. But like the gold band constricting her ring finger, the sensation only became more oppressive.

"Good morning, Mrs. Quindlin."

She jumped at the sound of Aidan's voice. She lifted her head to see him turning onto his side and propping himself up on his elbow. He touched her face with a big, gentle hand, raised himself up more so he could kiss her lips.

She adored his lips. But she didn't necessarily want to be married to them.

"Good morning." She managed to push the words through knotted vocal cords.

"You okay?" he asked.

No. I'm not okay. How can this be okay? Nothing will ever be okay again. Don't you understand that?

Not until they fixed this. And the only way they could fix it would be to somehow get unmarried. Kate glanced around the opulent suite, feeling like a cornered animal who needed a way out.

Surely lots of people who made the impetuous choice to let gangly Elvis marry them in a quirky little Vegas chapel had next-day wedding regret? Didn't they? Surely there was an escape clause? There had to be. You had ninety days to return a toaster to Target. Something as huge and life altering as marriage had to come with some kind of buyer's remorse safety net, didn't it?

The problem was, Aidan didn't seem to share her horror.

And he had called her Mrs. Quindlin. It was just registering.

"Talk to me." Aidan pushed himself into a sitting position mirroring hers. The muscles of his biceps bunched and relaxed in the process.

"What did we do, Aidan?"

"We got married." He reached out and tucked a strand of red hair behind her ear, letting his finger trail down her jawline.

"Talk to me," he said again. His voice was neutral, neither happy nor regretful, neither supportive nor reproachful. That, in itself, ignited a spark of hope in Kate. Maybe, for her sake, he had been holding in his regrets. Leave it to Aidan to be strong for both of them.

"How do you feel about it?" she asked, testing the waters. A smile spread over his handsome face and, in an instant, Kate's heart sank. She knew she was doomed—doomed to hurt him again, doomed to wreck the best thing that had ever happened to her. That was what marriage did to good people—to good couples who couldn't leave well enough alone. It started a slow erosion that destroyed even the strongest relationships.

"I'm happy, Kate. How else would I feel?"

Heavy silence hung between them.

He laughed, an uneasy sound. "Maybe I should be asking you how *you* feel about marrying me. Since that seems to be the burning question."

He was smiling at her in that good-natured way of his, but there was a note of caution in his eyes. He was so handsome. Anyone with a heart would melt at the sight of those brown eyes and that careless brown hair that was just a little too long but looked sexy as hell on him. Anyone with a lick of sense would realize she was the luckiest woman in the world to have the love of a man like Aidan Quindlin.

But did he love her? Love had never come up in their conversations. And she couldn't remember if either of them had mentioned it last night. Surely she would have remembered that?

Anyone who was less broken than she was would be making mad passionate love to that man right now and celebrating their marriage instead of sitting on the bed feeling sick to her stomach as she struck the first blows that would shatter this fragile new turn in their relationship.

"Aidan, we shouldn't have done this." Her eyes welled with the unshed tears she had been trying to hold back. "You deserve so much better than—" She couldn't bring herself to say it.

"Better than what, Kate? How can it get better than being married to you?"

"You don't love me, though."

He flinched. "Why would you say that?"

"Because you've never said the words *I love you, Kate*."

"They're just words."

"Yeah," Kate said. "Four big words."

"I guess I'm more of a believer in walking the walk rather than talking the talk."

His voice had an edge now. He leaned back against the headboard, crossing his arms over his flawless, bare chest. Kate hugged her knees even closer as she took in the sheer beauty of him, hating herself for ruining everything and trying to ignore the fact that he still hadn't said he was in love with her, even after she went so far as to prod him.

She died a little inside, thinking about how needy she must seem.

Of all things, she hated to seem needy.

"Aidan, you deserve better than an alcohol-induced, spur-of-the-moment Vegas wedding."

He frowned. "I wasn't drunk. Were you drunk?"

"No. Umm… I only had a couple of sips of that horrid drink. But I don't know, Aidan. Last night is a little fuzzy."

He squinted her. "Are you telling me you don't remember last night?"

Kate rubbed her eyes as if she could scrub away the gauzy veil that made everything hazy. "No, I do. Some of it, anyway. I just think we got caught up in the moment. I think we got carried away. And that drink they served didn't help. I think it hit me hard, Aidan. What's in a Love Potion Number Nine anyway?"

"For starters, nine shots of alcohol," he said.

"What? Nine shots? No wonder I feel like death this morning," she said. "That's enough to give a person alcohol poisoning. I'm glad I only had a couple of sips. Since I don't drink much, maybe it was enough to send me over the edge."

She shivered at the vile memory.

Aidan slid an arm around her and pulled her closer. She nestled into the warmth of him, breathing in his scent—hints of his cologne mixed with sleep and a manly note that was uniquely him. For a fleeting moment, she wished they could stay just like that. Just the two of them, safe from the harsh realities of the outside world. They were so good when it was just the two of them like this. No pressures. No marriage licenses.

"I'll go down to the lobby and get us some coffee. You probably need some water, too. You might be dehydrated. Water will make you feel better."

Maybe so. But probably not. Can you pick up an annulment while you're out?

Because it went a lot deeper than rehydrating. How could she feel better about something that should have never happened in the first place?

This was...permanent.

She braced her elbows on her knees and rested her head in her hands, covering her eyes, leaning away from him, shutting out the world. Aidan was such a good guy. He wasn't a pushover, but he was honest and patient, almost to the point of being overindulgent with her, cutting her slack for her moods and whims. Because she wasn't an easy person to love.

He was the steady force she so desperately needed for balance.

Maybe if she kept reminding herself of that, she could talk some sense into herself.

Look at how he was giving her a pass for freaking out over waking up married to him when he seemed so totally okay with it. That was a case in point for his goodness. He was even willing to go get her coffee and water, no doubt a subtle way to give her a chance to pull herself together. He would do that rather than get all bristly over the fact that she felt sick to her stomach rather than giddy with joy at realizing they were married.

"How can you not feel anything after drinking nine shots of liquor?" she asked, without raising her head. "I feel terrible. This is not how I envisioned the morning after my wedding would be. Actually, I never thought I'd get married, but here we are."

He was rubbing her back and she felt him tense a little when she said that. She wished she had kept that last little tidbit about never getting married to herself. The same way she was swallowing the urge to say it wasn't the kind of wedding she would have wanted—if she had ever wanted a wedding. And she hadn't. Yep. She was swallowing that right along with the bile that was stinging the back of her throat.

"They *say* there's nine shots of liquor, but I doubt it is true," he said. "Maybe the drink started out that way, but for a group like ours they probably mixed it by the batch and those batches get watered down with ice and there are mixers. I doubt anyone got nine shots of liquor in their glass."

Then what was wrong with me?

"Honestly, when we got our marriage license, my head was clear as glass," he said. "I knew exactly what I was doing. You seemed like you were fine. Otherwise, I would have suggested we wait. I would not have tricked you into marrying me, Kate. You believe me, don't you?"

She raised her head, hoping the change in position would quell some of the queasiness. It didn't.

"Did you put something in my drink?" She had meant it as a joke, but the delivery fell flat, as evidenced by Aidan's furrowed brow. He swung his feet over the side of the bed.

"Of course not. I would not do something like that. I would not drug you and drag you down the aisle. What kind of a guy do you think I am?"

"Aidan, that was supposed to be a joke. I'm sorry. It seemed funnier when it was in my head. Besides, if I remember anything it is that I was the one who proposed to you and dragged you down the aisle."

He glanced at her over his shoulder. His expression was proof that even the steadfast Aidan Quindlin had his limits. He raked his hand through his hair and cleared his throat.

"For the record, I went willingly," he said. "Are we still meeting Elle and Daniel for brunch?"

Ugh. That's right.

They were supposed to meet her sister and brother-in-law, who also happened to be Aidan's older brother, in the restaurant downstairs.

Gigi and Charles were off to Paris on their honeymoon. Her mother, Zelda, had ridden to the airport with Gigi and Charles so she could get back to work at the Forsyth Galloway Inn, the grand Victorian mansion that had been in the family for six generations and was now operated as a bed-and-breakfast. Her oldest sister, Jane, and her husband, Liam, had caught an early morning flight to New York to attend an event at Liam's restaurant, La Bula.

Kate and Aidan, along with Elle and Daniel, were flying out later that evening.

Her perfect sister Elle was the last person Kate wanted to see right now. Kate and Aidan had too much to sort out, before they faced others. What were they supposed to say to them—or to anyone, for that matter—"Good morning, we're married"?

She focused on Aidan's broad, tanned back. It looked so good she couldn't help but reach out and touch him, but as soon as she did, he flinched, and the sickening waves of nausea crested even higher. She put her hand over her mouth. "Ugh—" Uttering the sound was a mistake that sent her running into the bathroom.

"Are you okay?" Aidan asked through the closed bathroom door. His question was met with the sound of running water. He pushed open the door. The site of Kate hunched over the sink made his heart ache. She had wrapped herself in the cotton hotel bathrobe, which swallowed her slight body.

She was splashing water on her face. He walked to her and gathered her long, curly red hair in his hands, smoothing it away from her face, half expecting her to ask him to leave. Kate's fiery passion was one of the things that had always drawn Aidan to her from the first moment he had set eyes on her in Mrs. Wallace's high school AP chemistry class ten years ago.

Back then, it had been a rough go—a love-hate relationship. They had dated briefly, until Kate had fallen in with the cool crowd. Aidan had been called a lot of things in his life, but cool was not one of them. But they seemed to have a pattern of getting together and drifting apart again when she started to feel too claustrophobic. They had lost touch when Aidan went away to college and was married to someone else for a brief period of time.

They had found their way back to each other after his marriage failed and he ended up in the intensive care unit after crashing his Harley.

The accident had left him in a coma. When he had awakened, Kate's beautiful face was the first thing he had seen. At that moment, all the uncertainty and indiscretions of their youth had fallen away. The chemistry that reunited them seemed even stronger. This time, things felt a little more permanent.

Until she had claimed to not remember marrying him.

But like it or not, Kate was his wife. They were married. He glanced down at the slim ivory column of her neck, wanting to kiss her there, but he resisted.

He hated that she wasn't feeling well. Protectiveness swelled inside him. After she felt more like herself, she would realize they had been heading toward this since the day they met.

The only reason he hasn't proposed already was that her two older sisters had recently tied the knot. Then her grandmother had announced her plans for a quick wedding to her longtime love, which was why they were in Vegas this week.

Kate used to say that she never wanted to get married, because her father had abandoned the family when Kate and her sisters were young, and she didn't want to end up heartbroken like her mother.

He knew Kate well enough to know that while her father might have made her hard on the outside, she was a big softie on the inside. He was willing to bet that after she was feeling more like herself and things had a chance to sink in, she would be happy that they were married.

If she wasn't happy about the way the marriage had happened, they could rewind. They could do it again and invite family and friends. He would make sure she had the wedding of her dreams.

All he wanted was to spend the rest of his life with her.

Kate turned off the faucet and stood up looking ashen. As Aidan let go of her hair and the fiery red strands fell around her shoulders, he was certain she was the most beautiful woman in the world.

"You okay?" he asked.

She shrugged. No wonder she wasn't excited. She looked like she wanted nothing more than to crawl back into bed and sleep.

"Do you think it is food poisoning?" he asked.

She shook her head. "No, I don't have stomach cramps. I only had a couple of sips of alcohol, but I feel sick to my stomach. Maybe I picked up a bug on the flight out here. Or maybe I'm just tired."

She and her sisters and mother had flown in from Savannah, Georgia, a week before the wedding to get everything ready for Gigi and Charles. It was entirely possible that she had picked up something on the plane. Even though he didn't want her to feel bad, it was a hell of a lot more palatable than thinking that waking up to the reality of being married to him made her physically ill.

"Come in here and lie down." She let him steer her back into the bedroom of the suite. He removed the robe and tucked her into bed. "I am going to get you a cold cloth for your forehead. That always helps when you're feeling queasy. Then I'm going to go down to the lobby and get you some cold water and some of that pink stuff to settle your stomach. Try to sleep while I'm gone. After I get back, I'll call Elle and Daniel and tell them we can't make it to brunch. That we want to sleep in. They'll understand that."

It didn't seem like she had slept, but she must've dozed. Because the next thing she knew, she was waking up to Aidan sitting on the bed next to her, offering her cold water and Pepto Bismol.

She took a sip of the water and felt remarkably well again.

"It is weird," she said. "I feel a lot better. I appreciate you getting the Pepto, but I don't think I need it."

"That's great," Aidan said. "Drink more water. It will keep you hydrated. At least you'll have the pink stuff if you need it later."

He poured the cold liquid into a glass and handed it to her.

"I haven't called Daniel and Elle yet. Do you feel up to meeting them for brunch? Or do you still want me to cancel?"

Kate's stomach rumbled at the suggestion of food, and she suddenly realized she was ravenous. It was odd that one minute she felt like she was coming down with the flu and the next she was perfectly fine and starving. It would be a good idea to get some food in her stomach. Not to mention the fact that being around other people would get them away from the big marriage-elephant in the room. They didn't have to tell Elle and Daniel what had happened.

"I think I can make it," she said. "But let's not share our big news with them just yet. You know my family. If I tell one person and the others find out before we tell them, it will start an *uncivil* war. Besides, I don't want to do anything that might overshadow Gigi and Charles's wedding. This is their time. Let's let them have their moment, even though they're probably in Paris by now."

"Does that mean you're open to telling them at some point?" he asked.

Kate took a long sip, buying herself time before she answered. Aidan was looking at her expectantly. Unless she planned to chug the entire glass of water, she owed him an answer.

"Aidan, we have a lot to think about. A lot to talk about. Getting married the way we did changes everything, and I have to be honest, I—"

He held up a hand stopping her words. "I agree. We do have a lot to consider. And I'll be completely honest. While I was downstairs, some things dawned on me." He shrugged, and Kate realized he didn't look like the happy newlywed who had greeted her with a kiss when he had woken up. "I have Chloe to consider."

"Oh my gosh, Chloe," Kate said. "Of course. She has to be the first person to know."

Chloe was Aidan's six-year-old daughter from his previous marriage. Kate loved her like she was her own. They needed to handle this situation carefully.

Of course, he had to protect Chloe. Kate wanted to kick herself for being so self-absorbed and not thinking about the sweet little girl as soon as she opened her eyes. She had been trying to process everything as she coped with feeling like her insides were trying to wring her out. This marriage didn't affect her alone. They had to think long and hard about how this would impact Chloe.

Which brought to mind another delicate matter. Chloe's mother, Veronica, had walked out on the two of them just days after the child was born, leaving Aidan to raise her as a single parent all these years.

After his motorcycle accident, which was the catalyst that had brought Kate and Aidan back together, Kate had cared for Chloe as she helped nurse Aidan back to health and saw him through physical therapy.

Marriage was not something to trifle with. Of course, an annulment was always a possibility. Although they had consummated the marriage last night—a couple of times—and many times over the decade they had known each other.

After Aidan had recovered from his accident, he used to joke that making love to her was the very best kind of physical therapy and he owed his speedy recovery to it. She had certainly been eager to help him grow stronger.

Divorce or annulment, she couldn't shake the feeling that either one might damage their relationship beyond repair and it might hurt Chloe in the process. They hadn't talked about it yet, of course, but Kate sensed it. It very well might spell the end of them.

Just as marriage freaked her out, the thought of losing Aidan forever made her feel bereft to the core.

What was she going to do? There wasn't an easy answer.

For a fleeting moment, Kate considered what it would be like to stay married to him. For the three of them to be a family. Really, for almost a year, they had been spending a lot of time together. Of course, they had each kept their respective residences and he had been protective of Chloe. Even though he hadn't kept Kate a secret, he had been careful to let Chloe believe they were friends and nothing more. Kate had no idea how the little girl would feel if her daddy brought someone else into their close little family of two.

Also, it would mean that one of them would have to give up their home so they could move in together. The rest of the scenario played out as if her life was flashing before her eyes.

Suddenly, it felt as if it was hard to breathe.

"Let's not talk about it until we get home. Okay?" Aidan suggested. "And even then, it will be late when we get in. I say we sleep on it and get together tomorrow to begin sorting it out."

Aidan was right. It would be late when they got back to Savannah that night. Their best bet would be to wait until tomorrow and then set it right. In the meantime, living in marriage limbo was going to make this the longest twenty-four hours of her entire life.

The best thing they could do would be to meet Elle and Daniel and try to act like everything was normal.

"I've never seen a more beautiful bride," Elle gushed. "Gigi was positively radiant. And Charles was so handsome."

Dressed in a pink sundress with her blond hair pulled away from her face in a high ponytail, Elle looked pretty and dreamy as she sipped her mimosa while the others perused the menu.

Everything Kate considered ordering made her stomach churn. So she closed the menu and pushed it away.

"She was stunning," Kate agreed. "They looked so happy. I'm glad that everything for the ceremony and reception came together the way it did. Especially given that we planned it in pretty short order."

"I know," Elle said. "After planning three weddings in less than three years, I'd say we're getting good at this. What are you going to order for breakfast? I still can't decide."

"I'm just going to have toast," Kate said. "I'm not very hungry."

"Are you okay?" her sister asked. "You're not acting like yourself this morning."

Kate brushed it off by saying, "You know I never was much of a breakfast eater."

"I'm starving. I can't make up my mind between the French toast and the traditional breakfast. I wish I could get half orders of both."

"Order both and eat what you want," Daniel suggested. "Or maybe Kate would get one and you could get the other and share?"

"No, I'm good with toast." Kate sipped her tea and then changed the subject back to a safe subject. "I'm so happy Gigi and Charles finally have their chance at a life together. They deserve their own happily-ever-after."

Elle glanced at her watch. "They should be in Paris by now. Wasn't their plane supposed to land at nine a.m. Savannah time? Daniel, I want to go to Paris someday. We should just pick a date for the trip now. Because you know what they say. If you don't just do it, you'll never do it. You'll spend your whole life saying, 'Someday I want to go to Paris.'"

Daniel put his arm around Elle. "You know I'd give you the moon and Paris, if it would make you happy. However, we have our daughter, Maggie, to consider now. I don't know how much she'd enjoy the Eiffel Tower at this age."

Elle shrugged and sighed. "I suppose you're right. But don't think I'm going to give up on it."

She smiled up at her handsome husband and he leaned in and kissed her. Their affection made Kate all too aware of how stiff she and Aidan must seem. Aidan was still studiously perusing the menu as if the secret to eternal youth was buried somewhere in the text and Kate was sitting arms crossed, listing to the right in her chair, away from Aidan. Not that the two lovebirds sitting across from them would notice.

Kate sighed. It hadn't been love at first sight for Elle and Daniel. On the contrary. Daniel had been Elle's most disliked person at one time, when she believed, wrongly, that he had encouraged her former fiancé to jilt her at the altar. But it had taken a long time for her to find out the truth and accept it.

What if she had given up on him... Elle might have missed out on the love of her life.

Their story was romantic and, just that, a great love story. But it was *their* story. Kate and Aidan's long, tortured journey wasn't nearly as romantic. They had been on again and off again since high school. More off than on, if truth be told.

Aidan had taken a disastrous sojourn through marriage. It was a short-lived union that had ended when his wife walked out on him shortly after giving birth to their daughter, Chloe.

And now here they were.

Kate's heart ached to think that she would be following suit. Poor Aidan. She slanted a glance at him and caught him looking at her. She smiled and looked away, pretending to be fascinated by the restaurant and its coffered ceilings, thick alabaster columns and rust-colored, floral-patterned carpet, which matched the upholstery on the chairs.

It felt a little heavy and oppressive. Or maybe she was simply projecting her mood.

Aidan definitely deserved better than she could give him. Him and Chloe. The little girl didn't even know they were dating. Not that the traditional sequence of relationships mattered to six-year-olds. Kate had been around. They had told Chloe they were just friends. Would it seem strange to her if they came back from Vegas married?

Kate shook the thought from her head. It wasn't going to happen. They would look into an annulment as soon as they got home. In the meantime, she could slowly disengage from Aidan's life.

Well, except for the fact that her sister Elle was married to Aidan's brother. That made Elle Chloe's aunt. Since Daniel and Aidan didn't have other extended family, that meant Aidan and Chloe would be included in all the family gatherings because in Gigi's mind the holiday—be it birthday or Thanksgiving or Christmas or Groundhog's Day—wasn't celebrated to the fullest without a houseful of family.

Could this get any more awkward?

The server came and took their order.

When Kate asked for toast and more hot tea, Aidan leaned in. "I'm sorry you're still not feeling well. If you get hungry later, we can get you something. Or if you change your mind, you can share my huevos rancheros."

The mere mention of the spicy dish made Kate's stomach heave. She quickly lifted her teacup to her lips and sipped until the feeling subsided.

"He's so good to you, Kate," Elle cooed.

Kate hadn't been aware that her sister was watching them until now.

"You know, now that Jane and I are married, Gigi is going to zero in on you two," Elle said. "Be prepared."

Both Kate and Aidan laughed. Kate wondered if it sounded as nervous to Elle and Daniel as it did to her own ears.

"Did attending a romantic wedding make the two of you start thinking about taking your relationship to the next level?"

"Elle, don't," Kate said.

Kate couldn't look at Aidan, but out of her peripheral vision, she saw him shift in his chair.

"Honey," Daniel said. "Don't put them on the spot like that. I know you're happy and you want everyone to be happy, but I'm sure you'll be among the first to know, right?"

Kate couldn't even form words. All she could manage was a nervous squeak.

"Aidan, since my sister is impossible, I'm going to talk to you," Elle continued. She'd always had a determined, one-track mind when she latched on to an idea. "I think that if anyone could tame my sister, you could. It is obvious that the two of you are in love. Why don't you just do it? Why don't you just bite the bullet and get married?"

No one said a word. Elle took that as an opportunity to expand on her thoughts. "What time is it?"

She looked at her phone. "It is not even noon and our plane doesn't leave until eight o'clock. Let's go to one of those cute little wedding chapels and get you two hitched."

Kate wasn't sure if it was her sister's suggestion or the smell of the food wafting over from the table next to them, but suddenly she couldn't sit at that table another second more.

"I—I need to get some air," she said as she scooted back from the table and bolted for the exit.

Chapter Two

The next morning, Kate stood at her dressing table in her bedroom, holding her thin gold wedding band. It glinted in the ray of sunshine streaming in through her bedroom window.

She turned the ring from side to side, letting the smooth metal slide between her fingers as she stared at it. Now that she was home and had gotten a sound night's sleep, she still hadn't been able to mentally stitch together the pieces of her wedding that she remembered.

Memories of the night were like images from a blurry film. She remembered dancing with Aidan, and maybe even getting a little emotional over Gigi and Charles's wedding. She had a vague recollection of picking out the rings with Aidan. He had wanted her to get the diamond-encrusted band. She remembered that. He had been so generous, the way he had insisted. But she had maintained it was too expensive and questioned how they could prove the diamonds were real and not just a cubic zirconia rip-off. That had been a real sticking point for her. She had been such a judicious ring shopper. Where had all that good sense gone when it came time to say *I do*?

The rest was fuzzy and strange, as if she was watching a movie in her mind where two actors who were playing them in a zany rom-com had purchased the rings and gotten hitched by an Elvis impersonator.

If it wasn't so heartbreaking, she might've laughed at the ridiculousness of it. Her heart ached as she returned the gold band to the red velvet-lined box it came in and snapped the lid shut. As she tucked it inside her jewelry box, she felt as if she was hiding away Pandora's box. Because that was what it would be if her family found out—a source of a whole lot of trouble.

After they got over the shock, her family would want her to stay married. They loved Aidan. Everyone loved Aidan. Because what was not to love about him?

They would not understand that this had been a colossal mistake.

Her heart ached again. Aidan had been uncharacteristically stoic on their flight home last night. After they had landed, he had gone through all the Aidan motions while making minimal small talk—helping her with her bags and holding doors—but there had been a disconnect. Especially after he had deposited her luggage just inside the door. He had left her with the most paralyzingly platonic peck on the cheek, murmured good-night and walked away, leaving her standing at the door.

What had she expected him to do?

On the ride home from the airport, they had decided to meet the next evening to talk about the fate of their marriage. That was hardly cause for celebration or a toe-curling kiss.

Contemplating his cool demeanor and their talk later that evening, Kate felt nervous as a game show contestant. It felt like if she chose the wrong briefcase or gave the wrong answer, she stood to lose everything. And wasn't that telling? Was she really fit to commit if she equated this huge life decision with being a contestant on *Deal or No Deal*? Didn't that analogy speak volumes?

Her phone rang, making her jump and jarring her out of her morose thoughts. A photo of her sister

Elle's beautiful smiling face flashed on the screen. Kate was supposed to meet her for tea at the Forsyth Galloway Inn, their family's inn, which was located near Forsyth Park.

It would be a quick meeting before Kate's first appointment at the hair salon. Elle and their mom, Zelda, wanted to talk about plans for a special post-honeymoon homecoming celebration for Gigi and Charles.

Kate blinked at the time. Ugh, she was late, which meant Elle was calling to prod her along. Kate let the call go to voice mail and texted On my way. Be there soon. Now she had to get a move on so she didn't have to add lying to her list of transgressions—right below regretting her marriage.

Nothing like hitting the ground running on her first day back. Kate sighed. Better to stay busy than to dwell on the discussion that was coming later that evening.

Even so, Kate just didn't feel like making excuses for her tardiness. What was she supposed to say? She had gotten off to a slow start this morning because she felt flu-ish and exhausted again. She gave herself one last look in the vanity mirror. She looked tired. She undid the top button on the pink-and-red Kate Spade bubble-dot smocked dress, fluffed her curls and pursed her lips. Maybe the neutral pink lipstick was washing her out. She plucked a tube out of her makeup bag and colored her lips with the brightest red lipstick she owned.

If that didn't distract from the dark circles under her eyes, nothing would.

What was wrong with her? She was only twenty-six years old, too young to be sidelined by a virus or jet lag from a trip to Vegas. Stress really was a killer. She and Aidan had been married less than forty-eight hours and the honeymoon was already over.

Okay, so that wasn't exactly fair. Theirs wasn't exactly a typical wedding and they hadn't even taken a honeymoon. So, if there had been no honeymoon, it couldn't be over before it even started.

Unlike the marriage.

Keep talking, Kate. Keep thinking and talking and trying to explain it all away.

The bottom line was that she was not fit for marriage. Proof was…coming home from Vegas and having absolutely no idea what she was going to eat this week. Zero. *Nada.* Her cupboards were bare. If she didn't feel like grocery shopping after work, she didn't have to, since she was single. If she wanted to eat a pint of Ben and Jerry's Chocolate Chip Cookie Dough ice cream for dinner—which happened to be the only thing in her freezer right now—she need not answer to anyone but herself…and her bathroom scale.

Being single allowed her to fly off for the weekend at a moment's notice… That was exactly what she should be doing right now. Though she hadn't been that spontaneous since she and Aidan had gotten back together.

But she should be having fun, not planning meals and grocery shopping. She should be taking trips and enjoying her life. She worked hard at the salon and had built a steady clientele. She certainly wasn't rich, but she was making enough money that she had been able to buy a house without help from anyone, and she had even saved a respectable amount, adding yearly to her 401(k). If she wanted to use the rest of her hard-earned money to travel the world while she was young and unencumbered, she was entirely free to do so.

She grabbed the last bottle of water from the refrigerator and scooped up her keys and purse off the entryway table before letting herself out the front door. All the while, she tried to ignore the voice inside her that pointed out that even before the surprise wedding, she hadn't really been free and unencumbered. She had gotten pretty involved with Aidan… and his sweet daughter, Chloe.

It hadn't felt like she was shackled to Aidan until now. In fact, they had been doing so well. But true to form, in all of her matters of the heart, one day things were going well and the next…they were over.

A few minutes later, Kate had pointed her car in the direction of Forsyth Park. The short drive gave her time to let her mind squirrels run rampant, time to get out the raw emotion that was sitting on the surface and bury the rest of these strange feelings where she didn't have to deal with them. At least not right now. Not in front of Elle and her mother.

By the time she arrived at the inn, she had her game face firmly in place. She parked her red vintage Thunderbird in a space next to the inn's kitchen door. The sprawling butter yellow Victorian mansion turned bed-and-breakfast on Whitaker Street had been in her family for more than one hundred fifty years and had been a thriving business since 1874.

Kate and her sisters had grown up in the big old house with its ornate ironwork and creaking mahogany floors. Of course, each of them had moved on, pursuing her own dreams and identity separate from the inn. But all three of the Clark sisters loved to come home.

As Kate sat there behind the wheel of her car, she realized she felt like a fugitive. She and her mom and sisters had spent countless hours in the inn's kitchen dishing gossip and sharing their secrets. But today,

Kate couldn't even seek the counsel of the women she trusted most.

She couldn't tell them that she was married, but try as she might, she didn't love Aidan the way she wished she could—not the way her sisters loved their husbands. Not the way a wife should. Not the way he deserved to be loved. For the rest of his life.

It occurred to her that maybe her lack of love for him might be self-preservation. Was it? He had never said he loved her. Instead, he proclaimed that talk was cheap when it came to saying the three words that most people used as the basis for getting married.

The thought of tying herself to a loveless marriage made her stomach feel hollow and her throat ache with unshed tears.

She wished they loved each other. Why couldn't they love each other? Because she cared about him so much. But that probably wasn't enough. If this marriage of *inconvenience* hadn't happened, they probably would have broken up sometime. Kate felt the elusive tears that had escaped her earlier well in her eyes. Tears of frustration. Tears of anger—how could she have been so stupid to let this happen? Tears of sorrow because she didn't want to hurt Aidan…again.

She let the tears flow for a minute.

Then she blew her nose and fixed her makeup.

To buy herself a couple of extra minutes, she walked around to the front of the inn rather than using the kitchen doors, and climbed the steps to the stately wraparound veranda and let herself inside.

She mustered her best smile for a group of guests who were lingering in the lobby. Since Gigi's retirement, Kate hadn't been as involved with the inn as her mother and sisters, even though Zelda had a plan to draw all three of her girls into the family business, allowing each of them to continue doing what they loved, only doing it from the inn.

For Elle, it was art; the middle Clark sister, now Mrs. Daniel Quindlin, was in charge of art classes that were based at the inn. A graduate of the Savannah College of Art and Design, Elle also facilitated art and architecture tours around the city. She had temporarily shelved her talent as an artist when she moved to Atlanta to teach elementary school art, after her longtime boyfriend had left her at the altar. As fate would have it, that breakup had led her to her true soul mate, Daniel, whom she had previously blamed for causing her fiancé to change his mind.

Elle's classes and tours were drawing a lot of new business to the inn. They were nearly booked solid four months out.

For Jane, it was creating beautiful pastries and

delicious baked goods. She was the pastry chef for the tearoom at the inn, which they had opened last spring. She was creating quite a stir with her unique confections. Recently, she had won the Oscar Hurd Foundation award, a prestigious award that celebrated upcoming talent and those in the culinary business who were making a difference.

Now that her mother had implemented two thirds of her plan, she was determined to move into the final phase and build a small building in the inn's garden, which would house a spa. She wanted Kate to run it. With that, all three of her daughters would have their own unique place in the family business.

The only problem was, Kate already had a business of her own. She worked hard doing hair and had built a steady, loyal client base. She didn't own a salon but rented a chair from Kerrigan Karol, one of Savannah's premiere salons. As far as she was concerned, she had the best possible life as a hairdresser. The money was good. She loved what she did, and cherished her independence. She could set her own schedule. Such as today, when she didn't have to arrive until just before her first client's appointment. She loved not having to answer to anyone but her clients. When the salon drama got too thick, she could remove herself and let Kerrigan handle the mediation and the soothing of fragile egos.

Even if she didn't own the "walls" or the chair, she had built this business on her own. Nothing had been handed to her.

She didn't have to worry with the day-to-day operations of a brick-and-mortar building. No leases or rent or mortgage. No going in early to open the doors or locking up at night. No fretting about filling unrented chairs. No worrying about appeasing the clients of other stylists when those stylists decided to stay home nursing a hangover after a night of partying. With all those artistic personalities, it happened more frequently than the uninitiated might think.

Now Zelda was strong-arming Kate to give up her chair at Kerrigan Karol and take on all of the additional responsibility Kate didn't want. Zelda saw it as the ultimate gift that she could give her daughter. She couldn't understand Kate's apprehension—no matter how many times or how plainly Kate tried to explain it to her.

Because the spa meant so much to her mother, Kate had examined the possibility of running it from every angle. She could move her clientele from the current Kerrigan Karol Salon location to the inn, but she also would have to hire additional stylists. It would be frowned upon if she tried to poach her co-workers from Kerrigan. That meant she would need to run ads and take in hairdressers she didn't know.

Not only that, they would have to bring in licensed therapists and estheticians for massages, facials, manicures, pedicures and all the other traditional spa services, to accommodate a transient clientele. She would need to have stylists who could work guests into the schedule at a moment's notice. As it stood, most of her clients booked a year's worth of appointments in advance. She rarely had flexibility to work in walk-ins.

Then, there was the financial end of it. She hadn't had the heart to bring up finances with Zelda—as in who was paying for and installing the equipment needed to open a place like this. Since she had made the decision to skip college and go to beauty school, she had prided herself on supporting herself. She hadn't asked anyone for a single cent to make ends meet, not even in the early days when she was building her business. She might be financially independent now, but that "independence" fit within the realm of her budget. She wasn't in a position to take on the added expense of opening a place she didn't even want.

What if she gave up everything she had worked so hard to build—the lifestyle, the clientele, the independence—and then the spa at the inn tanked? That was a very real possibility because the dynamic would be completely different from what she was doing now.

But the Forsyth Galloway Inn was so special to her. It held so much family history. Shouldn't she do her part? Or at least care about leaving her imprint on the business, which was supposed to continue on for limitless future generations?

The prospect of tying herself to the inn made her itch the same way that the thought of being married for the rest of her life did.

What the hell was wrong with her?

She paused to look around. She had walked through the front doors so many times, usually in a hurry to get in and out, and now she realized it had been a long time since she had stopped and really looked at the place.

It was heartwarmingly familiar, but at the same time, it all looked new.

Next to the front door, a tall, galvanized metal container held an assortment of umbrellas. Its companion, a leaning coat rack, stood sentry on the opposite side of the door. A grandfather clock ticked rhythmically from the corner. The impressive staircase dominated the center of the room.

There was a plethora of dark wood, antiques and tchotchkes everywhere. A replica of the Eiffel Tower was perched on an end table next to a merlot-colored wingback chair. On the front desk, a porcelain figurine of a woman in a Southern belle's ball gown held court amid a garden of brochures and pamphlets about things to do in Savannah. Behind that, a collection of teacups and teapots perched on a shelf. There were several arrangements of artificial flowers—some had seen better days. Several paintings created by Elle adorned the dark, paneled walls; some depicted floral landscapes, and others were of local scenes such as the famous fountain in Forsyth Park and a streetscape of the historic downtown area.

"Hello, do you work here?" The voice came from behind her.

No, I don't work here, but—

The words were on the tip of her tongue and she turned around to see a man holding a huge arrangement of pink and white flowers, mostly roses, with some peonies and ranunculus rounding out the gorgeous work of art.

Flowers.

She loved flowers.

She had often thought that if money were no object, she would have vases of fresh flowers in every room of her house. It was a nice thing to do for yourself.

But she had to admit they were even sweeter coming from someone else. From a man.

Flowers were such a romantic gesture. They were totally impractical. A grand arrangement of cut flowers like these easily set back the sender a couple of hundred bucks.

They were beautiful and expensive and they usually faded within a week. But flowers like these could transform an otherwise ordinary week into something splendid.

Wait—what if they are from Aidan?

Kate's hand fluttered to her chest as her heart skipped a beat. Hope bloomed at the thought of Aidan making such a wonderful, romantic gesture.

Just as fast, her kicking heart clinched in her chest. Flowers—even if they were simply stunning— did not make a marriage work.

"I sort of work here," she said to the delivery guy. "I mean, my family owns the inn. How can I help you?"

The delivery guy turned the arrangement and glanced at the card, which was secured on a plastic holder.

"These are for Zelda Clark. Is she here?"

These flowers are for my mother? From whom?

Who was sending her mother flowers like these?

They were a bit too over the top to be from a vendor who might be courting her for business, or from a guest thanking her for a special getaway at the inn.

Kate cleared her throat, swallowing the disappointment that Aidan hadn't sent them to her, but then again, how would he have known she was here right now? He would have had them delivered to the salon.

"Yes, Zelda works here. I'll see that she gets them."

The man pulled a receipt and pen out of his pocket and held it out for Kate to sign. Then he transferred the flowers to her.

The heavenly aroma of roses and fresh-cut greenery tantalized her senses and enticed her to take deep breaths all the way to the kitchen.

She pushed through the double doors ready to begin the inquisition. Her mother and her sister Elle were seated at the wooden trestle table, sipping hot tea out of porcelain cups and giggling about something. Kate wondered if they were talking about the mysterious sender of the flowers. Their heads swiveled toward Kate as she entered the room.

"Aww, you shouldn't have," Elle joked.

"What in the world?" Zelda asked.

"I was wondering the same thing, Mom." Kate set the flowers in front of Zelda. "These came for you."

Elle's mouth formed a perfect O, and then her jaw dropped. "Who is sending you flowers, Mom? They're beautiful."

Zelda's eyes were wide, and she looked bemused as she took the card off the pick and opened the envelope. As she read, a pretty smile spread over her lips.

Judging from her mother's dreamy expression, they were definitely not from a prospective vendor.

Then she returned the card to the envelope, set it on the table in front of her, laced her fingers and placed her hands over the card as if that rendered it invisible.

"Where were we?" she said.

Elle and Kate looked at each other and then back at their mother.

"Um, hello?" Kate said. "You can't just jump back into the conversation like nothing happened. Who sent you flowers, Mom?"

"Just a friend," Zelda said, the secret smile still tugging up the corners of her lips. The wistful, far-away look in her eyes made it clear that her mind was somewhere else.

"None of my *friends* ever send me flowers like that," Elle said. "Do yours, Kate?"

"I know, right?" Kate said. "And I can't recall a single *friend* of mine who ever made me look the way you look right now."

That seemed to snap Zelda out of her reverie. "I'm sure I have no idea what you're talking about. The flowers are gorgeous. I was simply admiring them."

Her Southern accident was a little thicker than usual. It was one of Zelda's tells that signaled that she might be stretching the truth just a little.

With her long, curly copper hair, perfect smile and

apple cheekbones, Zelda resembled a slightly older Debra Messing. As Kate watched a range of emotions play over her mother's attractive face, it dawned on her that *this* was the way love should make you feel. This was why it had been a bad idea to marry Aidan the way she had.

It wasn't the flowers or the promise of heady romance. It was that undefinable something that was written all over her mother's face. It was the buoyancy that seemed to lift Zelda each time she glanced at the card and smelled the flowers sent by her mystery suitor. It was that palpable chemistry that zinged between Gigi and Charles as they had exchanged their wedding vows after waiting all these years. It was the *je ne sais quoi* between her sisters and their soul mate husbands.

It was something that Kate couldn't quite define, but she couldn't ignore it, either. Because when two people shared that kind of bond, the love between them radiated as naturally as the scent of roses filling the kitchen with romantic promise.

It was something that she and Aidan had always aspired to with each other but couldn't seem to find.

While she and Aidan were perfectly fine together and had mad chemistry in the bedroom, there was no magic between them in everyday life. Or at least not this kind of magic. Kate knew relationships didn't produce fireworks all the time. They were usually there in the beginning and settled down as they grew into something deeper. But if the fireworks and chemistry weren't even there in the beginning, what chance did that relationship stand when the honeymoon was over?

It seemed pretty clear that they needed to annul their sham of a marriage, and the sooner the better.

She would tell Aidan she had made up her mind tonight when he came over to talk about things.

"I know you two have full days," Zelda said. "Why don't we get down to business and start planning Gigi and Charles's party. Let's figure out what needs to be done and then think about how we should divide up the work. Sound good?"

"Works for me," Kate said.

Elle put pen to paper. "The way I see it, we need to come up with a guest list, decorations and food and drink."

"Oh! And we need to figure out how we're going to keep this party a surprise," Zelda said. "Someone will have to pick up Gigi and Charles from the airport and bring them here."

"I think it will be easy to keep it a surprise since they're out of town until the party starts," said Elle. "I'll volunteer Daniel to pick them up."

She jotted his name down on the list.

"It is a given that Jane and Liam should be in charge of food," she said as she wrote. "Do you and Aidan want to do the decorations?"

It would be a miracle if she and Aidan were still speaking by the night of the party. Annulments tended to have that effect on relationships.

"I think Aidan is pretty busy with work right now," Kate said. "Why don't you and I take on decorations together?"

Kate was relieved when Elle chirped, "That works for me. Now we just have the guest list and invitations. Mom? That sounds like a perfect job for you. Are you up for it?"

"Sure. Gigi keeps her address book in the office. I'll look through it and pick out her closest friends. We want to keep the party relatively small and intimate, don't we?"

As Elle and their mom chatted about the optimum number of guests, all Kate could think about was what would transpire when she met with Aidan tonight.

Regardless of what the two of them decided, they needed to hold it together so as to not cast a shadow over Gigi and Charles's homecoming. Then again, if they did this the right way, no one need ever know of their big Vegas mistake.

Chapter Three

"Are you ready to go?" Aidan asked after Kate pulled out of the stiff hello hug she had offered him in greeting. In his gut, he had known that things would be tense tonight. After all, they were meeting to discuss the fate of their marriage.

God, they were married. Kate was his wife.

But part of him had hoped that now that Kate had had a chance to process things, she might have had a change of heart.

Judging by her reaction, she hadn't. The reality made him tense up, too. He took a deep breath. He would make sure things were as normal as possible tonight. If he had to, he would hold it together for both of them.

She was worth it.

"I thought we'd go to The Hitch and get some dinner. How does that sound?"

He knew how much Kate loved the kitschy restaurant on Drayton Street. Over the year that the two of them had been back together, it had become their place. Tonight it would be neutral territory, where they could talk this out, but at the same time it would be a place that was special to them as a couple, a place that had history for both of them.

Maybe it would remind her that despite their ups and downs, the two of them were so good together. Their relationship may have been on and off over the years, but they always seemed to come back to each other. Wasn't that all that counted? That in the end, they couldn't stand to be apart?

Wasn't that what mattered?

"I'm not hungry, Aidan," she said. Her red curls hung loose around her slight shoulders. Her ivory skin looked a shade paler than usual. For a moment he thought it might be because of the stark black sweater she was wearing, but her beautiful sea green eyes lacked their usual sparkle. That had nothing to do with the contrast of ivory and black.

"Actually, if you don't mind," she said, "I'd prefer to not go anywhere tonight."

When he arrived, he had been starving, but his appetite suddenly went south. "Are you still feeling bad?" he asked as he followed her into the living room of her bungalow.

Unsmiling, she turned to him and crossed her arms over the front of herself. "It is not that," she said. "There's no easy way to say this. So I'm not going to make small talk. I'm just going to cut to the chase and come out and say it. I've thought about our situation all day today—in fact, I couldn't think of much else, and the only solution I keep coming back to is that we need to have the marriage annulled."

His heart dropped into the vicinity of his ankles, but he managed to keep his stoic poker face firmly in place.

"Can we talk about this, Kate?" he asked. "I know you think you've made up your mind, but, I mean, don't I at least get a say in this? It is my future, too."

"Of course, you do, Aidan, but I don't think there's much more to talk about. Is there? The last time you and I talked about marriage, we both agreed it wasn't for us."

Her words packed a punch that hit him hard in the gut. That wasn't exactly an accurate version of the story. She'd talked about how marriage wasn't right for her. She had told him the thought of a lifelong commitment to one person scared her to death. He'd listened, but he hadn't agreed. Because even though his first marriage had been a mistake, he wasn't about to let that misstep rob him of finding his soul mate and spending the rest of his life with her.

Despite everything, now, more than ever, he believed Kate was his soul mate.

"No, the last time we talked about marriage, we ended up married," he said. "Even if you don't remember it, you're the one who proposed to me."

"You said to me that after you watched your grandmother marry Charles, the love of her life, you had decided that we just needed to rip off the bandage and go for it. We needed to stop overthinking and just do it because you told me I was the love of your life and you didn't want to wait until you were eighty-five, like Charles and Gigi, before we could have a life together."

It was true. She'd said it.

"Here's another thing that I'm not sure if you remember, but when you first proposed your crazy plan, I said no. I wasn't up for it. Not at first. When I objected, you basically hit me with an ultimatum. You told me it was now or never. You don't remember that, either, do you?"

She dropped down on the sofa and buried her face

in her hands, shaking her head. "I don't remember it. I don't remember any of it, Aidan."

He sat in the chair across from her. They sat there without saying a single word for what seemed an eternity.

Finally she asked, "What are you thinking?"

Aidan shrugged. "I don't know. Would it even matter if I told you my thoughts, Kate? It seems like you've made up your mind for both of us. It doesn't appear as if you're going to give me a say."

"Of course, you get a say. I want to hear what you have to say." Then her face crumpled, and the tears fell and the hardline resolve Aidan had mustered quietly disintegrated. He closed the distance between them and pulled her into his arms. This time the stiff resolve was gone and she melted into him and sobbed.

"Hey, come on," he whispered. "I certainly don't want you to stay in a situation that makes you this miserable."

She looked up at him. Tears glistened in her eyes, making them look like sea glass. "Then you agree?"

No. He didn't agree, but he knew he needed to choose his words carefully.

"Aidan, don't you agree that this is no way to start a marriage?"

"I'm not sure I understand what you're saying, Kate. Is it the fact that you're married to me that has you so freaked out? Or is it the way it happened? A spur-of-the-moment Vegas wedding?"

She pulled away from him and stared at a spot somewhere in the distance. He let her have her space.

"Because you're the one who wanted to get married Saturday night," he said. "I don't know if you were just caught up in the moment or maybe you had too much to drink, but getting married in Vegas was your brainchild."

He knew he should have stopped and left it at that but holding his tongue when he should have spoken out was partially what had landed them in this predicament. Then she blinked and looked him in the eyes for the first time since he had arrived.

"I wasn't drunk," she said. "I had a couple of sips of one drink. That Love Potion Number Nine. You know me. I'm not a big drinker, but I've never blacked out. Aidan, it scares me that I can't remember much of what happened that night. I remember dancing with you at Gigi and Charles's reception. I vaguely remember us looking at rings, and that's all. I know that Elvis figured in there somewhere. The next thing I know, we were waking up in our hotel room married. You have to agree with me that that's no way to start a life together."

Or was it? "Sure, the way it happened wasn't ideal, but does a wedding ceremony really make the marriage?" Whether she wanted to admit it or not, they were good together.

As soon as he said the words, he knew he shouldn't have said them. The ceremony did matter to some women.

Maybe it wasn't the marriage that she objected to, but the way that it happened. Of course, he would have proposed to her. Sooner or later.

There had been a lot going on in both of their lives.

Two of her sisters and her grandmother had gotten engaged and married. Elle and Daniel had a baby.

Aidan had simply wanted to put some space between the happy family events and their own. He had been doing it for Kate. He had wanted her to have the engagement and wedding spotlight all to herself.

Maybe he hadn't realized that until now, but that was his reason for waiting to propose. Now it was crystal clear. He knew what he needed to do. He was going to give her the proper down-on-one-knee proposal with the traditional engagement ring and they could have another wedding.

If they weren't already married, he would ask her family for her hand, but that seemed like a moot point now. But she would get a more traditional wedding if that was what she wanted. The Vegas elopement would just be a precursor that could remain their secret if that was the way she preferred it. Or a funny story they could laugh about with their kids in the years to come.

"If we got the annulment, couldn't we just go on as before?" Kate said, jarring him from his thoughts. "Really, why does this have to change anything?"

Aidan looked at her like she had two heads. "Because an annulment would change everything, Kate. If we get this marriage annulled, what's the point in going on like before? I guess it is my turn to issue an ultimatum. We are married. As far as I'm concerned, we either need to live like we're married or we need to end things now. Permanently."

Kate flinched. Her reaction was visible and soul crushing. Aidan knew his words must've hit her like a slap in the face.

He didn't like being in this situation any more than she did. It wasn't the marriage he minded, because he wanted to make it work. It was her reaction to being married to him. Seemingly not even wanting to try to make things work. That cut.

As far as he was concerned, if she wanted to annul their union, then they had reached the end of the line.

She couldn't have it both ways. They had been drifting in and out of each other's lives in this limbo for far too long. Maybe a dose of cold, hard reality would wake her up.

He suppressed a string of colorful words. He

didn't want things to be like this between them. He wanted to bring home his bride, carry her over the threshold and start the rest of their lives together. Why did the simplest things have to be so damn complicated?

"I did some research about annulments," she said. "It is a little iffy, but a legal website I went to said that since we haven't *cohabited*, as they put it, we *might* be eligible to have the marriage dissolved."

He had fixated on the qualifier, *might*, because even though they hadn't formally lived together, they had made love. They had been discreet about their relationship, for the sake of his daughter. And good thing, too, since things seemed to be crashing and burning.

Even though his love for Kate was soul deep, his love for Chloe was in his bones, in his DNA. If Kate didn't want them to be a traditional family, Chloe had to be his first priority. His little girl had never known her mother. Veronica had chosen to not be a part of her daughter's life. How anybody could walk away from their own child was beyond comprehension to him. Veronica had her demons and her own issues, but at least the relationship had produced a sweet little girl.

For that, Aidan was eternally grateful.

It was also a mystery to him how a woman like Kate could walk away from the man she claimed to love. He'd thought he knew her. Was he really that bad a judge of character? Or maybe he was just a glutton for punishment. Two marriages and both of them down the crapper. One after a child was born. The other before they could even get out of Las Vegas.

So he had no idea if their physical relationship would prevent an annulment. But if Kate considered the marriage a mistake, he certainly wasn't going to force her to stay.

"Kate? Is that what you want? Do you want to start annulment proceedings?"

She kept her head bowed but looked up at him through thick, dark lashes.

"I don't know what I want, Aidan. From what I understand, the longer we wait the more difficult it could be."

"I don't know much about this since I've never been in this situation, but we might have a better chance if you filed and said that you were not in a sound state of mind to make such an important decision."

She shot him a dirty look and it brought up pin-pricks of irritation. He stood up and walked back to his chair.

"What do you want, Kate?"

"It sounds so irresponsible," she said. "*Not of sound state of mind to make such an important decision?* That's not who I am. Aidan, you know that."

"I know it is not who you are, but according to you it is the truth about what happened. You're the one who doesn't remember. You're the one who wants the annulment. So you're the one who is going to have to file, because I knew exactly what I was doing when I married you. You, on the other hand, did not."

Her face softened. "You're still saying you want this marriage?"

Of course, I want it.

He shrugged. "Would it make a difference if I did?"

"Maybe. I don't know, Aidan."

"We exchanged wedding vows. Are you sure you have no memory of it?"

She squeezed her eyes shut, and he imagined that she was trying to recall the night. But finally she sighed, a sound that made it seem as if she was carrying the weight of the world in her heart, and shook her head.

"That's why I don't drink," she said. "I've never had a problem with blackouts, but my dad was an alcoholic. Did you know that? That's why I'm not real big on imbibing. Maybe this kind of thing—this alcohol intolerance—is a gradual affliction?"

The silence hung between them like a guillotine.

"I just don't understand why it had to get its claws in me on that night, of all nights."

He wasn't going to say it, but what he didn't understand was why she had been so eager to marry him one moment, and now the thought of being his wife repelled her.

A week later, on the Monday evening of Gigi and Charles's homecoming party, Kate and Aidan were still in marriage limbo, and it appeared they might be in that holding pattern for a while.

They had hired an attorney who had helped them fill out the paperwork. He had said it could take a few weeks before he had word on whether the state would grant an annulment. Since they had been in a romantic relationship before the impromptu marriage, the attorney said it might be a difficult sell.

Since they had done all they could for now, Kate kept herself busy with her clients at the salon and threw herself into helping Elle and their mother plan Gigi and Charles's surprise party. Because of that, she and Aidan had not had much time to dwell on the fate of their relationship.

Stuck in this impasse, Kate had decided to find the silver lining. Because wasn't it just as well that they hadn't heard any news either way about their marriage? This way it would not cast a shadow over the happy occasion of the other newlyweds' homecoming.

Of course, Aidan would be attending the party.

Her family would not dream of having a get-together without inviting him. They loved him.

When Kate walked into the Forsyth Galloway Inn, Aidan was right there, endearing himself to Zelda and Elle, helping them hang the Welcome Home banner Kate had had made especially for the occasion. He had probably blown up balloons that were bobbing next to the helium machine. He would probably go back and group them into bunches and do all the other tasks he was asked to do with a smile on his face.

For all intents and purposes, as the guests arrived for the party, Aidan and Kate would be carrying on as they always had. They had never been ones for public displays of affection in front of the family, mostly for Chloe's sake.

Ugh, but the family—what was life going to be like after the annulment? Since Aidan's brother was married to Elle, which made Chloe her sister's niece, Aidan wasn't going away. He would be around long after the two of them were finished and their marriage mistake was a cautionary footnote in their personal annals.

The reality was a sobering thought.

And it caused a strange pang in Kate's heart.

For a moment, she found herself thinking about what it would be like to just go with it. To let herself love Aidan.

Because what the hell was wrong with her?

Yeah. What the hell was wrong with her? Why was she being so wishy-washy? Of course, it would be so much easier if the two of them could make a clean break, if they could go their separate ways and never see each other again. But that wasn't possible. Their lives would forever be inextricably intertwined.

Someday, Aidan would find a woman deserving of him and all he had to offer. Would he bring her to these family gatherings?

Kate knew her family probably would toss her out and keep Aidan and his perfect new wife. Kate laughed to herself, but there was nothing humorous in the silent chuckle. Her rational mind knew her strange need for independence would ultimately be her downfall. She would die alone, but by God, she would have her freedom.

Even Kate could see how ludicrous her own mind-set was, but it didn't change how she felt. She simply hated being hemmed in by anything or anyone— work or relationships. Being tied down made her feel like a caged animal.

She felt Aidan's gaze on her from across the room, and when their eyes met, he smiled.

After all they had been through, after everything she'd said, he could still spare a smile for her.

What was wrong with her? Why couldn't she be so generous? He really was the perfect man. He was kind and patient. What he lacked in swagger, he made up for in likable appeal and dependability. His was more of a quiet, bookish charm. Aidan Quindlin was never going to be the kind of guy who rolled up on his Harley and whisked you off to parts unknown. Nope, he had sold his motorcycle after the accident that had put him in a coma and nearly cost him his life. Not that she blamed him for ditching the bike. The bike had been out of character for him anyway.

And he had almost died.

When she had heard about the accident, she hadn't been able to bear the thought of losing him. At the time, they hadn't been seeing each other, but when she had heard that he had been hurt, she could not rest until she had made amends for the way they had parted when they had broken up all those years ago.

Where had that feeling that had driven her back to him gone?

Why couldn't she hang on to it?

Why couldn't she love him like he deserved to be loved?

Maybe it was for the best. Maybe it was for his own protection. Thanks to her past, she was broken. Since she was so tragically flawed on so many levels, maybe Aidan deserved better than the broken pieces of herself she had to offer.

"Are you doing all right?" He handed her a glass of red wine.

She accepted it graciously, but the thought of it made her insides roil. Normally she loved a good glass of red wine, but not so much right now. Maybe this was how her nerves were manifesting. Maybe it was the side effects of standing here face-to-face with Aidan.

"It depends on how you define all right," she said.

He raised a brow in that way that was so maddeningly attractive. She felt herself being drawn back to him.

She shook her head. She didn't want to talk about it. Tonight was not about her or even about the two of them. It was about Gigi and Charles.

It was about true love. She shifted the wine glass from one hand to another.

"I'm fine. Really, I am. Thanks for the wine. And thanks for all your help getting things ready tonight. I don't know what we would have done without you, Aidan."

She wished she hadn't said it.

He raised his brows and then slanted her a look. He opened his mouth as if he wanted to say something, but snapped his jaw shut, looking resigned.

She knew what he wanted to say.

She'd bet money that he had been about to tell her,

You don't have to do without me. Of course, he had way too much class to bring it up tonight.

Her sister Jane, who was setting out the appetizers, caught Kate's eye across the room and pointed toward the kitchen door. Jane and Liam had returned from New York City a couple of days ago after a business trip for their restaurant, La Bula, and, in short order, had managed to dream up a scrumptious feast for the party.

"Excuse me, Aidan, Jane needs me in the kitchen." Kate had never been so happy for an intervention.

"Of course," he answered. "Let me know if they need another pair of hands in there."

She just hoped her relief hadn't shown on her face as she walked away from Aidan and made her way toward the kitchen.

"Sorry to interrupt," Jane said. "We're a little in the weeds in here. I want to have all the food out before Gigi and Charles arrive."

Kate dumped the wine in the kitchen sink and rinsed the glass. She hated to waste good wine like that, but she still wasn't feeling well. Since she couldn't drink it, she didn't want to take a chance of passing along a bug that she might be fighting.

"Any word on their ETA?" Kate asked before Jane could say anything else about interrupting her conversation with Aidan.

"Daniel went to the airport to pick them up. Their

plane gets in around six thirty. They went through customs in New York, but they'll have to get their luggage at baggage claim. That could take a while if the flight was full. Daniel said he would text Elle when they were on their way."

Jane glanced at her smartwatch. "I figure we have about an hour…tops. Maybe not even that much. Could you help me set out the rest of the appetizers?"

"Absolutely. Just tell me what's ready to go out—"

Before Kate could finish the sentence, Jane had handed her a platter piled high with brie and mushroom crostini that smelled so delicious they made Kate's mouth water. She suddenly realized she was ravenous and wanted to eat for the first time today. If her hands hadn't been full, she would have insisted on sampling one before setting them out where they would surely be devoured before she could get back to them.

Instead of noshing, she made her way out into the dining room to find a place for the tray.

They were having the party in the Forsyth Galloway Inn's private dining room. The doors that separated private dining from the lobby room were closed, and a sign that read Dining Room in Use for Private Event rested on an easel to afford them some rare family privacy.

Even though paying guests who stayed at the inn basically had the run of the place, except for the family apartments and the kitchen, on special occasions the family would close the dining room for private celebrations.

Kate's gaze landed on the elaborate centerpiece of fresh flowers on the formal mahogany dining room table, which was dressed with their great grandmother's best tablecloth and pressed linen napkins. Though they weren't the flowers her mother had received, Kate couldn't help but think of them and how Zelda had managed to skirt the subject of the mystery sender. She still hadn't confided the identity of the new beau who had sent them.

Kate was sure they were from a man.

If it had been a vendor, Zelda would have said so right away, but there was something in the far-off, dreamy way she had smiled—and the way she had evaded the question of who had sent them—that made Kate sure they were from a man.

Plus, every time she saw her mother lately, Zelda had been glued to her phone. Tonight was no exception. Whenever Kate glanced in her mother's direction, she saw her reading a text or typing something on her phone, closing the screen when Kate or anyone else got too close.

Kate made a mental note to reopen the conversation about the flowers with her mother and ask about the text messages after the party.

Right now, everyone had plenty to do to put the finishing touches on tonight's festivities. The table was set for twenty-five using the heirloom crystal and sterling silver. Kate placed the platter on the sideboard and walked over to the table to straighten a fork at one of the place settings. She adjusted the place card at another. Then she stepped back and looked at the table, smiling to herself. They were pulling out all the stops for Gigi and Charles.

Exactly as it should be.

Tonight they were celebrating a love between soul mates who had waited nearly a lifetime to finally find their way back to each other. They had known each other most of their lives, but until recently, fate had had other plans for them.

Over the years, when Gigi, whose real name was Wiladean, had been free, Charles hadn't been. Then Gigi had been happily married to Kate's grandfather, and Charles, ever the gentleman, had respected the bonds of holy matrimony and buried his feelings for Gigi. Though it hadn't stopped him from naming his restaurant in downtown Savannah Wila, after her.

That little love note was one of those obvious tells that had been right out in the open, in front of everyone's faces, but no one had ever talked about the Wila and Wiladean coincidence until after Gigi's husband passed. And a few years later, Charles had confessed his love for her and had proposed.

Gigi had managed to find two great loves in the eighty-five years that she had been on the earth. She wanted nothing more than for her three granddaughters to fall just as happily in love.

In fact, she had said as much at her eighty-fifth birthday earlier that year, when she had announced that the only thing she wanted for her birthday was for all three of her grandgirls to find happiness with their soul mates. Elle had gotten a head start with Daniel and was the first to tie the knot. Jane, who had fallen in love with Liam, was next.

Kate was the lone holdout—

Her heart skipped a beat—and not in a giddy, romantic way—when she realized that, actually, she wasn't the holdout. She was *married*. All day long, the reality had been hiding behind her normal day-to-day activities, only to jump out and scare the bejabbers out of her. She'd be going about her business, cutting a client's hair, talking about their kids or their recent trip to a theme park, when—BAM!—the realization would wash over her that she and Aidan were married. She'd been busy and engrossed in her day but startled suddenly by the memory of what had happened.

And because of Gigi's birthday wish, it was going

to be all the more difficult if the family found out about the Vegas wedding only to learn that she and Aidan were trying to get an annulment.

She gave her head a firm shake. She was not going to think about that tonight. She actually wanted to forget about it for a while. Tonight belonged to Gigi and Charles. It was about true love and infinite happiness.

Gigi and Charles had insisted that there be no wedding presents, wanting only the gift of their family's time to help plan the wedding in Vegas and attend it. So the greatest gift Kate could give them was to be emotionally present for them tonight.

She would do that. She would be present and attentive and joyful—even if she felt shackled and weighed down by her big mistake.

In addition to the newlyweds and six of their immediate family and Aidan, the guest list that Elle and Zelda had drawn up included sixteen of Charles and Gigi's closest friends, who'd be here for the surprise welcome-home party.

Kate and Elle had handled the decorations, which were simple and festive. Jane and Liam were in charge of the food, which would be upscale and delicious, no doubt.

Kate had made several more trips to the kitchen to set out more appetizers that Jane and Liam had

prepared—pâté with toast points, a cheese and char-
cuterie board, mozzarella and cherry tomato kebabs
speared with a sprig of rosemary, homemade sweet
potato chips with Liam's famous hot mustard and
sweet chili dipping sauce.

Even though she and her sisters were as different
as their respective hair colors—blond, brown and
red—they completed each other, as evidenced by the
way they had come together to pull off this party for
their beloved Gigi.

Kate glanced at her watch. The guests would
begin arriving in the next few minutes. She needed
to get out of her head and into party mode, and help
with the finishing touches of the surprise.

Kate walked through the butler's pantry that connected the dining room to the kitchen. She pushed
through the swinging kitchen door and into another
world where Jane's husband, Liam, was barking orders at a skeleton staff that he had brought in for the
night from Wila, the restaurant he and Jane now co-
owned with Charles. It was fortuitous that the restaurant was closed on Mondays and the sous-chefs, who
were eager to make a little money of the side, were
available to help take some of the burden off Liam.

Jane was a pastry chef and had baked an elegant
two-tiered wedding cake that looked like a work of
art you would see in a Parisian bakery. She truly

was an artist, and the masterpiece she had created for the occasion was a rosewater-champagne confection with an arrangement of white roses and flecks of edible gold leaf cascading off the top tier. Jane had already mandated that when they served dessert, they would set aside the top tier for Gigi and Charles to freeze until their first anniversary. The gorgeous cake was sitting safely off to the side, well out of the way of the maelstrom swirling around in the kitchen.

Kate's heart melted a little when she thought about how Jane and Liam were putting heart and soul into this post-wedding feast.

She couldn't remember what she and Aidan had done after Elvis had pronounced them husband and wife. Her cheeks heated at the thought. They hadn't even fed each other cake.

It seemed like there was something a little shameful about that. About not remembering, and about the absence of cake.

Every bride and groom deserved a wedding cake.

Just as fast as the thought popped into her head, she blinked it away. Dwelling on it would not solve anything tonight.

"Would you grab the caviar out of the fridge?" Jane asked as she came up behind Kate. "There's a dish with crushed ice in it over there." She pointed with her elbow because her hands were full with a pot of something else. "The caviar sits on top of the ice. Is this the cheese fondue?"

"I don't know—" Kate said, but Jane wasn't talking to her, she was addressing one of the sous-chefs.

"It needs to go in the fondue pot over there. The stand is on the buffet table. Don't forget to light the Sterno. We don't want the cheese to cool and set."

The sous-chef took the pot from Jane and whisked it away.

"I love it when you're bossy," Liam said, pulling Jane into his arms and kissing her soundly in the midst of the kitchen chaos.

That. That right there was what she wanted, Kate thought wistfully. That passion. That fire. She wanted what Jane and Liam had. She wanted what Gigi and Charles had. She wanted what Elle had with Daniel and her mother seemed to have with her mystery admirer.

There wasn't a thing in the world wrong with Aidan. He would make someone a fabulous husband.

Just not for her.

Well, not for very much longer.

Chapter Four

"Aidan, it is so nice of you to help us tonight," Zelda said as he watched Kate disappear into the kitchen. Kate's mother was taking a stack of cocktail napkins out of the packaging.

"Of course," Aidan said. "I'm glad I could be a part of it. I'm always happy to help you all with anything you need."

"Anything?" Zelda's eyes flashed, and he had a feeling he had taken her bait and was about to be reeled in.

"Within reason," he qualified, with a smile.

"How about some professional advice about the inn?" she asked.

"What can I do for you?" he asked. Because, of course, he would do anything he could to help Kate's mother.

"Elle's art classes and tours are bringing in revenue and business is booming at the tearoom. I think we are finally in a good place to start planning the spa."

Daniel was the general contractor on the remodel of the Forsyth Galloway Inn. Aidan had served as the architect, drawing up plans for the first two of the three additions Zelda and Gigi had wanted: a classroom area for lectures, also serving as an open art studio, and the tearoom.

It sounded like they were ready to get started on the third phase—a spa, which would be built in the inn's backyard on a piece of ground that they currently used as a garden plot.

"What does Kate think about moving forward with the plan?" Aidan asked.

Zelda frowned and crossed her arms. "You know the world doesn't revolve around my Kathryn. Even if she would like to believe it does."

He smiled, but he wasn't about to touch that comment with a ten-foot pole. Everyone knew Kate was opinionated and stubborn. She knew what she wanted, and she wasn't easily swayed.

Kate's strong sense of self was one of the many

things Aidan found so utterly attractive about her. Her physical beauty was obvious: her long, curly copper-colored hair, her flawless ivory skin. Her heart-shaped face and those stunning sea green eyes. And those lips. Oh, those lips.

She could move mountains and break hearts with those eyes and that mouth. He should know. One moment she would be looking at him adoringly and the next minute her words would be cutting him to the core.

"Are you saying you want to get the ball rolling and start designing the spa?" he asked.

Zelda nodded.

"Does that mean you want to meet with or without Kate? Will she be involved in these plans?"

Zelda pursed her lips together for a moment. She looked as if she was weighing her words.

"Aidan, I believe Kate wants this more than she realizes," she finally said.

Aidan shrugged. "Kate knows her own mind. She's not going to be swayed or talked into doing something she doesn't want to do. We both know that."

Zelda shrugged, like she wasn't convinced. Her phone buzzed with an incoming text and she set down the stack of cocktail napkins she had been fanning and checked her messages, smiling as she dashed off a quick return text before she answered Aidan.

"Kate is a complicated woman, Aidan. That girl of mine is so headstrong, sometimes she's her own worst enemy." Zelda shook her head. "I love all my girls equally, but she's the one I worry about the most. I know she's perfectly capable and smart as she can be, and she thinks she doesn't need anyone, but I feel that she's too darn independent for her own good. She pushes people away."

Hear, hear, to that.

"And that's why she's her own worst enemy," Zelda continued. "Elle is my intuitive, empathetic child. Jane is the strongest of the three girls—she's one hundred percent no-nonsense. Then there's Kate. A lot of people think she's the strong one because she puts up such a front, but they don't know her the way I do. Kate likes to believe she's an island. It is all because of her daddy. Has she told you about Fred and what his antics did to her?"

Zelda's eyes darkened, and she gave her head another quick shake and held up her hands before Aidan could answer.

"Oh, would you listen to me being inappropriate? This is not the place or the time to dredge up bad memories of good ol' Fred. He's done enough damage to this family. I am not going to allow thoughts of him to cast a shadow over what should otherwise be a wonderful evening. But, Aidan, hon, I do want to thank you. Thank you for loving my girl. Thank you for loving her quirks and looking past her…her difficulties and seeing the best in her."

Zelda's words made Aidan ache inside. He was trying with all his might to love Kate, but there was only so much one person could do—he could only be shoved away like this for so long before he couldn't take it any longer.

If Kate didn't want him, he wasn't going to beg her to let him stay.

And he wasn't going to coast along in this limbo land in which they had been existing for so long.

On a normal day, he was a man of few words. Right now, when he should offer some sort of reassurance to Zelda, he was completely at a loss. He had no idea what to say because he didn't know where his relationship with Kate stood or where it was going. They were married, but she wanted an annulment. She wanted to erase their union like it had been a bad mistake.

Kate had mentioned her father in passing. She had said it wasn't a happy relationship. He hadn't been part of their life since he had left the family when she and her sisters were in elementary school. She had not offered many details, and Aidan hadn't asked her to relive something that had obviously hurt her. Maybe he should have, but Kate had put up her walls, as she so often did when things got complicated and uncomfortable. Just like she had done after Vegas.

Despite everything, Aidan still believed they were good together. If Kate could just give him some indication that she hadn't completely closed her mind— even if she couldn't see where they would ultimately end up—he would not give up on her. As long as they were headed in the right direction, they were staying together.

Even if it meant he had to keep caring about her in spite of herself, in spite of the way she was pushing him away right now.

The bottom line was that even Zelda could see how much he cared for Kate. Right now, he would remember that when he started giving up. He would be the glue that held them together right now, when Kate was doing her best to tear them apart.

When Gigi and Charles arrived and the dining room doors opened, and everyone yelled, "Surprise!" in unison, Kate's heart melted a little as she observed the astonishment on her eighty-five-year-old grandmother's pretty face. Hand on her pearls, Gigi gasped at the scene unfolding in front of her.

"Oh, my heavens," she said, before turning to Charles. "Did you know about this?"

"Who, me?" Eyes wide, Charles shook his gray head. "What makes you think I had something to do with this wonderful surprise? Which is just fantastic. Thank you, everyone for the wonderful welcome home for my bride and me."

With that, Gigi seemed to snap back into her normal gracious-Southern-lady mode. "Yes, what a wonderful thing for y'all to do for us. Thank you, each and every one of you."

Zelda and Elle were the first to move forward and hug Gigi. Charles stood next to his wife with his hand on the small of her back, looking like a magician who had pulled off a particularly amazing sleight of hand, even though he'd had no idea about the surprise, either.

When Kate stepped up to take her turn at welcoming home the newlyweds, Gigi hugged her tight. "Darling girl. How are you? This party has your name written all over it. Thank you, sugar. Where's that handsome boyfriend of yours?"

Kate gritted her teeth. "Do you mean Aidan?"

Gigi nodded. "Of course, I mean Aidan. Who else would I be talking about?"

"He's around here somewhere." Kate had to hand

it to him—he had been giving her plenty of space tonight.

Gigi gave Kate another squeeze and asked the question Kate knew was inevitable. "How long until we will have the opportunity to celebrate *your* engagement, sweetheart? I hope it is soon. I'm not going to live forever, you know."

"Oh, Gigi, don't say that. Especially not on such a happy night. And this night isn't about me. It is about you and Charles."

"Well, you're next, honey, and I can't wait to throw you a party that's just as magnificent as this one. When the last of my granddaughters gets married, I plan on throwing the wedding that will put all other weddings to shame."

Kate's heart twisted as she thought about how an annulment party was the most likely thing in her near future. And it would very well be the party that would end all parties.

At least for her.

"Gigi, I thought you prided yourself on keeping things equal. Elle and Jane aren't going to like it very much if you say my wedding will put their weddings to shame."

Gigi waved her comment away. "You know what I mean. As I said at my eighty-fifth birthday party, all I want is for all three of my darlin' grandgirls to be happily married and settled in relationships that made them as happy as my Charles makes me."

Gigi turned to her husband and smiled up at him. In that instant, she looked like a young, blushing bride.

Even though Gigi wanted all three of them to be married, it would crush her if she learned that Kate and Aidan had eloped. She wanted the chance to give each of them a wedding.

It was pretty much a given that her grandmother would never forgive her for having the marriage annulled. Not only was Aidan the best prospect for making Gigi's trifecta birthday wish come true, but she genuinely adored Aidan.

A very short-lived marriage certainly would not tick the box on Gigi's birthday wish list.

Kate wondered if it would help her cause to remind her grandmother that she had wanted them all settled in *happy* relationships. The *happy* part was key.

Would Gigi even care about the fact that marriage in general made Kate feel anything but happy? That it made her feel itchy and claustrophobic, like she wanted to run far away?

Thank goodness for Jane and Liam, who were holding trays of champagne and calling everyone for a toast, diverting Gigi's attention from what they had been talking about. Kate accepted the flute of bubbly Jane handed her, but as with the red wine that Aidan had handed her earlier, the thought of even sipping the golden liquid made her stomach churn. Love Potion Number Nine had really done a number on her.

"Mama and Charles," said Zelda. "If ever two people were meant to be together, it is you. You are an example and inspiration to everyone. You have waited so long to find your way to each other, but you are living proof that true love won't be denied, that true love is real. It exists. Even if we have to wait sixty-five years for the timing to be right. Here's to the two of you."

Zelda raised her glass and everyone else did, too. Kate felt Aidan's gaze on her. When her eyes met his, he raised his glass in a private toast to her. Did the look in his eyes telegraph that he was willing to wait as long as it took for her? Kate's stomach flipped at the romantic thought.

But just as fast, the hopeful feeling gave way to sorrow and shame. It was so unfair to even imagine something so one-sided.

It was selfish and wrong that in the midst of planning to dissolve their marriage, she would think the two of them might one day find their way back to each other.

Why couldn't she just let herself love him? Why

couldn't she just get herself together and realize that the perfect man for her was standing right in front of her?

He was her husband. Her mind could intellectualize it and make a solid argument for why staying married to Aidan was a good thing, but her battered heart and her self-preserving reflexes were not buying it.

Her heart had already packed its bags and moved out.

This was how it would go: she would lose him. Another woman with a whole lot more sense than she had would scoop him up and—

Kate tore her gaze away from Aidan's.

She had to put an end to that line of thinking right now. It was what it was and she needed to stop feeling sorry for herself, because she could not have it both ways.

She set her full glass of champagne on a side table and slipped out of the dining room into the lobby, and then exited through the beveled-glass front doors and made her way to the dark edge of the wraparound front porch. Maybe some fresh air would calm her upset stomach—and given the way she was feeling, it wasn't a bad idea to be close to a bathroom. Just in case.

No one would miss her before dinner was served.

They were all busy congratulating Gigi and Charles, listening to tales about their Paris honeymoon and filling them in on what had transpired in Savannah while they were gone.

The night air was balmy and what she could see of the sky through the moss-laden live oaks was clear and starry.

Kate had only been on the side porch for a few moments when she heard the front door open and close. For a split second, her heart raced when she worried it might be Aidan. She tried to disappear deeper into the shadows of the inn's magnificent front porch, hoping to remain out of sight.

"Kate?" It was Elle's voice. "Are you out here?"

So much for no one missing her.

"I'm here." Kate stepped forward.

"What are you doing out here? Is everything oaky?"

Elle was the most intuitive of her sisters. It didn't surprise Kate that Elle had picked up on her retreat. Kate now wished she hadn't left the party.

"I'm fine. I just need a little fresh air. I'm still not feeling great."

"Oh, I'm sorry. Yeah, I noticed you didn't drink your champagne. It is the good stuff. Jane and Liam brought it from the restaurant for the party tonight.

Do you want me to go get you some? Maybe the bubbles will settle your stomach."

"No, thanks. My stomach is still feeling a little off-kilter."

"Do you think it's the stomach flu?"

"I don't think so. It sort of comes and goes. A stomach bug is pretty consistent until it runs its course. I just have a lot of stress right now. Some things I can't really talk about."

"Really? You're not pregnant, are you?"

"Oh my gosh, no! Don't even joke about that. A baby is the last thing I need right now."

Kate laughed a nervous laugh, as if making light of it might ward off any bad juju that would swirl together and manifest the godforsaken possibility.

Even though their passion was strong enough to sweep them away, they'd always held on to good common sense, and made sure they used condoms. That was because Aidan had Chloe and she certainly didn't need a baby to further complicate already complicated matters.

The only thing that frightened her more than the thought of being someone's wife was being someone's mother.

"What are we doing today?" Kate asked as her client Karen settled herself in the salon chair.

"I don't know. I think I need a change, but I don't know what to do."

Yeah, I hear ya, sister. Isn't that the story of all of our lives?

Kate fluffed Karen's dark brown, shoulder-length bob. The woman had worn it this way for as long as Kate had been doing her hair—actually, for as long as Kate had known her.

At every appointment, Karen said she wanted to try something different, but she ended up second-guessing herself and leaving with the same cut freshened up, saying she'd think about it next time. But not before they went through the very same song and dance they were starting right now.

"Can you help me, Kate? I'd love some advice on what to do with my hair. I feel like I'm stuck in a rut."

Here we go again.

"How big a change were you thinking?" Kate asked. "Do you want a new style or a change of color? Or both?"

Karen's pretty, round face flushed. "Oh dear, I don't know. I've never colored my hair other than to touch up the gray. And you know that I do that myself at home. If I changed my color, like if I became a blonde or redhead, I probably won't be able to maintain the color myself, will I? I know hair color can be very expensive and it might be too drastic a change. Don't you think?"

Karen put her hands on either side of her face as if preparing herself for a mind-blowing answer.

Kate wanted to say, *Honey, I am not the one to ask. I am all about drastic changes these days. Even though I'm your hairdresser, I'm not the person to ask right now.*

But then again, this was about hair. Not life choices.

"It is true, color does require some upkeep. What about highlights? That would grow out more naturally."

Karen studied herself in the ornate gold-framed mirror, turning her face this way and that. The salon was busy today. Every chair was occupied, and the stylists were at various stages of their appointments. The place was buzzing with the sound of chatter, hair dryers and running water. A few chairs down, a client was having an animated conversation with someone about her cat. Or at least that was what it sounded like to Kate. That was the only thing she could imagine would climb the woman's curtains. Could be interesting if it was something—or some-one—else.

"Oh, Kate." Karen sighed. "You know me. I'm just not ready yet. I guess I'll need to think about it for a little bit longer. For now, let's just go with the usual haircut. Let's bring it up an inch." Karen tsked and raised her chin. "Wait. No, you know what? Let's live dangerously and bring it up an inch and a half."

"Are you sure? I could give you some layers. That would give your hair a little more lift."

Karen snagged Kate's gaze in the mirror. "I just— I don't know, Kate. You know I don't do much to maintain my hair. Do you think I should? Kate, tell me what I should do."

Irritation snapped at Kate's nerves, threatening to bite through her calm facade. How was she supposed to solve other people's problems when she didn't even know how to deal with her own?

Every time she and Karen did this beauty parlor two-step, Karen always decided to think about it. Kate never nudged her to try something different, because she was there to give her clients what they wanted, not to talk them into something they didn't want.

But today felt different. Maybe all these years, she had been doing Karen a disservice by not giving her that little push that would take her outside of her comfort zone.

Kate frowned and bit her bottom lip at the thought. Actually, running away from commitment was Kate's comfort zone.

"Okay, since you asked, yes. If I were you, I would go for it. You said you wanted a change. Right?"

Karen nodded, eyes large, as if Kate were talking her into jumping out of a plane. Then Riki Rollins, who had the chair next to Kate's, fired up her blow-dryer and proceeded to talk to her client over it, the noise encroaching on the confidence to try something new that Kate had intended to infuse into Karen.

Kate reminded herself to exercise patience. Karen was somewhere between her mother's and Gigi's age. Kate would hope that if either of them were sidelined by indecision, the person they were dealing with would be good to them and not try to sell them on something they didn't want.

She leaned in so Karen could hear her over the noise of the dryer. "I promise I won't do anything too drastic. Remember, if you don't like it, your hair will grow out."

Karen tugged at a piece of hair as if testing its ability to grow. Then with a flick of her wrist, she tossed it away.

"Oh, what the heck," she said with an adventurous glint in her eyes. "Let's go for it. You only live once, right? And you're going to come over every morning and fix it for me, right?"

Kate laughed. "Don't worry. I'll show you how

to style it. It won't be hard. Come on, let's get you back to the shampoo bowl so we can get this party started."

As she led the way, a tall, familiar masculine frame caught her eye. She turned to see Aidan standing in the reception area.

Darned if her body didn't override the common sense switch and experience that same visceral reaction she had every time she saw Aidan.

Heart pounding, she gestured to him that she would be there in a moment. She got Karen settled with one of the shampoo assistants and came back to meet Aidan.

"What are you doing here?" she asked. "Is everything okay? Is Chloe okay?"

"Chloe's fine," he said. "I came to see if you could take a lunch break."

Kate blinked as she realized that this was the first time since they had been dating that he had showed up unannounced at the salon to take her to lunch. And damned if it wasn't kind of sexy. Aidan was always so proper and polite. He was the type to call to make sure that she didn't already have plans or to ask what time was good for her so that he wouldn't interrupt her with a client. He never did anything spontaneous like showing up unannounced.

Until now.

"I'm getting ready to cut my client Karen's hair, but that should only take twenty minutes or so. She's back getting a shampoo right now. After Karen, my next appointment isn't until two o'clock. Do you want to wait?"

Kate motioned to one of the free seats next to the reception desk. "There's a Keurig over there in the corner. You can have a cup of coffee while you wait."

He glanced in the direction she was pointing.

"I have some things I need to do," he said. "I'll come back in a half hour."

"Oh, right. That sounds good."

She waited for him to lean in and kiss her, but he just smiled and said, "See you in a bit."

As she watched him walk out the salon doors and past the large picture window, a pang gripped her heart. Something felt different. Of course, it did. And it was all of her making. How was a man supposed to act when his new wife asked for an annulment? Aidan was being his normal, kind, classy self, with a little added distance.

Kate had to own it, but that didn't mean she had to like it.

Less than a half hour later, Kate had finished with Karen. She had just enough time to tidy up her station before Tasha, the receptionist, appeared and said, "That gorgeous hunk of yours asked me to tell you he is here."

On the few occasions that Aidan had stopped by the salon, he had just walked back to Kate's station. He hadn't waited for Tasha to announce him.

He was being formal. The pang that had previously made a guest appearance and quietly faded, morphed into a full-blown ache that took up residence under her rib cage.

She had really screwed up. Hadn't she?

If they could only go back to how it was before Vegas. If they could go back, she would keep a clear head and steer clear of all the cute little wedding chapels.

Maybe it wasn't as bad as she feared. After all, he had come to see her. He wanted to have lunch with her. It couldn't be all bad, could it?

Kate glanced at herself in the mirror. She fluffed her long, copper curls, swiped on some lip gloss and blush because she looked so pale. She still wasn't feeling like herself. Because of that, she hadn't been able to eat breakfast. The thought of food first thing in the morning turned her inside out. Maybe she was hungry. More likely, it was the stress of sorting out this mess with Aidan.

But he was the one who'd suggested lunch. So it couldn't be all bad, could it? She slung her purse onto her shoulder, checked her posture and went out into the reception area to meet Aidan.

"Hi, Kate." He smiled when he saw her. It was the same smile he always had for her. It reached all the way to his eyes, which lingered on her eyes in a way that made her feel special, as if he reserved that look just for her.

But once again, there was no kiss. He walked straight to the door and held it open for her.

"I thought we'd go to The Pig and Whistle." The Pig was a great little sandwich spot just around the corner from the salon, which was located on Abercorn Street.

It was early, just after 11:00 a.m. The place hadn't filled up. The hostess led them to a marble-topped table for two and handed them menus. "Jesse will be your server. He'll be right with you."

The smell of something frying hit her like a boat tossing on a rough sea, upending her stomach, making her glad it was empty. Her hand flew to her mouth.

"What's wrong?" Aidan asked.

Kate shook her head, drawing in a deep breath through her nose before she answered. "I don't know. I'm still not feeling one hundred percent. I don't know what's wrong with me. I might have a mild bug or something. Just when I think I've kicked it, it sneaks up on me again."

"Can I get you something?" he asked, all chivalrous, gentlemanly concern. "Some water, maybe?"

"Thanks, Aidan, but our server will be here any second now."

"And that would be me," said a tall, skinny guy who looked like he might've still been in high school. "I'm Jesse. Is everything okay?"

"Can you bring us some water right away?" Aidan asked. "She might be dehydrated. So, water first and then we'll decide what we want to eat."

"And some hot tea," Kate added. "Black tea, please. No sugar or lemon."

"Coming right up," Jesse said. In less than thirty seconds he was setting two glasses of iced water in front of them.

After sipping the water a couple of times and holding the ice cubes in her mouth, she felt the wave of nausea ease up a bit. They placed their orders and sat in silence for a few beats.

"Feeling better?" Aidan asked.

"I am," she said. Although she found the silence uncomfortable. "It is so strange. It comes and goes. Just when I think I've locked it. It rears its ugly head again. It is probably a bug. I probably picked it up on the flight out to Vegas. I'm sure it will pass."

"Since it is lingering, maybe you should go to the doctor," Aidan said. "You could mention the blackout."

Kate bristled. "It wasn't a blackout. I don't black out when I drink. Especially when I only have two sips."

"Okay, you had two sips of a strong drink and didn't remember marrying me. But it wasn't a blackout."

"Shhh!" Kate glanced around the restaurant. "The last thing we need right now is for someone to overhear us talking about it and for word to get back to Mom and Gigi."

"I'm just saying, if you're still feeling bad it would not hurt to get checked by a doctor. Why suffer if it is something that can be fixed?"

She made a face at him. "Yeah, maybe there's a problem with my brain. That would explain why my equilibrium is off and why I blacked out, as you put it."

Aidan shrugged. "Sorry. I don't know what else to call it. I'm concerned. I don't want it to be something serious."

He had a point. It wasn't normal. Feeling intermittently sick wasn't normal, either. Not remembering her own wedding was a real sore spot, and that certainly wasn't normal. What would it hurt to get checked out? If she had another wave of nausea between today and tomorrow, it might be a good idea to see a doctor. Maybe she was fighting off something that could be fixed.

Or maybe she was pregnant.

No!

Her mind replayed the conversation she had had with Elle yesterday.

There was no way she could be pregnant, because she and Aidan were careful. They used condoms. She was fanatical about it because she wasn't ready to be a mother.

No. There was no way.

No. Way.

Jesse brought their food and they made pleasant conversation while they ate. Kate polished off the bacon, lettuce and tomato sandwich she had ordered—the only thing on the menu that sounded good. She ate it ravenously, as if she hadn't eaten in days. It tasted better than anything she had ever eaten, filling her empty stomach in a gentle, soothing way.

Even though the bacon was a little greasy, it didn't bother her. It settled well.

After the bill was paid, Kate was still lingering over her tea, in no hurry to get back to the salon since it was still a while before her appointment.

Aidan didn't seem to be in a rush to leave, either. So it shouldn't have come as a surprise when he cleared his throat and said, "I need to talk to you about something."

Conversation during lunch had been a little strained, but when they reached the end of the meal without any major disputes or bombshells or mention of the annulment, Kate had started to believe that Aidan had asked her to lunch because he wanted her company. Even though Aidan had not been acting like his usual self since the time he'd appeared at the salon, in the back of her mind, Kate had let herself hope that maybe they could find their way back to good once the dust had settled.

But she'd thought too soon.

"I talked to a lawyer about our situation," Aidan said. Judging by the look on his face, he didn't have good news. "You're not going to like what I have to tell you."

"Oh. And what did the attorney have to say? Aidan, we haven't even had our hearing yet. I thought he said we'd have to wait a month before we could even request a hearing."

"He did say that. He also said that annulments in Georgia are very difficult to win. He consulted some of his colleagues on the matter and their opinion is that our case doesn't look promising. Of course, we can go ahead with the petition, but the attorney thinks the only chance we might have to win is by claiming that you were mentally incompetent the night we got married."

Wait. Hold on there. Mentally incompetent?

Kate made a face. "Mentally incompetent?"

"Yes. Even that's a long shot. The fact that we spent our honeymoon night together makes it even tougher to plead our case, and of course, our prior relationship doesn't help matters," Aidan continued. "He said if we really want to get out of this marriage, we should strongly consider divorce. Or at least start preparing ourselves for divorce being the only way to end the marriage, because it will likely be our only option."

Aidan stared at the table and traced a silver vein in the marble on the tabletop with his finger. He was already divorced from Chloe's mother, who had decided, right after giving birth, that she did not want to be tied down to a husband and child. She had left Aidan with a tiny newborn to care for on his own.

Aidan had confided in Kate that if he ever got married again—and it was a solid *if* because he didn't want to put himself and his daughter through that heartbreak again—the marriage would be forever.

While he sometimes talked like getting married

again was not very high on his list, he had not solidly ruled out the possibility.

But then why— Why, if he had been in his right mind, had he married her in Vegas under those circumstances? Of course, he had said that she had seemed to know what she was doing. Still, she longed to press the issue and ask him that question again, but right now, she couldn't move the words from her brain to her lips.

She didn't want to get a divorce. She wanted an annulment because it shouldn't have happened like that.

But even more, she didn't want to get the annulment by claiming mental instability. It wasn't true, and it felt like fraud. It felt disrespectful to those who did battle a condition. Something like that shouldn't be trifled with and certainly should not be used to get out of a sticky situation. She couldn't live with herself if she played that card. Surely, blacking out—er—*not remembering* one night wasn't the same as being mentally *incompetent*. Mentally incapacitated, sure. But not mentally *incompetent*. Saying she was would be a lie.

"If mental incompetency is our only way out, I have a feeling the judge isn't simply going to take my word for it. Wouldn't I have to see a doctor? Wait, don't even answer that. We both know it is not true and I don't think it is right to use something so serious to clean up the mess we made."

The moment the words fell out of her mouth, she regretted them. The look on Aidan's face was soul crushing. She wished she could reel them back in.

Aidan stood. "I wasn't suggesting that you lie or misrepresent a condition—because you're right, it should not be taken lightly." His voice was level and low as he bit off the words. "Then it looks like a divorce will be the only way to clean up our *mess*, as you put it. Though I never considered being married to you a mess or a mistake, Kate. I'll call him and have him get started on the divorce papers."

As he turned to leave, Kate felt as if he was walking out of her life forever. Her heart ached. "Aidan, don't go—"

"Yeah, I need to go. I'll talk to you later, Kate." He waked away and didn't look back.

Chapter Five

After Aidan left the restaurant, he didn't go back to the office. He walked around downtown Savannah, trying to burn off some of the anger boiling in his gut. Kate was right. This was a mess. Even though her calling their marriage a mess had pissed him off in a big way, that was exactly what it was. A big, fat, ugly mess, made worse by the increasingly clear reality that the only way out of it was straight down the divorce highway.

Sitting on the edge of the fountain in Lafayette Square, Aidan braced his elbows on his knees. He had calmed down to the point that he no longer saw red, and he was now able to do some soul-searching.

While he had never minded being the glue that held together his relationship with Kate, he wasn't going to force Kate into a permanent tie she didn't want. No relationship could make it if only one partner wanted it to work.

He had searched his heart and thought about his own motivation for staying in the marriage. It wasn't just because it would be his second divorce. While he felt like a two-time failure, he kept coming back to the fact that he wanted to build a life with her. He wanted to have kids with her. He wanted Kate, Chloe and him to be a family together.

Kate loved Chloe. Chloe loved Kate. God knew his little girl deserved a mother. While he and his daughter had done fine on their own, Chloe was getting to the age where she needed a female role model. Even as important as that was, it wasn't the tipping point that made him want to marry Kate.

They were good together.

He loved her.

Those were the reasons.

It was as plain and simple as that.

They fit. He was a better person with her. With her, he felt whole. As if every other relationship in his life—and there hadn't been many—hadn't worked because he was meant for Kate.

Kate was his soul mate.

He wished he made her feel the same way.

He would fight for them, but he would not try to force her to stay if she didn't want to.

But he couldn't help but hope that since it wasn't as easy for her to run away from her feelings this time, maybe she would have time to think about it—about them—and realize how good they were together.

The next morning, when Kate woke up with another bout of the nausea that had been sidelining her since Vegas, she decided it was time to visit the doctor. It had been going on for ten days now, more than enough time for a virus to run its course.

She got the first available appointment that morning since her first client wasn't coming until midmorning.

After peeing in a cup and allowing the nurse to draw blood, Kate sat on the exam table in a small room with cheerful yellow walls and framed paintings of colorful flowers. As she waited for the doctor to come in and offer the magic cure, she thought about how she had rarely been sick in her life. Except for the occasional cold, she was usually pretty healthy, which meant she wasn't super vigilant about going in for yearly examinations. She was only twenty-six and she took good care of herself. She walked to work several times a week and tried to watch what she ate. She didn't smoke, and except for the occasional social drink or celebratory toast, she stayed away from alcohol because of her father's dicey history with it and, for the most part, she didn't really like it. She would rather spend her calories on something sweet like chocolate or one of the masterpieces Jane created for the tearoom at the inn.

Had it been a mistake to forgo those regular checkups? What if there was something wrong that she could have prevented? Her heart thudded in her chest as a host of possibilities flooded her mind. She batted each one away with good, common sense reasoning such as her relatively clear family history. Her sisters, mother and grandmother were healthy.

But sometimes disaster struck. Having a clean family history didn't automatically exempt a person from being the first to be stricken with a disease—especially someone like her, who had her hands in chemicals such as hair color and perm solution day in and day out.

A few seconds later, a knock sounded on the exam room door, interrupting the spiral of hypochondria.

"Hi, Kate." Dr. Moore greeted Kate with a warm smile before she glanced at her chart. Olivia Moore was young and smart and had a great way with patients. On the rare occasion that Kate saw her, she never rushed Kate or made her feel bad for not making regular appointments. She made it clear that no question was a dumb question.

"Hi, Dr. Moore. Thanks for seeing me on such short notice. I have some kind of a bug that doesn't seem to want to run its course and get out of my system. It has been like ten days now. Is there something going around? Although I'd bet I picked it up on a recent flight to Vegas."

"How are you feeling?" Dr. Moore asked as she washed her hands at the sink in the corner of the exam room.

"I'm feeling frustrated. I'm tired all the time and I always have this vaguely nauseated feeling. Some days it is worse than others, but it always seems to be there."

Dr. More picked up Kate's chart.

"Do you know that you're pregnant? The test we just did came back positive."

The call from Kate came as he was dropping Chloe off at school. He was in the car line and hadn't quite made it to the place where the safety patrols helped the kids get out of the car.

He pushed the button that connected the call to the audio system so that he could keep both hands on the wheel.

"Good morning, Kate. I'm in the car with Chloe. You're on speaker."

"Oh!" was all she said for a moment. "Good morning, Chloe."

"Good morning, Kate," Chloe said. "We're having show-and-tell today. So I got to bring Princess Sweetie Pie with me. Say good morning to Kate, Sweetie Pie. She lets me call her Sweetie Pie instead of Princess Sweetie Pie. But only I can do that."

Aidan smiled as his little girl chattered on and on about her stuffed cat that she dragged around with her everywhere possible. Now that she was in first grade—big girl school, as they called it—she had to concentrate on her schoolwork and that meant that she couldn't cart the big white cat around. Except on special days like this.

It was sweet the way Kate listened to Chloe, interjecting all the right responses and asking questions that made her seem genuinely interested in what his little girl was saying. He had no doubt that it wasn't an act. Kate made it clear that she had a real affection for Chloe. Because of that—because of times like this—Aidan could put everything else that had happened since Vegas aside and feel nothing but love for Kate.

"We are almost at the drop-off point," Aidan said. "How about if I call you back in just a minute?"

"Please do, Aidan. It's important."

Important? That was when he noticed that her voice sounded a little shaky.

"Is everyone okay?" he asked. "Gigi and Charles? Your mom? Your sisters?"

"Oh. Yes. They're all fine."

She still sounded far away. Not in physical distance, but in demeanor, as if she was distracted and her mind was a million miles away.

"I need to talk to you. Is there any way you could come by my place after you drop off Chloe?"

"Sure. I have an appointment at ten, but I don't need to get to the office until a few minutes before then."

After he hung up the phone, Chloe said, "Look, Daddy, there's Miss Doris and Beatrice."

His little girl was bouncing up and down in her car booster seat as Aidan stopped in the drop-off zone. It warmed his heart and took his mind off the odd call with Kate as he thought about how little it took to make his daughter happy.

"I see them," he said. "I think they're waiting for you."

"I know! That makes me so happy. I can walk to my classroom with Beatrice."

The car line drill was that parents pulled up into the designated area and adults—a couple of staff members, but mostly parents who were volunteering as part of the PTA—helped the children out of the cars. That way the parents didn't have to get out and the line moved along quickly and safely.

Doris, who was the mother of Chloe's best friend, approached their car and opened the door for Chloe.

She leaned in. "Good morning, Aidan, I'm volunteering here today. Beatrice has just been chomping at the bit waiting for Chloe to arrive."

"Good morning, Doris," he said. "Chloe, don't forget your lunch. She's bringing in her stuffed cat for show-and-tell. I'm afraid she will forget everything else but that."

"No worries," sang Doris. "I have her backpack and lunch box. She has Princess Sweetie Pie."

Of course, Doris would know the cat's name. Chloe spent a lot of time at her house playing with her daughter.

"Are we forgetting anything?" Doris asked.

"No, I think that's all. Thanks, Doris. Have a great day."

Aidan turned around in his seat and prepared to drive away, but the woman lingered for a moment in his open back door.

"Per chance are you free to meet for coffee later? I finish my volunteer shift here in about twenty minutes. I was thinking we could meet up at The Sentient Bean. Are you up for it?"

"Sorry, Doris, I have to be somewhere in—" He glanced at his watch. "I should be there now."

The woman's face fell. "Oh, well. Of course. I'm sure you have a business to run. You can't just stop for coffee with the mom of your daughter's friend.

But maybe another time. It's that I like to get to know the parents of all of Beatrice's friends."

"As a good mother would," Aidan said. "Another time would be great, but I really do have to run."

They said their goodbyes and Aidan drove to Kate's house, pondering what was so important that she had to see him now.

Not that he minded. He longed to wake up and see her every morning, kiss her first thing and bring her coffee in bed.

He parked in the driveway in front of her bungalow. The gravel on the drive crunched under his feet as he made his way up to the door. Though it was still early, the sun was already heating up and the humidity clung to him like a heavy damp suit. It was going to be a hot one.

He knocked and swiped his hand over his brow to wipe away any beads of perspiration that might have collected as he waited for Kate to answer.

When she did, he started sweating for a different reason after he took one look at her tear-stained face.

"Kate, honey, what's wrong?"

"Come in." Her voice was barely a whisper. Her shoulders shuddered with the sobs she was trying to contain.

She shut the door.

He didn't know what to say or do—whether to

hug her or give her some space—as he searched his mind for the possible causes of her distress. She'd said her family was fine—

"Aidan, I'm pregnant."

Whoa. Okay. Wow. "Really?"

A baby? They were having a baby?

A warm glow slowly eradicated the cold dread he'd been feeling but a moment ago.

His heart suddenly felt so full that he couldn't help but beam with pride.

He and Kate were having a baby. He resisted the urge to yell *yes* and give the air a victory punch. Because one look at Kate and he realized that she was having a much harder time with this plot twist their lives had taken than he was.

Still, there was no getting around his happiness.

"Honey, this is wonderful news."

He pulled her into his arms, and to his relief, for the first time in a long time, she sank into him and let him hold her. Her body gently shook as she cried on his shoulder.

"Tell me what you're thinking," he said a few moments later, leaning back so he could see her eyes.

She shrugged. "I can't—I don't know. I can't quite get my mind wrapped around it. That there's a life growing inside me."

Tears filled her eyes and spilled over onto her cheeks.

"It is going to be all right," he said. "Everything is going to be fine. I promise. Kate. Oh my God, we're going to have a baby."

She swiped at her eyes. Aidan got up and returned with a tissue. She wiped her tears and blew her nose. "What are we going to do, Aidan?"

He smiled. "We're going to be a family. That's what we're going to do. This is the best news."

She blinked and then squinted at him. "Really? You're not upset?"

"No, I'm not. I'm the opposite of upset. I'm thrilled. This is something to celebrate. A baby, Kate. Our baby."

Maybe he should temper his enthusiasm. It seemed like she wasn't digesting the news quite as happily as he was.

"I was afraid you would be upset. After the Vegas wedding and now this—I was afraid you would think I staged the wedding because I was pregnant."

Her body shook with sobs.

"I didn't, Aidan," she continued. "You have to know I would never do something like that."

"I know you wouldn't do that." He smiled at her.

Kate sighed as if the weight of the world had been

lifted off her shoulders, but she still looked unsure. "You're really not upset?"

"No. Absolutely not."

Having a baby with Kate was one of the best gifts he could have imagined.

"Good, because I'm having this baby."

"Of course. As far as I'm concerned, there's no other option. However, you know that this means that there is absolutely no way we can get an annulment."

She nodded. "I figured as much."

They were quiet for a moment.

"I'm not sure what to do now," she whispered. "I mean, about us. What we should do."

"What if we give it a year?" he suggested. "By that time, the baby will be a few months old. That will give us enough time to think things through, so that we know we're doing the right thing."

She stood there quietly for a moment, as if she was processing her options.

Finally she nodded. "I think that sounds reasonable."

"How would you feel about moving in with Chloe and me?"

She shook her head as if he had suggested that she join him in swimming in a pool filled with rattlesnakes. "No, I don't think that's a good idea."

"Why not?"

"What about Chloe?"

"What about her?" he said. "She loves you. She would be thrilled for you to move in. I mean, we're married, Kate. It is not as if we'd be shacking up."

"Yeah, but we haven't even told her we're married."

"Well, then we need to tell her as soon as possible."

"Or do we?" Kate said. "Why do we have to tell her? We could live separately and see where we are at the end of the year."

"No." He shook his head. "This is where I have to put my foot down. We have to tell her because she deserves to know she has a little brother or sister. It wouldn't be fair to keep it from her."

"You're right. I know. I'm sorry."

"And your family will find out soon enough. We need to tell Chloe then because she is likely to find out after we tell your family."

"You're right. We need to tell my family, too." She looked panicked, but then her face settled into a look of resignation. She put her hand on her flat stomach. "I haven't had a chance to digest everything. It's a lot more complicated than I realized."

She closed her eyes and looked absolutely miserable.

"Aidan, I kind of like living here in our bubble— just you and me. And Chloe, of course. But what if

things don't work out after the year we're giving ourselves is over? I mean, I don't want to hurt Chloe."

"The only reason Chloe would get hurt is if we
break up," he said.

"Exactly. That's what I mean. It is a very real possibility that we need to consider," Kate said. "It could
happen. You said yourself we would give it a year,
a trial run. Who knows? At the end of the year, you
might not be able to stand me. You might be the one
who wants out."

Aidan raked his hand through his hair. "I highly
doubt it. I'm coming at this with the intention of making it work. That means I'm not going into it with a
defeatist attitude. I'm not going to think that we're
doomed to fail before we've even given it a fair shake.
I believe you're worth the investment, Kate. We are
worth the investment. Our baby, Chloe, the family
that we are forming. It is all worth the ups and downs.
Don't you think so? How could you not think so?"

Kate sank into the corner of the couch and pulled
her knees up to her chest. She looked tiny sitting
there. It was as if she was trying to disappear.

"You're putting a lot of pressure on me, you
know?"

Maybe he was. He didn't mean it that way. But
by God, if she couldn't bring her all, then maybe he
should tell her she was free to go. That she could

call him when she had decided what she wanted to do. But he didn't want to do that. Because this child was as much his as it was hers. He was going to be part of their child's life whether or not she wanted them to live like a traditional family.

But he wasn't going to say that out loud. He couldn't. Because all it took was one look at her face, and he could see how much she was hurting. And the fact that she hurt made him hurt, too. It turned his guts inside out.

Right now, he would be strong for both of them.

"That's why we're going to give it a year. We're good together, Kate. Even if you don't know it right now, I really believe we can make it work."

She was silent for a moment, resting her forehead on her knees.

"I have been thinking about something." She lifted her head and looked him square in the eyes.

She shook her head. Her eyes filled with tears again. "I've been avoiding facing the real deep-seated reason marriage scares me."

"What is the real reason?" he asked. "I'm sure there's nothing we can't fix if we work together."

"I wish it was that simple, Aidan. But I don't think so. Actually, I didn't realize it until now, but I think the reason I'm so terrified of marriage is that I'm afraid deep down that I will turn out to be just like my father."

"Kate, I don't know your dad, but I know you and you seem nothing like what you've told me of him."

Granted, she didn't talk about him much, but from what she'd said, Aidan could tell he was a louse.

"I don't deserve you, Aidan." Tears were streaming down her cheeks now, and he reached up and tried to swipe them away.

"I don't know why you would think that," he said. "Because it is not true. We are so good together."

"Maybe I should say that you deserve better than what I have to offer you and Chloe."

She closed her eyes and drew in a deep breath as she brushed an imaginary piece of lint off her black pant leg. Finally she cleared her throat.

"You know that my father left my mother, sisters and me, right?"

"Yes. I remember you mentioning it. And later, your father tried to take the inn away from your mother. Or at least he tried to sue her for what he believed was the half he was entitled to—"

"He wasn't entitled to anything," Kate snapped.

Aidan reached out and took her hand. "I know that."

He wanted to ask what that had to do with them or her turning out to be like her father, but by the grace of God, his better judgment kept him silent until she was ready to speak.

"When my father left us, it really did a number on me. You know how some girls are born daddy's girls? I think that was me, but not in the traditional sense of daddy being the first guy I fall in love with and no guy ever measuring up to him. I'm afraid that I inherited his mutant gene—that selfish defect in his personality—that makes it impossible for me to commit to one person or stay in a situation for a prolonged period. I mean, I will commit to raising the baby. There's no question about that. Between the two of us and the help we'll get from my family, the baby will never want for anything. But I'm afraid that if I move in with you and Chloe, I'll end up leaving and hurting the two of you in the end. In fact, I can almost guarantee you that's what will happen."

"Almost." Aidan took care to keep his voice gentle, even though he really wanted to scream. Not at her, but at the situation.

"What?" she asked.

"You said you could *almost* guarantee that you would leave. That means the door isn't completely closed. As long as there's even a small margin of hope for us, I'm not giving up on you, Kate."

She gave her head a quick shake.

"When my dad left and then, years later, tried to take the inn away from my mom and my sisters and me—I mean, he knew it was our birthright—it crushed me. He expected Gigi and my mom to sell this place that had been the only home my sisters and I had ever known. That was bad enough. But the worst part was after he lost the lawsuit, he just disappeared. My sisters and I haven't heard from him since.

"Not only didn't he want to be married to our mother, but he completely washed his hands of his daughters. But there's more.

"In a really sick way, I can understand how making a clean break would be easier. It's not that I excuse him for doing it, but it's like I can step back and see how he could do it. The fact that I can relate to him on that level crushes me almost as much as him abandoning us. I'm afraid that I will pull the same thing and hurt you and Chloe the way he hurt me."

"He's already taken enough from you, Kate. Don't let him screw with your head and make you afraid that you'll do the same thing to someone you love. You're better than that."

"I wish I could be that resolute, Aidan. But I can't."

She gave her head another quick shake. Then she leaned forward and retreated into the position she'd been in before, resting her arms on her knees, then putting her forehead on her arms—a move that allowed her to escape into herself and not look Aidan in the eyes.

"Why not? What are you afraid of?" he asked.

"My father's leaving us affected my sisters. It made them wary of being hurt the same way my mother was. But not me. It made me afraid of turning out just like him."

"That's why you're still not sure, then? That's why you can't decide whether or not you're staying?" Aidan raked his hand through his hair and tried to tell himself to quell the irritation crawling up the back of his throat. If he ever needed to dig deep and find his patience, this was the time. "I'm sorry it happened to you, but having been there, wouldn't it be even more important to you to make sure you never let that kind of pain happen to your own child? I just don't see how your way of thinking makes sense."

"I care so much about Chloe and you. The last thing in the world I want to do is hurt the two of you. But I have a lot of issues that I need to sort out. I hope I can do that before…before the baby…before I hurt you and Chloe."

"Then don't hurt us. Don't leave us. Just stay and love us."

She shook her head. "I wish it was as easy as just

saying I will not do that, that I could make up my mind to not leave. I'm trying to be—"

"No. There's no such thing as *trying*, Kate. You either stay or you go. And that is one hundred percent in your control. You're either part of this family or you're not. It is not a hard decision to do the right thing. Or at least it shouldn't be."

A tear slid down Kate's cheek and he hated himself for making her cry, but it was slowly becóming clear that handling her with kid gloves was not the answer. Still, he reached out and brushed her tear away with the pad of his thumb.

"I need to work this out in my head," she said.

"Do you know where your father is?" he asked.

She shook her head.

"I think we need to find him. Maybe you need to go see him. See if he's happy with the decisions he made. Confront him and tell him what a crappy thing he did to you, your sisters and your mom. Because it was crappy. And I think if you can tell him that, you'll realize you're better than that, Kate."

He wanted to use stronger language than that. He wanted to call Fred Clark a lot of words he wasn't in the habit of using because he'd tempered his vocabulary in the interest of setting a good example for his daughter.

"Kate, he was a crappy father. Just like Chloe's

mother was a crappy mother. I know in my heart that you're not like them. You're so much better than that. If you were like them, you would not be here now. You owe it to yourself and you owe it to our baby to exorcise this demon so that you can get on with the life you deserve. I can ask my friend Randy Ponder, who owns a PI agency, to track him down, if you want. Randy employs private detectives who do that kind of thing. I'll go with you to talk to him."

"I don't think that's a good idea," she said. "I don't know if I want to see my father. What am I supposed to say? Hey, thanks for ruining my life?"

Before Aidan could answer, Kate shook her head and buried her face in her hands again.

"Think about it," Aidan said. "I know it is scary. I know it is a lot. You don't have to decide right now. But I think confronting him is the only way you're going to get past this thing that's keeping you from enjoying your best life."

Kate looked at him with a storm of emotion raging in her green eyes. But Aidan felt as if he might have gotten through to her.

"I do need to decide pretty soon," she said, tears streaming down her cheeks. "I need to figure out what I'm going to do so we can both get on with our lives. I owe it to you and Chloe and the baby. Thanks for not giving up on me, Aidan."

Chapter Six

After a restless night spent tossing and turning, Kate called her sister Elle as soon as the hour was decent.

"Are you free?" she asked. "I know it's last-minute, but I took the day off because I only had two clients scheduled and I was able to move them to later in the week. I need some sisterly advice."

"Sure, Daniel is already at work. Patrice is handling the tours today. It is just Maggie and me at home this morning."

Patrice Crowder was the college girl Elle had hired to help with the tours. She was a student at

Savannah College of Art and Design, and she was talented enough that Elle even trusted her to take over some of the art classes they now offered at the inn, giving Elle the ability to balance work and motherhood.

"Is everything okay?" Elle asked.

Kate was silent. She didn't want to alarm Elle by saying no, but technically, things weren't okay. Everything was upside down. But she certainly didn't want to tell her sister her monumental news over the phone.

"It is not a matter of life or death," Kate said. "So, no need to worry, but I do need to talk to you."

"Okay. Good. Come over and I'll fix us an early lunch," Elle offered. "Or a late breakfast. Have you eaten?"

"I haven't and I'm starving." Technically, that wasn't the entire truth. At the moment, the thought of food repulsed her, but based on how things had been going since the morning sickness first started, it was likely that she would be ravenous by the time she got to Elle's house.

Elle answered the door with baby Maggie in her arms. "Say hello to your auntie Kate, Maggie." The tiny girl took one look at Kate and burst into tears, her adorable, cherubic, chubby-cheeked face turning puce.

Wonderful.

If this wasn't proof that she was not qualified for motherhood, Kate didn't know what else the universe needed to show her. Wasn't there some sort of maternal standard women had to meet before they could bring a child into this world? If not, there should be. And Kate knew she certainly would not pass the test, if there was one.

Even her own niece had taken one look at her and cried foul.

I know, little baby. I get it. I want to cry, too.

"Don't take it personally, Kate," Elle said, bouncing little Maggie on her hip. "She's overtired. Let me put her down for a nap and we can talk. Go on into the kitchen and make yourself at home."

Elle closed the front door and headed down the hallway toward the baby's nursery. "I'll be right back," she said over her shoulder. "Okay. But what makes you think I took Maggie's crying personally? She loves her auntie Kate."

Maybe if she said it out loud she'd start believing it.

"Yeah, well, sorry, the look on your face gave you away."

So she was that obvious. She had never had a good poker face. Her mom had always sworn that she could read everything Kate was thinking simply by looking at her face. What in the world was she going to do between now and the time she and Aidan broke the news to the family?

Maybe she should hide out. Or take an extended vacation. Yeah, and look at where her Vegas vacation had gotten her. No, she and Aidan would be much better off not waiting and just telling everyone as soon as possible. The sooner the better. That way they could get used to their new reality.

She took a seat at the kitchen table in Elle's cheery kitchen. Her sister and Daniel had recently remodeled it to look like a Tuscan farmhouse kitchen.

From the white farmhouse sink to the marble countertops, travertine tile and wood floors, it really was a show place.

Daniel had built a large fireplace in the room—the opening was at least six feet by six feet—along one wall. There was a built-in pizza oven on the left side of it.

The centerpiece was a top-of-the-line eight-burner gas range, which Jane and Liam coveted. Every time they set foot in Elle's kitchen, Jane bemoaned the fact that she didn't have an appliance as impressive, even though she was the cook in the family. Elle always said that she and Liam were welcome to come over and cook in her kitchen every day if she wanted to make dinner for her and Daniel.

Of course, Jane and Liam spent most of their time at their restaurants and the tearoom, but still, it was a dream kitchen. Custom features like that were one of the many perks of being married to a builder.

And since Aidan was not only Daniel's brother but also his business partner, Kate, too, could have— Reality suddenly reared up in her in the face, giving her a start. Aidan was not just her brother-in-law's business partner, Aidan was her *husband*.

All of this—husband, family and a life of security and happiness—was hers to lose. Why was she so eager to throw it all away, ensuring that her worst fears came true, that the worst possible version of herself, the one with all of the qualities of her father, defined her after all?

Elle returned five minutes later. "She fell asleep the minute her little head hit the pillow. She was so tired."

Trying to get her mind off herself, Kate marveled at Elle's special way with children. She really was the kid whisperer. It was as if she had some kind of magic touch with the under-thirteen set, which, of course, was what had made her such an excellent teacher back in the day, when she used to teach elementary school art in Atlanta.

"I was thinking of making grilled cheese and tomato basil soup for lunch," Elle said. "Does that sound good? Of course, the soup is from a can. I'm not Jane, after all, but it is a good brand."

Elle held up the soup can with the blue label.

"Sounds delicious." Right on schedule, Kate was suddenly ravenous. She couldn't think of anything that sounded better.

"How can I help?" Kate asked.

"You can start talking and tell me what's on your mind."

Kate glanced around the kitchen as if someone might be hiding and secretly listening. Of course, no one was home, but she still weighed her words.

"Is marriage hard?" she asked her sister.

Elle set a block of cheddar cheese and a butter dish on the cutting board she had placed in the middle of the kitchen island. Cheese slicer in hand, she looked at Kate thoughtfully.

"It depends on what you mean by hard. I mean, it is not always easy. It is not all hearts and fireworks, and honestly, sometimes it gets pretty darn difficult, but at the end of the day, there's no place else I'd rather be, anything else I'd rather be doing or anyone else I'd rather be doing it with. I've never enjoyed working this hard for anything in my entire life. So the short answer is, yes, it is hard. But it is more than worth it. It's everything."

As Elle buttered the bread for the grilled cheese

sandwiches, she had a dreamy, faraway look in her eyes and a smitten smile on her face.

That's what I want. That, right there.

And that was what Aidan deserved. He deserved someone who got all warm and fuzzy and dreamy when she thought about him.

Was Aidan the love of *her* life? Had she been so busy pushing him away that she couldn't even see the good that was right in front of her? Maybe she needed to start rethinking things.

Now, especially with the baby on the way, it wasn't just about her. Not anymore.

"Well, I'd say that's a pretty good endorsement of marriage." Kate hated the way her voice shook.

Elle snapped out of her reverie and pinned Kate with a hopeful look. "Are you and Aidan—"

"Are Aidan and I what?" Kate snapped before Elle could finish.

Elle shook her head. "For a moment, I thought that maybe you had some news you wanted to share."

Why couldn't she just say it? It was the reason she had come over here this morning. To talk to someone compassionate who would not judge her or get overly celebratory before it was time.

Would there ever be a time when they could celebrate?

Elle walked over to the stove and started grilling the sandwiches.

"Aidan and I got married when we were in Vegas." The words poured out. She couldn't stop them.

The spatula fell from Elle's hand and clattered against the skillet. She didn't bother to pick it up. Instead, she turned to face Kate.

"You did what?"

"You heard me. Aidan and I are married."

Elle stood there rooted to the spot for a moment before she ran over and flung her arms around her sister. "That's wonderful! Congratulations!"

When she pulled away and looked at Kate, Elle's face fell. "Why is it not wonderful? What's wrong? Why are you crying?"

"Because I'm an idiot. Or maybe it's just my hormones, because I'm pregnant, too."

Elle gasped and hugged her again. "Oh, Kate. It is wonderful. Really, it is. A baby. You're going to be a mother. I'm going to be an aunt. Maggie and your baby will be so close in age, they'll be best friends. This is so exciting."

"Is it?"

Elle nodded.

"Good. Keep telling me that because I'm not so sure."

Elle's eyes narrowed. "How does Aidan feel about it?"

"He couldn't be happier." Kate squeezed her eyes shut, knowing she needed to tell her sister the whole story. So she did, starting with the marriage she didn't remember in Vegas and how they had looked into an annulment, ending with how she had gone to the doctor to find out what was wrong with her only to discover that she was pregnant.

"Dr. Moore said that my blackout was likely an alcohol allergy exacerbated by pregnancy hormones. I only had two sips of that awful Love Potion Number Nine. I wasn't drunk."

"It was pretty awful, wasn't it?" Elle agreed. "Or maybe it was just divine intervention to keep you from drinking too much since you're pregnant. Oh, Kate, I think you and Aidan are made for each other. I've always thought so."

Kate crossed her arms over her middle. "I wish I could share your confidence. I don't know that I am made for anyone."

Elle waved her hand as if clearing the air of Kate's words. "Don't be ridiculous. You know the old saying, 'There's a lid for every pot.'"

"You're saying Aidan is my lid?"

Elle nodded, a sweet smile turning up the edges of her lips. "I've thought that for a long time. You guys have known each other for such a long time, and you keep finding your way back together."

"I have to give him credit for that. He hasn't given up on me yet."

"Do you think subconsciously you've been testing him? To make sure he won't break your heart the way Fred broke Mom's heart?"

Kate shrugged. Elle and Jane called their father by his first name because they both agreed he didn't deserve to be called Father or Dad.

"God knows Mom has been beating herself up for far too long," Elle said. "You can't let her bad experience make you think all men are bad."

Fred Clark was an alcoholic. He had been unemployed more often than he had held a job. At one point, Zelda had finally given up trying to collect child support. She had decided cutting ties and making a clean break was better for her daughters than the occasional check. But even so, Fred would come around occasionally, wanting to see his girls. He'd carried on that way for several years until he decided to sue for half interest in the Forsyth Galloway Inn and lost the case.

They hadn't seen or heard from him since, saddling their mother and Gigi with mountains of legal fees they were still trying to pay off.

The lawsuit had inspired Gigi to have an attorney strengthen the terms of the trust, to protect the inn from husbands of future generations if they tried pulling a similar stunt. Ever the optimist, Gigi had said that being able to add extra protections to the ownership of their beloved inn had been the silver lining to an otherwise horrible situation.

Zelda, however, simply saw it as a heartbreaking ending. She hadn't been the same since the divorce. It was as if he had stolen their mother's spirit.

"It is not just the men that can be bad."

Elle scrunched up her nose. "What?"

"I worry that I inherited the same defect that made him leave Mom. That weird thing that makes me terrified of love and unable to commit to anything. Elle, I'm that flawed. I know it, and I don't want to break Aidan and Chloe's hearts."

"Oh, and you think divorcing him when you're pregnant with his child is going to somehow set him free?"

The ripple of silence between them widened as if Elle had just dropped a rock in what had otherwise been a still pool.

She took the skillet off the heat, turned off the burner, walked over and sat on the stool next to Kate.

"Okay, you know I love you. And I'm only saying this because I do. But you need some tough love right now. You need someone to be real with you.

You have a child on the way. Life isn't about you anymore. Actually, let me rephrase that. You and Aidan have a child on the way. This can be the start of a new life for you. A brand-new path full of adventure with a child and a good man who wants to be your husband. It can change your life in ways you never dreamed possible. You are lucky to have Aidan, Kate. Now you have to make up your mind. You have to commit and come to the table prepared to hold up your end or be willing to live with the consequences that you are mirroring Fred. And it is your choice."

The next morning, Kate stood on Aidan's front doorstep with coffee in one hand and a paper bag of bagels in the other. When she had called Aidan about getting together to talk—asking if he had time to talk when Chloe wasn't home—he had suggested this morning.

Aidan had arranged for the parent of one of his daughter's friends to take her to school this morning. With that set, Kate had offered to stop by and bring breakfast. Aidan had wanted to go out for breakfast, but she needed to have this conversation in private. Aidan had sounded dubious, but he had agreed.

Even though Kate had made up her mind by the time she left Elle's house yesterday morning, she wanted to give herself the night to sleep on her decision and consider it with a fresh head the next day. Because she knew that with this talk, she was giving Aidan her final answer. There was no going back after today.

She rang the doorbell, taking care not to spill the coffee in the open white ceramic mug she was carrying. She had seen the mug in one of the novelty shops on Bull Street, which was located not too far from the salon.

It was plain white, with the word *Dad* emblazoned in big, black letters. Underneath was the year. She had stopped at the store and purchased it after her visit with Elle. Although, of course, Aidan was already a father to Chloe, and a wonderful one at that, raising her on his own without a bit of help from Chloe's mother.

Boy, Aidan sure knew how to pick them, didn't he? Maybe where Chloe's mother had failed, Kate could do better. It said something that Aidan hadn't let one bad relationship experience sour him on trying to make it work with her. And that was before he had learned she was pregnant. He was either a fool or the best thing that had ever happened to her.

Her throat was so tight she almost couldn't speak. Instead, she hoped the "Dad" mug would do the talking for her. Or at least break the ice.

When he opened the door, she held out the coffee cup and her words spilled out. "I know you're already a dad. But see the year on the cup? It signifies the year we became a family. All four of us."

"Are you saying what I think you're saying?" he asked cautiously.

Kate nodded. "But I have stipulations. I'm not giving up my business. I need to make my own money. And I am keeping my house. I don't want to sell it."

He scrunched up his face. "You want to be married, but live separately? We already talked about that, Kate"

"No, I want to live with you and Chloe, but I don't want to sell my house. I saved for a long time before I could afford to buy it. And I don't want to let it go."

"Okay, we can rent it out."

Kate shrugged. "I guess so. The extra money would be nice."

Aidan smiled. "So we're really going to do this?"

Kate took an audible deep breath and nodded.

"Elle knows we are married, and she knows about the baby. So we have to tell the family as soon as possible."

"Why? Before you change your mind?"

"Very funny," Kate leaned in and brushed a featherlight kiss on his lips. "Don't tempt me."

Aidan deepened the kiss and white-hot volts of

electricity shot through her, waking up her lady parts. "Okay, you can tempt me that way. But let me set this down. You're going to make me spill the coffee."

Aidan took the bag with the bagels and set it and the mug on the table in the foyer.

Kate stepped inside. "I trust my sister to keep our secret, but things happen. Tongues slip and happy news finds a way of spilling out. And if my mother and Gigi find out we're married and having a baby before we can tell them, they will disown both of us."

Aidan pulled her into his arms, somehow managing to close the door in the process.

"Okay, when do you want to tell them?"

"How about this Sunday at family brunch?"

"That sounds like a plan," he said.

"There's something else," Kate said. "I hope you won't think this is silly because it's important to me. I want you to propose to me, and I want a do-over with the wedding. I want a traditional wedding. Because we eloped, I didn't get to buy bridal magazines and I didn't get to say yes to the dress and cry when I found the perfect one. I want all of that, Aidan. I want my sisters to be bridesmaids and I wanted Charles to give me away. I don't want our marriage to be defined by a bad Elvis impersonator and a ceremony that I didn't remember."

"I want you to have all of those things, Kate. You deserve to have the wedding of your dreams." Aidan reached out and put his hand on her arm and gave it a loving squeeze. "If that's what has been hanging you up about us, it is all easy to fix. I would get down on one knee right now and ask you to marry me, but I want you to have a real proposal and I intend to surprise you with it."

Her heart swelled, and then he kissed her for real.

The connection cut through the jangle of nerves that had been rattling her since she woke up married. In an instant, she was one hundred percent certain this was right. That he was not going give up on her or tell her to leave because she was too difficult to deal with.

In turn, she would give her best to him.

He deepened the kiss and her body responded immediately. Her heart pounded and her body sighed, *oooh, yes.*

Or maybe she had said it out loud. She hoped she hadn't said it out loud. Even if she had, it didn't matter because that was the thing about them. They were so good together. Physically, they just worked. While the physical part of their relationship wasn't the only thing to build a relationship around, it was something. An important something. And they had it.

She slid her arms around his neck and pulled him

close. She opened her mouth and invited him in. He turned her so that he could deepen the kiss even more.

In contrast to how he tended to let her run the show outside of the bedroom, in the bed he was the one who was in control. Maybe that would be their saving grace?

She was vaguely aware of him gently but deftly walking her backward away from the front door, all the while not breaking the electric connection that was this kiss.

Somehow, her back was against the closest living room wall. His hands had found the back of her neck, and his touch was tender but firm, in contrast to the fiery, lingering kiss. He tasted of toothpaste with just the slightest hint of coffee, and that taste that was uniquely Aidan. How was it that sometimes she forgot the exquisite deliciousness of him? Thank God for reminders like this.

Kate fisted her hands into his hair and pulled their bodies even closer. Why did it take almost walking away and losing him for her to remember that Aidan was her touchstone, her constant? He always had been. Why did she sometimes forget that?

But all of the difficulties leading up to this moment didn't matter anymore. Aidan's mouth was on her lips, and his hands were on her breasts, making her entire body sing.

Oooh, yes. Oooh, hell yes.

For a moment the entire world telescoped and disappeared until it was just the two of them, his lips devouring hers, his strong hands, which had somehow slipped down to cup her bottom and pull her even tighter against him…and the proof of how much he desired her.

And she wanted him, too. His hard body felt so good under her hands. She slid them across his shoulders and down his muscled arms. Her hands pushed their way between them, finding the waistband of his trousers. She dipped her fingers below, working the button and fumbling with it, determined for nothing to stand between them. There would be nothing but skin on skin. Him inside of her. And the sooner the better—but before she could finish unzipping him, Aidan broke the kiss.

He stood there for a moment, stock-still, his forehead resting on hers.

"Is this a good idea?" His eyes, dark with need and hunger, like a mirror reflecting back everything she was feeling, locked with hers.

"Of course, it is a good idea," Kate said. "When has the two of us having sex ever been a bad idea?"

"Never." He kissed her again. "Until now. I don't want to hurt the baby."

She took his bottom lip between her teeth, let go and then kissed it. "The doctor said that gentle lovemaking in the early stages of pregnancy is fine as long as there are no problems. She said this pregnancy doesn't appear to have any problems. And I certainly don't have any problems with you making love to me."

Aidan scooped her into his arms and carried her into the bedroom.

She heard the ragged edge of his breathing just beneath the blood rushing in her ears. He smelled like heaven: subtle aftershave with grassy notes and something leathery and masculine. The seductive mix nearly pushed her over the edge. It teased her senses, made her feel hot and sexy and more than a little bit reckless as he eased her back onto the bed, his gaze transfixed on hers.

No…she wasn't feeling reckless. She was feeling…safe and protected. As he tasted and teased, she melted into him and let go of the last bit of hesitation she possessed. If she let herself, she could love him. Couldn't she? Because if ever she could love a man, it would be Aidan.

And hadn't it always been Aidan? Even if her conscious mind hadn't realized it, hadn't her subconscious mind always wanted him? Yes. For as long as she had known what it meant for a woman to want a man.

His fingers lingered on her stomach, slipped underneath her blouse and worked their way up to her breasts. He loved the way she seemed to melt at the feel of his touch. Explosions of desire and fiery need spiraled in his gut.

She looked so beautiful and vulnerable lying there—his wife. This was his wife. Kate was his wife. And she was going to have his baby.

He kissed her lips, her gorgeous eyes, her jaw, her cheeks, the delicate ivory column of her neck, and tenderly bit down on her earlobe. Her head lolled to the side in approving bliss.

"I've wanted this for so long," he whispered. "I've wanted you for so long. I've wanted us. I promise you I will do everything in my power to make you happy and be the best husband I can be."

He had never felt such all-consuming longing in his life. He needed to show her how much he ached for her, how much he desired her, not just in this moment. He would crave her for the rest of his life. He wanted to show her with his lips and hands and body why they were so right together.

He touched her, and in response, his own body

swelled and hardened. He had to be careful, gentle. They had to take things slowly. That was why he focused on how much he loved the feel of her body, her curves, so strong, yet so pliable to his touch. When he moved, his hands found her breasts again, cupping them through the silky material of her blouse, savoring their full curves before teasing her hard nipples. She gasped and arched against him, seeming to lose herself in his touch, fueling his rigid desire.

The thought of making love to her sent a hungry shudder coursing through him. It racked his whole body. But that was nothing compared to the feel of her hand on the front of his trousers. She teased his erection through the layers of his trousers and boxers. The sensation was almost more than he could bear. He needed her naked so that he could bury himself inside of her.

Again he reminded himself to go slow, savor the moment, protect their child. He took his time undoing each button on her blouse. In one swift, gentle motion, he lifted her so that he could remove it. Next, he unhooked the front clasp of her bra. He freed her breasts, lowered his head and worshipped them with his mouth until she cried out in pleasure.

The sexy sound almost undid him.

She must have sensed as much, because she made quick work of picking up where she had left off with his trousers, sliding down the zipper. He helped her rid him of his pants and boxers. They fell to the floor, freeing him.

When he settled himself beside her, she looked like the most beautiful woman in the world. He knew at that moment that he had been waiting his whole life for *this* moment. It was just like the first time all over again, and in a way, it was, because this really was the first time they were making love as husband and wife.

And then they were kissing each other deeply again, tongues thrusting, ravishing each other. When he was sure she was ready, he turned her on her side, spooning her and burying himself inside her. That was when he knew without a doubt that this was where he wanted to be, where he needed to be. Always.

Chapter Seven

Every Sunday, the family had a standing brunch date. It wasn't mandatory, but it was appreciated when every effort was made to attend, because they all led busy lives and this was the way they connected once a week.

Kate and Aidan decided family brunch would be the perfect time to share their double dose of good news with the family. Everyone would be there except for Chloe. She was at her friend Beatrice's house for the afternoon. They would tell her the news after she got home this evening—after the rest of the family knew, so that the little girl didn't spill the beans before Aidan and Kate had a chance to tell everyone themselves.

Elle was still the only one who was in on their secret, and in true Elle form, she had been a champ about helping them keep it under wraps until they were ready to announce it.

Kate had finally decided that she would move into Aidan's house with him and Chloe, but she didn't want to start packing up and relocating until they had officially informed the family.

She knew that her elopement might not go over very well with her mother and grandmother. Never had two women loved planning weddings as much as her Zelda and Gigi. Kate was preparing for the worst—hurt feelings that she had robbed them of their last chance to throw a wedding for the youngest of the three girls.

But she and Aidan planned on placating them with the consolation that even though they were already officially married, they wanted to stage a more traditional do-over in Savannah.

They had agreed to skip over the part about Kate not remembering the Vegas wedding—they would keep that little tidbit to themselves—and go right into the joyous news of the baby and how Gigi was getting her eighty-fifth birthday wish after all. All tied up in one beautiful package with a pretty bow.

Because it felt best to have the home field advantage, Aidan and Kate had agreed to host this week's brunch, with the help of Elle, who had prepared a festive fruit salad, and Jane, who was none the wiser but whipped up delicacies such as scones, brioche and quiche from her tearoom.

After everyone had eaten, Aidan began uncorking the champagne. They had decided to make the announcement with a toast. It was, after all, a happy occasion. They needed to present the news in a happy, upbeat manner and everyone would be happy and upbeat about the news.

At least in theory.

Even so, Kate was a nervous wreck. Her hand shook as Aidan handed her a champagne flute that he had surreptitiously filled with ginger ale when he was in the kitchen.

Oh, come on. Get ahold of yourself. You're a twenty-six-year-old grown woman who has married a wonderful man. You're not a teenager who has gotten herself in trouble. If Mom and Gigi take issue with things, they will just have to get over it.

And even that tough self-talk wasn't helping.

"Family is everything to us," Aidan began. "That's why we are so happy we could all be together today."

Kate was standing next to him and he slid an arm around her waist.

"When Daniel and I were young, we lost our parents. Our grandmother took us in because we had no other family to turn to. Even if we'd had other options, she probably would have insisted on raising us. But what I'm trying to say is that a family bond is everything. Now that she's gone, Zelda, you and Gigi have made me feel like part of your family. When Daniel married Elle, you so warmly welcomed Chloe and me into the fold without even blinking an eye. Now Kate and I are happy to announce—"

"Oh my goodness." Gigi's hand fluttered to her mouth and then she clapped her hands like a child who had just spotted the pony she'd gotten for her birthday. "Are you two engaged?"

She looked so thrilled that Kate imagined that she might float away on an imaginary heart balloon that bloomed from her happiness.

"Actually," Kate said, sliding her arm around Aidan for support. "We are already married. We were so inspired by your Vegas wedding, Gigi and Charles, we decided to follow suit."

Kate watched her mother's and Gigi's expressions turn from elated to confused, and then to something unreadable. She snared Elle's gaze and telegraphed, *Help me!* Elle must have gotten the message because she jumped up from her seat, and hugged Kate and Aidan.

"Congratulations! This is the best news. It is so exciting. Isn't it great, Jane?"

Jane immediately did her part, and while not quite as effusive as Elle, she helped rally the family with her congratulations. Zelda and Gigi still looked stunned, but Liam and Daniel came through with backslaps for Aidan and good wishes and hugs for Kate.

"Bro, you're better at keeping a secret than I thought you were," said Daniel. "How long has it been? Like three weeks? I didn't even have a clue. You've got some kind of a great poker face."

At least *he* did. Kate knew she had a terrible poker face and that she probably looked crushed when Gigi finally found her voice. "Daniel is right. You two have kept this from your family for three weeks. I don't understand why you would do that, and frankly I'm a little hurt."

"I was thinking the exact same thing." Zelda looked downright angry, while Gigi seemed merely upset. "Why did you do it this way?"

"We didn't want to horn in on Gigi's and Charles's big day," Kate explained. "We wanted them to have a chance to get back and get settled in and be the newlyweds before we broke the news."

Her mother and grandmother did not seem moved by the reasoning. Sadly, it dawned on Kate that she shouldn't have to apologize for eloping. Even if the reason they had given for sitting on the news was only half the truth—there was no way she would divulge the rest of the story about how they'd ended up married. If she didn't owe them an apology for getting married, she certainly didn't owe them the dirty details.

This time, Jane came to her sister's rescue. "You know what, Mom and Gigi? I love you both dearly, but Kate and Aidan are adults, and if this is the way they wanted to get married it is their choice. You don't get a say."

Jane's smile blunted the edge of her words, and it seemed to better drive home the point.

Bless her.

Gigi looked as if she wanted to say something, but she snapped her mouth shut, pressing her lips into a tight, thin line.

"Jane is right, you know," Charles said. He raised his glass. "If this is the way they wanted to do it, who are we to question it? I'd like to propose a toast. To the newest newlyweds. May they have a lifetime of happiness."

Everyone raised their glasses. Zelda and Gigi looked a bit subdued, but they did, too.

"I noticed that neither of you are wearing wedding rings," Zelda said. "Are you going to wear them now that the secret is out?"

Kate's finger went to the back of the naked ring finger on her left hand. Since she'd stashed her wedding band in her dresser, she hadn't thought much about it.

She glanced at Aidan, who was nodding.

"Of course, we will."

"But wait," Kate said. "There's more. Very soon, Aidan, Chloe and I will be a family of four."

She hadn't meant for the announcement to rhyme. Maybe if doing hair didn't work out, she could start a greeting card company.

"And believe it or not," Aidan was quick to add, "we did get married before we found out we were expecting. We just learned that good news the other day."

Kate caught her grandmother's eye. She was smiling and wiping happy tears. So was her mother, who was murmuring, "A baby. A grandchild."

"Wishes do come true," said Gigi. "It looks like I did get my eighty-fifth birthday wish after all. All three of my granddaughters are married. Even if Kate and Aidan did buck tradition." Gigi laughed. "Oh, what am I saying? This is *Kate* we are talking about. She doesn't have a traditional bone in her skinny little body."

Kate kept the smile plastered on her face. That wasn't true. In fact, it was one of her most personal, closely guarded secrets. She wanted nothing more than to have a traditional proposal and wedding. She wanted to buy bridal magazines and go dress shopping. She wanted to be moved to tears when she found *the dress*.

Most of all, she wanted a marriage so firmly held together by love that it would never break, that would keep her from ever feeling the urge to run, like her father had.

"Whether you know it or not," she said. "Deep down I really am a traditional girl. I absolutely swoon at the thought of a big, fat traditional wedding. And because it's so important to us and to Mom and Gigi, Aidan and I are going to have a ceremony right here in Savannah. I'll need your help to plan it. Are you on board?"

As everyone hugged her, she thought about how in all other aspects of her life she wasn't traditional. She'd cultivated a lifestyle based on marching to her own tune. She needed a flexible career, and above most things, she valued independence.

But a traditional wedding felt like the right way to start the rest of her life with Aidan.

She said a silent prayer that marriage wasn't so traditional a lifestyle that it would drain the life blood out of her—and send her running in search of the freedom she had always cherished.

The brunch wrapped up around 1:30. Afterward, Aidan helped Kate move some of her things to the house. It wasn't much—her clothes, shoes, toiletries and makeup. She brought a couple of special accessories and a few kitchen must-haves.

Just enough to allow her to get settled in and to make Aidan's house feel like it was her home, too. She could move over the rest of her things as she realized she needed them. Even then, she probably would not end up bringing over everything, because that would feel like she was abandoning the life she had worked so hard to build for herself.

But now that they had a baby on the way, her life wasn't her own anymore. She and Aidan were starting a life together, which would be so much better.

Wouldn't it?

If so, then why does it feel like I'm abandoning myself, leaving my own life behind and stepping into his life?

Everything will sort itself out.

She had been repeating that promise like a mantra. Reminding herself why she wanted to make the marriage work and why moving in with him was the best decision. How could a marriage work if the couple lived apart? Marriage was a blending of lives; it was sharing, and sacrificing a certain amount of personal freedom was part of the equation.

Really, it was the only way to go.

Plus, it was the best thing for Chloe. It would not be fair to take her out of her home, and away from her familiar surroundings.

She had been through a lot in her short life—her mother abandoning her and Aidan's accident this year. He had been in a coma for several days and recovering in a rehab center for a few weeks. There had been months of physical therapy. Kate, Elle and Daniel had worked hard with the help of Zelda and Gigi, to keep Chloe's life as normal as possible.

Despite Kate's uncertainty, apart from everything else, one thing was undeniable: she couldn't love that little girl more if she was her natural daughter. When she started fretting over everything, she would picture Chloe's sweet face, and it would all make sense.

Maybe there was hope for her in the motherhood department after all.

Only time would tell. In the meantime, they were planning on renting out Kate's furnished house, which meant she would have to box up the rest of her possessions and store them if she didn't move them to Aidan's place. The extra income would be nice, and she clung to the false sense of security it would give her—that she had saved a piece of herself—preserved a segment of the life she had built for herself before she had messed—

No!

She had not messed up. She had to stop thinking of her life that way.

The truth was, she had thought everything would snap into place after they told the family about everything. It had helped for a little while, mostly during the brunch, after Zelda and Gigi had wrapped their minds around her elopement and arrived at a place of acceptance. But now that she was actually moving out of her house into Aidan's, everything felt daunting again.

"I put everything from the fridge into the cooler, and I put the food that was in the pantry and cabinets in boxes," Aidan called from the hallway. "Do you want to bring anything else over tonight?"

In her bedroom, she walked over to her dressing table and lifted the lid of her jewelry box. She pulled out the red velvet-lined ring box and opened the lid. The sun streaming in through the blinds glinted off the pretty gold band as if it was urging her to put it on her finger, where it belonged.

She did just that, sliding it onto her left ring finger. To her surprise, it didn't feel heavy or cumbersome, it felt...fine.

Tucking the box back inside the jewelry box, Kate resumed packing. She took the last of her dresses out of her closet and put them into a hanging bag she had laid out on the bed. "I put some gadgets and coffee mugs in that box near the front door. But I think that's all. For now, anyway."

"I have coffee mugs," Aidan called. "You don't need to bring them unless you want to."

"I like my coffee mugs," she said as Aidan appeared in the bedroom doorway. He looked sexy, and Kate's heart performed a little cha-cha. "Oh, hey there."

Her voice was low and husky.

She was a lucky woman. She needed to remind herself of that every time doubt reared its ugly head. Aidan was a good man. And a very nice-looking one at that.

"Hello, Mrs. Quindlin." He picked up her left hand and kissed it just above her wedding band. "I'm glad you're wearing your ring. I'll put mine on, too, when we get home."

"Good," she said. "But my coffee mugs and I are a package deal. Nonnegotiable."

His laugh was low and sexy and he smiled that half smile that did magical things to her insides, and her heart melted a little more when he pulled her into his arms and kissed her soundly. Her body responded and so did his. She said a silent prayer that this chemistry between them was one of the things that would survive as they blended their lives.

Conventional wisdom dictated that eventually attraction waned, giving away to something deeper. What could be deeper than the pull of attraction that had brought them together all those years ago and reunited them after Aidan's accident?

"Do you love me?" The words escaped as the kiss ended, before Kate could register what she was asking. She felt Aidan tense ever so slightly. With that, she really wished she hadn't asked. She hated looking needy and insecure.

"Of course," he said stiffly. "Why would you ask?"

"Because you've never mentioned it." She took a step back from him and crossed her arms and shook her head. "Just… Oh, never mind. We'd better get back to your house before Chloe is dropped off."

Aidan glanced at his watch. "No worries, we have plenty of time."

Did he look a little relieved that she hadn't pressed the "Do you love me" issue? That she hadn't said, *Because when a woman marries a man it would be nice to know that love was the foundation of the relationship.*

Could she start blaming irrational thoughts like these on pregnancy hormones? Because they certainly seemed to be coming from out of the blue. Before Aidan, she had had a couple of serious relationships, both relatively short-lived and both ending badly, but when things were good, she had never asked the men if they loved her. It had never crossed her mind.

"Well, shouldn't we have the car unloaded before Chloe gets home? I don't want her to see me moving my things in before we have a chance to talk to her and explain everything."

"Good point." He smiled, and that simple gesture took away some of the former uneasiness. "I really appreciate how much you care and think about Chloe."

"Of course. She is important to me. We are going to be a family. I want us to get started the right way."

Aidan stepped closer and put his arm around Kate and spread his other hand on her belly.

"You're already a wonderful mother."

She was glad that one of them was so very sure of that.

On the way back to Aidan's house—er—*their* house, they decided it would be fun to fix Chloe's favorite dinner for their first meal together as a family. On the menu: chicken nuggets cut into the shape of dinosaurs, macaroni and cheese, baby carrots and applesauce. The plan was to heat up the food and take it to the park and have a picnic.

The spread sounded strangely appealing to Kate, and she attributed the appetite to pregnancy hormones. She had heard about women craving for strange things when they were pregnant. She had never dreamed that she would be yearning for dinosaur chicken nuggets.

After Kate and Aidan had unloaded the car, they discovered they were out of baby carrots and were running low on honey mustard, apparently a must-have for dino nugget dipping.

Aidan decided to make a quick run to the store. "Would you pick up some barbecue sauce, too?" Kate asked. "And would you check in the deli and see if they have some ambrosia salad? It is that sweet salad with the coconut, mandarin oranges and mini marshmallows. It would be in the refrigerated area where they keep the prepared salads—you know potato salad, coleslaw and such. That stuff."

"Anything for you, my darling," he said, feathering a kiss on her lips. She noticed he had put on his wedding ring. "Are you sure you're going to be okay here alone while I'm gone?"

"Of course. Why would I not be?"

"I don't know. Just making sure. Doris Watson is dropping Chloe off. She'll probably get here while I'm gone. Is that okay?"

Kate laughed. "Of course. Chloe and I will be fine. It's not like you will be away overnight."

"I know you will. And Doris is great. She's been so nice to help out with Chloe lately. Will you tell her I said thanks?"

"You got it."

While Aidan was at the store, Kate hung her clothes in the walk-in closet in the master bedroom and arranged her toiletries in the en suite bath. She had just finished when the doorbell rang. When she answered the door, she would have thought the woman standing on the porch was at the wrong house, if not for Chloe and another little girl with dark blond hair. The girls giggled and ran past Kate, presumably headed for Chloe's bedroom, saying something about getting a doll who wanted to go home with Beatrice.

Kate turned to face the model-perfect woman. She was tall and had the kind of lean, toned body that screamed personal trainer, daily Pilates and regular 5K runs. On top of all that, she was probably captain of her tennis team. It made Kate tired to think about it. Her hair was long and honey brown with perfect, sun-kissed streaks that must've cost a fortune because they looked so natural paired with her tanned skin. Vivid blue eyes regarded Kate with a question. "Hi, is Aidan at home? I'm Doris Watson."

This was Doris Watson? She was not at all what Kate had envisioned. The name Doris had called to mind someone much more…mature. Never had a woman this beautiful entered the mental picture that had popped into Kate's mind when Aidan mentioned her. At the moment, Kate couldn't even recall what her original picture had looked like.

"Hi, Doris," Kate said. "Aidan had to step out for a moment, but he told me you would be dropping off Chloe. Thanks for doing this. I hear she loves playing at your house."

Doris stood there for a moment, regarding Kate. It felt as if the woman was sizing her up. That was when Kate noticed a piece of paper in Doris's hand. Kate gestured to it. "May I give Aidan a message for you?"

"Oh, yes, thank you. This is an invitation to our parent-child rock group." Doris thrust the paper at Kate and Kate accepted it.

"Rock group? As in music?"

"Oh, bless your heart, no. It's a rock-painting group some of the other mothers and myself are organizing. We think it will be a fun chance for the girls to get together weekly. We will paint rocks and write inspirational sayings on them, then place them around town for people to find and tag us on Instagram. The paper has the details of our first meeting. After that, we'll plan on short weekly meetings and— I'm sorry, who are you?" Doris asked.

There was a challenging note in her voice, as if rambling about the rock group had allowed her to add up all the pieces and she ended up not liking the sum of the parts. "Are you Chloe's nanny?" Doris asked.

"Oh, heavens, no," Kate said. "My name is Kate. I am Aidan's wife."

Aidan stopped his car in front of the house in time to see Doris on the porch talking to Kate. It was good for them to meet since Chloe enjoyed spending so much time with Beatrice. Doris had been so good about having Chloe over and driving her here and there. Now they would have a better chance to reciprocate and have Beatrice over so Doris could have some free time.

"I understand congratulations are in order," Doris said when Aidan approached. "I didn't know that you had gotten married."

Doris reached out and took ahold of Aidan's left hand and made a show of looking at his wedding ring—as if she needed proof. She gave her head a quick shake, as if she was trying to wrap her mind around the idea. "Well, look at that. Matching bands and all. I guess I never noticed your ring, and I'm usually pretty observant when it comes to things like that."

When neither he nor Kate said anything, Doris broke the awkward silence.

"I'm sorry this is throwing me for such a loop. I didn't even realize you had someone special in your life."

Kate crossed her arms and shot him a look with raised brows and pursed mouth.

He hadn't wanted her to be a secret. Not on purpose. He and Kate had been seeing each other for nearly a year, but Kate had been adamant about keeping things casual. Friends with benefits, they had joked, even though he had wanted it to be so much more.

Still, he had decided he wasn't going to push her. Because of that, he had done his best to keep Chloe's world, with her school and teachers and friends and their parents, as separate as possible from his life with Kate. Introducing Kate into that mix would have only muddied the waters.

In retrospect, maybe he should have done it anyway. Though he never would have dreamed they would find themselves in a situation like this.

"Yeah" was all he said about the matter, following it up with "Thanks for letting Chloe come over today, Doris."

Doris wrinkled her nose and smiled. "I'm sorry I seem so surprised. This is so odd. Chloe has never mentioned you, Kate."

Kate inclined her head. "Until Aidan and I made things official, we wanted to protect Chloe. As a mother, I'm sure you understand what I'm talking about."

"What on earth do you mean by *protect*?" Doris asked. "What would Chloe need to be protected from?"

Despite the stiff smile on plastered on Kate's face, Aidan could sense that she was getting her back up.

Before the exchange could go any further, they were interrupted by the sound of two giggling six-year-olds. Beatrice and Chloe joined them on the porch. Beatrice had a doll tucked under her arm. Chloe was carrying Princess Sweetie Pie.

"I am letting Beatrice take Annie to her house so she can spend the night there," Chloe said. "She's letting her doll, Iris, stay with Princess Sweetie Pie and me. It's a doll sleepover."

The girls jumped up and down, hugging the dolls.

"That sounds like a fair exchange," Aidan said. It suddenly dawned on him that because of the way Doris has been questioning them, she might say something in front of Chloe about him and Kate being married.

"Chloe, I need you to go inside and help Kate find the picnic basket because the three of us are going on a picnic for supper."

He telegraphed to Kate that she should take Chloe in the other room. She seemed to understand, because she gave him a subtle nod and then whisked the little girl away.

Of course, Kate was the one who'd told Doris about them being married. How else would Doris have found out? Judging by what he had read in Kate's eyes, she had realized it had been risky for her to let the cat out of the bag before they could tell Chloe.

"Who was that lady, Mama?" Beatrice asked, as Kate took Chloe inside and shut the door behind her. And not a moment too soon.

"That's Chloe's new mommy," said Doris. She locked gazes with Aidan. Her gaze and her bemused smile wore a question, as if she expected Aidan to explain. But what else was there to say?

"Again, thank you, Doris. I need to get inside. We will see you and Beatrice soon. Maybe next time the girls can play over here."

As Aidan was letting himself inside the house, Doris put her hand on the door. "I gave Kate a piece of paper with information about our rock-painting group. It is a mother-and-daughter thing, but fathers are always welcome, too."

"Thank you for the invitation."

"I do hope you will bring Chloe and join us," Doris said.

She looked like she wanted to say something more. Instead, she let go of the door and stepped back. "Let me know if you ever need anything, Aidan."

Kate walked into the living room as soon as Aidan closed the door.

"I'm sorry," Kate said. "I shouldn't have said anything to Doris until we had a chance to talk to Chloe. But she was grilling me. Doris certainly was surprised to discover that we were married. But maybe not as surprised as I was to discover that Doris is so young and pretty. I'm not going to lie. I had a mental picture of her being more of a grandmotherly type or like Mary Poppins." Kate shrugged. "I guess that just goes to show you what preconceived notions will do. But I think she likes you."

Aidan flinched. Surely she wasn't meaning that the way he was inferring it? He decided to hedge, to play dumb, because the thought made him uncomfortable.

"Doris and I get along just fine. I am the father of

her daughter's best friend. She would not let Beatrice play with Chloe if she didn't like me."

Kate crossed her arms and pinned him with a steely gaze. "You know that's not what I'm talking about."

He let his face go blank. "No, I don't have any idea what you're talking about. What do you mean?"

"Are you blind?" Kate asked. "You have to know what I mean, or you are blind."

"Then if I'm blind, does that mean you're jealous?" Aidan laughed. Just as he hoped, the question threw her off her line of questioning.

"Why would I be jealous? Or maybe I should ask if I *should* be jealous? As I said, Doris is beautiful, and she is obviously interested in you."

Chloe seemed to materialize from out of nowhere with her stuffed white cat tucked into the crook of her arm. He wanted to hug his little girl for saving him. "Why are there boxes in our kitchen?" she asked. "Where did they come from?"

He and Kate exchanged a glance. They needed to talk to Chloe before the news of their marriage came out the wrong way. They needed to make this happy news. Because it was a happy thing. But first, he and Kate needed to be on the same page. And there was no room on that page for Doris Watson.

Aidan kneeled down in front of his daughter so that he was eye level with Chloe.

"Remember how I told you we were going on a picnic for dinner tonight?"

Chloe nodded and plucked at the fur on Princess Sweetie Pie's face.

"Kate and I have a big surprise for you. And we were going to tell you about it on the picnic, because it is something very special and very exciting that the three of us are going to celebrate."

The little girl's eyes grew large and her mouth fell open. "What is it, Daddy?"

"It is a surprise," Aidan said. "Go get your shoes on while Kate and I go into the kitchen and finish getting the picnic ready and we will get this party started."

Chloe jumped up and down and clapped her hands, then scampered off toward her room, leaving Kate and Aidan alone.

"Let's just tell her about the wedding now," Aidan said. "I want her to digest that and then we can tell her about the baby later, when she's ready. Are you okay with that?"

Kate put her hand on her middle and nodded. "Of course. You know Chloe and if you think that's the best way to handle it, I'm right there with you."

He reached out and ran the pad of his thumb along

Kate's jawline. "Don't worry. Everything is going to be fine."

"Do you really think so?" she asked. "I mean, are you sure Chloe isn't going to feel like I'm an intruder in the life that the two of you have built together?" Kate whispered the words.

"I hope not. I mean, I can't imagine that she would feel that way. Her mom has never been a part of her life. Since she's been hanging around Beatrice and Doris so much lately, she's asked me a couple of times why she doesn't have a mother like her friends."

Kate's face softened. "*Oh*, poor little girl. I hope I can live up to the task and be a good mother to her."

"You already are," Aidan said. "All you have to do is…love her. I think you'll be good at that."

The word *love* made him think of how they hadn't resolved Kate's question, which seemed to have come from out of the blue. Of course, he cared for her. He wouldn't have married her if he didn't. Then he saw Kate's throat work as she swallowed. When she looked up at him, emotion swam in her eyes.

He pulled her into his arms and kissed her softly on the lips.

"You're going to be a great mother," he said.

The sound of Chloe's feet scampering on the hardwood floors made Kate tense and pull out of his arms.

"It is going to be fine," he said. "I promise."

* * *

A half hour later, Kate, Aidan and Chloe were seated on a quilt in Forsyth Park. As Kate helped Aidan set out the food for their dino nugget dinner along with six gourmet cupcakes he had picked up at the store for the celebration, the little girl danced around them on the grass.

"Princess Sweetie Pie wants to know when we can have our surprise," she said. Now she was jumping up and down. "Can we have the surprise before dinner? *Pleeease, Daddy? Pleeease.*"

"It is not exactly something that you have," Aidan said.

Chloe stopped jumping and blinked. Not in a disappointed, spoiled-child way. It was more of a look that said she was trying to understand what he was telling her.

"What is it, then?" she asked quietly, holding her cat by one arm at her side.

Aidan glanced at Kate, as if looking for the answer. She shrugged and gestured back at him. She had nearly blown it once today when she had spilled the beans to Doris. He needed to figure out the right way to break this news. She would be right here for moral support.

He must've understood, because he finally said, "It is something that Kate and I have to tell you."

Chloe dropped down onto the quilt that they were using as a picnic blanket and stared up at them, her face solemn.

"Don't look so upset," Aidan said. "It is good news. It is happy news."

Kate's heart was hammering in her chest as if it was trying to break out and run away.

Then Aidan reached out and took Kate's hand.

"You know how you told me that you wished you had a mommy?"

Chloe nodded.

"Well, now you do. Kate and I got married when we went away—remember when we went away, and you stayed with Beatrice?"

The little girl nodded again, her eyes looking hopeful.

"Since we're married, Kate is your mommy. What do you think about that?"

Chloe's hands flew to her mouth. "Really?" The words were muffled behind her little fingers. "Are you really my mommy?"

"I would be honored to be your mommy, if you want me to be," Kate said.

Chloe nodded earnestly. Then she jumped up and threw her arms around Kate's neck.

Suddenly she pulled back and tilted her head to the side. "Does that mean you're going to live with us and tuck me into bed and eat dinner with us every night?"

"It sure does," Kate said around the emotion that had knotted in her throat. "I'll even take you to school every morning if you want me to."

Again Chloe nodded enthusiastically. "Will you take me to school tomorrow?"

"I would love to take you to school tomorrow, as long as it is okay with your daddy."

Both heads swiveled to looked at Aidan. He held up his hands in surrender. "Hey, it is two against one. Majority rules. It looks like I'd be outnumbered if I said no, but I would not have said no anyway. Not to my two best girls."

He locked gazed with Kate and hot tears stung the backs of her eyes. She blinked them back and bit the insides of her cheeks until the temptation to cry passed. She had never been a big sap like this. She had prided herself on being stoic and cynical. One look at the happiness on Chloe's face—the little girl made it seem like getting a mother was the best gift anyone could have ever given to her—and Kate was about to become a blubbering mess.

Was this what kids did to you? Soften your hard heart and strip away your defenses? Because that was what was happening to her as she realized that

Chloe—and Aidan—and their baby were the best gifts she could have received.

From where she sat, she could see the Forsyth Galloway Inn across the grassy expanse and through the moss-laden trees on the other side of the street. The place that had belonged to six generations of women in her family. It felt as if each one of her ancestors who had come before her was smiling down on her right now, approving, welcoming this formerly motherless little girl into their female-centric fold.

It was overwhelming, and, at the same time, the most divinely right feeling she had had in her life. Well, except for one. When she looked up and saw the look on Aidan's face, she felt like she was finally home.

Chapter Eight

"How is married life?" Daniel stood in the open doorway of Aidan's office, startling him out of his thoughts.

"Considering that we have had one week of normalcy under our belts, now that Chloe and the family know, so far so good."

"Good thing you're an architect," Daniel said. "Because you make a terrible actor."

Aidan's knee-jerk reaction was to pretend like he didn't know what his brother was talking about, but why? One thing he had learned with Kate was you didn't solve problems by pretending life was perfect. Kate had taught him that you had to come at the situation head-on.

"The other day you said I had a good poker face."

"That was when you were keeping the marriage a secret. You were good at that. But I can tell that something's bothering you."

Aidan sighed.

"Okay, marriage is hard." He shrugged. "We are adjusting. Or, at least, we are trying to and I'm trying to keep a positive outlook. You know, set a good example for everyone."

Aidan pushed back from his desk and placed his hands behind his neck and shrugged.

"Chloe is happy. So that's good. She loves Kate. She loves finally having a mother and Kate is a great mom to her. She's good with Chloe. We haven't told her about the baby yet. We wanted to break the news to her in digestible bites. You know, let her get used to us being a family first. Let her feel safe, and then we'll tell her our family is going to grow some more. That she's going to have a sibling."

Daniel lowered himself onto the chair across from Aidan's desk.

"That's good," Daniel said. "So what's the problem?"

"Kate's…quiet. You know, distant. I don't know. I guess we're still adjusting to living together. I'm not sure how I thought life would be, but I thought it would be different than this. I don't know whether to give her space or if I should try harder."

"Marriage, even under the best circumstances, can be difficult. Or maybe I shouldn't say *difficult*. *Difficult* has a bad connotation. It can be challenging. *Challenging* puts a better spin on it."

"But should you have to *spin* something like marriage?" Aidan asked. "Shouldn't she and I just be happy to be together? We're newlyweds."

"Are you saying you're not happy?"

"No."

He had answered too fast, he knew it, which placed his answer squarely in the "doth protest too much" territory.

"I don't know," he amended. "I don't know that we would have gotten married had the circumstances been different."

"I thought you said you didn't get married because of the baby."

"We didn't."

"But you just said you would not have married her if she wasn't pregnant?"

"I didn't say anything about marrying her because she was pregnant."

"Okay, I'm confused," Daniel said. "Did you and

Kate plan this Vegas elopement, or did you just get caught up in the moment?"

Aidan clasped his hands together tightly on top of his desk. Then he loosened them and steepled his fingers, tapping them together as he thought of how to best answer his brother's question.

He inhaled a long and slow and steady breath as he chose his words. "It is more complicated than that."

"My next appointment isn't until after lunch. So I've got all the time in the world if you want to talk it out," Daniel said.

Aidan explained about Kate's wedding amnesia, following up with how the doctor said Kate's pregnancy hormones could have created an allergy to the alcohol, causing her memory loss.

"She wanted an annulment before we found out she was pregnant. She didn't want to be married—to anyone—but the baby changed everything. The pregnancy meant we couldn't have annulled the marriage. We would have had to get a divorce. Looking at things honestly and with clear eyes, I believe the judge would not have granted the annulment anyway—even without the pregnancy—because of our personal history. But once Kate found out about the baby, it was clear that she resigned herself to staying married. Still, it feels a little precarious to know my wife had to resign herself to marrying me. I can't shake the feeling that we're living in a house of cards. You know, one wrong move and it will all come crashing down."

Aidan knew what a mess it was when all Daniel did was sit there and nod. Squint at him and nod some more. Aidan didn't expect his brother to have the answer, but he would have loved some positive insight.

"I don't know what to say, man," Daniel said.

Aidan waved away the comment as if he could clear the air with the gesture. "Look, it is fine. I don't expect you to solve my problems. You've got enough on your own plate."

Daniel held up his hand. "But I like my plate. My plate does not include a house of cards. So if you're saying you want to make this marriage work, maybe you need to stop looking at it as if it is a problem. Try to put a positive spin on it."

There was that word again. *Spin.* As much as Aidan hated to hear it, his brother was right. He had been turning this issue around and around, looking at it from every possible angle. He needed to spin it in the right direction.

"I guess you have a point," Aidan conceded. "I don't know why the word *spin* bothers me so much."

"It is just semantics, dude," Daniel said. "Call

it whatever you want. Situations live up to the way that you see them. Is the glass half-empty or is the glass half-full?"

Aidan shook his head. "This is surreal. Between the two of us, I've always been the more positive one. Here we are and you're giving me lessons on optimism."

Daniel shrugged. "A good marriage can change a man."

But what did a bad marriage do to a person? Or even more apt, what happened if one person was happy in the marriage, but the other person felt trapped?

The unspoken questions hung in the air. Aidan knew he could be happy making a life with Kate. He would move mountains to make her happy and make the marriage a good one. But he certainly could not make it work if Kate didn't try too.

"You have to concentrate on the good, not the problems," Daniel continued. "If that's spin, then I don't know why it is such a bad word. It is worth it. You love Kate, don't you?"

Aidan took a moment and let the words of wisdom sink in. He thought about his brother's question. Did he love Kate? Since Veronica had walked out, he hadn't let himself love anyone except his daughter.

He'd been open to seeing women and the possibility of relationships. But love?

"What does love even mean?" Aidan deflected. "It is just a word. Veronica promised she would love me until death parted us and look how that ended up. Kate promised the same thing in Vegas and then she didn't even remember what she'd said. The next day, she wanted to pretend like it didn't even happen. *Love* is a disposable word. I think it's nothing more than a fleeting feeling."

"But you love Chloe, right?" Daniel said.

"Of course, but a father's love for his daughter is different than the kind of love we're talking about."

"Or is it? I can see that you believe in love. You just don't like the word."

Aidan shifted in his seat, bracing his forearms on the desk. "I believe in walking the walk, not talking the talk. Love is just a word. Actions mean a lot more than words. And when did you become a shrink?"

Daniel wasn't just talking the talk, either. He was probably tapping into something that Aidan had buried deep in his psyche. Even if that wasn't the case, Daniel and Elle were an example—living proof— that a couple could overcome seemingly insurmountable odds and come out the right side of love after Daniel caused Elle's former fiancé to leave her at the altar.

Aside from romantic love, in the familial arena, Daniel had been the one to brood over the losses they had sustained when they were younger. Aidan had always taken the view that the random hand that fate had dealt him would never define him. Though he had mourned the loss of their parents who had been killed in an automobile accident, leaving them alone, he had been able to believe in love until Veronica had abandoned Chloe and him.

She had left him with a newborn baby and hadn't looked back. Aidan had been too busy to brood over the loss. He had been too in awe and a little afraid of the beautiful little life that had been left in his inexperienced hands. Maybe subconsciously he had been determined to be unfazed by Veronica's walking out because he didn't want Chloe to feel any less loved or like it was her fault. He had channeled all his time, energy and love into his baby girl.

"It doesn't take a PhD to see that you're more affected by the past than you're admitting," Daniel said. "If you don't love Kate, how do you expect this marriage to work? Is it even fair to her? It is like you're saying, *Be my wife, but by the way, I don't love you.*"

The words hit Aidan in a vulnerable place. In his mind he heard her voice and the question she had asked him that day they had been packing up her house.

"I didn't say I don't love her. I just don't like saying... I just don't—" Aidan made a growling sound and scrubbed the heels of his hands over his eyes. "Just because I don't live in the past doesn't mean I haven't come to terms with it. Maybe I'm better at the *spin* than I gave me credit for. Because rather than moping, I've moved on, but I just refuse to repeat the same mistakes—"

Like tying the knot with a woman who doesn't want to be married to me?

A litany of words that Aidan had conditioned himself never to say in front of Chloe exploded in his head like a long string of fireworks.

Okay. Fine. That was exactly what he had done by marrying Kate in Vegas. He had repeated the exact same frigging mistake.

At least Daniel, who sat there with a knowing look on his face, had the good sense not to point out the obvious.

This conversation was going nowhere. Or at least nowhere he wanted to go.

"You know, you're right," Aidan said.

Daniel's brows arched, and he could virtually read the *Glory, hallelujah* sounding in his brother's mind at Aidan conceding the fight.

"If my marriage is going to work—and I'll be dammed if it won't—I need to come at this from a more positive place. Kate's aloofness is not a *problem*. It is a *challenge*. *Love* is a ridiculous word and it has nothing to do with this. I need to make a big gesture to show her that I'm in this for the long haul. I'm going to get her an engagement ring and propose the right way. I know she will love that, and we will start planning that wedding she wants to have with her family and friends. Before we told the family about the marriage, she told me she was worried about losing herself if she got married. She's independent and that's one of the things I love about her. I think it might help if she had something that was just hers. Something in addition to the salon. And I know exactly what that thing is."

"Do tell," Daniel said.

"At Gigi and Charles's party, Zelda pulled me aside and said they were ready to move forward with the spa at the Forsyth Galloway Inn. She asked me to draw up plans for the building. Which also means we need to get Anna to put the project on the schedule."

Anna Nolan was their very part-time, very capable office manager. When Aidan and Daniel first opened the doors to Quindlin Brothers Renovations, they had handled all aspects of the business themselves, including scheduling and planning. But as their company grew at a rate faster than they could have ever expected, they'd brought in someone who could keep them organized and on the right track in the two days a week that she came into the office.

"Sounds like a plan," Daniel said.

Aidan explained the projected timeline. "Keep it on the down low for now," Aidan said. "I want to surprise Kate with it. I think I'm going to get her a ring and make this a reverse proposal."

Daniel laughed. "What does that mean?"

"We're already married. But she never got the down-on-one-knee proposal, and since we're going to have another wedding for the family, why not do it right and propose the old-fashioned way?"

"And the spa business is part of this old-fashioned proposal?"

Aidan smiled. "Sure. What's wrong with that? It will be an engagement present."

When Kate let herself in the kitchen door of the Forsyth Galloway Inn, she was greeted by her mother yelling, "Don't let the puppy out!"

"What in the world?"

A tiny red-and-white corgi puppy appeared at her feet just as she shut the door. For as long as her mother, sisters and she had lived at the inn, her grandmother had staunchly insisted there would be no pets allowed. That was the reason why growing up, the girls had never had a puppy despite how much they had begged and pleaded.

Now that Gigi had retired, had Zelda lifted the no-pet policy?

"Whose dog is this?" Kate asked as she set her tote that contained the shampoo, conditioner, hair cape and curlers she used for Gigi's weekly hair appointment. Usually Gigi came into the salon, but she had asked Kate to come to the inn today. It was such a beautiful day that Kate had been happy to have a valid excuse to get out of the salon. She had even walked the short distance from downtown to the inn.

She squatted down and took the puppy's sweet face into her hands, taking care to scratch behind the ears and on the fluffy white chest. The pup returned the favor by alternating licks and gentle nips on Kate's hands.

"That's your mother's dog," Gigi said, her voice tight with disapproval.

"What?" Kate asked as she stood up to face Zelda. "Seriously? When did you decide to get a dog? And a corgi—" Kate's voice went up an octave as she drew out the last syllable of the dog's breed. She was unable to contain her excitement.

Zelda looked sheepish. Not at all like Kate expected her to look after pulling rank on her grandmother so victoriously. After all, Gigi was officially retired and Zelda was in charge, which meant she made the rules.

"Well, I didn't exactly decide to get a dog—"

"It was a gift," Gigi said with a scowl and lowered her voice. "Ask her about it. Go on. Ask her. It is a gift from that *man*."

The way Gigi uttered the words *that man*, as if it was sinful, made Kate laugh out loud.

"What? Really?" Kate asked. "What man?"

"Yes. Really," Gigi answered. "Apparently, your mother has a boyfriend that she's been keeping a secret."

Zelda rolled her eyes. "Oh, Mother. Can you not—"

"The only reason I found out was because of this thing." Gigi curled her lip and pointed at the dog with her slippered foot. The puppy immediately mistook the gesture for an invitation to play and pounced, yanking the slipper off Gigi's foot and doing a victory lap around the kitchen with it in his mouth.

Gigi shrieked. Kate laughed. Zelda called after the puppy, "Bear, come here! Give that back. Give that slipper back to Gigi and play with your own toys."

The puppy's name was Bear?

Awwww. Be still, my heart.

That was exactly what he looked like, a tiny mischievous bear up to no good and winning over every single heart at the same time. Well, except for Gigi's.

As Kate watched her mother laughing and chasing the little dog around the kitchen, in pursuit of Gigi's slipper, Kate realized she couldn't remember the last time she had seen her mother look this happy. She looked young and beautiful and…in love.

Obviously, this boyfriend knew her mother well enough to know a corgi puppy meant more to her than gold and diamonds.

"Okay, so, I'm away from the inn for—what?— three days? And suddenly Mom has a puppy *and* a boyfriend? What alternate universe have I fallen into? Wait, is this who sent you those flowers?"

Hands on her hips, and trying hard to hide her smile, Gigi tsked.

"Seriously, Mom, who is this mystery man and when do we get to meet him?"

"Oh, I don't know, Kate. We'll have to see. I want to wait until I know where things are going with him. Right now, I'm not sure."

"Can I tell my friends that you're my new mommy?" Chloe asked, as Kate helped her get out of her car seat at her friend Beatrice's house. She and Aidan had decided that Kate would take Chloe to the rock-painting group that Doris had invited them to join.

Kate smiled at the little girl. "I would love it if you called me that." She kissed the little girl on the top of her head and smoothed her curls away from her pretty little face. Chloe smiled up at her as she put her hand in Kate's, and they started up the cobblestone walk toward the mansion that was situated on Monterey Square.

Nice neighborhood.

Kate felt pinpricks of nervous energy as she worried about exactly what sort of situation she was walking into, meeting all the young mothers.

Doris's mansion was within walking distance of the Forsyth Galloway Inn. But while Kate's family had been forced to open their home to travelers to afford keeping the big old house, Doris's people had obviously had the luxury to retain it as a private residence. Although, despite the various setbacks, each generation of Kate's ancestors had discovered creative ways and means to keep the house in the family and pass it down.

Actually, Kate couldn't imagine the inn being anything but a bed-and-breakfast. The family had always had their private quarters, and the guests who'd stayed with them over the years had left behind interesting stories that had become part of the house's rich tapestry of history.

As a native daughter of Savannah, Kate had

passed by Doris's house dozens, if not hundreds, of times in her twenty-six years, but she had never known who lived here. She had certainly never been inside. She made a mental note to ask Gigi and Charles what they knew about it. Between the two of them, they knew practically everyone in the historic district.

Based on the address, Doris wasn't hurting financially as a single mother. Because places like this—even the grand old houses that had fallen into the worst of disrepair, and this one looked impeccably preserved—didn't come cheap. Suddenly Kate wondered about Doris's story.

Kate hadn't allowed herself to think too much about the woman since meeting her last weekend. Because that would have forced her to examine the fact that Doris obviously had a crush on Aidan. If she had thought about it too hard, she would have had to talk to Aidan about it and that would have made her seem jealous, or needy and territorial.

The only time Doris had come up in conversation was when Aidan had asked Kate if she would be willing to take Chloe to the afternoon gathering. It was her day off. He had said it would be a good chance to meet Chloe's friends and their moms.

If Aidan had been interested in Doris, he could

have gone to the gathering himself or come along with the two of them.

Because of that, she had pushed back the little voice that nagged in the dark corners of her brain—that beautiful, wealthy Doris Watson had a lot to offer a man.

But obviously, Aidan had had his chance to be with Doris if he had wanted to.

He swore he had been in his right mind when he had married Kate in Vegas. He was the one who had been determined to stay in the marriage and make it work.

Funny, as she walked up to the grand front entrance of Doris's house, Kate realized, for the first time ever, that she wasn't worried about being the one who was like her father. She was worried that Aidan might pull a Fred.

Actually, no. She wasn't worried about that. Not at all.

Aidan Quindlin was nothing like Fred Clark.

When Aidan married her, he had promised to be faithful—she knew this because she'd revisited the keepsake book from the Elvis wedding chapel that contained a copy of the vows they had supposedly exchanged.

And he would remain faithful unlike her father, who, after cheating and leaving her mom, had returned years later to sue her for half of everything, left them in financial ruin and had broken Zelda's heart, though he'd lost the case.

No. Aidan was nothing like Fred Clark.

She wasn't going to insult him by letting petty insecurities make her doubt him.

She and Aidan were married now. Even if the marriage wasn't based on love—even if he had just married her so that Chloe could have a mother—he had married her. Not Doris.

Kate lifted Chloe so she could used the lion's head door knocker to knock on the large double doors that were painted in candy apple red lacquer.

Right away, a petite older woman dressed in a crisp white tunic blouse and cobalt blue pants that skimmed her ankles answered the door. Her small, manicured feet were encased in bejeweled thong sandals. Her jet-black hair was styled in a sleek bob. She looked as if she had stepped out of a Talbots ad featuring mature women.

"Hello! You must be here for Beatrice's rock-painting party," she said. "I'm Candice Watson, Beatrice's grandmother."

It didn't escape Kate that the woman hadn't called herself Doris's mother. Same last name. Was Candice the paternal grandmother?

"I'm Kate Clark. This is my daughter, Chloe."

"Of course, I know Chloe. She's been over here to play with Beatrice many times since the girls moved in."

Since the girls moved in?

"Come in, come in," Candice said. "The party has started already. Everyone is in the kitchen."

Were they late? Kate had made it a point to be here right at the time stated on the invitation. She could hear the sound of children laughing and female voices in another room.

The rich-looking foyer was all dark polished wood and Persian rugs. A mirrored, antique buffet with a marble top stood sentinel along the parallel wall and oil paintings with thick, ornately carved gilded frames graced the persimmon-colored walls on either side.

Candice walked ahead as if she expected them to follow.

Suddenly shy, Chloe clung to Kate's hand and pressed her cheek against Kate's hip, half hiding behind her. Kate gave the little girl's hand a gentle and reassuring double squeeze, hoping to telegraph, *No worries. I'm here for you.*

Kate felt a bit nervous herself. Like she was walking into the lioness's den.

Chloe had always seemed like such a good-natured child. Even during the time that Aidan had been in the hospital and she, Elle and Daniel had cared for her, she had seemed remarkably well adjusted. This was the first time she was noticing the more reticent side of Chloe.

Until now, it hadn't dawned on Kate that this brave little girl had previously had no choice but to boldly march into mother-daughter get-togethers like this one alone, without a mother at her side. Or, at best, as the guest of another mother-daughter duo.

For Kate, being surrounded by the protective love and support of her sisters, mother and Gigi had always been such a given that sometimes she unwittingly took it for granted. She couldn't imagine what it was like not to have them in her life, on her side. To be a motherless daughter with no feminine guidance.

Something shifted inside Kate. A fierce, protective feeling bloomed and her heart was promising to be there for Chloe. To love her and guard her. She would never have to walk alone in this world again.

"Are you okay?" she asked Chloe.

"I think we're late," she said.

Kate remembered that uneasy feeling of walking into a party that had already started. Especially when she was a girl. Alliances shifted, and new bonds formed in the blink of an eye. At this age it felt awful to be the odd person out.

"Naaa," Kate said, bending down so that she was

eye level with Chloe. "The party doesn't start until we get here."

Chloe's eyes got large.

"It is true." Kate nodded. "Let's not keep them waiting."

Chloe laughed and visibly relaxed. Kate squared her shoulders and raised her chin a notch. "Ready?"

The little girl did the same, standing a bit taller and looking more confident, holding Kate's hand as they found their way to the kitchen.

Candice was standing next to Beatrice at the largest kitchen island that Kate had ever seen. The older woman appeared to be helping Beatrice with something.

"Chloe's here!" Beatrice got down from her stool at the kitchen island.

"There you are," Candice said. "Did I lose you? I was just about to come look for you."

"We just needed a moment." Kate smiled at the woman.

The kitchen at her family's inn was roomy, but this one, which looked like it had been remodeled to include every top-of-the-line modern convenience, was vast. Five other little girls, each wearing a painter smock, were seated at the island, painting rocks. Five women, presumably, the girls' mothers, were clustered in the kitchen, each of them holding wine glasses, talking and picking at a spread of food arranged on one of the counters.

Beatrice hugged Chloe and then took her hand and led her to the stool next to hers. "I saved this seat for you so you could sit next to me."

She seemed like a sweet little girl. Kate felt bad for expecting less of her. She had to be careful not to project her own vulnerabilities onto Chloe. Such as how she felt out of place standing there by herself as the women continued to talk.

"Dori, look who's here," Candice said as Doris entered the room carrying a handful of paint tubes, which she deposited on the island.

Dori—er—Doris—yeah, she did seem more like a Dori, Kate decided. That name suited her better.

Dori smiled at Kate, but there was no mistaking the way her gaze swept beyond Kate. Dori's eyes searched the room and flashed disappointment when she didn't find what—or *who*—she was looking for. But to her credit, she recovered quickly.

She cocked her head to the side, reminding Kate of Zelda's corgi puppy for an instant. "Kate, isn't it?" She had managed to muster a sincere-looking smile, all traces of her disappointment at finding her instead of Aidan neatly vanishing without a trace of animosity. "Welcome. I'm so glad you could come." She walked toward Kate, arms outstretched, palms upturned. Was it a sign of greeting or of conceding? *You married Aidan, I accept.* When she reached her, she planted a double kiss on Kate's cheeks, an intimate gesture for not being sure she remembered her name.

The women who had previously been unaware of Kate's presence had turned to see the newcomer.

"Everyone," Dori said, "this is Kate… Quindlin? Did you take Aidan's last name?"

They hadn't really talked about it. She had been so busy moving in and making life as normal as possible for Chloe that she hadn't really thought about it.

"It is Kate Clark…"

Kate saw two of the women exchange glances, which made her feel as if this wasn't the first Dori and her friends had discussed Aidan's surprise marriage.

"Um… Kate Clark Quindlin," she amended. Saying the words aloud made her realize that the double name did have a nice ring to it.

Dori put an arm around her and walked her over to her friends, and made the introductions. There was a Pam and a Heather, and Janet, or was she Janelle? And because she had been pondering the Janet-Janelle question, she had missed the last introduction completely. She was opening her mouth to ask for clarifications and redo, but Dori said, "Everyone, this is Kate. Kate, I'm sort of the new girl, too. Beatrice and I moved here from Charleston a couple of months ago. I started this rock-painting group so Beatrice could make friends, and, okay, if I'm perfectly honest, I want to make friends, too. I know everyone is busy, but I'm hoping we can make this a weekly after-school thing."

The other women nodded their enthusiasm.

Did they work? Probably not—Kate reminded herself not to jump to conclusions.

"I work," Kate said, wanting to establish that up front. "My schedule can be flexible, but it all depends on my clients."

"What do you do?" asked Janet, or Janelle.

"I do hair." Kate punctuated the declaration with a rise of her chin.

There was a chorus of oohs and "I see"s. Pam said, "I know how valuable a good hairdresser is. I've been going to my girl for ten years. If she left, I think I'd have to leave my husband and follow her."

Kate was tempted to say that she wasn't there to recruit, but she bit her lip instead.

"So you and Aidan are newlyweds?" the one whose name she had missed asked.

"We are."

"Congratulations," Heather said. "You got yourself quite a catch with that one."

Kate's gaze dropped to Heather's hand. She was wearing a big, fat halo diamond with ring guards. *Married*, she noted, and wondered why she was so up on Aidan's catch-worthiness.

Maybe Heather read it on Kate's face, though she had never thought she was quite *that* transparent, but the woman said, "Okay, we have to confess. We had no idea that Aidan had anyone special in his life. We had our eye on him for Dori. Her husband died and we think it is time for her to get back in the saddle."

Dori snort-laughed. "Well, let's just usher that big elephant right out of the room. Now that that's out of the way, I hope we can all be great friends."

That was probably one of the most awkward conversations she had ever had, but the raw honesty of it was refreshing.

Chapter Nine

Later that night, after the girls had gotten back from the rock group and they had put Chloe to bed, Aidan and Kate sat together on the sofa.

"After everything that has been going on," said Aidan, "it feels like this is the first chance we've had to be alone in a long time."

He put his arm around Kate and pulled her close, leaning in for a gentle kiss, testing the waters. Things were still so uncertain between them, but he realized they were never going to move forward if he kept acting like he was walking on eggshells. He wanted her. He wanted this life with her, and he believed she wanted it, too. Especially given the way she was kissing him back.

They stayed like that for hours, or maybe it was minutes. Time seemed irrelevant when they were like this, because they were so good together. As one, rather than fighting each other. Right now, for the life of him, he couldn't remember why he ever doubted that they could make it. When the kiss ended, he leaned his forehead against hers, keeping his arms around her.

"That was nice."

She made an agreeable sound. Her eyes looked dreamy, and for a moment, he was tempted to scoop her up and carry her into the bedroom—their bedroom—and show her exactly how happy he was that things had turned out this way. The right way.

In an effort to make himself slow down, he said, "Are you thirsty? I picked up some freshly squeezed orange juice from Brighter Day on the way home."

Brighter Day was the health food store on Bull Street that supplied fresh orange juice to the Forsyth Galloway Inn.

Kate smiled and put her hand on her still-flat belly. "That sounds delicious. Thanks for picking it up."

She seemed a little subdued tonight. If not for the unmistakable way she had returned his kiss, he might've worried that something was wrong. Of course, she might be tired. That was why he had to stop jumping to conclusions like that. There would be ebbs and flows in their conversations. Even someone as strong and outgoing as Kate needed time to herself to recharge. As the quieter of the two, so did he.

"How was the rock painting?" he asked from the kitchen as he got the container out of the refrigerator and juice glasses from the cabinet.

"It was…nice. Dori and her friends are really… *nice*. Did you know, that's what they call her? Dori?"

"No," he called. "I didn't know that. She introduced herself to me as Doris. I'm not in the habit of giving people nicknames." He laughed to make sure she knew he was joking.

He could imagine her rolling her eyes in that way she so often did when he cracked a corny joke.

"Well, yeah, that's what they call her. I met her mother, Candice. Their house is just around the corner from the inn. But I'm sure you know that."

"I did," he said.

"Of course," Kate said. "You would not let Chloe go off with a stranger without knowing where she was going. Anyway, Dori and her friends were so welcoming to Chloe and me. I mean, you never know what you're walking into in a situation like that. Where people already know each other. I mean, I wasn't exactly invited."

He entered the room, carrying two glasses of juice. He handed her one and sat down next to her.

"Actually, I think she was counting on you coming over rather than me." Aidan didn't know what to say and he was glad when Kate shrugged. "Until she got her mind wrapped around the fact that you and I really are married. You know she had her eye on you?"

"No. I didn't know that. And yes, you and I really are married. As far as I'm concerned, you are the only woman in the world for me."

"Aww, that's sweet."

He couldn't read the look in Kate's eyes.

"The kids seem nice," she said, "which is important. This is a good group of friends for Chloe. I was watching them interact and they really were very sweet to each other. I know you would approve."

"That's good to know," he said. "But why are you changing the subject?" he asked.

"I'm not changing the subject. I was telling you about the play date. Fair warning, I think we'll eventually have to offer to host this rock-painting group over here. They're meeting in the park next time, but they want to start a rotating schedule."

"That's fine, but I need you to know that you really are the only woman I care about having her eye on me."

Kate sipped her juice. He saw her throat work. She licked her lips. "I just don't want you to feel trapped in this marriage."

"I knew exactly what I was doing when I said 'I do.' Kate?"

She met his eyes. "Are you the one who feels trapped?" he asked.

"No."

She smiled. "Apparently, my mother has a boyfriend. Had you heard about that?"

He chuckled and shook his head. "No."

"I didn't know if you would have heard through Elle and Daniel."

Again, he shook his head. "Good for Zelda. Who is he?"

"I have no idea. He's some sort of mystery man. She wants everyone to meet him Friday night. Do you have plans?"

"If I did, I'd cancel them."

"Me, too. I haven't seen her this happy in ages. Not since—" her eyes darkened "—not since before my dad left."

Fred Clark was such a thorn in her side. Aidan wished there was some way that he could take away the pain that even the mere mention of Fred's name caused her. He had given Fred Clark's name to Randy Ponder, his PI friend, but he hadn't heard whether or not he had been able to locate him. He made a mental note to follow up with Randy.

"I'm sorry," Aidan said.

"Don't be sorry," Kate said. "Zelda is so happy, there's absolutely no reason to be sorry."

"I just hate it that it caused you pain when you think of him."

"Here's the thing." Kate leaned forward. "Zelda's happiness is such an inspiration. If she can be happy after going through hell, maybe there's hope for the rest of us."

Aidan blinked. He loved the sound of that.

She reached into her pants pocket and pulled out something.

"Chloe made this for me tonight," Kate said. "While all the other little girls were painting rocks to leave in Forsyth Park, Chloe came up to me and pressed this into my hand. She told me she had painted it for me and wanted me to keep it."

Kate handed the small, colorful stone to Aidan.

On one side, it said, "I love my family," in rudimentary bold blue letters. On the other side, Chloe had painted a man, and a woman with flowing red hair. Between the two of them was a little girl with curly blond hair holding the hands of the man and woman. The three were encircled by the outline of a red heart.

"This is just…." Her eyes glistened with tears, but she was smiling as she looked at the rock. "You and Chloe mean the world to me, Aidan." She put her hand on her stomach. "This little baby and I are so lucky to be part of this family. It is overwhelming, really."

"We're lucky to have you. You complete us. Or maybe we should say that we complete each other. Let's never forget how fortunate we are."

Kate closed her fingers around the rock and nodded. He pulled her into his arms and held her like that for a long time.

"I know you wanted things to be different. You wished that the wedding could have been more traditional."

"At the very least, I wish I could remember our wedding rather than waking up married. It is as if I wasn't even there."

"I want you to remember it, too. You deserve that and a real proposal. Let's do it again. Let's have a real wedding. I will surprise you with a proposal. I want you to buy bridal magazines and pick out the dress of your dreams and have your sisters next to you as bridesmaids."

"Chloe can be our flower girl," she said, her head still resting on his shoulder.

He was going to make that happen. He was going

to make sure Kate had a proposal she would never forget and the wedding of her dreams.

The tall man exiting Aidan's office looked familiar, but Kate couldn't place him as she watched him walk to his car, which was parked ahead of her car, on the street in front of the Victorian townhouse that housed Quindlin Brothers Renovations.

It was after 6:00. She had just dropped off Chloe at Dori's house.

Dori had invited Chloe to join her and Beatrice for dinner.

Since Chloe would have a much better time with her best friend than attending the formal dinner to meet Zelda's mystery man, Kate had taken Dori up on the offer, with a promise to reciprocate as soon as things settled down.

She watched the man get into his car and then texted Aidan to let him know she was waiting for him outside. Two minutes later, he greeted her with a kiss that curled her toes in the pointy flats she was wearing.

When they came up for air, she asked, "Who was that guy that just left? He looks so familiar."

"That's my friend Randy Ponder."

"The private investigator?"

"The one and only."

Kate frowned. "Please tell me you are designing a house for him or he has some other business here because I still haven't made up my mind about whether I want to open the Pandora's box that is my father."

Aidan grimaced. "Yeah, about that. He, uh, found your father." Aidan opened the folio he had brought with him and took out a sealed manila envelope He tried to hand it to her, but she held up her hands and refused it as if the missive would burn her fingers.

"I don't want this, Aidan."

"Then put it away, because you might change your mind."

"I am not going to change my mind and it was presumptuous of you to do this since I never gave you the go ahead. In fact, I thought I asked you to drop it."

Aidan frowned. Kate's heart was beating so fast she thought it might break through her breastbone and fall into her lap.

"You didn't ask me to drop it. You didn't make a decision at all. But you did acknowledged that you needed to sort out your feelings so we can both get on with our lives. Since you were having such a hard time deciding what to do, I took matters into my own hands."

"I told you I did not want to find him."

"Kate, I don't think you're going to be able to put everything behind you until you talk to him."

Kate saw red and it threatened to engulf her. "Just because we're married, it does not give you the right to decide what is best for me. We are late. I don't want to talk about this anymore. I'll pretend like this never happened as long as you agree not to overstep bounds like this again."

Before Aidan had a chance to respond, she started the car and headed toward the Forsyth Galloway Inn. She saw him tuck the envelope beneath the sun visor on the passenger side of the car.

Okay, fine.

She grabbed the envelope and shoved it into her purse. When she got home, she would throw it away the without opening it. The last thing she wanted was to talk to the man who broke her heart and did his best to ruin her family's life.

Even though they shared the same blood, it didn't mean she had to call him family. He had certainly forfeited the privilege of being called Dad. As far as she was concerned, he was a sperm donor. Nothing more.

They rode to the inn in silence. The entire way, she tried to calm down by telling herself that Aidan only had good intentions. But how would he feel if she insisted that he contact his ex-wife, Veronica?

Okay, that would be a dumb idea.

That was for Chloe to decide when she got older. Veronica had rejected her own daughter once, before Chloe knew that she was being rejected. No need to give Veronica the opportunity to hurt the little girl.

Kate's cheeks burned with the realization of how parallel Chloe's situation was to her own. A swell of conflicting emotions bubbled up, stinging the back of her throat, making her eyes water. Kate bit the inside of her cheeks to keep the tears from multiplying. She cared so much for Chloe—okay, she *loved* her. She didn't want her to go through what Kate had gone through, knowing that one of the people whose love you were supposed to take for granted hadn't loved you enough to stay. If she could, she would protect that sweet little girl so that Chloe could grow up without the pain and anxiety of wondering who the next person would be to abandon you—Aidan was such a stable force in her life that she might not have the same trust issues with men that Kate had developed.

Aidan was steadfast and good and reliable…and he obviously loved his daughter. A father's love for his daughter was different than a man's love for a woman. He would never leave Chloe. But— Kate blinked as realization dawned. Aidan had never said he loved her. He had told her he cared and that he wanted them to work and that they believed they were good together, but he had never professed his love for her.

She stole a glance at him. He was tapping out something on his phone.

Her mouth opened, ready to ask him point-blank, but she couldn't make the words come out. She felt like she was being needy and vulnerable, which she hated. On the rare occasion that happened, she removed herself from the situation that dredged up the feelings and went inside herself. Self-reliance. That was the key. She knew she would not let herself down. Other people…they were a gamble. That was why she tried to not pin her hopes on others. If you didn't have expectations, you would not be disappointed.

"Are you all right?" Aidan's voice was clipped and level, and that irritated her, too. He didn't even have to say it— *Just leave Kate alone and eventually she'll come out of her snit soon enough, as long as you don't poke the bear.* She had lived with that her whole life. Maybe it was sound advice on how to best deal with her, but… She inhaled a long, deep breath.

"I'm fine." She gave herself an inward shake. *Get yourself together. This is a big night for Mom. You don't need to ruin it with your own baggage.*

"I'm fine," she repeated as she parked the car in

an empty space on the street that ran along the side of the inn.

"Good." Aidan leaned over and dusted a feather-light kiss on her lips. Even the brief brush of his lips on hers made something shift inside her. It lifted the weight of the earlier irritation. It made the better part of her remember that he was a good guy if he could put up with her moods. She couldn't take him for granted because surely that generous forbearance had its limits.

Aidan was a good man. She didn't need to rip open the scars left by her father to realize that.

"Let's have a good evening, okay?" he said.

She sighed. "Of course. Aidan, I'm sorry. I'm not upset anymore, but I just need you to not push me when it comes to certain things." She shrugged. "Namely, my dad."

Aidan nodded.

"I don't need to see him again to get on with my life. In fact, I worry that if I do reopen this closed door, he will think it is an invitation to be part of our life. *Our* life. Not *his* life. Not *my* life. *Our life.* That's what I want to protect."

God, she hadn't even fully realized that until the words had presented themselves. But they weren't just words. It was the truth.

She, her mother and her sisters were all finally

getting on with their lives after living through the hell Fred had put them through. Fred Clark had no place here.

Aidan was smiling that lopsided smile of his. It was just for her. He reached out and touched her face, ran his hand around to the back of her neck and pulled her closer. This time, he kissed her soundly and thoroughly and her lady parts sang. She wished there was a way she could sneak him up the back steps to her old room and....

A quiet little moan escaped at the thought. But there was probably someone staying in her old room because she had been on her own since graduating from beauty school. And tonight was about her mother and her new beau. Not about reliving her teenage years with Aidan.

"Come on," she said. "We need to go inside before I have my way with you right here in the car like a couple of teenagers making out."

"And why would that be wrong?" His hand had found the hem of her skirt and was inching its way up her thigh, sending spirals of longing that intensified the closer he got to her center. Out of the corner of her eye, she happened to catch movement in the sideview mirror. It was Liam and Jane, and their presence snapped her back to reality.

"Because my sister and her husband are walking up." She pulled her skirt back into place in the nick of time.

"Rain check?" Aidan asked.

"You bet."

As they greeted Jane and Liam, Kate noticed that Aidan was carrying his briefcase. "You can put that in the trunk, if you want," she offered. Savannah was a safe place, but given as many tourists and other people that came and went through the historic district, everyone knew it was smart to not leave anything that might tempt someone to break in. His case should be safe in the trunk.

"No, I'd rather take it inside," he said. "I'll stick it out of the way in a closet."

That seemed reasonable.

Soon enough, they were shaking hands with Zelda's special friend Stephen Windsor, a handsome businessman from Lexington, South Carolina. They had met when he visited Savannah on business. Stephen looked to be about six foot four. He had dark hair graying at the temples. He could have been Pierce Brosnan's stand-in, if he was looking for that kind of work. According to Zelda, he was a self-made man.

"It was love at first sight," Stephen said, placing a kiss on Zelda's temple. Her mother blushed a pretty shade of pink. She was absolutely glowing tonight, like Kate had never seen her before.

"Elle and Kate," Jane said. "Can you please come help me in the kitchen?"

Jane's eyes sparkled as she gave a quick jerk of her head, indicating that it was time for a sisterly summit. No one except the three of them would have noticed. It was that secret language of sisters that allowed the three of them to decode the subtext when others weren't the wiser.

"What do you think?" Jane asked, once they had made it through the butler's pantry and were safely tucked behind the kitchen doors, where something smelled delicious. Apparently, coq au vin was on the menu tonight. Jane had mentioned that she and Liam had prepared it earlier today. She went to a large pot on the stove and stirred it.

"I love him," Elle said.

"I want to love him, but—" Kate said.

Elle made a face and waved away Kate's words as if they smelled. "I had a chance to spend some time with him this afternoon and he is a fantastic guy. He really is. I just love him and there's no disputing that Mom is so happy."

"I just hope he doesn't hurt her," Kate said.

"Okay, Eeyore." Jane rolled her eyes. "This is

a happy night. Please check your negativity at the door."

Kate's thoughts skittered back to the envelope that Aidan had tucked beneath the visor. Then she remembered how happy her mother had looked. The way she and Stephen looked at each other.

Jane was right. If their mother was happy, she needed to be happy for her.

"Kate, are you in here?" Gigi's voice preceded her into the kitchen. "Oh, there you are. Girls, please come out to the dining room. Your mother has an announcement."

The sisters looked at each other.

Surely it wasn't what they were thinking? Could it be? Stephen and Zelda had only known each other a couple of months. If they were announcing their engagement, things were moving a little fast.

"I hope this won't take too long, because I need to prep the potatoes and green beans."

"That can wait a moment," Gigi said. "We need you."

"What's going on, Gigi?" Kate asked.

Gigi smiled a knowing smile before she sashayed out of the kitchen, calling over her shoulder, "I guess you'll just have to wait and see."

Kate looked at Elle. If anyone would have a hint about what was going on, it would be Elle. Because of the art classes she taught at the inn, she was around their mother more than Kate and Jane.

Jane must've been on the same wavelength. "What do you know?" She directed the question to Elle, who shrugged. "I have no idea what's going on. Let's go find out."

The sisters made their way out of the kitchen, through the butler's pantry and back to the dining room where everyone had gathered. Aidan, Daniel and Liam were filling glasses with champagne and handing them out.

Aidan walked over with two flutes—one with sparkling white grape juice, the other with champagne—and handed the grape juice to Kate, standing next to her.

Uh-oh. Champagne meant news and it was usually of the relationship variety.

She hoped her mother wasn't making a colossal mistake by rushing things before she really got to know Stephen. Anyone could be on their best behavior, present their best self over eight weeks... especially when it was a long-distance relationship.

"May I have everyone's attention, please?" Zelda said. Everyone in the room quieted down and turned their gazes to her. "Thank you so much for making time to come tonight and meet Stephen. You're definitely going to be seeing more of him as he explores business ventures in this area." Zelda rose up on her tiptoes and planted a kiss on Stephen's cheek.

Oookay, here we go.

"But right now, we have something else to celebrate." Zelda's gaze fell on Kate and Aidan. "Aidan doesn't know I'm doing this, and I hope it is okay. But even if it isn't, I'm just too excited to keep this to myself much longer."

"Zelda?" Aidan shook his head. "Is now the best time?"

Zelda didn't answer. She turned around and picked up the cardboard tube that looked suspiciously like the one Aidan had carried in his briefcase tonight. Kate had been so busy meeting Stephen and saying hello to everyone else that she hadn't noticed him give it to Zelda—or where he had put his briefcase for that matter.

Kate shot Aidan an inquisitive look and whispered, "What's going on?"

Zelda brandished the tube like a scepter. "Kate and Aidan, everything has been so crazy since we returned from Vegas, I haven't had a chance to give you a wedding gift."

A wedding gift?

"Aidan helped me with this," Zelda said. "So it will be a surprise for you, but not so much for him, though he will benefit from it as much as you will, because it will bring goodwill and prosperity to your marriage and allow you more time to stay home with that baby."

Kate laughed. "What in the world are you talking about, Mama?"

Zelda looked like the cat who ate the cream as she handed the cardboard tube to Kate. "See for yourself."

Kate removed the plastic cap and turned the tube on its end. A roll of papers fell out. They were blueprints.

"Unroll them and look." Zelda appeared barely able to contain her happiness. "Isn't it a beautiful design? Now, of course, we want your input. Don't we, Aidan? After all, you're the one who will be running the spa at the Forsyth Galloway Inn. We want to sit down with you before we start building it."

The spa at the Forsyth Galloway Inn? What?

Kate felt all the blood drain from her face. She rolled the papers up and took a deep breath trying to diffuse the fury that was rattling her nerves. "I can't run your spa, mom. I have my own business. My own clientele." She slanted a look at Aidan. "Aidan knows how important it is for me to keep that business. We've talked about it."

"Aidan and I thought that with the baby on the way, you would not want to be on your feet so much,"

Zelda said. "And, of course, you'll need to take time off when the baby comes. This way you can have a staff who can help take the load off you and free up your time."

So this was what it was like to be ambushed. Obviously, Aidan hadn't listened to a single word she'd said.

If not for Chloe, Kate would've left the dinner party and let Aidan find his way home alone. But she didn't leave. She simply did her best to avoid talking to him at the party and was mostly silent as they walked to the car.

What she realized was that she could've left without him and picked up Chloe early, but something made her stay.

Wasn't that what marriage was all about? You could be seething on the inside, but to the rest of the world, everything was fine. It was all fine. One big facade. Of course, she wasn't going to get into it at the party with her mother about how disappointed she was that Zelda and Aidan were trying to railroad her into giving up what little freedom she had with her business. She had made it clear that she did not want to take on the responsibility at the inn.

Aidan steered the car into a space along Forsyth Park.

"What are you doing?" Kate asked.

"We need to talk about this before we pick up Chloe."

Dori's house was just around the corner. "I don't know if we should get into this right now. We can't be too late picking her up. And really, what's there to say, Aidan? Except that I don't know what part of 'I want to keep my job' you didn't understand. If it wasn't clear, I meant I don't want to work at the spa. I don't want to own my own salon. I want to keep my client base and keep at least one part of my life normal. I feel like you and my mother are trying to railroad me into something that you want."

"I'm sorry you feel that way. It wasn't what I intended."

"You're kidding, right? Then why did that even happen tonight?"

"Why? Because your mother is a client. She asked me to draw up plans for the final phase. She did not ask me to kidnap you and force you to do anything you don't want to do."

He sounded irritated. The barbed words hung in the air between them.

"Kate, I can't shake the feeling that this—what we're doing right now—isn't solely about the spa, is it?" he said. "Because you know it is your call whether or not you want to work there. I'm not railroading you into anything. Especially not into a life with Chloe and me. But I do have to say that I can't take these mercurial ups and downs. I cannot walk on eggshells wondering if the next thing I do is going to make you feel fenced in or railroaded or otherwise forced into a situation you don't want. What do you want, Kate?"

"I don't know what I want." Her words were barely a whisper. "I know I don't want to hurt you or Chloe. I don't want to feel like I'm being fenced in or ambushed or forced into something that should be so good. It shouldn't be this difficult. I know that. But I can't seem to get my head together and that's not fair to you. I know that's not fair to you. But I don't know what to do about it."

Aidan stared straight ahead, weighing his words, silently testing out what he would say before he said it. Because once the words were out, he couldn't take them back. But really there was no other way.

"You need to take some time and figure out what you want," Aidan said. "You need to figure out if you're staying or going because if you want us to be a family, things can't always be about you."

She inhaled sharply. "You're right. It can't be that way and I've made it that way and I'm sorry. I wish I could make myself feel differently. But it isn't fair to you. I'll do my best to sort out my head and get myself together."

The glow from one of the streetlights perfectly illuminated Kate's face. He saw something flash in her eyes. "How do *you* feel about our arrangement, Aidan? We've been so focused on how I feel, that you haven't said much about how this is affecting you."

"I told you. I want this marriage to work."

"I know. You've said that several times. But *why*, Aidan? *Why* do you want this marriage? Because it certainly isn't the easiest path you could have chosen. I'm not the easiest person to live with and sometimes I think you deserve…more."

Her voice broke on the last word.

"As far as I'm concerned, divorce isn't an option. Unless you want out. I won't keep you in a marriage you don't want to be in. I said 'til death do us part and I'd like to keep that promise."

"That." Kate jabbed her finger in the air. "That right there."

"What?" Aidan asked, genuinely confused.

"This isn't a 'you broke it, you bought it' situation, is it, Aidan? Are you in this because you're keeping a promise? Or because you don't want a second divorce on your record?"

"Kate. Don't."

"No, Aidan. It is a perfectly legitimate question. Are you trying to make me the bad guy, the one who wants a divorce so that it is not on you? Shouldn't love be a factor? The word *love* has never come up the entire time we've been together. And now we're married. I witnessed firsthand what happened in my parents' marriage. My dad didn't love my mother and eventually he left. Even three daughters couldn't make him stay. Because he didn't love us. I know you're not my father, but I don't want to be in a marriage of obligation. Despite what you seem to think, it is not good for the kids. Kids can sense when it is wrong and they're usually the ones who end up getting hurt."

Aidan felt himself bristle. Then his walls went up. They needed to pick up Chloe. It was already getting late, and if they opened this can of worms, they had to be here longer. For a moment, it crossed his mind to say the words she wanted to hear. But he couldn't find the right words. The ones that wanted to come out asked, *What is love anyway? And what is* I love you *but three meaningless words strung together? A hollow promise.*

If Kate couldn't see how he felt— If his actions didn't speak louder than three empty words, maybe this marriage would not work because she needed more from him than he could give.

"I think you need to take a couple of days and decide what you want," Aidan said.

"So that's how it is going to be? You're putting everything on me again? The fate of this marriage is on my shoulders? Whether we stay married or go? I'm not the only one who needs to think about it. I need a marriage based on love. Not on obligation. I'm going to go away for a few days. And when I come back, we both need to have figured out what we want."

Aidan nodded. Then they sat in silence for what seemed like an eternity. He watched a couple strolling in the park hand in hand. The other side of the park, near the basketball courts, was illuminated and he could hear distant cheers. Someone's small victory.

He wished for a victory of his own.

He wanted to pull her into his arms and remind her why they were so good together. But that would only muddy the waters. Obviously, it wasn't enough for Kate. She needed more than that.

"What will we tell Chloe?" Her voice was small.

"Tell her that you're going to be away."

Tonight he had realized that as much as her leaving now would hurt his daughter, if she was going to leave anyway, the longer Kate stayed, the worse it would be.

He glanced over at her and tears were streaming down her cheeks. "Can I stay tonight?" she asked. "So I can tuck her in and tell her myself? I'll pack some of my things in the morning after she's gone to school."

"Of course. It is your home, too. For as long as you want it to be. But please don't tell Chloe you'll be back, if you can't guarantee that you'll keep that promise."

Chloe looked so tiny and angelic in her little white lace nightie, with Princess Sweetie Pie tucked underneath her arm.

Kate pulled the covers up over the little girl, taking care to bring the pink sheet and blanket only up to the stuffed animal's chin. As Chloe had explained, "Princess Sweetie Pie doesn't like to have her head covered up."

Kate sat on the side of Chloe's bed and listened to her chatter on and on about the night's adventure with Beatrice. They had built a blanket fort and Miss Doris had allowed them to eat their macaroni and cheese in the fort.

"It was the funnest time ever!" Chloe exclaimed. She threw her stuffed cat into the air and then wagged her finger and scolded. "Princess Sweetie Pie, get back under the covers. It is past your bedtime."

Both she and Kate laughed at the naughty animal, and Kate repeated the tucking-in and read Chloe's favorite book, *Good Night Moon*. Finally she noticed that Chloe's eyes were getting heavy and she knew she couldn't postpone what she had to do any longer.

For a moment, as she took her time putting the book on the nightstand and straightening the lamp and the small glass of water they kept by Chloe's bedside in case she got thirsty in the middle of the night, Kate tried to talk herself out of going away, only to have the split-second decision washed away by the pull of her reality with Aidan. He didn't love her. Not the way she needed a man to love her if she was going to give her life to him.

Doing her best to act normal, she said, "Chloe, I have to go away for a little while, but your dad will be here, and he can take you to your rock group, and maybe Miss Doris can let you come over after school. Doesn't that sound like fun?"

Kate held her breath as she waited for the little girl to ask her when she would return. Instead, Chloe clapped her hands and rattled off the plans that she and Beatrice were already making. Kate managed a smile. As she leaned down to kiss Chloe good-night, it dawned on her that maybe Dori was a better fit for Aidan. If Aidan married Dori, Chloe and Beatrice would be stepsisters. Kate knew firsthand the power of sisterhood. Maybe she was holding them both back by trying to make this sham of a marriage work.

Her heart ached as reality unfolded: maybe she would be doing everyone a favor by ending things now.

"Good night, sweetheart," Kate whispered in Chloe's ear.

"Good night. I'm so happy you're my mommy. I love you."

The words uttered by that sweet, sleepy little voice knocked all the wind out of Kate, but still she heard herself saying, "I love you, too."

She turned around before the tears started falling and turned off the light and shut her door.

Aidan's face drained of color when he saw the state that Kate was in.

"What's wrong? What happened?" His voice was accusatory.

"She said she's happy I'm her mommy, and she loves me."

She could tell by the look on his face he was as shocked and moved as she was. Though she had never heard Aidan tell Chloe that he loved her, he had always acted warm and caring toward her. What spoke volumes was how happy and well adjusted Chloe was—even before Kate had come into her life. This little girl whose mother had abandoned her at birth still had a pure, unblemished heart.

Granted, she had never known what it was like

to miss her mother because Aidan had protected her from the fact that her mother didn't want her. Kate didn't want to be the mother who affected Chloe the way Kate's own father had damaged her.

"I can't stay tonight," Kate said. "Will you please tell Chloe that I had to leave earlier than I thought? Don't worry, she didn't ask when I was coming back."

After spending a restless night in her house, Kate got to the salon earlier than she had expected. She had had an all-call text from Kerrigan Karol, summoning everyone to come in for a staff meeting before the staff opened. He did this every once in a while. Not often, but when he called meetings, there was usually some point of contention that needed to be aired—someone was stealing the Keurig cups or the toilet paper or dipping into another stylist's supplies, the ultimate taboo. Staff meeting–worthy infractions were never a crisis. Usually, a terse "Somebody has been doing *x*, please stop it" righted the ship without further discussion.

Kate figured she might as well go in and endure the group scolding and then use the time to organize her station. She knew she hadn't borrowed anyone's flat iron without returning it or taken something that didn't belong to her—unless you counted taking

Aidan and Chloe away from Dori and a chance for them to be a loving family—

No! Stop. I'm not thinking about that now.

She had this meeting and a full day of clients. If she thought about it now, she would cry and then everyone would ask her what was wrong. She didn't want to talk about it. She didn't want to think about it—even though the heartache of choosing was a physical ache that tightened her throat and made her feel like she had a hole in her chest where her heart should be. Tonight, after her last client, she would get take-out Japanese food and go home and face her issues.

Although she hadn't found comfort there last night, in her own house—her own space. The bed had been cold and too big. The walls felt strange, like she didn't belong there anymore. She had felt nearly as fenced in there as she had at the inn last evening, when Zelda had unveiled her plan to manipulate Kate into taking on the spa.

She wasn't going to the inn for a while. She was still too irritated with her mother for ambushing her. Zelda had called three times already—twice last night and once this morning. Kate hadn't able to listen to the messages. If there had been an emergency, her sisters would have called. She and her mom would talk eventually, once Kate had a chance to cool off, but right now, she needed to sort out her head.

Kate joined her colleagues in the small kitchen at the back of the salon. Since the front of the salon featured a large plate glass window, where they were on full display to passersby, the kitchen was the one place where they could gather without a client knocking on the door and asking to be let in.

"Good morning, lovelies." Kerrigan was ten minutes late. But at least he was carrying boxes from the Tearoom at The Forsyth. There would be loads of comfort in her sister's fresh-made pastries. Kate fully intended to eat her feelings. "Gather round, children, get a yummy and settle down. I have big news."

Big news? Does that mean no one's in trouble?

Her coworkers must've been wondering the same thing because they were fast to settle in.

Kerrigan was a small man in his midforties. His hair was dyed blue-black, his bangs a stark contrast with his ivory skin. He was clad in all black—skinny jeans and a silk shirt that clung like a second skin to his toned body. He had accessorized with black cowboy boots and a studded black leather belt.

"Y'all are a talented bunch and I have been honored to have you in my salon—some longer than others." He nodded to Kate. "Some of you have been with me since I opened my doors eleven years ago, right, Katie girl?"

God, has it been that long? It has been that long. What is he saying?

"A few months ago, I learned that the landlord of this building wants to raise my rent to an obscene amount. At first, I was devastated. Then I got mad and thought about moving the salon. But the greedy bastards that own the buildings in downtown wanted crazy rent, too. I didn't want to move out to the suburbs. That's just not who I am. So, after a lot of soul-searching and talks with my financial planner, I decided it is time for me to retire. I am moving to Costa Rica, babies. Isn't that wonderful?"

Kerrigan clapped for himself, as if to drive home exactly how wonderful. Everyone else stared at him blankly, in various stages of realization that they were going to have to relocate.

"But wait, there's more," Kerrigan said. "The reason I'm moving to Costa Rica is because I've met someone. I'm getting married and we're starting our lives together there."

Finally everyone snapped out of it, clapping and making congratulatory noises, demanding details.

They met online. Three months ago.

First, her mother had fallen head over heels in love. Now Kerrigan? Had someone put something in the water to make people fall in love so fast? She had known Aidan since high school. They were married and she still wasn't sure.

How could her mother and Kerrigan be so sure after such a short time?

Just as pressing was the thought, where was she going to go now? Where would she move her clientele?

Zelda would eat up this news like one of Jane's pastries.

It dawned on her that her sisters had succumbed to Zelda's master plan to move her three daughters and their careers into the Forsyth Galloway Inn. They seemed happy. Kate hadn't asked too many probing questions for fear that Zelda would mistake her curiosity for interest in securing her own place at the inn. The mere thought made Kate itchy with claustrophobia.

Still, it felt as if the fates had been conspiring with Zelda and Aidan to herd her and keep her close to home. Making her settle down with responsibilities that made her chafe even thinking about them.

Could she do hair in her kitchen?

Her clientele liked luxury. That was why they were willing to pay the prices they paid that allowed Kate to live comfortably. They would not want to sit in her kitchen.

If she did go to the inn, it sure would simplify things, and it would be a good time to see if some of her favorite colleagues might want to join her. Granted, the spa was a few months from opening but if she planted the seed now—

She shook her head. It was all too much, coming at her too fast.

Maybe she should talk to her sisters and get the inside scoop on what it was really like to work at the inn under their mother's well-meaning but intrusive watch.

Carrying one of Jane's famous colossal cinnamon rolls, Kate walked back to her station and opened her bag to get her phone out, but she was waylaid by the sealed manila envelope that contained her father's contact info. It had been in her purse—unopened—since the day Aidan had presented it to her. While she was at it, maybe she should talk to her sisters about him, too. They had all been hurt by him. Each of them carried the scars of his abandonment in her own way. The main difference between Kate and her sisters was that Elle and Jane had gotten on with their lives. They had found love and happiness and fulfilling places in their community.

Kate was admittedly stuck on an island of her own making, unhappy and unable to move on. That was evidenced by the fact that she hadn't realized she had been at the Kerrigan Karol Salon for eleven years. Doing the same thing day in and day out. Life had been passing her by. More than a decade was gone and what had she done? She was still in the same spot, treading water. It took Kerrigan draining the pool to make her make a change.

Kate plucked the envelope out of her bag and contemplated it. What was the harm in looking at the information Randy Ponder had gathered. It wasn't as if he would have to face him. But it might be the first step toward a better life. She glanced at her watch. It was still early. Her first client wasn't due for a half-hour. Envelope in hand, Kate hitched her bag onto her shoulder, and approached the salon's reception desk. "I have to step out for a minute. If my client arrives early, please tell her I'll be right back."

She to the coffee shop across the street to read private detective's report.

Chapter Ten

"They're over there, Daddy!" Chloe pointed toward a group of girls and moms at a picnic table. "Can I go?"

Aidan nodded and watched Chloe set out across the park with her stuffed white cat tucked under her arm, running toward her rock-painting friends. When she reached the table, Doris greeted her and then immediately walked toward Aidan to meet him halfway.

"I'm so glad you could make it," Doris said. "Where's Kate today?"

He knew they had to ask this question. He had been prepared, but for a moment he lost his words.

"She is away right now, but Chloe still wanted to come. I hope it is okay that I'm here. I know this is a mom-and-daughter thing."

He wished she would offer to keep an eye on Chloe so that he could go back to work for a couple of hours. He didn't want to ask since Chloe had already spent so much time over there. Apparently, his returning to work wasn't in the cards, because she had linked her arm through his and was walking him to the table.

"Nonsense," she said. "You are absolutely welcome to join us. We won't be here very long anyway since a couple of the girls have commitments tonight. We're just going to paint a few more rocks and let the girls place them around the park for people to find. I had little labels made with our collective Instagram handle @savannahrocks2754."

"Does 2754 have a significance?" he asked.

Dori shrugged. "It was available."

He nodded, not quite sure what else to say.

At least there would be something to do, a way to keep busy. He could help Chloe paint and then they could hit the road. His heart was heavy thinking about going back to the house and Kate not being there. He hadn't heard from her today. A couple of times, he had had his phone in his hand with her number up, his thumb hovering over the Call button. But he had managed to come to his senses before doing anything stupid, like calling her. She wanted space. Or maybe he had told her she needed space. It was all so convoluted that the lines were beginning to blur.

All he knew was that she needed space and he needed to give it to her.

Speaking of personal space, Doris still had her arm linked through his, and as they approached the picnic table, he wasn't quite sure how to pull away without offending.

By the grace of God, Chloe called, "Daddy, come here and look at my pink rock. Isn't it pretty?"

When he reached Chloe's side, his daughter held up a bismuth-pink rock, beaming at him as if she had painted a replica of the Sistine Chapel.

"It is gorgeous, Chloe," Doris said. "What inspirational saying are you going to write on it?"

Chloe squinted toward the sky, pursing her little mouth and tapping her chin as if giving Doris's question careful consideration.

Then her face brightened, and she said, "I'm going to write, 'Come home soon, Mommy. I miss you.'"

"That's very sweet, Chloe, but that will be the second rock you've painted for your stepmother. Don't you want to write one you can leave in the park?"

Chloe's face clouded. "I was going to leave this

one in the park. I want her to find it so she knows how much I miss her and how much I want her to come home."

Doris flashed a smile that didn't reach her eyes. "Oh. Okay. Do whatever you would like."

Aidan's heart twisted. Good grief, they were little girls. How many universally inspirational sayings did a six-year-old know? He wanted to kick himself from one side of the park to the other for allowing Kate to hurt his little girl. Chloe had been through enough already. Now he had allowed her to form an attachment to Kate and Kate was going to leave, too. What the hell was wrong with him?

Chloe tugged at his sleeve. "What is it, sweetheart?"

She got up on her knees on the bench of the picnic table, cupped her hand and whispered, "What is a stepmother? Why did Miss Doris call Mommy that?"

Aidan drew in a deep breath, buying time to sort out his thoughts. "It is just another name for a mommy."

He braced himself for her to push for a better explanation. Instead, Chloe cupped her hand again and whispered into Aidan's ear again. "How do you spell 'Come home soon, Mommy. I miss you'? Will you help me write it?"

Aidan debated whether he should try to talk

her out of painting that on the rock, but he decided against it. Chloe seemed pretty set on writing a message to Kate. If he tried to steer her in another direction, she might get upset and he didn't want to push her into a meltdown.

Choose your battles.

Doris walked up and stood next to Chloe. "Sweetheart, I have an idea. What if you paint 'Throw kindness like glitter'? You could use the silver paint for the lettering, and I brought some glitter glue that you could use to decorate it. It would look so cute if you decorated your pink rock that way."

Chloe frowned. "But my mommy is already kind. She already does that. I don't have to tell her to be that way."

Aidan's heart twisted. Leave it to a kid to see the best in people. Of course, since day one, Kate had been nothing but kind to Chloe. If Kate couldn't bring herself to stay in this marriage, he hoped that somehow, Chloe would not take Kate's leaving personally. Couldn't Kate see that, in a sense, she was doing to Chloe exactly what her father had done to her, even though she said she didn't want to be like him.

"What if this rock wasn't for your...um... mommy." Doris glanced at Aidan. He gave his head a subtle shake, asking her to let it go. Either she didn't understand or she was ignoring him because she continued. "The purpose of this group is to paint rocks so that strangers can find them and the positive messages we write can bring happiness into their lives. Don't you want pictures of your rocks on the Instagram page? We can't post pictures of ones we don't leave for people to find."

"My mommy needs some happiness," Chloe insisted, her voice suddenly defiant.

Doris flinched.

"How about if I paint the rock with the glitter message and Chloe can paint her rock the way she wants to?"

Doris's eyes flashed as she looked at Aidan. Obviously, she didn't agree, and for a moment, Aidan thought she might challenge him. She didn't, and it was a good thing. He didn't think that this little rock group of happiness should be quite so stringent and inflexible. Good grief, the girls were barely six years old. Doris took a deep breath and blinked several times in rapid succession.

"I'm sure that's fine." Her voice was cool. She placed a package of multicolored glitter glue on the table. "I'll just leave this here in case one of you wants to use it." She made quick work of moving around the table and helping the other girls.

"Is everything okay?" asked the mom who was sitting next to him. Her eyes looked hungry for gossip.

"Sure," Aidan said. "Why would it not be?"

The mom shrugged. "I've never seen…." she nodded sharply in Chloe's direction "…quite so…" She made a face that Aidan guessed meant difficult, or maybe she was trying to show her concern? Chloe was busy smearing gold glitter glue on her pink rock and seemed oblivious. Still, Aidan didn't want to talk about his daughter as if she wasn't there.

"You know how six-year-olds can be. Could you pass the pink paint please?"

"Daddy, can you help me with my message to Mommy?"

Again, questioning whether he was doing the right thing by not steering her away from making that rock for Kate, he spelled out each word slowly. In the middle of the process, he caught Doris and the mom to his right exchanging a look. He didn't react. Instead, he kept spelling for Chloe and lettering *glitter* and *kindness* over his own pink painted rock.

Finally, after all the rocks had been photographed and dispersed around the park, he and Chloe were on their way to the car. "Daddy, I need to go over there." Chloe was pointing to the Forsyth Galloway Inn, which was standing there like a specter he had been trying to ignore all day. From this vantage point, the yellow Victorian was clearly visible through the oak trees laden with Spanish moss.

"No, honey, we need to go home."

"*Noo*, Daddy, I have to give this rock to Gigi to give to Mommy."

Since Kate hadn't been in touch in the almost twenty-four hours since she had taken leave and he had no idea what the family knew about the latest bump in their relationship, he didn't want her family—or his brother, for that matter—to discover him skulking around the grounds of the inn.

It was on the tip of his tongue to tell Chloe to hang on to the rock and give it to Kate in person. But what if Kate decided not to come back and Chloe didn't get the chance to give it to her? The last thing his little girl needed was a souvenir from the heartbreak.

Why not leave it there? If he ran into the family, he would let Chloe give it to them to pass it on to Kate. Let Kate explain why Chloe was missing her. He took his little girl by the hand and let her lead the way.

Chloe left the rock by the kitchen steps, half-hidden by one of the flowering potted plants lining the brick steps.

"Don't be disappointed if someone else picks it up, Chloe," he said on the way back to the car.

"No one else will. It is for Mommy. She'll be the one who finds it."

At least the damn rock was out of his little girl's hands. Aidan hoped that out of sight would mean out of Chloe's thoughts.

After work, Kate went to the inn.

"I have news," Kate said after she and her sisters were settled at their table tucked away in a corner of the tearoom.

As luck would have it, Liam was working at Wila, while Jane was still here at the tearoom. Elle had just finished a late afternoon art walk with a group of guests and was in the lobby answering follow-up questions when Kate had walked in.

After her last appointment of the day, Kate had stopped by the inn, hoping to catch her sisters there. She had been booked solid with appointments after Kerrigan had dropped the retirement bombshell earlier in the day, which meant she hadn't had much time to think about the implications or her next move. Her first thought after her last client was that she wanted to talk to Aidan about what has transpired. She had swallowed her pride and called him, but her call had gone to voice mail. She knew Chloe had her rock-painting session that afternoon. Knowing Aidan, he had probably silenced his phone to give his daughter his undivided attention. He was good about things like that. She hadn't left a message because after the way they had left things—the way she had run out last night—she felt as if she had no right.

Her heart ached at the thought of another night away from Aidan and Chloe. For someone who'd felt as if she needed her space, she was feeling awfully shaky without them.

The only other people she could turn to at a crazy, mixed-up time like this were her sisters. Though she wasn't sure how much she wanted to tell them about what was happening with Aidan.

What could she say when she didn't even know what she wanted?

Still, Kate needed their steadfastness, their understanding, and maybe even a dose of their tough love, because they would not simply tell her what she wanted to hear.

As Elle poured tea from a porcelain teapot into delicate matching cups, Jane grilled Kate.

"News, huh?" Jane counted off on her fingers. "You're already married and there's a baby on the way. What other news—Wait, the baby's okay, right? You're okay?"

"The baby's fine. I'm fine."

Of course, that was only partially true. The baby was fine, thank God for that. Kate put a protective hand on her stomach. Like a beacon of light in the storm, this little person growing inside her was a bright spot in an otherwise murky future.

"How are you feeling?" Elle asked.

"A lot better. I'm right at thirteen weeks. The morning sickness has stopped. Actually, I feel great. But what I wanted to tell y'all is that Kerrigan announced today that he is closing the salon."

Her sisters gasped, as surprised by the news as Kate had been.

Kate explained that it was the landlord's decision to raise the rent and… Kerrigan's falling in love that had led to his decision to retire.

"Good for him," Elle said. "I'm happy for him, and the timing couldn't be better. Now you're free to bring your clients to the spa at the inn. I know your loyalty to Kerrigan was holding you back, but now you can do it guilt free. Maybe some of your coworkers want to relocate here, too. It seems like it was meant to be."

"Does it?" Kate asked. "I don't know if it is the right decision for me."

Jane and Elle exchanged a glance.

"What are you afraid of?" Elle asked.

"She's afraid of Mom and Gigi." Jane turned to Kate. "Am I right?"

"Maybe," Kate said. "They do have a history of getting into our business."

"Is that what you're worried about?" Elle asked. "You know they only mean well."

"I know they do." Kate glanced around the tearoom. Its black-and-white marble floors and formal dark, polished wood contrasted with the light airiness of the glass from the windows and mirrors, which reflected the crystal chandeliers and the pops of color from the red banquettes lining the back wall. They had consciously decided to have the decor echo the look of the restaurant Wila, to tie the places together.

"I don't mean any disrespect to them. You know I love them. But I'd be lying if I didn't admit that I like my independence. I've worked hard to build my business without anyone's help. It is mine. No one can take it away from me."

Like Dad tried to take the inn away from Mom and us.

"Yet, isn't it crazy how Kerrigan's decision to close his shop at the end of the month has left you scrambling to find a new home?" Jane arched a brow at Kate. "Do you have any other salons in mind? If you get too far away, your clients might not follow you."

It was true. She had been so comfortable renting a chair at Kerrigan's salon for so long that the possibility of having to relocate had never entered her personal equation. For nearly a decade, she had booked her own appointments and come and gone as she pleased. If she wanted a day off, she scheduled herself off. There was no asking for time off, no co-ordinating days or coverage. No standing in for other stylists if they didn't show. That was the beauty of being an independent contractor. She rented a chair, minded her own business and life was grand.

"I don't know if I want to give away my independence by running the spa," she admitted. "That's more like punching a time clock. Will you level with me? How much do Gigi and Mom get in your business?"

"I can honestly say it hasn't been a problem," Elle said of the art classes and tours that she ran out of the inn.

Jane shrugged. "Same here. I had the same worries when they started talking to me about opening the tearoom. I made it clear that I needed my independence if the arrangement was going to work. If you think about it, the three of us have defined ourselves in niches that Mom and Gigi know very little about. They respect that. I've found that they leave the pastry decisions to me because I know what I'm doing. Sure, they might ask for a batch of blueberry scone or a specific cookie, but they let me look at what's selling and what's not and they trust me to make the decisions that make the business work."

They all sipped their tea for a moment. Jane was the most no-nonsense of the Clark sisters. Like Kate, she had put herself through school and had been making her own way before their mother and grandmother had come up with the grand plan to involve the three more closely at the inn. Elle had been an elementary school teacher. She could easily get a teaching job at one of the local schools if she found the arrangement too constricting.

"Kate, why don't you talk to them?" Elle said. "Be up-front with them. Let them know your feelings and your trepidation. Honestly, since Gigi got married and turned over management of the inn to Mom, she's not really into micromanaging. Mom is happy that Jane and I are back at the inn, and she's a little distracted with Stephen, so she hasn't been a problem, either."

"Yes. Talk to them," Jane urged. "Now that the three of us are happily married, and they have men in their lives to distract them, too, I think you're going to see a world of difference. Their buttinsky quotient is a lot lower than it used to be."

Happily married. Kate's heart twisted.

And what if things didn't work out with Aidan?

Would they think that gave them a license to remind her daily of what an idiot she had been to let such a great guy get away? Because Aidan was a great guy.

What was wrong with her?

Was she trying to push him away to prove her point that all men were like her dad or was she so self-destructive that she was hell-bent on carrying on her father's legacy of heartbreak and dysfunction? It would serve her right if she ended up being the spinster sister who lived with her mother in the old Victorian house on the park.

Then again, at the rate her mother's and grandmother's love lives were going, Zelda and Gigi would probably be too busy to worry much about Kate's sorry state of affairs. It seemed that she was the only one who was still obsessing over what Fred Clark had done to their family.

"Have you ever thought about contacting our father?" The question slipped out of Kate's mouth before she could think better of it. When Jane and Elle shot each other alarmed glances and then looked at Kate as if she had invited them to go dumpster diving for their dinner, she wished she could have reeled the question back in.

They didn't know about her trial separation from Aidan. Was that what it was? A trial separation? Kate didn't even know. The only thing she was sure of right now was that both of her sisters were blissfully married, happily working at fulfilling careers and starting families of their own. Of course, they didn't give their father a second thought.

"Are you talking about the father who left Mom and us high and dry and then tried to sue for half the Forsyth Galloway Inn?" Jane asked.

That was why. He was why.

"There's no other father that I'm aware of," Kate said. "So, unless you know something I don't know, yes. He's the one."

Since Kate seemed to be the only one haunted by the past, logic told her she needed to face the ghost head-on, look him in the eyes, tell him what a rotten excuse for a father he had been and then move on. The problem was, every time she went through the mental exercise of doing that—where the meeting would happen, what she had to say and how she had to say it—she wanted to put a pillow over her head and forget about it.

Now she had more to think of than herself. Kate put a hand on her stomach. Her mind skittered to Aidan and Chloe and her heart ached. One night away from them and she missed them like she missed a limb or a vital organ. But the odd push-me-pull-you force that seemed to control her like a puppet master manipulating a marionette reminded her that it was easy to miss them from this vantage point. Every time she thought about settling in—be it moving her business to the inn or fully committing to be part of the Quindlin family—she felt the walls closing in, and utter terror warned her to get out before the claustrophobia could suffocate her.

But was this what she wanted for the rest of her life? To keep running when life got to structured and real?

It shouldn't be this difficult. She loved Aidan and Chloe. She was carrying Aidan's child. Her place was with them. Why was she making life so hard on everyone?

If she could answer that question, she would not be nearly sick with dread right now.

Elle was frowning into her glass of water. "Why would you ask that?"

Kate shrugged. "Because I can't stop wondering how a man could just walk away from his family."

She heard herself saying the words and it didn't escape her that it might have been not so dissimilar from the way that she had walked away from Aidan and Chloe. But it wasn't the same. Was it?

"You know what?" Jane asked. "I don't care why he did what he did. I don't want to know. So I guess the answer is no. Not only have I never wanted to contact him, I don't care if I ever see him again. I truly don't care."

Elle shot Jane a look seemed to say she was being too harsh.

"Are you thinking about getting in touch with him?" Elle asked. "Is it because of the baby?"

"No…yes." Kate scrunched up her face in frustration. "I don't know. Maybe I do need to work through some things before the baby arrives."

"And you think seeing him will help?" Jane looked like she smelled something foul. It dawned on Kate that maybe her sisters weren't as unaffected by the trauma of their childhood as they seemed. Obviously, they were better at compartmentalizing their feelings. Lucky them. If only Kate could do that—box up the memories of their mother trying her best to explain that their father had left but it wasn't because he didn't love them. Trying to justify his actions and make excuses for a man who had been such a coward that he couldn't even say goodbye to his own children.

"I thought it might," Kate said. "I don't know. His leaving us is something I still haven't come to terms with. Even all these years later. I think it is part of my problem—why I have a hard time committing to situations like the spa."

And Aidan and Chloe.

"You know he can't take the inn away from us," Jane said. "The judge made that final. And the spa doesn't mean prison. Just have a plan and work it. Mom and Gigi will respect you."

Kate gave a one-shoulder shrug. Jane might be right.

"What do you think will happen if you go see him?" Elle asked. "Are you looking to reestablish a relationship with him…as in letting him back into your life?"

Kate shook her head. "No, that's not what I'm looking for."

"Good," said Elle. "It would be one thing if he had contacted us…or you, but he hasn't, Kate. The sad truth of it is it's been years and he hasn't cared enough to get in touch with us. He's moved on. Frankly, as far as I'm concerned, so have I. That door is closed."

"Forever?" Kate asked. "Even though you're married and have the baby?"

Elle pursed her lips and looked thoughtful for several beats, as if she was deeply contemplating the question. Finally she said, "Especially because of Daniel and the baby."

They were quiet for a moment. Kate let her sister's declaration sink in.

"I have a confession to make." Elle folded her

hands and stared at them, clearly gathering her thoughts and maybe her courage. "Daniel and I ran into Fred right before Maggie was born. We were in Pooler at the outlet mall shopping for the baby. I turned a corner and nearly bumped into him. My stomach was out to here and we literally almost ran into each other."

"Are you serious?" Jane said. "Did you talk to him?"

"Why didn't you tell us?" Kate asked.

"I didn't tell you because other than a mumbled *excuse me*, we didn't talk. He was with Bev and they just kept right on walking."

Beverly was the woman for whom he had left his wife and family.

"Wow," said Jane.

"They're still together, huh?" Kate asked.

"Apparently so," Elle said. "And his actions spoke loud and clear about where his loyalties lie. There's no relationship left to salvage."

Elle's voice broke, but her words hung in the air.

"I'm not saying the door is nailed shut. If he came to me or to one of us, I'd try to meet him halfway, but until then, out of self-preservation, I had to quit letting him live in my head rent-free. I have a family—a great husband, a sweet daughter. I have the two of you and Mom and Gigi. I have a wonderful, full life. So many blessings. I had to make a conscious decision that I wasn't going to let him rob me of current sweet, happy moments."

"Yoo-hoo!" someone called. Kate looked over her shoulder and saw her mother and Stephen standing at the entrance to the tearoom. Zelda had Bear, the corgi puppy, on a leash. "We've just returned from a walk. I'm going to take Bear upstairs to the apartment since dogs aren't allowed in the tearoom. Honey, why don't you wait down here and talk to the girls. I'll be right back."

Zelda tilted her face up and Stephen planted a kiss on her lips and whispered something in Zelda's ear that made her giggle like a schoolgirl. After another quick peck, she walked away with her puppy and Stephen made his way to their table.

"I'm not interrupting, am I?"

His interruption was welcome after the heavy turn their conversation had taken.

"Not at all." Kate patted the empty chair next to her. "Join us."

Stephen looked handsome in khaki pants and an expensive-looking cobalt blue button-down. He was clean-shaven, and his thick brown hair was cut short. Despite the hint of gray at the temples, Kate wondered if he might not be a few years younger than her mother. Maybe even as much as five or seven years.

You go, girl.

Age aside, he seemed nice and he was clearly crazy about Zelda. He made her happy and that was all that mattered.

"Would you like some tea or something else to drink?" Jane stood.

"No. Thanks, though," he said. "Please sit down. I don't want you to go to any trouble."

"Really, it is no trouble," Jane said.

Stephen glanced over his shoulder at the place where he and Zelda had stood. "I was hoping to speak with the three of you. I need to ask you something before your mother returns. It is fortuitous that the three of you are here right now."

The sisters exchanged looks. Kate had a feeling she knew what Stephen was going to say even before he said it. Although she hadn't quite expected it the way he delivered it.

"I would like to ask the three of you for your mother's hand in marriage."

Jane gasped. Elle's hand flew to her mouth. Kate opened her mouth to say something, but Stephen said, "Family is important to both of us and the three of you are so important to your mother. I want you to know how important it is to me to have your blessing. I love her."

Jane and Elle were making the appropriate happy noises, murmuring things like *Yes, of course,* and

She's going to be so happy, and *When will you propose?* and *Where will you live?*

Kate was silently beating herself up because the first thing that crossed her mind after she heard the news was *Mom said she never wanted to get married again.* Her sisters seemed to have forgotten that declaration because they were all but planning the wedding.

"Shhh," Elle said. "Here she comes."

Stephen stood. "Thanks, ladies. We're going to get a bite to eat. I would invite you to join us, but—" he winked "—I have something I have to do. More very soon."

The sisters nodded and watched him walk away toward their mother, who was standing at the entrance of the tearoom.

"That was so sweet of him to ask for our blessing," Elle gushed. "Oh, and speaking of things that are sweet, Kate, didn't you say that Chloe was involved in some sort of rock-painting club?"

"Yes, it is with friends from her school. Why?"

Elle fished in her pocket and pulled out a pink painted stone. "I think she left this for you on the kitchen steps at the inn. It is so cute. I'm sure she wanted you to find it. I saw it this afternoon on my way back from the art walk, and I was afraid if I put it back someone else would pick it up. Look, she wrote her name on the back—Chloe Quindlin. On the other side is a message for you."

Elle held up the rock and Kate took it from her, first examining the side with Chloe's name lettered in gold paint, then flipping it over and seeing the message: "Come home soon, Mommy. I miss you."

Kate's heart leaped into her throat, lodging there. Her hand fluttered to her mouth.

"What does that mean?" Jane said. "*You're still living with them, aren't you?* Wait—Kate, are you crying? Why are you crying?"

"Kate? What's going on," Elle asked.

Kate gave her head a sharp shake. If she uttered one word right now, she knew she'd lose it.

Suddenly, it was as if everything snapped into sharp focus. She was an idiot for allowing her father to hold her heart hostage all these years. With the way her heart ached at the thought of Chloe missing her—and Aidan, no doubt, taking her to the inn to leave the stone, there was no way that she was like her own father, who clearly didn't give a damn about his own flesh and blood. The truly perverse thing was that he had moved on. He and Beverly were still together. They were probably happy, in their own way, in their own little world, which did not include them. If he had come face-to-face with Elle, the sweetest and most forgiving of his daughters, and had treated her like a stranger, he had made a choice.

Now, the question wasn't *why* she had given him so much power over her all these years, but *how* she would move forward.

"I have to go," Kate said.

"What's wrong? Is everything okay?" her sisters asked as Kate scooted out of her chair and gathered her purse, all the while holding tight to the rock.

"I'll explain later, but right now, I have to go."

Ten minutes later, Kate steered her car onto Aidan's street. Since it was difficult to find street parking, she parked in the first space she could find, which was about three houses down, and got out and walked. Maybe she should have called, but she needed to see Aidan and talk to him face-to-face. She needed to tell him she loved him, and she was sorry she had let this ridiculousness go on too long. She finally knew what she wanted, and she wasn't going to waste another day.

When she cleared the mammoth azalea bush that separated Aidan's yard from his neighbor's, she stopped short. Dori Watson and Beatrice were walking hand in hand up the walk that led to Aidan's door. Dori looked cute in a red sundress that showed off her figure and offset her tan. She was wearing matching high-heeled wedge sandals that added to her height and made her look like a glamazon.

She set down the picnic basket she was carrying and knocked on the red lacquered door. When Chloe answered and threw her arms around Beatrice, Kate stepped back into the cover of the azaleas. The little girl looked so happy to see her friend.

That was a good thing. The last thing Kate wanted was for Chloe to look dejected or as if she had been pining away in Kate's absence.

However, her heart had a different thought when she saw Aidan appear in the doorway after the two little girls had disappeared inside. When he leaned down to pick up the picnic basket, Dori flipped her glossy long, brown hair over her toned shoulder, leaned in and planted a kiss on Aidan's cheek.

Kate couldn't see his reaction because she didn't want to get caught sneaking a peek and she would have melted in a puddle of mortification if he'd seen her lurking in the bushes. But as it ended up, her heart began dying a long, slow death after Aidan invited Dori inside and closed the door behind them.

Chapter Eleven

"After I got home from the park today," Doris said from her seat at Aidan's kitchen island, where she had settled herself to unpack the picnic basket she had brought. "I thought to myself, Aidan looked so sad. I think he could use a little help tonight. You know, a little pick-me-up, even though he would never ask. So I went home and packed a picnic supper for us."

He must've made a face, because she quickly amended, "Or just for you and Chloe, of course, if you're not up for company. And there's plenty for Kate if she'll be back later?"

When Aidan didn't bite, she continued, "I brought

some fried chicken. I whipped up some mashed potatoes and sautéed some green beans. And for dessert, I have homemade brownies."

This time she waited for a response.

"This is nice of you, Doris," he said. "You didn't have to go to all this trouble, but thank you."

"Oh, call me Dori, please." She crossed her legs at the ankles. Aidan realized she had changed clothes since they were at the park. He didn't remember what she had been wearing, but it wasn't this red dress. It made him a little uncomfortable.

"And really, it was absolutely no trouble at all."

"Well, thanks, again, Dori—" Aidan cleared his throat. "How did you pull all of this together so fast?"

Dori laughed and flipped her hair back over her shoulder.

"Okay, you caught me," she confessed. "I might have had a little help, but what matters is that you and Chloe are taken care of while Kate is away. When will she be back?"

Doris's eyes shone a little too brightly. Her questions, coupled with the red dress and heels, made Aidan wonder if she had an ulterior motive or, at the very least, she was here on an info-gathering mission. He couldn't figure out what she wanted. Was she being sincere? Or, worst-case scenario, was she fishing for something he just couldn't give her? Beatrice was Chloe's best friend, one of the constants in an ever-changing sea of uncertainty. He would not allow himself to ruin that for his daughter.

"I appreciate you going to all this trouble, but I have to be honest, I'm not up for company tonight."

"Oh." The shine in Doris's eyes dimmed a bit. She pursed her lips. "Of course. Bea and I don't have to stay. I just thought it might be fun for the girls to play for a while. You know, a distraction for Chloe."

How was she so certain that there was trouble in paradise after Kate's absence from one rock group?

A text came in and Aidan pulled his phone out of his back pocket and checked to see if it was Kate. Once Doris left, he was going to call Kate and ask her to come home.

The text wasn't from Kate, but he noticed there was a missed call from her. When had she called? It must've been when he and Chloe were at the park. How had he missed her?

"Dori, I'm sorry, I have to make a phone call. Will you please excuse me?"

He started to leave the room.

"Aidan, I hope I haven't given you the wrong impression. Um… I don't mean to pry, but you really do look so sad. If you need some time… I mean, if you need to go…somewhere. What if Chloe came over tonight and spent the night with Beatrice? I know Beatrice would love to have her best friend over. And for the record, Aidan, I like Kate a lot. I just want to make sure she's okay. That everything is okay. It is obvious how much you love her." She shrugged and smiled. "I guess this is me trying to help. Admittedly, not very eloquently."

Aidan glanced at his phone again, at the alert reminding him that Kate had called, and he had missed her. She hadn't left a message, but obviously she had wanted to talk to him. She had reached out. He hated to impose on Doris. But she was offering, and after her admission, she did seem sincere. If she had come here for…whatever…he hoped he had made it perfectly clear that he had nothing to offer because his heart belonged to Kate.

Chloe would love to stay over at Beatrice's and play with her. It would be a safe place for his daughter, and if Chloe was there, it would give him a chance to go see Kate face-to-face. It would give them a chance to talk things out. Chloe didn't need to be there for that.

But he needed to tell Kate how he felt. The sooner the better.

He loved her.

He had never told her that before. They were married. They were having a baby. But he had never allowed himself to express the depth of his feelings.

Maybe it was because after the losses he had suffered—his parents dying, Veronica walking out—he didn't want to spend those sacred words like small change.

But Kate deserved the wealth of his feelings. After all that she had been through with her dad, she needed to know how he felt. How could he expect her to feel safe if he had never told her that she and the child growing inside of her and Chloe were what anchored his life? It was time he made things right.

It certainly hadn't taken Dori long to scope out the situation and move in for the kill. Had it?

As Kate washed a handful of arugula under cold water, she mentally kicked herself because she knew it was her own fault. Dori had made it clear that she found Aidan wildly attractive—what woman with a libido would not? What hurt the most was that she had finally made up her mind to open her heart to Aidan. She was willing to believe his "actions speak louder than words" philosophy and accept it.

She had even been ready to keep an open mind when she saw Dori in her sexy red dress and little Beatrice walking up the path to Aidan's door, but it was that kiss on the cheek that ruined everything. It wasn't flagrant, and admittedly she hadn't witnessed Aidan's reaction. It had been intimate, and he had invited her in.

That kiss was an action that spoke much louder than the three words Aidan couldn't speak to her.

Kate's phone sounded an incoming text. Even after everything that had gone down, her heart leaped. *Aidan?*

No. It was a group text from her mother.

Stephen proposed and I SAID YES!

Oh! That was fast. Well, good.

They must still be at the restaurant, because Kate had only been home from Aidan's house for about a half hour.

She pushed aside the vegetables she had been chopping to add to her arugula salad, dried her hands and picked up her phone.

Congratulations! This is such wonderful news!

Kate added her good wishes to the texts pinging through from her sisters and Gigi.

She was so happy for her mother. Really, she was. Zelda was finally moving on with her life.

Zelda was in love.

Kate was, too. But per usual, it was so complicated she couldn't see how it could work out. Maybe some people just weren't destined for traditional relationships. She grappled with the mixed emotions boomeranging through her stomach, ricocheting off her broken heart. It was strange how one part of her could be elated for her mother. Because she really was truly thrilled that Zelda had found happiness. Zelda deserved to be with a man who treated her right. She had devoted so many years to raising her daughters, trying her best to be both mother and father to them, putting her own life on hold to cocoon her children from their father's misdeeds. This was her time.

The part of Kate that was heartsick shifted a bit. It was clear that she needed to borrow a page from her mother and stop worrying about love. All these years, she had allowed her father to hold her hostage. And for what? It was finally clear that instead of protecting herself from the hurt he had caused—or inadvertently inflicting her father's brand of pain on someone else—she had let him continue ruining her life. Only, the adult years that she had allowed him to color weren't his fault. That was all on Kate.

It was time for a change.

This little baby already had a leg up from Kate's own upbringing. Aidan would be part of his child's life, even if Kate and Aidan couldn't sort out things well enough to make a life together.

She gathered up the vegetables she had been chopping and returned them to the refrigerator. She had no appetite. The best thing she could do for herself was draw a hot bath and take a long soak, then put herself to bed early.

Tomorrow was another day. She would have a clearer head that would allow her to start thinking about possible new directions she could explore. The first task was accepting the offer to manage the spa at the inn. In this storm of uncertainty, returning to the Forsyth Galloway Inn felt like entering a safe harbor. She would wait a few days for her mother to come back down to earth after the engagement before she broached serious talks about logistics and moving her clientele to the spa.

Of course, she'd want to be involved in outfitting the place. She had no idea what sort of timeframe they were looking at for opening the spa. She would have to figure out where she could service her clients in the meantime.

Putting a positive spin on it felt like a fresh start. She'd like to think it took the edge off the pain of her broken heart, but only time could do that. As she picked up a dishrag to wipe off the countertop, someone knocked on her front door.

She glanced at her phone to see if her mother or one of her sisters had texted to say they were coming over, but there were no new messages.

When she answered the door, Aidan was standing

there with a bouquet of roses in his hands. A nervous smile curved his lips, making his eyes sparkle.

"Hi," he said. "I'm sorry to come over without calling, but I just saw that I missed your call and what I have to say to you, I have to say in person, because I love you, Kate. We have to find a way to make this work because I don't want to spend another night without you."

"Aidan!" Kate threw her arms around his neck. "I love you, too," she whispered. "I'm so happy you're here. Can I come home?"

He nodded as tears made his eyes glisten even brighter.

"But first, there's something I need to do." Aidan handed Kate the roses. He reached into the pocket of his jacket and pulled out a small red box. As he lowered himself down on one knee, he took Kate's hand.

"Kate Clark, I love you with all my heart. Will you make me the happiest man in the world and marry me again—this time in a more traditional setting—and spend the rest of your life with me?"

With happy tears streaming down her cheeks, Kate nodded and watched as Aidan slid a gorgeous emerald cut diamond on the ring finger of her left hand. It struck her that even though her father might have lived in her head and affected all of her past relationships, he hadn't hijacked her subconscious.

Suddenly she realized that maybe part of the reason she had blocked their Vegas wedding was because that part of her knew it was the right thing to do.

If she and Aidan hadn't eloped in Vegas, maybe they would not be standing here like this now, with him on one knee and her heart overflowing with love for her...her husband.

"It is beautiful, Aidan. When did you get the ring?"

"I bought it right after you moved in with Chloe and me. I was waiting for the right time to propose, because I wanted to give you the proposal you deserve. I know how important it is to you. Maybe it could have been grander—"

"No. It is perfect."

"And we can start over and plan a traditional wedding," he said.

"You really do know me, don't you? Better than my own mother. Oh my gosh! Speaking of, my mother and Stephen got engaged tonight. I'll have to ask her, but what would you think of us having a double wedding? Chloe could be our flower girl."

"I think it would be a perfect wedding. I'm up for anything as long it makes you happy and we get to spend the rest of our lives together. I love you, Mrs. Quindlin."

Epilogue

One month later

On a perfect day in April at the Forsyth Galloway Inn, Kate and Aidan and Zelda and Stephen prepared to stand in front of Gigi, who had become an ordained minister for the occasion, and exchange wedding vows.

Zelda had been thrilled with the idea of a double, because she would finally get her wish of seeing her third daughter get married.

"Thank you for wanting to share this special day with Aidan and me."

"For Stephen and me, having a double wedding is the best of both worlds. We get to share our special day with you and Aidan," she said as she straightened Kate's veil. She smiled, blinking back tears, then she kissed her daughter on the cheek.

"Oh, Mom, you're making me tear up, too. We're going to ruin our makeup."

They laughed, holding on to each other's forearms.

Zelda looked gorgeous in a sleek, sleeveless, blush satin A-line gown. It skimmed her slender body, showcasing her toned figure and all her best features. Instead of a veil, she had opted to wear a spray of orange blossoms tucked into her classic chignon.

Kate, on the other hand, had chosen to go traditional, with a beaded champagne-colored strapless fit-and-flare gown. Her baby bump was just starting to show, and Kate accentuated it like a badge of honor. Kerrigan Karol had done Kate's hair, taming her long red curls into a sophisticated updo fashioned around the chapel-length veil, which sat on the back of her head.

Jane and Elle entered the bridal room looking beautiful in silk tea-length dresses that were a shade darker than Zelda's gown. Each of them held one of Chloe's hands. The little girl wore a champagne silk shantung dress with a wide pink sash that tied into a large bow in the back. Elle had Zelda's puppy, Bear, on a crystal-studded pale pink leash.

They handed Kate and Zelda beautiful bouquets of white and blush pink roses, hydrangeas, peonies and freesia. The long green stems were cut blunt at the end and tied with a satin ribbon. Zelda bent down and loved on Bear before taking the leash so the puppy could accompany her down the aisle.

"Mommy and Grandma Zelda, you look so pretty," Chloe said, holding her little basket.

Together, the brides and their attendants moved from the bridal room into the dining room, which looked out into the garden where the ceremony would take place.

Since they had been able to make the plans for the double wedding come together so quickly, they had delayed construction on the spa. It would start as soon as the couples returned from their respective honeymoons, which they were taking separately.

Kate had agreed to assume ownership and move her clients over. In the meantime, she was going to put the chairs she had purchased from Kerrigan in an empty guest room. She and a handful of the colleagues she had worked with at Kerrigan Karol's would be able to operate until the spa was fully operational and open for business.

Elle, Jane, Chloe, Kate and Zelda stood at the French doors in the dining room, hugging and blinking back tears and remarking about how beautiful the garden looked. The camellias in white, peach and pink were splendid, and the azaleas, which were usually at the height of their glory in March, were still flourishing. It was as if they had stayed just to bless the wedding with their brilliant tones of red and fuchsia, which popped against the green vines spilling over the wrought iron fence surrounding the Forsyth Galloway Inn's garden. Delicate white dogwood blossoms dotted the trees and stood out resplendently against the brilliant blue sky.

The most creative florist in all of Savannah could not have offered wedding flowers that were more beautiful.

Through the sheers on the French doors, Kate could see Aidan standing by the fountain at the other end of the garden. Her gaze homed in on him like a light guiding her home. Could there be any greater honor than to be Aidan's wife and a mother to Chloe and their unborn child?

Remarkably, she wasn't nervous—at least, not in the negative sense of the word. A calm excitement had her heart beating at the same rate as Pachelbel's "Canon," the processional song for the bridal party, which had just begun. Jane and Elle had started their walk down the cobblestone path to the fountain.

Rows of gold chiavari chairs lined both sides of the aisle. There wasn't an empty seat in the house, but Kate couldn't take her eyes off Aidan. Seeing him looking gorgeous in his tux, a serene smile on his handsome face, made Kate feel cocooned in the most delicious love and warmth. She knew down to her bones that this was right.

That *this* was the moment she had been waiting for all her life.

Anna Nolan, Aidan's and Daniel's office manager, was serving as wedding coordinator for the day. When Elle and Jane had almost arrived at the fountain, she put her hand on Chloe's shoulder, indicating it was time for her to begin her trip down the aisle.

"Remember to walk slowly and take your time scattering the flower petals," she whispered to the girl.

Chloe nodded, then turned to Kate and threw her arms around Kate's middle, spilling a handful of rose petals out of the basket.

"I love you, Mommy." She put her hand on Kate's stomach. "And I love my baby sister, too."

It was too early to tell if the baby would be a boy or a girl, but since telling Chloe she was going to be a big sister, the little girl had made up her mind that the baby was a girl. Kate and Aidan hadn't had the heart to correct her and say it might be a boy, because Chloe had such a capacity to love, and they knew she would love her sibling no matter what.

"I love you, too, Chloe." Kate kissed the top of

the girl's head. "Grandma and I will be right behind you."

Zelda blew a kiss to Chloe and the little girl set out down the aisle.

Zelda and Kate had decided to walk down the aisle together to the traditional wedding march. On her walk down the aisle, all Kate could see was Aidan and the promise of their future together. What once had felt so uncertain, a life out of her reach, was finally theirs. It had taken a long journey, complete with years of moving closer to each other, gangly Vegas Elvis and a baby to bring them together, but that was fine. It was their journey, their love story, and Kate couldn't love it any better if she had written it herself.

After they exchanged their vows and Gigi pronounced them husband and wife, Aidan took Kate into his arms and they danced to "I Can't Help Falling in Love with You." Kate smiled up at him. "No one can accuse us of rushing into anything."

"No, they can't." Aidan chuckled, then pulled her closer. "It may have taken a decade and a practice wedding for us to get this right, but Kate Clark Quindlin, you were worth the wait."

* * * * *

COMING SOON!

We really hope you enjoyed reading this book.
If you're looking for more romance, be sure to
head to the shops when new books are
available on

Thursday 26th
June

To see which titles are coming soon, please visit
millsandboon.co.uk/nextmonth

MILLS & BOON

MILLS & BOON

Coming next month

CINDERELLA'S NEW YORK FLING
Cara Colter

The sales assistant, Meredith, swept up all the clothes and left them.

"I feel like Cinderella," Jessica said, sinking into the chair beside him. The dress hitched up on a slender leg. He tried not to look. Failing in that, he tried not to be obvious about looking.

"But it's just about midnight. The glass slipper falls off, and I see what it all costs. I probably can't even afford one thing from here."

Jamie looked at his watch so she wouldn't see the pleasure in his eyes that he was going to play a part in her fairytale.

Not the prince part, of course. Though something about seeing her in all those clothes could tempt any man to play that role, even one as cynical about fairytales as him.

Meredith came back. She held out a piece of paper to Jessica.

Jessica took it, looked at it, and blinked. "Oh," she said. "It's so much less than I expected. Still, I don't need two skirts. So, I should probably take out the pencil-line one and keep the navy slacks."

Meredith snatched the paper back from her. "I forgot to add our preferred customer discount."

Jessica took back the paper with the adjusted price. Her mouth fell open with shocked surprise.

"Alright," she cried, beaming, "I'll take it all!"

As Meredith handled the transaction – giving the one

bill to Jessica and putting the real amount on Jamie's credit card, Jamie realized this was probably the most duplicitous thing he had ever done. But Jessica was absolutely radiant.

"I'll pay you back, of course. The insurance representative said I'll have some money by this afternoon."

How could something feel both so very wrong and so very right at the same time?

When they left the store, Jessica was wearing the brand new sundress. Jamie couldn't help but notice that, in a city where no one paid any attention to anyone else, Jessica was receiving subtle – and deeply appreciative glances – from the men of New York.

A man on a construction site whistled at her. Jamie threw him a warning glance, and then noticed Jessica was blushing as though she had been propositioned.

How could he turn her over to an assistant when it was so complicated? Jessica now looked like a sophisticated woman of the world. But she was the furthest thing from that. He couldn't just cast her out on her own. A still small voice, somewhere in the region of his heart, whispered to him, *admit it, pal, you don't want to.*

Continue reading
CINDERELLA'S NEW YORK FLING
Cara Colter

Available next month
www.millsandboon.co.uk

Copyright © 2020 Cara Colter

LET'S TALK
Romance

For exclusive extracts, competitions
and special offers, find us online:

 facebook.com/millsandboon

 @MillsandBoon

@MillsandBoonUK

Get in touch on 01413 063232

For all the latest titles coming soon, visit
millsandboon.co.uk/nextmonth

JOIN THE
MILLS & BOON
BOOKCLUB

* **FREE** delivery direct to your door

* **EXCLUSIVE** offers every month

* **EXCITING** rewards programme

50% OFF
YOUR FIRST
PARCEL

Join today at
Millsandboon.co.uk/Bookclub

WANT EVEN MORE

ROMANCE?

SUBSCRIBE AND SAVE TODAY!

'Mills & Boon books, the perfect way to escape for an hour or so.'

MISS W. DYER

'Excellent service, promptly delivered and very good subscription choices.'

MISS A. PEARSON

'You get fantastic special offers and the chance to get books before they hit the shops.'

MRS V. HALL

Visit millsandboon.co.uk/Subscribe and save on brand new books.

MILLS & BOON

HISTORICAL

Awaken the romance of the past

Escape with historical heroes from time
gone by. Whether your passion is for
wicked Regency Rakes, muscled Viking
warriors or rugged Highlanders, indulge
your fantasies and awaken the
romance of the past.

Six Historical stories published every month, find them all at:

millsandboon.co.uk/ Historical

MILLS & BOON

MEDICAL
Pulse-Racing Passion

Set your pulse racing with dedicated, delectable doctors in the high-pressure world of medicine, where emotions run high and passion, comfort and love are the best medicine.

Eight Medical stories published every month, find them all at:

millsandboon.co.uk

GET YOUR ROMANCE FIX!

MILLS & BOON
— *blog* —

Get the latest romance news, exclusive author interviews, story extracts and much more!

blog.millsandboon.co.uk

MILLS & BOON

THE HEART OF ROMANCE

A ROMANCE FOR EVERY KIND OF READER

MODERN

Prepare to be swept off your feet by sophisticated, sexy and seductive heroes, in some of the world's most glamourous and romantic locations, where power and passion collide.
8 stories per month.

HISTORICAL

Escape with historical heroes from time gone by. Whether your passion is for wicked Regency Rakes, muscled Vikings or rugged Highlanders, awaken the romance of the past.
6 stories per month.

MEDICAL

Set your pulse racing with dedicated, delectable doctors in the high-pressure world of medicine, where emotions run high and passion, comfort and love are the best medicine.
6 stories per month.

True Love

Celebrate true love with tender stories of heartfelt romance, from the rush of falling in love to the joy a new baby can bring, and a focus on the emotional heart of a relationship.
8 stories per month.

Desire

Indulge in secrets and scandal, intense drama and plenty of sizzli hot action with powerful and passionate heroes who have it all: wealth, status, good looks…everything but the right woman.
6 stories per month.

HEROES

Experience all the excitement of a gripping thriller, with an inten romance at its heart. Resourceful, true-to-life women and strong, fearless men face danger and desire - a killer combination!
8 stories per month.

DARE

Sensual love stories featuring smart, sassy heroines you'd want as best friend, and compelling intense heroes who are worthy of the
4 stories per month.

To see which titles are coming soon, please visit

millsandboon.co.uk/nextmonth

JOIN US ON SOCIAL MEDIA!

Stay up to date with our latest releases, author news and gossip, special offers and discounts, and all the behind-the-scenes action from Mills & Boon...

 millsandboon

 millsandboonuk

 millsandboon

It might just be true love...

